STRONGER

— THAN A —

BRONZE

DRAGON

STRONGER

— THAN A —

BRONZE

DRAGON

MARY FAN

PAGE STREET
PUBLISHING CO.

PAGE STREET
PUBLISHING CO.

FOR MY FAMILY

CHAPTER ONE

MY FATHER'S SWORD

Moonbeams frost the dark water of Dailanjiang, and I imagine the great River Dragon passing beneath its skittering ripples. It's said that he visited our village generations ago and granted our ancestors an enchanted pearl as a sign of his favor. If I hadn't seen that pearl with my own eyes, glowing like the moon upon its jade pedestal, I would have thought the story false. He certainly hasn't visited again since. And no one seems to be favoring Dailan lately.

As I walk along the riverbank, Father's sword bounces against my hip. I wrap my fingers around its hilt and feel the magical energy pulsing within. Beside me, Pinghua adjusts the holster carrying her clockwork pistol; at eighteen she's only a year older than me, but her sharp cheekbones make her look more mature. We turn onto a dirt path and head for the makeshift watchtowers that top several sloped roofs. They're little more than hastily constructed bamboo platforms since Dailan never needed watchtowers until recently. Our village had always been too small and remote to draw enemies.

Until the Ligui came.

I scan the glittering sky for any sign of the shadowy monsters. No one knows what they really are. We call them Ligui—powerful ghosts—because they're not earthly beings, but for all we know, they aren't ghosts at all. Unlike the souls of the dead who have visited before, the Ligui are mindless, hungry things that appear in many shapes and attack without reason. Yet unlike other monsters we've encountered, they can't be killed with ordinary weapons. They're creatures of smoke, spirits of darkness.

And tonight it's our job to warn the village if they attack again. I almost hope they do. It's been weeks since their last attack, which has meant many long nights of boredom.

Pinghua glances at me. "Do you think Mr. Gao made it to the capital?"

I shake my head, and my two long black braids brush my cheeks. "Even if he did, the Emperor won't send aid. He has no soldiers to spare thanks to the border war in the north. Besides, no one outside Sijiang Province believes the Ligui are real."

"That's true. I wonder why they strike our village so often."

I shrug. That's a question our elders have pondered often over the past few years, but even the spellmasters, with their vast knowledge of the supernatural, haven't been able to come up with a satisfactory answer. "You might as well ask a typhoon why it strikes one shore and not another."

"We're not their only targets, though. Maybe Mr. Gao can convince the nearby cities to help. They've seen the Ligui too."

"They'll say they need their warriors to defend themselves. We're on our own, Pinghua. I don't know why Headman Su keeps sending out messengers when they always return with the same bad news—if they return at all."

Pinghua sighs. "Especially since there are so few men left."

"Soon he'll have to start sending women." I give a cynical smile.

"Su would never go that far." Pinghua pats one of the twin knots on the sides of her head. "Letting girls join the Guard was one thing. Our numbers were so few, he had no choice. But women traveling without chaperones . . . Even if he allowed it, no one would volunteer."

"I would. Traveling alone hardly frightens me."

"That's not the point. It would be inappropriate, and you'd lose any hope of finding a husband. I'm still surprised your mother let you join the Guard; mine wouldn't have if my husband hadn't agreed."

I let out a derisive noise. "Who has time to worry about such things when the Ligui could kill us all? There's no one left to marry anyway."

"Tradition is important. We've already lost so many of our ways. Five years ago it would have been unthinkable for us to be armed and dressed like boys."

"Five years ago the Ligui were only a rumor, and my father was still alive." A pang slices my heart. I reach the ladder leading to the watchtower on Headman Su's roof and start climbing.

Pinghua continues down the street, heading to a different watchtower. She pauses and glances at me. "May the Gods of Heaven and Earth protect you tonight, Anlei." There's a weight to her voice—I think it's sorrow.

It isn't until I've climbed onto the platform that I realize I should have returned the blessing. A movement catches the corner of my eye. I whirl, drawing my sword, but the shadow across the moon is merely a cloud—not a Ligui about to materialize.

Moonlight prances across my enchanted weapon, which looks ordinary with its nicked hilt and well-worn blade. Only the bronze cross guard—shaped like a lion's face with the blade protruding from its wide, fanged mouth—sets it apart from a hundred weapons like it. I peer at the white gleams on the blade's surface, recalling what Mother used to tell me about how, if you look closely, you can see the Yueshen in the moon's reflections. Once the laughter and songs of the lunar spirits whispered across the night breeze, but no one's found any sign of them since the Ligui first attacked, slaughtering two dozen men in one night. Some say they slaughtered the Yueshen as well and that even the blessed beings aren't safe. I prefer to think the Yueshen fled back to the moon, where they're safe in their mysterious kingdom in the sky.

A distant screech pierces my thoughts. Shimmering, otherworldly vibrations shake me to the core.

A Ligui is approaching.

This is it—a chance to fight at last. I seize the clockwork pistol strapped to my belt, aim upward and pull the trigger. Red streams into the air, whistling as it flies. An instant later Pinghua fires a flare from her watchtower. Within seconds ruby blazes fill the sky, bathing the rooftops in fiery light as guards spread the signal.

Having alerted the village, I shove my pistol back into its leather holster. Sword in hand, I search the dark for the source of the screech. Heat crackles through my veins, and my body itches for a chance to slay the monstrous beings.

A black tendril rises, reaching for the platform I'm standing on.

I leap and slide down the sloped roof. Friction from the clay ridges heats my skin through my clothes. I push off, launching myself into the air as a giant black dragonfly appears before me. I slice its wing. My blade glows gold when it touches the being of smoke, and a satisfying sizzling noise envelops my ears.

The Ligui's shrill cry splits the air. Cringing, I grab the edge of the roof with one hand. My palm burns as I swing toward the house and land on a balcony. Thick columns support the roof, and a waist-high, latticed wall separates me from the flailing monster. No moonlight reflects off its long body, and its wings appear to be made of dripping tar.

I slice downward, chopping off its head with a fierce cry that I barely hear over the creature's screech. It dissolves into black fog, and a grin creeps onto my face. This is what I was born to do: fight evil.

Where Ligui go after I slay them, I do not know, but if there's any justice in the universe, they spend eternity suffering the torments of the Courts of Hell.

Screams of terror pepper the dark, interspersed with the whistles of flares and the battle cries of my fellow guards. The air reeks of the acrid smoke of gunpowder and the sulfurous stench of the Ligui, and it's exhilarating. Barrier spells to repel the Ligui glow in golden lines around the edges of several houses.

Heavy hoofbeats pound nearby. My blood rushes as I leap over the latticed wall, twisting as I jump. In midair I face the thick column supporting the balcony, seize the column with both hands, and slide down. Splinters slice the skin off the knuckles of my sword hand, but I don't care. I kick the column and release my grip. The movement whirls me to face the street as I land.

The ground trembles. A bull made of shadow charges toward me, driving its horns into the houses on either side of the narrow street. Gold sparks fly from the barrier spells in the walls, but the horns nevertheless tear gashes through the brick. It must be an especially strong Ligui. Smoke trails after its running form, and the smell of sulfur is so thick I nearly gag. Fear creeps up my chest, but I set my jaw, determined not to let it sink in. The Ligui have taken enough from us. No more of their kind will harm my people—not if I have anything to say about it.

The ground seems ready to leap to the rooftops under the weight of the bull's hooves. Its ferocious, glowing eyes fix on me, and I snarl. "Come on! *Lai ba!*"

Before I get my chance to strike, Pinghua leaps from a balcony above and lands on the bull's back, burying her blade into its body. My eyes widen in surprise; I've never seen her attempt such a bold move before. I wish I'd thought to do that. The bull bucks, but Pinghua keeps her blade embedded, hanging on with her thighs. Her sword, like mine, possesses magic that allows her to treat the Ligui as if it's an earthly being.

Heart pounding, I charge. The bull rears. I leap and plunge my sword into its throat, relishing the crackle of magic that arises. My weight draws the blade downward, and orange sparks fly. The bull jerks, flinging the blade from its body and throwing me into a wall.

The impact knocks the breath from my chest. I force myself to get back up. Though pain pulses through my back and knees, I don't have time to be hurt. I glimpse Pinghua standing in one of the wide doorways lining the street; she must have been thrown off too but had a better time landing than I did.

Two of the Guard's men race past me toward the bull. I exhale. Four against one . . . even though this Ligui is stronger than most, we stand a chance of defeating it.

A flash of movement catches my eye and I whip around as a man-shaped shadow disappears around a corner. Though his silhouette suggested an everyday tunic rather than the warrior's armor he wore the last time I saw him, the glowing crescent on his neck told me everything I need to know: This is the Ligui that killed my father. The Shadow Warrior.

The world vanishes behind an explosion of wrath. All I see is that crescent. Though the Shadow Warrior has appeared often in my nightmares, this is the first time he's returned while I'm awake.

May the Gods of Heaven and Earth witness my oath: I will avenge you, Father.

I sprint after him, rage pulsing through my body.

Somewhere far away, a girl's voice calls, "Anlei! Come back!"

The words are a meaningless buzz beneath the blood thundering in my ears. All I know is that my father's killer is at last within reach. And, by the Gods of Heaven and Earth, I will destroy him. Like the legendary Warrioress, I will slay my enemy and reap the glory.

As I follow the Shadow Warrior through alleys so narrow they nearly scrape my shoulders, red edges my vision. I don't care if there are other guards who could fight him—this victory will belong to me alone.

I stop in my tracks as a single rational thought cuts through my fury.

He's heading toward the River Dragon Shrine.

I know every house, every street, every forgotten corner of my village. If the Shadow Warrior thinks he can outrun me in my own territory, then he's dead wrong.

I whirl to my left and race toward the open window of Mr. Hong's house, leaping over the golden line of the magic barrier surrounding it. I sprint across a wide room, jump out the window on the other side, and cross the street. If anyone protests, I don't hear it. After zooming across a bridge over one of the many little rivers running through Dailan, I arrive at the miniature island dedicated to the River Dragon.

A lone willow stands by the bridge, bowing its branches toward the water. At the island's center stands a small, round shrine with a three-tiered roof and a wide entrance supported by red columns. A stone statue depicting the River Dragon, with his serpentine body and long horns, sits inside. Before it stands the River Pearl he granted our ancestors, guarded from outsiders by his lingering magic. Only residents of Dailan can enter the shrine, but though the pearl's power protects itself, it's never done a thing for us.

The Shadow Warrior runs at it from the main road. I don't know if it's the River Pearl he's after or something else, and I don't care. I rush into his path.

Before I can strike, a burst of yellow explodes against the ground. The force knocks me off my feet, and I land painfully on the stones. Heat pours over me. I spring up, determined not to let anything—not even a mysterious explosion—keep me from my revenge.

But as a stream of golden light falls from the sky, the Shadow Warrior takes off in flight, vanishing into the dark. Frustration grinds at my insides. I've failed. Though the monster that murdered Father was right in front of me, I let him get away. All my hopes for glory suddenly seem foolish.

Clunking and whirring noises swirl above, and the smells of metal and a strange, bitter smoke waft toward me. I look up.

Five mechanical dragons made of bronze with red and green accents soar above the village. Their long bodies twist through the air like a snake twists through water. Yellow eyes glow beneath sharp horns, and metal claws extend from wide paws attached to short legs. Fire streaks the night as more blasts spew down from their mouths. For a moment I fear they're attacking us, but then I hear the wild screeching and feral bellowing of the Ligui as the fireballs strike them. The popping noises that follow make the crackle of my sword seem like whispers.

What are they? Where did they come from? I stare in amazement as a sixth flying machine emerges from behind a cloud: an enormous cruiser, resembling the great ocean-faring warships I've only seen in pictures. Three tall masts with scalloped sails rise above it, flanked by giant propellers protruding from either side of the hull. Long cannons extend from the ship's body, and additional propellers spin at the keel. A dragon's head adorns the bow. White steam pours from its flared nostrils. A bronze tail curls up the back.

I watch in awe as the ship draws closer. I've heard rumors of flying machines like this, powered by a combination of science and magic. But I never dreamed that one would find its way to a village as remote as Dailan.

Whoever controls these mechanical dragons, whoever is responsible for the great fleet in the sky . . . I can't help feeling as if my life's about to change forever.

CHAPTER TWO

THE VICEROY

I race along the riverbank over mud and stones, heading for the spot where I saw the flying cruiser land, burning to know whose it is and why it came. Bronze dragons hover above the ship's massive form, which now floats in the widest part of the river; the vessel nearly spans the water.

I'm covered in mud by the time I get close enough to see four automatons striding down the ship's gangplank with a litter on their metal shoulders. Each machine bears the vague shape of a person, with long skeleton-like limbs of bronze. Their faces are painted like opera masks, with sharp, angled eyes surrounded by swirling patterns of red and black. Enchanted red lanterns hover to either side of the litter, illuminating the broad-shouldered man seated upon it. He throws me a disgusted look, and I stop in my tracks. His elaborately embroidered robe of black silk, which reaches his ankles, indicates he must be rich.

A graying queue extends from under a bowl-shaped hat topped with a blue button from which red tassels cascade. It's the hat of a government official.

The man glares at me as if expecting me to drop to my knees and press my forehead to the ground. I glare right back. Whoever this stranger is, he hasn't earned my respect yet. His mechanical dragons may have chased away the Ligui, but until I know why he did it and what he wants in return, I won't trust him. His proud cheekbones and sharply angled chin might have been handsome were it not for the condescension marring his expression. With his narrowed black eyes, he reminds me of a serpent.

Six soldiers, each carrying a sword in one hand and a pistol in the other, follow his litter. For a moment, I believe them to be automatons as well. Metal plates cover half their faces, and yellow lights glow in place of their left eyes. Their arms appear to be mechanical, made up of silver plating, complex wiring, and exposed gears. But the rest of their bodies look human, and unlike the automatons, they actually seem alive.

Cyborgs! I gasp. I've heard tales of these half-man-half-machine beings guarding the wealthy, but this is the first time I've seen them myself.

Headman Su approaches the riverbank via the paved path leading to the main road through the village. His mechanical left leg hisses and clanks as he moves. Though he managed to throw on a plain blue tunic, his white queue appears mussed. He bows his head in deference.

The man faces Su and orders the automatons to set down his litter. I stare, wondering how it's possible for a machine to listen. Even the most complex creations I've seen must be commanded by buttons and switches . . . for an object without ears to hear someone's words and do as they say is unheard of.

This man must be a powerful spellmaster . . . or employ one. Who is he?

"Viceroy Kang." Su keeps his chin lowered as he speaks. "You honor us with your presence. We are deeply grateful for your assistance."

He's the viceroy? I inch closer. I've heard of the great Viceroy Kang, of course—everyone has. He governs Sijiang Province and won many victories for the Emperor in his youth. It's said that he'd still be fighting to this day—defending our nation's northern border—but for a battle wound that prevents him from wielding a sword anymore. So he sends his generals to fight in his stead but is still known as one of our nation's greatest war heroes. But if that old injury hinders his movements, I can't tell from the way he walks.

I never thought that such a high-ranking official would find his way to Dailan. I once hoped, along with everyone else, that he'd send his army to protect us, but as the years passed with no help I thought he'd forgotten about us—or decided we weren't worth saving.

So what changed his mind?

The same thoughts must have occurred to Su, because he says, "Forgive me for my impertinence, Your Honor, but I must ask why you've come now. We've sent many messengers to Tongqiucheng pleading for help but were always told that you had no troops to spare."

Viceroy Kang lets out a long sigh. "I deeply regret my past inability to protect your village. You must understand that I had to protect the cities first."

"Of course."

"But now, I've unlocked new secrets of science and magic that have allowed me to build this mechanical fleet." Kang gestures at the bronze dragons, sweeping the wide cuff of his gleaming sleeve. "They are far more powerful and effective than human soldiers alone, which means we'll be better equipped to fight the Ligui. Soon I hope to have a mechanical army large enough to protect the entire province."

I narrow my eyes. It's always bothered me that the viceroy knows the Ligui are real, but the Emperor, whom he advises, still believes them to be superstition. Either Kang isn't a very effective advocate, or he's purposely leaving something out when he sends his official reports to Zhongjing.

Su bows his head. "Forgive me once again, Your Honor, but would the Emperor allow so great a force to exist outside Zhongjing when the law states that no magic is to be greater than his own?"

I huff impatiently. Dailan is so isolated, the rest of the Empire sometimes feels like a faraway tale that has nothing to do with me. I certainly don't care about its politics.

"How dare you question my plans?" Kang scowls at Su. "I know the law better than any village headman ever will."

"I meant no offense." Su clasps his hands. "So little news reaches us here. I was merely curious."

"I will remind you, then, that the Emperor's own army wields many powerful enchanted weapons and boasts many mighty vehicles." The viceroy gives Su a disdainful look. "Any rumors claiming that my fleet has the potential to be greater are utter nonsense. I even shared my designs with the Emperor's engineers, and though they've been unable to replicate my success so far, they should be able to with time. I have nothing but respect for the Emperor, and I won't have you questioning my loyalty."

"My deepest apologies, Your Honor. That was not my intention." Su's continued deference stirs my frustration. He should be demanding protection for us.

"Though my resources are limited, I am not ignorant to Dailan's struggles," Kang goes on. "I was passing over on my way back from a diplomatic trip when I saw the Ligui attacking your village, and I had to intervene."

Though he sounds earnest, churning discomfort remains in my gut. A powerful man like Kang doesn't grant favors without desiring something in return. What could Dailan possibly offer him?

"I have a matter of official business to discuss." Kang gestures up the cruiser's gangplank. "Please, join me on board my ship."

"Of course, Viceroy." Su's gaze pans over the gathered villagers, who stare at the first visitors we've had in years. "Everyone, go back about your business!"

The villagers scatter. Su waits for Kang to return to his litter then follows the automatons into the dragon-shaped vessel. Too curious to leave, I watch them board. The automatons retract the gangplank. The whoosh of steam and the clang of machinery pour from the ship as the gangplank telescopes into a narrow slot in the cruiser's hull.

"Anlei!"

Hearing Pinghua's voice, I turn. A red gash cuts across her cheek, and the left leg of her trousers is torn and bloodstained. From the way she limps, I know she's injured, and I briefly wonder what happened to her before the bull-shaped Ligui flashes through my head.

She was fighting it, and I . . . I abandoned her to chase the Shadow Warrior.

What was I thinking, leaving in the middle of a fight? All I remember is that one moment, I was facing the bull, and the next, I was chasing the Shadow Warrior.

Pinghua glares at me. "Why did you run?"

"I'm so sorry. I . . . I saw the Shadow Warrior—the one that killed my father."

"That's no excuse. If you can't be part of a team, then maybe you don't belong with the Guard."

My jaw drops. "I'm the best fighter here!"

"You're arrogant and selfish. It doesn't matter how well you can handle a sword if you lack discipline."

Shame winds through my chest. I look away. Headman Su told me the same thing during my training, and Father used to lecture me for my impulsiveness and conceit as well. I don't mean to think only of myself . . . I just have trouble connecting with the rest of the world and sometimes forget it's there, especially when powerful urges drive me to action and drown out my thoughts.

"I'll do better," I murmur, more to myself than to Pinghua.

"Good." She gestures for me to follow her. "We should return to our posts."

I glance doubtfully at her wounded leg. "Are you sure you can—"

"I'm fine."

Though there seems to be little point in going back to the watchtower with Viceroy Kang and his fleet here, I walk with Pinghua.

When I reach my post, I gaze down at Kang's enormous cruiser. Somewhere inside, the viceroy and the village headman are discussing matters that could change all our fates. I yearn to hear what they're saying.

The mechanical dragons land on the water and float placidly beside the flagship, their bodies forming arches above the ripples. Watching their smooth, undulating movements, I almost forget for a moment that they're machines like my pistol.

If the River Dragon returned now, would he welcome them as his brothers, or would he see the artificial creatures as a threat?

CHAPTER THREE

WARRIORESS

Qi lai!"

My little sister's high-pitched voice pierces my ears, telling me to get up. Sleepiness sits in my head like a bag of rocks, and my muscles feel as if someone replaced them with clay.

"*Qi lai!*" Insistent hands seize my shoulders and shake me. "*Jiejie*, we have to prepare our act!"

"No, we don't. The next festival isn't for months." Without opening my eyes, I shove Anshui back. Though she and I once showed off our acrobatic skills regularly, since the Ligui started attacking we do it only for special occasions. I miss our days of journeying, when we'd accompany our parents on their errands for Dailan and perform for neighboring villages to earn extra money. Even though we never went far, it was still *something*. Now, it's too dangerous for anyone but a few select messengers to leave Dailan. If Mother weren't so passionate that my sister and I keep performing to preserve her family's traditions, we'd probably have given it up years ago.

"*Jiejie!*" Anshui's voice takes on a whiny tinge.

Weary as I am, I'd rather get up than return to the dreamscape, where the Shadow Warrior taunts me within an inch of my sanity. I can still see his menacing white gaze glowing against an otherwise faceless darkness. The crescent on his neck burns in my memory, and I can almost hear him say, "You had me right in front of you. But you failed, and because of that, I will slaughter many more fathers while yours lies deep underground."

I blink against the sunlight streaming through the window in our small wood-paneled room. My sister's face peers into mine. Two bright black eyes tilt gently toward a delicate nose, which bisects a watermelon-seed face. Like me, she takes after Mother, with her pointed chin, cherry mouth, and mildly arched brows. I wouldn't be surprised if, when she grows the last inch between our heights, people start asking if we're twins.

"*Kuai qi lai!*" Anshui shakes my shoulders again. "We have to rehearse, and there's not much time!"

"What are you talking about?" I reluctantly sit up. The sun was already rising when I finished my guard shift, and judging by its present angle, not much time has passed since.

Anshui grins. "We're throwing a festival in honor of Viceroy Kang, and Headman Su requested that we perform! Can you believe it? We're performing for an *official!*"

I smile back, but I'm not nearly as excited. While I'm grateful that Kang's forces spared our village further tragedy, I still wonder about his intentions.

Anshui grabs my hands and tries to pull me up. "The show is *this afternoon*, and it's been forever since we practiced our routine. What if I can't do it anymore?"

"Don't be ridiculous. I remember *my* part, and you're much smarter than me."

She looks away. "No, I'm not. I don't know why you always say that."

I cock an eyebrow. "You can read through miles of characters without pausing and understand every meaning of every sentence. But to me, characters don't look like words—they're just meaningless lines unless I concentrate hard and absorb each stroke one by one. Anything that requires reading hits a wall in my head."

"But you're a *warrior*. Like Father." Admiration shines in Anshui's eyes. "Intelligence is about more than reading."

"I suppose that's true." I'm an expert at recalling the intricate movements of a martial artist and can recite epic tales word-for-word. But though she's only thirteen, Anshui already possesses enough skill in science and magic to craft gadgets like the ones Grandfather used to make. Before disease took him a few years ago, Grandfather was the village's greatest spellmaster; "I only wish I could understand Grandfather's notes like you do. Maybe someday you can explain them to me."

Anshui shakes her head. "Magic can't be learned through oral teaching alone. You have to know how to treat strings of characters like mathematical equations."

Just thinking about that makes my head hurt. "I hate that I'll never fully understand the magic that powers my weapons."

"You could if you wanted to."

"But it would be extremely difficult. You make it look so easy."

Anshui shrugs. "We're all gifted in our own ways. Don't forget, Father once failed to master *his* father's craft before finding his calling as a soldier in the Emperor's army. Grandfather and I may have been blessed with intellect, but you and Father were blessed with ferocity."

I smile. "It seems you were blessed with wisdom too, *meimei*."

Anshui blushes. *"Xie xie."*

As I pick myself up off the bamboo mat I glimpse a pair of spectacles with copper frames sitting on the ground surrounded by tools and stray gears. Apparently my sister turned our bedroom into a workshop this morning. Unlike ordinary spectacles, the ones she's been tinkering with have multiple lenses layered on top of one other. Each is perfectly circular, and bronze gears adorn the sides. I point at them. "Are you still tinkering with those? It's been weeks!"

Anshui twists her mouth. "The magic still doesn't flow through the gears as well as it should."

"Are you ever going to tell me what they're for?"

She grins. "It's a surprise!"

"Well, they don't belong on the floor." I give a teasing smile.

"If you don't put your things away, the Yueshen will steal them."

I expect my sister to be annoyed by the common village saying, but instead her face takes on a wistful expression.

"I wouldn't mind if they did. It would mean they were back."

Her eyes flick over to the corner, where lines of red ribbons sit on a small wooden table. They're an offering she's left out since the Yueshen vanished. It's said that if you leave out trinkets or food for the Yueshen, they'll grant you favors. They can carry small objects across great distances in an instant, and so you might ask them to bring you medicine when your mother is ill. Or since they can move invisibly, you might ask them to whisper to the boy or girl you like that you're the one to pursue.

Anshui was too young to request anything like that before they disappeared, but she told me that a Yueshen girl visited her when she was seven, and I know better than to doubt her.

She smooths out one of the ribbons with a sigh. "I don't even want any favors. I just want to see my friend again. I just . . . "

She doesn't finish, but I know what she wants to say.

She just wants life to be normal again. She was only eight when the Ligui came, but that was old enough to remember how fun it was to see new places with Father, old enough to be aware of how carefree life seemed, knowing that no matter where we went, Father would keep us safe.

"So do I." I wrap my arm around her and give her a squeeze.

Mother appears under the wooden doorframe holding an unfinished baby garment. It's probably for our pregnant neighbor, who's been too fatigued to do housework and whose fisherman husband agreed to give us a share of his daily catch in exchange for Mother's help. She lifts her thin black brows at me. "I thought you'd be dressed by now. I want to review your routines before the performance, and we only have a few hours before then."

I grimace. While I enjoy performing, Mother, who was an acrobat herself when she was young, is a relentless perfectionist. Ordinarily I don't mind her strict instruction or the grueling rehearsals, but I hate the idea of putting in so much effort for the pleasure of that pompous viceroy, especially since I'm still weary from last night's battle. "Why does it matter? We aren't true professionals."

"As long as my family's blood flows in your veins, you will honor these traditions to the best of your ability." She approaches, and the streaks of gray in her tightly wound black hair catch the sunlight.

Anshui bows her head with respect. "Yes, Mother. We will always honor our family's art."

"If your family is so important to you, why did you leave them?" I've asked Mother this question many times, but she has yet to give me a satisfying answer.

Anshui rolls her eyes. "Because she and Father wanted to settle down in his hometown. How many times must Mother explain this?"

I cross my arms. "I know what *happened.* But it still doesn't make sense to me that two people who'd traveled the entire country—Mother with the troupe and Father with the Emperor's army—would choose to settle down in a middle-of-nowhere river village."

Anshui scowls. "Dailan is our *home*! It may be small and mundane compared to the great cities, but it's *ours.*"

"Of course, that's why I defend it with my life every night. But . . . what have we missed? If Mother and Father hadn't settled down, our family would still be journeying—maybe even as far as the West." Imagine those strange nations where men cut their hair short and women bind their waists. Anshui's lips quirk.

"Yes, it would have been exciting. I've dreamed of it too . . . performing in exotic cities full of tall stone buildings with colored-glass windows. But we would never have known Dailan—we would have been born on the road."

"We wouldn't have missed much."

Her scowl returns. *"Jiejie!"*

"We'd have seen so much more! And . . . we'd have been miles away before the Ligui attacked . . . Father would still be with us."

Anshui's expression falls, and tears fill her eyes.

Mother, who's been watching us with a patient look, places a hand on Anshui's shoulder. She kisses her forehead, then mine. "I miss him too. But it will do no good to dwell on what might have been. I never inherited my parents' wanderlust and disliked the dangers of the road. When your father told me of Dailan, I asked him to bring me here because I wanted to raise our children in a quiet, peaceful place."

"Your plan failed, then," I grumble. "Look at us now."

"That's enough." Mother's jaw tightens. "Get dressed. We have work to do."

She strides out of the room, covering her face as she walks out of view. Anshui wipes her eyes and leans down to clean up her tools.

I glance in the direction Mother left in, then turn back to Anshui. A sense of misery weighs on both of them, and I know I caused it. I never meant to hurt them—I only spoke what was true to me. But I should have considered how my words would affect them.

I lean down beside Anshui. "I'm sorry."

She sweeps the stray gears into a little cloth bag but doesn't look at me. "It's Mother you should apologize to. You made it sound like it's her fault that Father's gone."

"That's not what I meant!"

"But it's what your words implied."

I press my fist to my lips. So often the meaning of my words comes out all wrong, but this is the worst thing I've ever said, even though I didn't mean to say it.

I rush to find Mother. She sits in the small but well-lit main room of our house, her expert fingers working at the baby garment. I walk up to her, twisting my hands nervously behind my back. "I'm sorry for what I said. I didn't mean it."

"I know." Mother looks up. "You must watch your words, Anlei. And you must consider the perspective of others."

"Yes, Mother." But understanding the unspoken meanings behind words, like reading, is something I can only accomplish with great focus and effort. I wonder if I'll ever learn how to do what comes so naturally to everyone else.

Red lanterns line the streets, dripping from thin strings that hang off the wooden balconies and wide doorframes of Dailan's low buildings. Each is carved with the characters and symbols that invoke the barrier spells at night. Brightly hued kites in the shapes of butterflies, sparrows, and dragons soar over the rooftops, and little clockwork birds flutter between them. Ordinarily Dailan is a simple village of brown and gray, but today's festival decorations have given it splashes of red, gold, green, and blue.

"*Zhou kai!*" A man's gruff voice strikes my ears.

A mechanical cart chugs toward me and Anshui, belching steam from its engine, its wheels clattering against the uneven stones. I grab my sister's arm and pull her to the side of the street, careful to avoid the stinking gutter.

Mr. Cheng, one of Dailan's spellmasters, sits in the driver's seat, frowning behind his white beard. Judging by the earthen pots in the back of the cart—each of which is marked with characters and symbols—he's probably on his way to congregate with the other spell-masters and work on enchantments to better protect our village. Though he and the others know their craft well, they've never been as adept at combining magic with mechanics as Grandfather, who built that cart years ago, and who once traded his inventions for the rare knowledge and costly ingredients needed to conjure the barrier spells.

Mr. Cheng speeds past us, and I leap out of the way to avoid mud splashing on my costume for the performance Anshui and I are to give shortly.

"Man dian!" Anshui cries. "If you don't slow down, you could ruin the engine!"

Mr. Cheng doesn't seem to hear her.

I chuckle. "You sound like Mother."

Anshui makes a face. "If the cart breaks down again, I'm the one who will have to fix it. Grandfather didn't like what they did to it last time and made me promise to take care of his favorite machine."

"Grandfather visited you again?" I turn to her with a twinge of envy. Though the ghosts of friends and family have visited many in our village, they have yet to speak to me.

My sister nods. "I saw him in my dream last night. He also wanted to make sure I was keeping up with my studies and said he was sad he couldn't be there to teach me himself."

"That's . . . wonderful. I wish he would visit me too."

"Maybe he did, but you were too busy obsessing over the Shadow Warrior to see. I know you had another nightmare about him—you were cursing him in your sleep."

I grimace. "I saw the Shadow Warrior right before the viceroy's fleet arrived. I almost had him."

"I know. Mother told me what happened." Her expression becomes stern. "You shouldn't let the Shadow Warrior dominate your thoughts. He's only one Ligui, and there are so many out there. What would destroying a single one do?"

"I swore I'd avenge Father."

"Father wouldn't want you to if he knew how vengeance consumes your thoughts."

I touch the jade pendant around my neck, running my finger across the tiny carved scales of the three koi splashing across its smooth surface. Father gave it to me when I reached my first hundred days of life, and I've worn it ever since. Now the pendant and my sword are all I have to remember him by. "You weren't there when he died . . . You wouldn't understand."

"I guess I don't." Anshui sighs. "Come on. We don't want to be late."

She continues down the road, and I follow, shaking my head. This need for revenge—it's a hunger that gnaws at me every day, and only when the Shadow Warrior is destroyed will it be satisfied.

I can't help wishing the Shadow Warrior would attack again so that I might have another chance to finish him.

Joyful music curls through the air. From my spot backstage, I watch the small band of mechanical instruments performing on the village stage in the center of the square. The stringed lutes lean on metal stands, plucked by clockwork picks, and the long flutes dangle from strings with valves that open and close over the holes in place of fingers. Yellow sparks dance above them, telling of enchantments at play. The perfect blend between the old and the new, the earthly and the magical, fascinates me, and I marvel at the genius of the spellmasters who created it. When I close my eyes, I forget that the light, skipping tune is being produced by machines.

Our three old spellmasters sway their heads as they watch from the audience, their long, white beards bouncing against their simple gray tunics. Several villagers surround them, having crowded into the square for the show. Above, on a wide platform shaded by bamboo slats, Viceroy Kang sits on an ornate gilded chair. He must have brought it from his ship, since we have nothing so fine in Dailan. My jade pendant, which Father received from a Zhongjing lady as a gift for saving her life, is probably the most valuable thing in the village. Other than the River Pearl, of course.

Cyborg soldiers flank the viceroy, each surveying the crowd with one natural eye and one glowing mechanical one. Automatons guard the base of the platform, their expressionless, painted faceplates still. I glance at them, then at the mechanical band. Wonderful as the spellmasters' creation is, it pales in comparison to everything the viceroy brought.

When the instrumental performance concludes, the spellmasters walk up the wooden steps to the stage and flip switches on each. Mechanical legs unfold from their delicate forms. They crawl off the stage, spider-like, gears clicking and feet clattering. The spellmasters follow.

Now it's time for the last act: my solo performance. My body still aches from the sister act I performed with Anshui earlier—much of which consisted of me folding myself into elegant shapes while she leaped on top of me and performed the real stunts. Since she's the smaller and more flexible one, she gets the glory when we perform together. But this next act will be mine alone, and it's one I love performing so much, I don't need a holiday—or an important official's visit—to motivate me to practice it.

Holding out my prop sword, I stride onto the stage. The red ribbons woven into my hair, which sits in two twists on the sides of my head, trail behind me. My embroidered white tunic glints under the fading sun. Though its edges are yellowing, it's still the finest thing I've ever worn, and it makes me feel like an empress.

"Have you ever heard the tale of the great Warrioress?" The question is rhetorical; *everyone* knows the legend of Warrioress. I sweep forward until I'm standing at the very edge of the stage and look the viceroy right in the eye. "Let me tell you."

I sprint upstage. A bamboo pole stands at the back, towering like a narrow tree trunk. I drop my prop sword, leap upward, and seize the pole. Several feet above the ground, I curl my knees into my chest.

"She was the daughter of a Yueshen prince and his beautiful bride—a pair so pure, Heaven granted them the powers of the stars." Though the strain of holding myself up makes my arms ache, the rehearsed words flow seamlessly from my tongue. "But the evil Mowang, the demon king, grew jealous of them and cursed them with his dark magic. Any children they bore would fall to Earth and be trapped in a human form."

To illustrate Warrioress's fall from the moon, I push off the pole and flip backward. When I land in a crouch, the audience applauds.

"The place where the infant Yueshen princess landed was once a battlefield, and the ghosts of the great warriors who'd died there took pity and raised her." Slowly, I rise, picking up the prop sword. "With their training, she learned to fight as well as any man—and better than most!"

I flip across the stage, slashing my sword, then twist and kick in several theatrical martial arts movements. They would never work against a real enemy, of course, but they impress the audience, which claps approvingly. I tumble some more, sweeping my sword over my head and tossing it from hand to hand for extra effect.

In this moment, I'm a bit of both Mother and Father. Mother choreographed the acrobatic parts, and Father taught me some real swordplay to make it feel more authentic. Spotting Mother in the crowd, I flash her a smile. She beams at me.

My heart soars as I strike at an invisible enemy. I love this act, love embodying the tale of the legendary woman who battled wicked humans, fearsome demons, and evil spirits long, long ago. Even before the Ligui came, I dreamed of being like her. Though joining the Guard brought me one step closer to her physical feats, I'm nowhere close to matching her intelligence, and defending one village seems so insignificant next to the stories of how she saved entire nations. But when I'm onstage, I can pretend . . . and if the audience believes it, then so can I.

"But the girl knew she couldn't stay among the spirits forever. So she left the protection of the ghost warriors to seek out the humans." The next segment allows me to recover a bit as I stride across the stage, acting out Warrioress's journey. "Mowang, realizing how powerful she'd grown, sent a demon soldier to kill her the moment she struck out alone."

Ideally, another performer would play the enemy. But finding a suitable actor in Dailan proved impossible, and so Mother arranged the choreography so that I could play both parts—Warrioress and the demon soldier.

"The demon soldier attacked!"

I twist my face into a grotesque expression. My next set of tricks involves bolder movements and cruder execution as I imitate the wicked being. I march across the stage and stab my sword at the air, then perform a few simple turns.

"But he was no match for her skills."

This is my favorite part: the young Warrioress defeating her first real enemy. I feel her determination and courage flow through me as I strap the prop sword to my back and leap onto the bamboo pole, then use the momentum to swing around and throw myself into a complex flip. Wind whips past me, and elation fills my heart as I fly. For this one instant, I, too, am more than human.

In midair I grab the sword from my back and, as I descend, grip the hilt with both hands. The moment my feet land on the stage I kneel dramatically and stab the blade into the ground.

"She defeated him, and from that moment on, she was known as Warrioress."

Of course, the tale of Warrioress would go on for much longer than what my one-person show could express, but it's a satisfying ending nonetheless.

Cheers break out. Though my neighbors have seen this performance many times before, I apparently still impress them. I stand with a grin and take a moment to bask in my success before bowing and walking off. Out of breath, I collapse against one of the wooden posts propping up the stage. My bangs cling to my sweaty forehead.

"Attention!"

Hearing Headman Su's voice, I force myself to straighten. Though I wish I could remain back here—I can hear him fine, after all—I've been told many times that it's rude not to show my face when the headman is speaking. I need to be *seen* listening, which seems silly, but I drag my weary limbs around the stage and join the crowd.

Su waves from the elevated platform, standing beside the viceroy's chair. "Viceroy Kang and I have reached an agreement. He will honor us by taking one of our daughters as his eighth wife if we will grant him the River Pearl."

Gasps ripple through the crowd. I furrow my brow. Viceroys don't marry village girls . . . or any girls who aren't the daughters of nobility. But more bizarre is the price—how can Su give up Dailan's sacred gem? I've never thought much of the River Pearl before—it was always just some ancient relic to me—but now that someone wants to take it, I feel invisible fists rising in my chest, ready for a fight. That gem belongs to my village, and no condescending government official should have it.

Su motions for silence. "Quiet! I made this agreement for the good of all in Dailan. Though Ligui continue to attack cities and villages across Sijiang Province, Viceroy Kang has agreed that in addition to a generous bride price, he will station a permanent battalion here to protect Dailan once he's married. For then this will be his wife's village, and he will be duty-bound to ensure the safety of all who live here."

The invisible fists drop. An old, useless object in exchange for the safety of hundreds . . . it's obvious what the right thing to do is. Though the River Pearl is said to carry great magic, I've never seen it do anything other than sit in its shrine. Many who prayed to it for protection, hoping to reach the River Dragon through it, have fallen to the Ligui. And it's continued to lie there, no different from any rock, while the Ligui kill again and again. Some blessing it turned out to be.

No one mentions why Kang might want the pearl, and honestly, I don't care. The only thing I want more than the destruction of the Shadow Warrior is for no more of my people to die at the hands of his kind.

Su waits for the information to sink in. After a beat, he continues. "We are very fortunate that the viceroy is willing to take a woman of such humble lineage into his household. All eligible women are to be presented to him for consideration. The—" He breaks off as Kang stands abruptly and steps in front of him.

Kang mutters into Su's ear, and an uncomfortable feeling snakes through me. I wish fiercely that I were close enough to hear what the viceroy is saying.

Su looks the viceroy in the eye, nods, and turns back to the crowd. "The presentation will not be necessary, as Viceroy Kang has already chosen his bride."

So quickly? I feel sorry for whichever poor woman will be forced to leave with that man. The crowd titters, echoing my curiosity.

Headman Su glances around. "Liang Anlei!"

My eyes widen. *Why is he calling me?*

Viceroy Kang's gaze finds me first. A hungry look glitters in his eyes, and a subtle sneer plays across his lips.

My heart stops. *It's me . . . He wants me . . .*

My legs start running before the realization fully hits me. And when it does, I urge them to run faster.

CHAPTER FOUR

MY HOME, MY HEART

I don't know where I'm going . . . I just can't stay here. My heart urges me to run. *Kuai pao . . . Kuai pao . . .* it's all I know how to do.

"Anlei!" Mother's voice rings in my ears, but I don't stop.

How could Viceroy Kang have chosen *me*? I'm hardly the kind of girl a government official would want to marry . . . My manners are crude even on my best days. Does he realize that I'm the same mud-covered peasant he looked down upon last night?

Glimpsing a bridge, I turn sharply toward it. I duck under the arched wood. The tide is low enough for several inches of land to stand between the base of the bridge and the stream it spans.

Panting, I lean back. *What do I do?*

Every inch of me revolts at the prospect of marrying the viceroy. Not only is he old enough to be my father, not only does he clearly look down upon me and my people, but the way he regarded me—as if I'm some piece of property he can buy—and the way he had Headman Su call for me like a dog showed me his character.

The thought of marrying him makes me sick. I *cannot* spend the rest of my life under his roof, forced to entertain his whims and bear his children . . . The very thought makes me gag.

For several minutes, I stand in the shadow of the bridge, wishing I could melt into it. My mind whirls, and my heart pounds. I can refuse the viceroy all I want, but the choice isn't mine. It's Su's. With both Father and Grandfather gone and no other male relatives in the village, the headman is effectively the patriarch of our family—a role he's taken on for more and more households as the Ligui have devastated the population. We mostly provide for ourselves between Mother's sewing skills, Anshui's tinkering, and my role in the Dailan Guard, but when that's not enough, Su's the one who sees that we have what we need. It's his right to marry me off to whomever he pleases, and there's nothing I can do about it. The injustice roils my blood.

Thoughts race through my head. If I can't refuse, maybe I can run away. I wouldn't need much—just a weapon and a change of clothes. I could disappear into the countryside and never see Kang again.

"Anlei!" Mother peers down at me from the bridge above, disappointment clouding her lined face.

"I can't marry him." I shake my head vigorously. "I *can't*."

Mother approaches, joining me in the bridge's shadow. "Anlei—"

"It's not fair! Why must I marry someone I don't even know? What does the viceroy want with a village girl anyway?"

"It was Headman Su who insisted upon a marriage alliance. He feared that without that kind of permanent bond with Dailan, the viceroy would break his word and fail to provide the promised protection after receiving the River Pearl. Since he is a powerful man, such a transgression would have no court for justice." Mother's thin brows tilt with sorrow. "I didn't want this fate for you either. I wanted you to meet a nice boy who makes you laugh, to fall in love without meaning to and marry after realizing you couldn't live without him. . . . I wanted you to have what I had with your father."

"So don't make me do this! Can't you convince the headman to leave me alone?"

"I understand how hard this must be for you." Her voice is gentle. "You've enjoyed a lot of freedom in Dailan. I always thought you'd be married by now, but you never showed any interest in being a wife, and I would never push you to be anyone but who you are. Things will be different if you marry the viceroy . . . what's being asked of you is nothing short of a sacrifice. Under different circumstances, I would never ask you to accept his hand. But it's not your fate alone that's at stake."

"But . . . there are plenty of eligible women in Dailan! Surely one of them *wants* to be a viceroy's wife! We can convince him that I'm unsuitable. . . . I—I dress like a boy and fight Ligui! My hands are blistered and my skin's too dark. . . . What viceroy would want a wife like *that*?"

Mother sighs. "Headman Su offered to find him a girl more suited to being a lady. But Viceroy Kang is a proud man, and you insulted him when you ran. He'll lose face if it looks like you can refuse him. Even our attempts to persuade him to choose someone else offend him, for it calls his original judgment into question. He stated that he will marry the girl he chose or leave for good."

"And he'll take his army with him." My heart sinks. "What about the River Pearl? He'd be abandoning that too."

"He is a *viceroy*, Anlei. You've lived here all your life, so it may be difficult for you to grasp how important appearances are to a man of his rank. No prize is worth losing face for. If it were known that he caved to a village girl's wishes, he would never be respected by his peers again."

"He'd let all of Dailan fall to the Ligui for the sake of his pride."

"Exactly." Mother places a gentle hand on my shoulder. "The question is: Would you do the same?"

I knit my brows, startled that she'd even ask. "I risk my life every night to protect our people!"

"Yet your refusal to marry the viceroy would doom Dailan to remain vulnerable."

I drop my gaze. Though I'd be glad to fight the Ligui until my dying breath, they would claim many more lives than just my own. The viceroy's forces could provide a hundred times the protection of our ragtag group of villagers; just one of those mechanical dragons could protect Dailan better than the entire Guard.

Viceroy Kang is offering the lives of my entire village in exchange for me—and the River Pearl. He'd have taken the pearl without my being part of the deal, but Su was right to distrust his word. A marriage alliance would seal the promise.

"But why did he have to choose *me*?" I wonder aloud.

Mother gives me a sad smile. "You're a beautiful and talented young woman, and you dazzled in your performance as Warrioress. Is it really such a surprise?"

Despite everything, Mother's praise warms my heart.

Her expression falls. "If I'd known that the viceroy was looking for a bride, I would have forbidden you and your sister from performing. But it's too late now, and as much as I wish it weren't so, you have a choice to make."

A heavy feeling descends in my chest. If I don't agree to this union, then I'll truly be as selfish as Pinghua accused me of being. "No, I don't. I swore I'd do anything to protect Dailan. Even if it means marrying the viceroy."

"I'm proud of you, *baobei*." She kisses my forehead. "Try to see the good in this arrangement. Even if you don't care for the viceroy's riches, you've always said you wanted to see the world. He'll take you to his palace in Tongqiucheng, and perhaps, if he favors you, he'll let you accompany him on his travels. You may even find in his household what you couldn't in Dailan: friendships."

"I have friends here!"

She gives me a patient look. "You have family and neighbors, but I don't think you've ever had a true friend in Dailan—someone you trust and confide in. Am I wrong?"

Sometimes I wonder what would have happened to me if the Ligui hadn't killed so many of our men, giving me a chance to become a warrior. As a girl, I would never have had the chance to prove my worth in battle if not for them. I'd have been pressured to marry or treated as an outcast for refusing to. I understand what traditional womanhood means to everyone else—including Mother and Pinghua and maybe Anshui—but it isn't what I was born for. I used to think I'd grow into it; when I was younger, I'd watch older girls become wives—spending their days tending to their homes and husbands and children—and think that when I turned their age, I'd want that life too. But now that I'm seventeen and still have no interest in being a traditional wife, I realize that while it's something I respect, it's not something I can become without changing my very soul.

"I've never really belonged here," I murmur. "Dailan is my home, but . . . I've always wanted something else."

Mother nods. "I know. You inherited my parents' adventurous spirits. This journey will give you a chance to expand your world—and those in it. There are only so many people in Dailan to meet. Perhaps, once you leave, you'll learn to connect with and even love another."

"I love plenty," I grumble. "I love Dailan enough to marry that viceroy for them."

"That's different. You love your home as a whole, but not the individuals in it, apart from those you were born to. So often you treat even people you've known for years as if they were strangers." She strokes my hair. "I don't mean to criticize you. I only hope you can see this marriage not as an end to your life here, but as a beginning to a new one."

Though I know there is wisdom in her words, I take little comfort in them. "I'll try."

I force myself to return to the square with Mother. Viceroy Kang sits in his chair with a deep scowl, and Headman Su paces along the platform edge, quivering with nervous energy. When he spots me, he waves his arm in an urgent, beckoning gesture.

I grit my teeth. Part of me hates him for making this deal. Yet I can't blame him for doing what he thought he had to for the sake of Dailan. Drawing a breath, I walk up the wooden steps to the platform. Kang's gaze flicks over me, and a satisfied smirk curls his lips. I long to punch it off his face. But though he'd let a village die for his pride, for the sake of my home, I swallow mine.

"Forgive me, Viceroy." I drop to my knees before him, schooling my features into something humble. "I was so intimidated by your greatness, I did not know what to do when my name was called."

"You should not have run from me." Kang's voice is light, and I detect mockery in his tone. "You nearly cost your village my protection."

Though disgust coils through my stomach, I manage not to scowl.

Kang places his long, cool fingers under my chin and lifts it. His harsh eyes meet mine. "Your village headman has agreed to our union, but I want to hear it from you."

What kind of sick game is this? It's not enough for him to claim me . . . he needs me to *want* to be his. He probably expects me to swear unconditional loyalty and devotion to him.

Since I can't bring myself to do that, I say, "If Dailan has your protection, then you'll have your bride."

Kang nods, apparently satisfied, and turns to Su. "You will be her guardian until the wedding and accompany her to Tongqiucheng. We leave at dawn."

"Yes, Viceroy." Su bows his head.

As I climb to my feet, I look over the platform at the faces of the villagers in the square. A myriad of expressions greet me, and I wonder what they're feeling . . . maybe sympathetic to my plight, maybe puzzled as to why I ran, maybe a bit jealous. I suppose, in the eyes of some, I've received a great honor. I'll be royalty, living in luxury. If only they knew how quickly I'd trade places with any one of them. Though I try to take comfort in what Mother told me, all I see in my future is a gilded cage.

It's for my people that I do this. All of them—whether they love me or hate me or resent me. For them, I'll play the part of a humble bride. Even though I'd rather dive into the Courts of Hell.

CHAPTER FIVE

LADY JIANGZHU

Morning light gilds the viceroy's dragon-shaped cruiser, brightening its bronze and red hull. As I follow Headman Su up the gangplank, I feel like I'm walking into a giant fire. Two automatons clank and whir as they walk beside me, carrying my plain, wooden trunk between them. After I'd gone home to pack yesterday, Su came by with a message from Kang saying that I didn't need to bring anything, since he'd provide me with new clothes when I arrived in Tongqiucheng. In other words: *The viceroy thinks everything you own must be garbage and has no place in his palace.*

I insisted upon bringing a few things anyway. They'll be my one connection to my home after I leave.

I glance back at the shore, where Anshui watches me with mournful eyes. She did such a good job of pretending she was happy for me yesterday, I almost believed her.

"You're so lucky!" she said with a grin. "You'll get beautiful clothes and servants who will comb your hair with jade! Everyone's so jealous of you!"

I bit down bitter words and tried to play along. "I'll be sure to write and tell you all about it."

"Maybe your husband will let me join you someday." Anshui's voice quivered. "I could work in the palace . . ."

After we went to bed, she sobbed quietly into her pillow, and it shattered me. I wanted to go over and comfort her, but what could I say? I couldn't promise I'd be back someday, couldn't pretend I have any choice over what will happen to me once I reach Tongqiucheng.

My life is no longer my own . . . I as good as belong to the viceroy.

I wrap my fingers around my jade pendant and blink back tears. I tried to give it to Anshui, but she insisted that I keep it.

"Father gave it to *you*, and now it's something you can remember all of us by." She then handed me the spectacles she'd been tinkering with. "I made them to help you see better in the dark. They're not quite finished, but . . . they mostly work."

"I love them." I embraced her, touched. She'd spent hours working on that little device, experimenting with machinery and magic. And whether they work or not, they're now my most precious possession beside my pendant.

As I step onto the cruiser's deck, I pause to take one last look at my village; its sloping rooftops, the humble boats tied against the riverbank. Though part of me is excited to see Tongqiucheng, no matter how great the city turns out to be, it will never match Dailan in my heart.

"Anlei!" Su throws me a stern look. "*Kuai dian.* You mustn't keep the viceroy waiting."

I scowl but say nothing as I follow him. Viceroy Kang and his entourage boarded last night, and by the looks of things, he has no intention of coming out of his chambers to greet us.

Glancing around, I feel like I've just walked into a small town carried on the back of a dragon. Rectangular houses line the deck, and a large building with a red, three-tiered roof rises from the center. Colorful paint brightens its ornately carved façade, as if the whole thing is embedded with rubies and emeralds and brushed with gold leaf. I wonder if even the Emperor has a flagship so resplendent. Kang must be inside. Cyborg soldiers guard the bronze doors, and this close, I realize that their mechanical arms haven't *replaced* their human ones, but instead cover them in metal casing with embedded machines.

Su leads me to one of the small houses, his mechanical foot clunking against the deck. As an automaton opens the door, he gestures for me to enter.

"This is where you'll be staying for the duration of the journey," he says. "My cabin will be on the opposite side of the ship. Should you need anything, instruct the automaton to fetch me, and I'll do what I can."

I nod. It feels odd to be traveling alone with the headman. Though he's been a presence in my life for as long as I can remember, we aren't exactly close.

Su meets my gaze. "I know this isn't easy for you. You're a very brave young woman."

I try to smile but don't quite succeed. "How long will the journey take?"

"Because of the viceroy's magic, this ship is several times faster than the quickest horse." Su looks around the ship with admiration. "We should be in Tongqiucheng by this time tomorrow, and the wedding is to take place the day after."

So fast? I blink in astonishment. It would take weeks to reach Tongqiucheng by horse. I can't believe that in less than two days I'll be the viceroy's eighth wife. Nausea sweeps over me.

This journey will expand my world . . . I repeat Mother's words over and over, wishing I could take comfort in them. But too much uncertainty stretches before me, and all I know is what's being taken from me—my family and my freedom.

Automatons place my trunk in the corner of the room, which is empty except for a chair and a desk. A rectangular doorway leads into a second room containing a narrow bed. Golden light spills through a square window facing the shore, and through it I spot Anshui standing beside Mother. I wave vigorously. Anshui brightens when she spots me and waves back.

"Anlei!" A man's voice whispers my name.

Whirling, I expect to see Su standing in the doorway, but he's already halfway across the deck. Only an automaton stands by my door, its gears and joints still. Su watches as a cyborg soldier carries a jade pedestal containing the River Pearl, which is the size of a large grape and glows pure white even as dawn tints everything else. As he directs the cyborg to place the pearl in his chambers—he'll be its custodian until the wedding—I imagine I can still smell the smoke of hundreds of pieces of paper burning in a ceremonial bowl before the River Dragon Shrine.

For the ritual to break the enchantment binding the pearl to Dailan, each person born in the village mixed a drop of his or her blood in ink, then wrote his or her name on the paper. Those too young or infirm to write their own names were guided by their parents or relatives. When my turn came to take a stick of incense and light the paper on fire, I almost ran again. One refusal—my refusal—would have been all that was needed to make the viceroy leave and never return.

He'd let all of Dailan fall to the Ligui for the sake of his pride . . . Would you?

With those words echoing through my head, I threw my burning name into the bowl. Now, anyone can possess the River Pearl.

"Anlei!" The man's voice whispers again, interrupting my thoughts. This time, I know it's not Su because the headman is talking to one of the soldiers.

"Who's there?" I whip around, but unless it was the automaton that spoke, no one's near enough to have whispered. I peer at the machine's theatrically painted face, wondering if it *had* spoken. Maybe the magic that powers it gave it a voice as well.

"Anlei!"

The voice is louder this time. And it sounds . . . it sounds so familiar.

"Father?" My chest tightens. Though I've often prayed that Father's ghost would speak to me, visits from the departed are supposed to take place during prayers or in dreams . . . for a ghost to appear randomly, without being called upon, is virtually unheard of.

Whatever the circumstances, I'd give anything to see Father again. "Father!"

For several moments, I stand there hoping and waiting. But all I hear are the whispers of the wind outside and the voices of the ship's crew as they prepare for launch.

The silence slices my heart like a knife. I can't help wondering if maybe it was my own guilt calling to me, accusing me of failing to avenge him. Now that I'm to marry the viceroy, I've lost my chance. The viceroy would never let one of his wives run around slaying Ligui. I'll be kept locked up and safe—no different from the River Pearl.

Knowing that didn't keep me from hiding Father's sword at the bottom of my trunk. Even if I never wield it again, I couldn't bear to part with it.

The floor vibrates as an engine starts rumbling. Realizing that we're about to leave, I rush back to the window. My family remains on the shore, along with what looks like the entire village. Water splashes as the boat's propellers begin spinning, surrounded by golden, crackling flecks of magic.

I remain by my window as the cruiser rises, flanked by mechanical dragons, and I keep watching as Dailan shrinks below me.

White clouds and blue sky fade into a speckled night. Outside my window, the not-quite-full moon glows. I've spent all day watching the sky outside my window—the slow, deliberate dance of the clouds, the contortions of colors as varying shades of blue transformed into the fiery hues of sunset. Beautiful as it is, having nothing else to do is driving me mad. Ordinarily, I would have spent the day helping

Mother with chores or training in combat. But a lady does none of these things, and though I'm not married yet, I'm supposed to start acting like one.

At one point, Su arrived to inform me that after the wedding, I'll be known as Lady Jiangzhu—Lady of the River Pearl. All I did was nod in response. I couldn't exactly object.

Leaning my elbows against the windowsill, I release a long sigh. I'm so bored, I almost want to jump out just to see what would happen. My fingers itch to grip Father's sword and run through a few drills.

A warrior must be disciplined, on and off the battlefield, Father told me once, and I've been repeating those words in my head all day. In my mind, I see his face—powerful jaw, inky beard, stern, focused eyes. If he were here, he'd tell me that even though I won't be fighting anymore, I must still practice discipline. Which means no jumping out windows and no practicing sword drills in my room. *But I'm so bored . . .*

A wisp of black crosses one of the clouds outside. I straighten, my instincts leaping to action. I've seen enough Ligui to recognize one about to materialize.

Excitement courses through me. I dig Father's sword out from the bottom of my trunk. My wide tunic—a woman's tunic—allows me almost as much movement as my guard outfit would have, even though the high collar, decorated with knotted buttons, chokes me somewhat when I move.

A gong's ring splits the air. Cyborg soldiers leap into action. By the time I make it onto the deck, several are already battling Ligui in various forms. Explosions ring through the night as the mechanical dragons blast entire swaths of the creatures with their fiery breaths.

My blood cries out for action, and I race into the fray. Seeing one soldier locked in duel with a man-shaped Ligui, I slice through the monster from behind. The satisfying crackle of my enchanted sword against its shadowy body is music to my ears.

The soldier carries an ordinary sword. Yet he had no problem dueling the supernatural creature . . . My gaze falls on his mechanical arm, and I realize that his cyborg enhancements must allow him to wield *any* weapon as if it were enchanted.

"Lady! What are you doing out here?" The soldier grips my arm, metal fingers digging into my sleeve. "You must stay inside."

I open my mouth to protest but glimpse another man-shaped Ligui heading toward the cabins on the other side of the deck. The sight of a glowing white crescent on his neck sends a burst of energy through me. I tear out of the soldier's grasp.

May the Gods of Heaven and Earth witness my oath: I will avenge you, Father.

I won't fail this time.

The shadowy figure with the white crescent climbs onto the roof of one of the cabins. I sprint across the deck and spring off the ground, grab the edge of the roof, and pull myself up.

The Shadow Warrior is several cabins down now, running along the narrow beam across the sloped rooftops. I follow as quickly as I can, holding my arms out for balance.

When I catch up, I bring my sword crashing down toward him. He holds up his own weapon to block me, and our weapons sizzle against each other. A few hot sparks hit my skin, but I don't care. His glowing eyes take on that mocking glint. Though I can't see the rest of his face, I know he must be grinning. Fury flares through me. I swipe his weapon to the side and strike again. This time, he parries hard enough to send me stumbling off the beam. My foot slips, and I tumble off the roof.

I land in a heap on the deck. The Shadow Warrior vanishes over the roof, and before I can begin my pursuit strong hands seize both my arms.

"What is the meaning of this?" Viceroy Kang glares down at me, his harsh eyes boring into mine.

"Let me go!"

"No wife of mine will behave like such a barbarian!" Kang drags me toward my cabin while explosions tear the darkness above. The mechanical dragons wind through the air, their serpentine bodies clunking as they twist and curve over the ship. The Ligui scatter, their screeches rattling the night.

When we reach my cabin, Kang tries to take the sword from my hand, but I hold it tight.

"No!" I yank it away from him. "It was my father's!"

Kang reaches for the weapon again but pauses. An aura of coolness descends upon him. "No doubt your father taught you the value of discipline."

I grit my teeth, hating that he'd use my father against me.

"I will allow you to keep the sword as a reminder of his lessons." He gives me an indulgent smile, as if he's granting me the greatest favor in the world. "But you must never wield it again. Behave yourself, and you will receive many such favors. Refuse, and you'll find I'm not always so generous."

He strides out toward the deck where the Ligui are all but vanquished. The Shadow Warrior is nowhere in sight. I don't know if one of the mechanical dragons destroyed him or if he escaped, but one thing's for sure: I failed again.

Dejected, I sink down into my chair. The sword slides from my grasp, and I bury my face in my hands. That was my last chance to fight, my last chance to claim glory.

Liang Anlei is gone. I'm to be Lady Jiangzhu.

CHAPTER SIX

THE CITY OF COPPER AUTUMN

The streets of Tongqiucheng—the City of Copper Autumn—stretch in amber lines outside my window, though I can only see a sliver at a time. Because I own nothing befitting a lady, Viceroy Kang ordered me to keep the curtain of my carriage down. The ruby silk flutters as my mechanical carriage moves along, humming and hissing on large wheels. Through the crack between the curtain and the wide window frame, I catch snatches of the city outside. Buildings line the streets, each two or three stories high with sloping roofs supported by red or yellow columns. Ornate carvings and colorful paint embellish the trims in snaking patterns of flowers or dragons or tigers. Even the market stands, from which merchants sell everything from fruits to beads, are richly decorated. The midday sun glints off gilded accents. Mother was right about one thing: agreeing to this marriage has given me a chance to see this magnificent place.

High above, mechanical dragons twist through the blue sky. According to Kang, nothing supernatural can cross Tongqiucheng's borders without one of them noticing. Any Ligui are stopped before they can harm anyone here. Soon, that will be true for Dailan as well.

The streets bustle with people from all walks of life. In the short time between leaving the viceroy's ship and this moment, I've seen more individuals than all of Dailan holds. Some are dressed in simple white or blue tunics not unlike those my neighbors wore, while others sport fine embroidered silks. The men all wear their hair in the customary queue, and the women flaunt twisted hairstyles adorned with ribbons and carved pins. They all look like royalty to me, and I find it puzzling that they're walking around the streets alongside ordinary people. I guess Tongqiucheng is so wealthy that these people hardly even count as elite.

Several people throw curious glances in my direction and mutter to their neighbors. They must be speculating about who the viceroy's new bride is. I want to throw up the curtain and let them see me for exactly who I am: the poor village girl with messy braids, rough hands, and sun-browned skin. Why should I hide until the viceroy's servants dress me up and paint my face? He was the one who chose me, and his people should get to see exactly who their new Lady Jiangzhu is.

But my father's words about discipline keep circling through my mind.

Self-control today is a gift for tomorrow. Be kind to your future self.

Provoking my future husband's temper can lead to nothing good.

The carriage's engine belches white clouds of steam that briefly obscure what little view I have. A thin, sparkling haze hangs over the entire city, softening its edges. At first, I wonder if it's some kind of fog, but then I notice just how many machines puff out white wisps from metal exhaust tubes and give off little sparks of magic. Though I was accustomed to seeing the mechanical wagon rolling down Dailan's streets, hauling crops or transporting people, in Tongqiucheng, it's as if ten thousand spellmasters spend all day and all night creating all manner of devices. Bronze animals gallop up to storefronts or trot alongside their owners. Automatons amble alongside the people. Children chase clockwork butterflies that flash yellow lights, and metal birds with blade-like wings soar between windows, carrying rolled-up messages in their talons.

Anshui would love this. I bite my lip, wondering if I'll ever see my sister again.

A flash of movement outside catches my eye. Something's wrong—I feel it in my gut. I press one eye up to the crack between the curtain and the window frame.

Then I see it again—a figure darting into one of the shops ahead. The person moves so quickly, all I catch is a grayish blur of motion as they vanish through the elaborately decorated doorway of a store selling jade sculptures and other such fineries. Though two well-dressed men stand inside, apparently haggling, neither seems to have noticed a third person enter.

As the carriage rolls past the store, I keep my gaze fixed on it, certain that something is amiss. Seconds later, the figure appears in the alley to the store's left, apparently having emerged through a window. He pauses for a second, which is just long enough for me to realize that he is a *he*. Or at least he's wearing a man's tunic. Something yellow sits clutched in one hand . . . something that looks an awful lot like a silk coin purse.

"*Zei!* "I stick my head out of the carriage and point emphatically at the thief, but since I've made myself visible to the entire street, people seem more interested in ogling at me than hearing what I said.

The thief whirls toward me, but a gray cloth covers most of his face. To my surprise, the front of his head is unshaved . . . in fact, he has no queue at all. Thick black locks brush his shoulders. It's the hair of a foreigner—I've never seen any man fail to conform to the Imperial style before. Maybe he isn't a *he*—I've worn a man's tunic often enough. But the hair is still odd; I've never seen any women or girls with their locks unbound either unless they were in mourning.

Two glinting black eyes dart toward me, and for the briefest of moments, we lock gazes. Then the thief winks and sprints down the alley.

Hundan! The arrogance sparks my fury. This thief won't get away with stealing.

I leap out the carriage's window, barely hearing the gasps of the people in the street. The whole world blurs except for the path I need to take, which focuses in perfect clarity before me. I follow it through the crowd, heading in the direction I saw the thief take off in, and zigzag between men, women, and automatons. I race into the alley beside the store, which I reach in time to see the thief turn a corner.

Somewhere faraway, people are exclaiming words like "Who was that girl?" and "Is that the viceroy's new bride?" and "Lady! Come back!" Though my ears catch their sounds, their meanings vanish in my mind. All I know is that a thief is getting away with a crime, and I have to stop it.

I glimpse the lithe, fleeing figure ahead. A quick laugh, bright and clear, jingles past my ears. Apparently, they think it's funny that I'm chasing them. *Fool! We'll see how funny they find things when I catch them!*

The streets grow narrower and dirtier the farther I go from the main road. The buildings I whip past are no longer painted and carved, but simple wooden houses similar to those in Dailan.

The thief darts around one of them. I follow—then come to an abrupt halt.

Instead of fleeing, the thief now crouches in the muddy street. A dirty, barefoot old man in ragged clothing sits against the wall with a cracked clay bowl before him. *A beggar.*

To my surprise, the thief places the coin purse in the bowl.

The beggar bows his head in gratitude. "*Duo xie*, Masked Giver." He picks up the purse with frail, wrinkled fingers and looks up at the sky. "The Gods of Heaven and Earth, bless this boy."

My fury peters away as I realize what's happening. A man in a fancy shop, a silk coin purse, an old beggar in the street . . .

A mix of dismay and admiration whirls through me. I can't capture the thief *now*. I couldn't bear to snatch the purse away from the old man, and without it, I have no evidence that the masked man even *is* a thief.

He stands and turns to me. From the way his eyes twinkle, I know he's grinning at me beneath that mask. "You should return to your carriage, Lady."

He dashes off, and this time, I don't pursue. My heart pounds from the chase, and with the rush of action gone, weariness settles into my limbs. The Masked Giver disappears behind a rickety wooden house as I stare after him, wondering who he is. What kind of arrogant idiot steals in broad daylight—and right in front of the viceroy's convoy? And what kind of thief takes such a huge risk only to give away his prize?

He's still a criminal, I remind myself. Part of me wonders if I made a mistake in letting him go. But what kind person would I have been if I'd taken money from an old man in need when I knew it came from someone with plenty?

"Lady Jiangzhu!"

A man's voice booms through the street, accompanied by footsteps. For a moment, I wonder who he's calling to before I realize it's me.

I'm not Lady Jiangzhu yet! For one more day, I'm still Liang Anlei.

I face the approaching soldier—one of the cyborgs from the flying ship. Pounding hoofbeats ring out behind him.

Viceroy Kang approaches on horseback, flanked by two guards. His harsh voice explodes like thunder. "How dare you leave the carriage after I instructed you not to?"

"I saw a thief!" I square my shoulders. "In Dailan, it's every person's duty to stop a crime in action."

"You're not in your village anymore." Kang glares down at me. "This kind of behavior will not be tolerated."

You don't command me! I bite back the words. Much as I wish they were true, a sinking part of me knows they're not.

Swallowing hard, I lower my chin. "I'm sorry. I should have controlled my impulses."

Kang's lips curl. "Good. You are learning. But if anything like this happens again, you will be disciplined. Understand?"

Hatred burns in my chest, and I dig my nails into my palms. *If he thinks I'd let him hit me or lock me up, he's dead wrong.* Yet I can't stop the fear from trickling down my spine.

Turning to the soldier, he says, "Take her back to the carriage and tell everyone that she's a servant—a decoy for my actual bride, who is already inside the palace."

"Yes, sir!" The soldier seizes my arm as the viceroy and his guards ride off.

The soldier drags me through the streets, treating me like the servant girl he tells everyone I am.

My new title might be Lady, but even after they scrub me clean, paint my face, and clothe me in silk, I'll still be little more than a slave.

CHAPTER SEVEN

PAINTED DOLL

A strange girl stares at me from within a large, golden frame molded to look like a dozen koi swimming in a circle. The fish's scales flash under the muted sunlight on the other side of the paper window, and they almost appear to move over their lacquered red stand. They're trying to drown her—the grotesque doll that stands where my reflection should be.

Though I've worn heavy makeup for performances before, this *feels* different. Then, I was transforming into a figure from legend or a mythical creature. It was all part of the showmanship, meant for entertainment and exaggeration. And it was always my choice to participate.

But the chalky girl with the unnaturally bright lips and garishly flushed cheeks—that's who I'm being forced to turn into. Lady Jiangzhu, the viceroy's wife. If I'd chosen to be her, I might have found her beautiful. Instead, she's a mutilated version of me. Though she's dressed in luscious red silk embroidered with golden dragons, she looks as if she's fading away. Wide sleeves cover her hands, and her long skirt drags on the ground. It will be just the right length when she slips on her shoes, which glimmer with colorful embroidered flowers and balance on jeweled blocks. They resemble a horse's hoofs and seem impossible to walk in. Not that Lady Jiangzhu will have anywhere to go, since she's forbidden from leaving the viceroy's palace.

Though it looks magnificent—a sprawling city within a city surrounded by red walls—the palace might as well be a prison. No—a tomb. I find it hard to admire the red one-story houses with golden roofs and the covered walkways decorated with painted flowers when they are keeping me from the life I want. Even the beauty of the viceroy's central hall, which has golden dragons snaking down its red columns and painted carvings of the zodiac animals along its eaves, looks gloomy and menacing to me. The statue-lined stone terraces, the brilliant flowers and sculpted mountains in the gardens, the intricate, multi-layered roofs of the important halls . . . all are tainted by the knowledge of my fate among them.

Any hope that something good might come out of this marriage has disappeared. It's not the journey Mother hoped for, and it never will be.

My heart quivers as the girl in the mirror obediently allows strange women to bedeck her for her wedding. I don't know why this shard of fear remains embedded in my chest. Except for the day I watched the Shadow Warrior murder my father, I've never been so frightened in my life.

The women—who serve the viceroy's other wives and were lent to me for my wedding—twist my hair into elaborate knots. Other than to instruct me to stand or lift my arms or tilt my head, they haven't spoken to me; if their loyalties are to their mistresses, then they hardly have reason to welcome another wife. Though I stand among others, I'm completely alone.

I picture the long, empty days ahead, broken up only by the viceroy's visits. I imagine that horrible man touching my skin and demanding his rights as a husband . . . The thought sends bile up my throat. How will I survive this? If he tries to kiss me, I might find myself strangling him before I know what I'm doing.

But powerful officials are known for exacting revenge on generations of families for the misdeeds of one individual. Viceroy Kang could destroy my entire village if I wrong him, and with his army of bronze dragons, Dailan wouldn't stand a chance. He's as good as holding them hostage—my family, my neighbors, everyone I've ever met. I'll have no choice but to yield to his wishes and restrain my rage. I doubt any of the Courts of Hell hold as excruciating a torture as my future holds for me.

In the mirror, Lady Jiangzhu meets my gaze. Her eyes are dead.

I'm worse than dead.

A powerful swelling presses against my heart, and though I clench every muscle in my body, I can't stop my trembling.

"Are you all right?" One of the women glances at me with concern.

I breathe hard, trying to contain the flood surging against my heart. But it's no use; the dam is cracking. And no one can be here to see the deluge. "Get out of here. All of you."

The woman knits her eyebrows. "But—"

"Gun!" I point emphatically at the door. "Get out!"

Her eyes widen with fright. "If you're late for the ceremony, the viceroy will punish all of us."

"I–I just need a few minutes." My voice cracks. "Please—just five minutes."

The woman hesitates, then nods. She turns to the others and motions for them to follow as she leaves.

As soon as she's out of sight, my legs collapse beneath me. Unwelcome tears stream down my cheeks, and I press my hands against my eyes, trying to push them back. The air seems to drown me, and I gasp for breath.

It's over . . . It's all over . . .

I'll never again run through the streets of Dailan, not caring about messed-up hair or muddied shoes, never again stand watch with the Guard. Everything I know is gone forever.

And what's replacing it? An eternity of fearing that any wrong move I make will doom my family, my people. Of biting my tongue and binding my warrior's instincts.

Of living with Viceroy Kang as my husband.

If only the Shadow Warrior had cut me down.

I grasp at my jade pendant, which hides beneath the high collar of my wedding dress. Though my fingers meet silk, I feel its smooth groves. The stone calms me, and I picture Father's face. He gave his life for Dailan. I can do the same.

I draw a deep breath and force myself to stand. In the mirror, the grotesque doll appears even more absurd with her smudged makeup. She's a pathetic, self-pitying thing, and I never want to see her again.

Tomorrow won't change because I'm afraid of it. I might as well maintain what little dignity I have left.

I hastily brush my cheeks. No doubt the women will be back soon, and I can't let them see me like this. From my performing days, I know how to fix bad makeup, and I rush to erase the smudges on my cheeks. There's nothing I can do about the redness in my eyes.

Sudden shouts cut through the air, punctuated by rushing footsteps. I turn toward the door as two of Kang's guards, accompanied by one of his cyborg soldiers, burst in with their weapons raised. Their long queues whip over their shoulders as they whirl this way and that, apparently looking for something.

I furrow my brow. "What's going on?"

One of the guards glances at me. "There's a thief in the palace—a masked man without a queue."

The Masked Giver? He must be arrogant indeed to rob the viceroy himself on the day of his wedding.

"Have you seen anything?" the guard asks.

I shake my head. Even if I had, I wouldn't have told them. Let that idealistic idiot take the viceroy's knickknacks and hand them to beggars. What do I care?

"Search everywhere!" Kang's voice thunders through the hallway outside. He strides into the room, his face purple with rage. "You! Did you have anything to do with this?"

My jaw drops. "Of course not!"

Before I can ask why he'd even think that, Headman Su scurries in after him, his mechanical leg whirring frenetically. "I assure you, Your Honor, we want the thief caught as much as you do! We would never dishonor our people by breaking the oath we made to you!"

"What happened?" I ask.

He turns to me with a fearful, quivering expression. "The River Pearl has been stolen. One of the guards glimpsed a masked thief running off with it, but he vanished."

I gasp. I knew the Masked Giver was bold, but I never imagined he'd take the River Pearl. It wasn't the viceroy he robbed—it was Dailan. *Gai si! I shouldn't have let him go!*

Kang's eyes flash. "Without the River Pearl, I cannot marry her! And neither will I send my army to Dailan. The pearl and a marriage alliance for my protection—*that* was our deal."

"And we will honor it!" Su clasps his hands and holds them out before him in a gesture of pleading. "We want the thief caught as much as you do—more so, even! It is our village's honor and safety that's at stake, and we will do whatever we can to get the River Pearl back."

"Yes, we will!" Anger burns like an ember in my chest. Whatever the Masked Giver's intentions, he could destroy everything I am willing to sacrifice myself for. "If marrying you means protecting my village, no thief will stop me!"

Kang's countenance relaxes, and he gives me a thin smile. "Apologies, my bride. Of course you'd be as eager to marry me as I am to wed you."

I bite my teeth. *Discipline . . .*

He approaches. "Both you and the River Pearl *will* be mine, and I'll let you sit beside me when we behead that troublesome thief."

Nausea rolls through my stomach. I don't want the Masked Giver *dead*. But I'm not about to protest right now—especially since the thief apparently doesn't care that my whole village could die because of him.

Kang turns to his guards. "I want the thief alive so I can execute him publicly as an example to other criminals. And most importantly, I want the River Pearl back. Understand?"

"Yes, sir!" The guards rush out of the room, either to spread the word or continue their search.

Viceroy Kang strides out after them, his long gold tunic swishing behind him. Headman Su follows. I can only guess that he'll continue to beg forgiveness, even though he's done nothing wrong. I feel awful for him. He wants Dailan safe as badly as I do, yet he's helpless to do anything other than plead with the viceroy to keep to our agreement. He'd probably tell me to keep quiet while the guards search for the thief.

But I've never been very good at waiting.

CHAPTER EIGHT

THE MASKED GIVER

Headman Su was right when he said that it's our village's honor and safety at stake; I plan to use those very words if Viceroy Kang or his men catch me. In the quiet of the night, I can make out the distant whirring of the mechanical dragons patrolling the sky and guarding the city from Ligui. Moonlight glazes the ornate storefronts lining the city's streets, and paper lanterns dance above me, glittering with the magic that illuminates and buoys them in place of flames. No one gives me a second glance as I wind through them, retracing the steps I took yesterday when I chased the Masked Giver. Back in my plain tunic and scrubbed clean of a lady's makeup, I look too ordinary to pay attention to, which is how I want it.

Kang's guards march up and down the streets, questioning every other person they encounter about whether they've seen a man in a mask. Those with cyborg parts stare into the faces of the people they interrogate with glowing mechanical eyes. My pulse quickens as I pass them. Fortunately, none seem to notice me.

The streets grow narrower, the buildings plainer, and the lanterns scarcer. A stench wafts through the air—sewage and rotting garbage. I'm reaching the poor area where I last saw the Masked Giver, but I can barely see a few feet in front of me. Since I don't want to risk drawing attention to myself, I didn't bring anything to light my way. *Time to see how well Anshui's spectacles work.*

I pull them from the pocket of my baggy trousers and place them on my face. The street appears a little lighter, as if a solitary lamp glows somewhere above. Anshui never had the chance to tell me how they work, but I know the little gears on the sides aren't for decoration, so I turn one of them experimentally; the rest click in response. The unseen lamp glows brighter. Not by much, but just enough for me not to trip in the shadows.

As I continue forward, the heavy gold hairpin in my pocket bangs against my thigh. It was part of my wedding ensemble, but I doubt anyone will miss it. Enough wealth fills the viceroy's palace that the loss of a single adornment would hardly be cause for alarm. And if it is . . . well, I'll deal with the fallout later. Right now, it's more important that I locate the River Pearl.

I find the old beggar man sitting against the same wall as yesterday. He glances up at me and clasps his hands. "Please, Lady. Please help an old man."

I cock my head. "I'm no lady."

"Perhaps not yet, but soon."

He must remember me. I crouch before him and pull the gold hairpin from my pocket. "I've come with an offer: this for anything you know about the Masked Giver."

The old man recoils. "No . . . No, Lady. I will not betray him."

I scowl. "Why not?"

"He's a hero to the forgotten parts of the city." The beggar sweeps his arm. "No one here would send him to his death."

"He's no hero!"

I hold up the pin. "There are thousands of treasures like this in the viceroy's palace, yet the Masked Giver took the *one thing* my village is counting on to survive. If Kang doesn't get the River Pearl, the Ligui could wipe out my home!"

The old man's white brows tilt with sympathy. "The Masked Giver must not have known of the pearl's significance."

"I don't care. If I fail to return it . . . " I shudder.

"It's only the pearl you want? You don't want to see the Masked Giver executed?"

I shake my head. I may want to make the thief pay for the agony he's caused me, but not with his life.

The old man strokes his long beard. "I'll tell you where you can find the Masked Giver, but only if you'll help him escape the city. Swear on your father's soul that you'll keep the viceroy from killing him."

I bite the inside of my cheek, considering, then nod once. "I swear."

His eyes crinkle, and he motions for me to draw closer. I lean toward him, and he whispers in my ear, "There's an abandoned house where he hides . . . You'll probably find him there. Tell him Lao Gu sent you to help him."

"*Xie xie.*" I nod in thanks. I doubt the thief will want my assistance, but I keep my oaths. Whether it was greed or foolhardiness that led him to steal the River Pearl, I just need it back. Even if it means helping the man who took it escape. Placing the gold pin in the beggar's bowl, I say, "Keep that. Now, how do I find this house?"

I slip through the shadows, searching for the abandoned house Lao Gu directed me to. Spotting a cyborg soldier, I duck behind a cart. He stops several people, demanding to know if they've seen the thief, but none reveal any information. I wait for him to move on, my heart jittering.

Finally the guard's heavy footsteps fade into the distance, and I continue through the streets until I reach the building matching Lao Gu's description. I don't pass any more guards along the way; my guess is that they're spread too thin to guard *every* street. Thanks to Anshui's spectacles, I'm able to move through the blackest shadows and stay out of sight.

A carved lion roars against a rotting panel above the building's cracked door. This part of the city is so dark and lonely; not a single ray of lantern light spills over. I tuck the spectacles into my pocket and use a few moonbeams to guide me the rest of the way.

I push the door open, and its rickety hinges creak. As I step into an empty room with wide windows, a shadow darts up the stairs.

"Stop!" I bolt after it.

I reach the second story and spot the thief leaping off a windowsill, about to climb onto the roof. I seize his ankle and yank back hard, pulling him down.

Instead of stumbling, he uses the momentum to launch himself inside, knocking me flat. Cursing, I spring up and tackle him from behind, clasping his waist. He twists abruptly, throwing me off. My warrior's instincts spark to life, and I turn the fall into a barrel roll.

Enough moonlight spills through the window for me to glimpse a length of bamboo on the floor. I snatch it up. As the thief speeds toward the window, I sweep it into his ankle, tripping him.

This time, it's his turn to curse. I stand and point the stick at him, but before I can speak, a loud *clack* pierces the air as something solid meets my stick. Apparently there was more than one on the ground.

Spotting movement, I quickly raise my stick to block his strike.

He presses down, trying to force me back, and his masked face moves into a patch of moonlight. Black hair cascades down his cheeks, and thick eyebrows cut straight lines over intense eyes, which glint with amusement as they meet mine. "Why is it that every time we meet, you're trying to kill me?"

"If I wanted you dead, you'd be dead!" I arc my stick downward, swiping his off. "I'm not trying to kill you!" I lift one foot and send my heel into his gut. Compared to what I'm capable of, it hardly counts as a kick, but it's enough to send him staggering back.

Instead of crying out, he laughs. "Are you sure?"

He swings at me again. I want to yell, "Idiot! I came here to help you!" But I don't get a chance to between blocking his blows and attempting a few strikes of my own.

Our bamboo sticks clatter and crack as we move through the room in an absurd dance. The lack of light keeps me from seeing all the openings I could take, though I suspect the same is true for him. He keeps trying to get me out of the way so he can escape out one window or another, but I refuse to let him, and as our weapons crash against each other once more, his quick laugh flutters through the darkness. I realize with indignation that he's toying with me, that this is all some great joke to him. Furious, I strike harder.

I manage to drive him against the wall, our sticks locked against each other.

"Just *listen* for a moment!" I say through clenched teeth. "Lao Gu sent me to help you!"

He knits his brows. *"Shen me?"*

"If you give me back the River Pearl, I'll help you get past the viceroy's guards!"

"No deal." He tries to shove me back, but I drive my knee into his gut, knocking him against the wall. Though he doubles over, he keeps his weapon up. He laughs again, though there's a strange edge to the sound. "You really are determined to be the viceroy's wife, aren't you? He won't marry you without the pearl . . . That's why you're fighting so hard to get it back, right?"

The mocking in his voice sends wrath shooting up my chest. A bolt of energy jolts me. I twist hard enough to force his weapon out of his grip. "My village's fate depends on that pearl!" I shove the edge of the stick against his throat, standing close enough to feel his breath on my face even through the mask. "I need it to save my people!"

"So do I." All levity vanishes from his tone. "Without it, they're doomed."

"What do you mean?"

"I'll tell you if you let me go."

"As if I'd fall for that."

"Then we'll have to keep fighting." The teasing returns to his voice. "I'm tired, though. Wouldn't you rather talk for a change? I thought ladies preferred civilized conversation to stick fights."

I scowl. How dare he make fun of me when *I'm* the one with the advantage? "All I need to do is press harder to strangle you—then I could take the River Pearl off your dead body!"

"So why haven't you?" He lifts his brows. "If you're as ruthless as you claim, I'd like to see you try."

"Is this all a game to you?"

"Life is a game, Lady. So are you going to kill me or not?"

I glare at him. Furious as I am, I could never kill a person in cold blood. And he must be banking on that.

We stand there in silence, our faces inches from each other. With the adrenaline fading, weariness weighs down on me, and sweat trickles down my forehead. His heavy breaths tell me that the fight has exhausted both of us, yet I doubt either of us will surrender.

Maybe it wouldn't be a bad idea to back off and negotiate. That's what I came here for, after all. But if I release him, he could make for the window again, and we'd be right back to where we started. I need some kind of leverage. "Take off your mask and tell me your name. Then I'll lower my weapon and we can talk."

"So, you've decided to play. What good will seeing my face do? I'm easily identifiable." He blows a lock of hair off his eyes.

"Hair can be changed. Faces can't."

"I'm not so sure about that. As for my name—you don't expect me to give you a real one, do you?"

"Why not? You must know mine."

"Liang Anlei." The way he says my name makes it sound like a song, and I wonder if he's making fun of me again. "Or do you prefer Lady Jiangzhu?"

I narrow my eyes. "Anlei. Now, tell me yours. It's only fair."

He gives me a wary look. After a moment of hesitation, he says, "If those are your terms, then very well. Though if you want me to remove this mask, I'll need my hands."

Narrowing my eyes, I cautiously take a step back but keep my weapon raised. He reaches behind him and unknots the gray cloth mask, then sweeps it down to reveal a striking face with prominent cheekbones. I know at once that it's a face I'll never forget. His untamed locks give him a wild look. With his smooth skin and youthful attitude, he can't be much older than I am.

I slowly lower my stick. "I completed my part of the bargain. Your turn."

He gives me a crooked smile. "My name is Tai."

"What's your family name?"

An odd expression—something akin to sorrow yet carrying more heat than weight—flickers across his countenance. "It doesn't matter."

Considering that he's a thief, I wonder if he's an orphan. But

I came for the River Pearl, not a tragic backstory. "Fine. Now, tell me: What did you mean when you said you needed the River Pearl to save your people?"

CHAPTER NINE

LOCKED IN CONFLICT

Still leaning against the wall, Tai sinks to the ground. Shadows swallow him, and all I can see is a dark figure outlined by a few traces of moonlight.

I stay on my feet, ready to spring into action again if he tries anything. "Well?"

He draws an audible breath. "You know of Mowang, don't you? The Courts of Hell?"

"Of course I do." Everyone knows of the dark underworld that the wicked are damned to, whose entrance lies at the base of the legendary Heihuoshan—the Black Volcano. Ruled by the ferocious demon king, the place carries untold tortures. Each Court of Hell punishes a different kind of sin, and since there are infinite ways to do wrong, there are also infinite Courts. Many have written about what lies within them but since it's a one-way trip for most, no one really knows what it's like.

The few ghosts that escape and return to the earth are so twisted by torment they scarcely know how to speak. "What do the damned have to do with any of this?"

"Mowang trapped my people in the Courts." A single moonbeam traces the outline of Tai's face, just enough to reveal a tightening jaw. "I don't know how or why . . . All I know is that I must find a way to free them."

"Mowang damned your entire village?"

"Not exactly. Because of the divine laws that bind him, he couldn't kill them, and so he settled for capturing them. They're doomed to remain among demons and the damned unless I can get them out."

A tremor runs through me as I picture innocent people being forced to endure torments meant for the worst of humanity. Even just witnessing them would be a monstrous horror. "That's . . . terrible."

He tilts his face toward me, and the moonlight catches his eyes. A mix of anger and pain fills their depths. "I'm the only one who escaped, and I've been searching for a way to free them for years. Only recently have I learned of the River Pearl's powers."

"You think the River Pearl can free your people from the Courts of Hell?" I snort. "That relic couldn't even protect the village it was dedicated to. As far as I can tell, it's no different from any other gem."

"Scholars of the past, realizing its potential, feared what would happen if the knowledge fell into the wrong hands, and so they destroyed their writings. But I've recently discovered that long ago, there was much written about the River Pearl's power—and how to harness it."

"That can't be true." I shake my head. I've never heard of lost ancient writings. "I've known the River Pearl all my life, and it's never done more than sit on its jade pedestal."

"That's what those ancient scholars *wanted* you to think." He leans toward me. "It's not only me who believes this—if Viceroy Kang were here, and if he were an honest man, he would tell you the same. It's why he's so determined to get the River Pearl—determined enough to enter into a marriage alliance with a poor, inconsequential village."

I glower. "How dare you—"

"That's how the viceroy thinks of you. Or did you think he saw your village as an important ally?"

I clench my fists, seething—but not at Tai. The viceroy spent years acting as if my home didn't exist, ignoring our desperate messengers. Though he claims that he was passing over when he saw the Ligui attack, the speed with which he entered into the agreement with Headman Su makes me wonder if he was after the River Pearl the whole time. "How do you know this?"

"This wasn't my first time in the viceroy's palace." He sits back. "I've spied on him plenty of times while relieving him of his extraneous wealth."

"I see."

"The viceroy's had his eye on the River Pearl for years. He didn't know exactly what it was capable of, so he didn't pursue it in earnest, but ever since an oracle named it among the few items he could use to solidify his power, he has, on some level, wanted it. Only recently did he discover an ancient scroll describing the pearl's true power. I saw it when he first unfurled it . . . He didn't know I was there, but I read the same characters that he did. I'd been told, a while ago, that a dragon's magic would be the key to freeing my people from Mowang. It wasn't until I read the scroll that I realized the River Pearl was what I'd been seeking. The very next day Viceroy Kang left for Dailan. And I waited for an opportunity to claim it for my own."

The story sounds almost too fantastical to be true—an entire people trapped by Mowang, the hidden power of a relic I believed useless. Shades of doubt cloud my mind, yet at the same time, why would he lie? *Maybe he's trying to earn my sympathy so I'll let him keep the pearl.*

That's something I can't do. Whatever Kang wants the pearl for, he can have it as long as he protects Dailan.

"You don't believe me, do you?" Tai lets out a cold laugh. "Of course not . . . why would you listen to me when I'm getting in the way of your marriage?"

A slight movement catches my attention as his hand closes around the end of his stick, which still lies on the floor where it fell. How did I fail to notice him reaching for it?

I point my stick at him. He quickly raises his to shield himself, but I don't strike. "You've been so keen to tell me why *you* need the River Pearl to save *your* people. Did you forget the part where I told you I need it for the same? I only agreed to marry Kang so he'd protect my village. The Ligui have already killed too many—including my father—and if a relic and my hand in marriage are what it takes to stop them from killing more, so be it."

"I'm sorry. I didn't realize." His expression and voice seem sympathetic, earnest even, but I don't trust my ability to read him. It only lasts an instant. Letting out an exaggerated sigh, he says, "So, it looks like we're once again locked in an unresolvable conflict. Maybe we should cross sticks again and duel it out."

I'd almost prefer that. "You're not going to try convincing me that you were telling the truth?"

"Would it make a difference?" His weapon remains raised in a defensive position. "Even if you believed me, would you choose my people over your own?"

I don't answer. Though I sense that he's hiding something, I can't persuade myself that he's lying about the fate of his people. Maybe it's because I know what it's like to have a story so unbelievable; after being refused help by the nearby cities, Dailan's messengers went to the Emperor with tales of the Ligui, only to be dismissed as superstitious fools. Who am I to do the same?

I'm left with a choice between my people and Tai's. He's obviously chosen his own, and his situation is certainly more dire. Dailan still stands, after all. Perhaps there's a way to save both.

"If Kang knew of what happened to your people, he might be willing to lend you the pearl. That way, he could both protect my people and give you what you need to save yours."

Tai lets out a dry laugh. "Do you really believe what you just said?"

I bristle. "It's worth considering."

"Kang never does anything unless he stands to benefit. Just look at what your village had to give up in exchange for his protection, even though it's in his province and should have been protected in the first place."

I hate how naïve I must sound. I furrow my brow, searching for another solution. "How about this: You return the pearl for now, but steal it again *after* Kang marries me and sends protection to Dailan. I'll even help you get it."

"Kang will surely place more security around it after this incident. Who knows if either of us will be able to access it again?" Tai rises, keeping his stick between us. "I'm not giving up this chance to save my people."

I watch his every move in case he tries to attack. "You keep talking about your people, but who are they? What's your village called?"

"Before Mowang took them, my people lived in Baiguang."

That's not a village I've heard of before, and I think I'd remember one named after light, but the Empire of the Pearl Moon is a vast place. Most people have never heard of Dailan either. I chew on my bottom lip, contemplating what else we could do. "How do you plan to use the River Pearl?"

"There's a powerful spellmaster who knows how to make a sword that could defeat Mowang. But a dragon's magic is needed to make it work." A lock of hair falls over Tai's eye. He keeps both hands on his stick and tosses his head. "I plan to take the pearl to the temple so the spellmaster can construct the sword, then go down to the Courts of Hell and free my people."

I almost laugh. "You want to kill the demon king?"

"Don't be foolish. No one can kill an immortal." He moves slowly to the right.

I step to block him and glare. "What, then?"

"Mowang can't be killed, but his physical form can be destroyed." Apparently realizing he can't slip past me, he relaxes against the wall. "When this happens, he's forced to retreat so he can regenerate . . . which takes a hundred years."

"Why couldn't you have just said that?"

Tai shrugs.

He's the most frustrating person I've ever met. Not to mention the most ridiculous. Journeying to Hell and going up against the demon king himself—tales like these are what legends are made of. And to think, when I first spotted him, I took him for a simple thief. I'm not sure if I admire his audacity or find it idiotic. "Just how do you plan to reach the Courts of Hell?"

"The spellmaster has an enchanted map that will guide me there."

"What happens to the River Pearl if you succeed?"

His mouth tilts slightly. "I suppose I could pop it out of the sword and give it back to you. I only need to defeat Mowang once, after all."

That could work. I worried that defeating Mowang would somehow involve destroying the River Pearl—grinding it into a powder for a spell or something. If Tai only needs to borrow the relic, we may be able to reach an agreement. I don't know who's more foolish—him for proposing his plan or me for believing he can pull it off. "One more question: where is this temple, and how long will the journey take?"

Tai's lips twitch. "That's two questions."

I snarl. "Answer me!"

"I've already been more than generous with answers. Don't you trust me yet?"

"No."

He chuckles. "Very well. The journey will only take a few days." He taps his fingers against his stick. "I've . . . procured one of the viceroy's flying ships. It'll get me to the temple in a day or two, and assuming I don't get lost in Hell or dismembered by the Demon King, I could return the pearl to you within a week. Then we'll both get what we want."

"And the temple's location?"

"I'll tell you that *after* I return from my journey. What do you say, Lady?"

I'm not about to trust a thief to return to a city that's hunting him. Also, this adventure he's describing . . . it's the kind of journey I've always craved, one worthy of Warrioress. *I* want to be the one to travel across the land, dive into danger, and face off with the Demon King himself, even if it's not my people who need rescuing. I want to take Tai's place in his own quest.

Perhaps I can at least be part of it . . . and claim one last chance at glory before vanishing into the viceroy's household. Dailan can survive for a week. And maybe in journeying to Hell I can find answers about the Ligui and discover how to stop them for good.

"On one condition: I'm coming with you."

Tai laughs, but not in a condescending way. "I should have known you'd say that. You heard the part where I said I'm journeying to Hell and fighting Mowang, right?"

"Of course I did—I can hear perfectly well. Do you expect Hell to frighten me?"

"If I did, I'd be an even bigger idiot than you think I am."

I almost let that flatter me but warn myself that he's probably making fun of me again.

"It sounds like we have an agreement, then," he says.

"Only if you'll give me your oath." I don't know whether oaths mean anything to thieves, but it's better than nothing.

Tai looks me in the eye. "I swear on my mother's soul that I'll return the River Pearl to you once Mowang is defeated and my people are freed from his realm." The smile returns. "Do you trust me now?"

"Still no."

"I'll do my best to prove your distrusting instincts wrong, Lady." He bows his head.

I roll my eyes. "First, we have to get you out of Tongqiucheng."

"You too."

"*I'll* have no trouble escaping. Unlike you, I can blend into a crowd." I cock my head. "Why don't you simply dress like everyone else and do the same? Cover your hair with a hat, attach a fake queue, and go out without your mask?"

"I can't tell you."

"Why not? You want me to trust you, yet you won't tell me anything about yourself!"

"I prefer to be the mysterious type. The less you know about me, the more interesting you'll find me." He winks.

I have half a mind to tackle him again and forget our plan. If seeing it through means I'll have to put up with his smug face for the next several days, I'm not sure it's worth it. "If you don't start taking this seriously, then you won't have to worry about the viceroy executing you. I'll kill you myself!"

"I don't doubt it, Lady."

"Stop calling me Lady. You know my name."

"Apologies, Anlei." He pushes off the wall and straightens. "I have an idea, though you're not going to like it."

"What is it?"

"In the dark, most people look the same, and even Kang's cyborgs have trouble discerning one person from another when they're moving fast. If you cover your face, all they'll see is a masked thief."

"You want me to be your decoy?" It's not a bad idea. Especially if I let my hair out of its braids to flow wildly around me—the hair of a foreigner. Of course my locks are much longer than Tai's, and my clothing is dissimilar, but if I move quickly enough no one will have time to notice.

"Kang's men won't come after me if they're too busy chasing you. And you're faster than me, so you'll have an easier time evading them. I can meet you outside the city, where I've stashed the stolen ship." Tai grins. "I knew you wouldn't like it."

I arch my brows. "How do I know you won't run away with the River Pearl?"

"Because you trust me?" He widens his eyes into a look of innocence.

I want to smack it off his face. "How about this: You give *me* the pearl first, and then you trust *me* to bring it to you outside the city."

"Here we go again . . . Maybe we really should just duel it out."

Out of patience, I swing my bamboo stick. "If that's what you'd prefer."

Tai blocks, and a *clack* rings through the room. "I was joking!"

"I'm not. Don't you take anything seriously?"

"Not if I can help it."

I glare. "If you won't give me a real reason to trust you, then we might as well go back to where we started."

Tai releases his right hand from his weapon and lowers it, letting it dangle from his left. It looks like he's surrendering, but I keep my guard up. "You know my name, and you've seen my face . . . That's all the leverage you need to make sure I hold up my end of our agreement."

"What does that *mean*?"

Instead of answering, Tai pulls his mask over his nose and mouth. "The stolen ship is hidden in the East Forest, by the lake—Huimaohu. I'm leaving for the temple at sunrise, whatever you decide. You can help me, or you can try to stop me, but either way, remember that the fate of my people depends on your decision."

A sudden blow sweeps my ankle out from under me. It isn't hard enough to hurt, but it causes me to lose my balance. I land gracelessly with a yelp.

Tai drops his stick and darts to the window. I scramble to my feet and move to grab him, but he's too fast this time.

Ta ma de! Cursing, I chase after him as he leaps off the windowsill, but by the time I make it onto the roof, he's gone.

I put on Anshui's spectacles and look around, certain he must be around somewhere. This house isn't connected to any others, so he must have scaled down the side and run into the streets.

The arrogant, ridiculous, irritating fool! I pace along the rooftop, wondering what to do. He may have escaped me, but he told me exactly where he'd be—assuming he was telling the truth.

Shouts rise from below. Thanks to Anshui's spectacles, I'm able to see several guards and a cyborg racing down the streets, and I wonder if they spotted something I missed and are now chasing Tai.

If they catch him, Kang will kill him.

Angry as Tai makes me, at least he showed some decency, and he did give to a beggar. And he's on a quest to save his people. The thought of watching my hateful husband-to-be kill him over a mere object sends fire shooting through my veins.

Besides, I swore to Lao Gu—on my father's soul—that I'd help Tai escape.

Fine! I'll do it! After stashing the spectacles in my pocket, I unbind my braids and shake them loose. Yanking hard, I rip the edge of my tunic, then tie the tattered fabric over my nose and mouth. I tuck the frayed edges of my tunic into the waistband of my trousers so I'll at least be shaped like I'm wearing the shorter tunic of a man. I'll have to move quickly so no one can get a good look at me and realize that I'm not Tai.

I must be as ridiculous as he is.

CHAPTER TEN

OUT OF THE CITY

My lungs burn from the effort of running through alleys, ducking into corners, and jumping over the low walls that surround some of the buildings. Since Tai's heading for the East Forest, I lead the guards and the cyborg soldiers toward Tongqiucheng's west side—or at least what I *think* is the west side, based on the little I know of the city's layout.

The cyborgs' heavy footsteps ring off the buildings lining the wide street. There's not much cover here, and if I were really a thief trying to escape, I'd never be foolish enough to take this route.

"There he is!" a man shouts.

Good, I got their attention. I turn into an alley. Based on what I hear, I estimate that I have about half a minute before Kang's men catch up. I whip Anshui's spectacles out of my pocket and put them on—one of the taller buildings has a narrow balcony I missed in the dark.

I shove the glasses back into my pocket, and jump onto the column supporting the balcony and pull myself up. My arms ache from having scaled many similar columns tonight. I don't know how much longer I can keep up this pattern of running, getting the guards' attention, hiding, and then doing it all over again.

I flatten myself against the balcony's floor and hold my breath as Kang's men pass beneath me. The torn cloth over my face feels like it's trying to smother me, and I wonder how Tai can stand wearing one.

Who could he be? Maybe he's the wayward son of an elite household and he worries what consequences his actions might have for his family. I suppose it doesn't matter as long as I get the River Pearl back by the end of all this.

After several moments, the sounds of Kang's guards fade away. I climb back down the column.

A metal hand seizes me. Gasping, I spin to find myself staring into the face of a cyborg soldier. The mechanical casing over his arm gleams under the yellow glow of his artificial left eye. I twist hard, but his grasp is too tight. With his other hand—the human one—he yanks the mask off my face.

My heart stops. I suddenly understand why Tai might fear someone knowing his identity. As long as I was just a masked person, there was still a chance I could return to Viceroy Kang as if nothing had happened. But if I'm recognized as Liang Anlei—the future Lady Jiangzhu—things will be much, much worse for me and everyone I know.

The soldier narrows his human eye. "You're too short to be the thief."

Relief seeps down my chest.

"Who are you? And why are you running around in a mask?" His mechanical eye stares into mine. "I can see when someone's lying."

When someone asks a woman or a girl who she is, they're really asking who her family is.

I swallow hard. "I'm just a poor girl from the countryside. My father is Liang Liwei."

Liang is a common enough family name and neither Kang nor anyone in his entourage ever asked about my father other than to confirm that he's dead.

I pause, trying to think of a way to tell the truth without giving away my identity—or letting the soldier know that I'm helping Tai. "I heard about the man who stole from the viceroy, and I was outraged by the thief's audacity. In my village, it's every citizen's duty to stop criminals, so I left the house hoping to catch him. But my father would disapprove if he knew his daughter was running through the streets at night. I masked myself so no one would know who I am."

Yellow light from the cyborg's eye fills my vision. I tense, wondering if he can hear my pounding heart or detect the sheen of sweat forming on my brow.

Finally, he releases my arm. "This is not your village. Leave the law enforcement to the professionals and return to your home."

"Yes, sir." I exhale.

"And do not put that mask back on. You might be mistaken for the thief again."

"Of course. I'm sorry, sir."

The soldier waves me off and runs down the alley to join the others.

I tug at the scrap of cloth around my neck. *That was too close.*

How did I fail to hear him approach? He couldn't have been among the group that was chasing me initially . . . He would never have believed me if so. He must have been searching on his own and happened to be there when I dropped down in front of him.

I'm so tired that I'm starting to make stupid mistakes. Next time I won't be so lucky. And I still need to get back to the viceroy's palace without being seen, since I'll need a few things before I can head off for Baiheshan with Tai.

Surely Tai must be out of the city by now. Deciding I've bought him enough time, I head back toward the palace.

Candlelight flickers across the page as I write a letter to Viceroy Kang explaining that I've gone after the thief myself. Which is true, if not the whole story. Hopefully he'll accept my explanation that since the River Pearl was given to him by my village, it's my duty to ensure that he gets what he was promised. I'm glad I don't have to say all this to him in person; it's much easier to lie on paper, even though drawing each character is a laborious task. I'm sure I've made mistakes, but I don't have time to correct them. Even when I try to read back my own writing, the characters seem to twist and flip. I keep the letter as short as I can.

Discomfort gnaws at me. Kang won't be happy when he reads this note and discovers that I'm gone. It shouldn't make a difference since he won't marry me without the pearl anyway, but he seems to desire complete control over me, and I fear he might take his wrath out on Dailan and refuse the alliance even after I return.

He'd let all of Dailan fall to the Ligui for the sake of his pride.

I add in a deferential sentence begging him to forgive me for any impertinence and assuring him that once I return, I'll be the obedient bride he deserves. Writing those characters leaves a foul taste in my mouth, but it may be the only way to salvage this situation and get my village the protection it needs.

I end the note with: *I swear on my father's soul that I will return with the River Pearl. As proof, I'm leaving behind my most precious possession: the jade pendant he gave me.*

I pull the carved stone out of my tunic and lift it over my head. Immediately, I feel as if a part of me is missing. I've worn that pendant every day since I was a baby. I can't remember ever *not* wearing it. Kang won't appreciate what it means to me, but Headman Su will. And he'll certainly be called upon when the letter is discovered.

Guilt stings me as I imagine how distressed he'll be in the morning. I'm leaving him to deal with the viceroy's wrath—I'll be long gone by then.

I only hope the Ligui will stay away from Dailan until I'm able to bring the River Pearl back, or that the Guard will be strong enough to keep them from killing anyone else. Each day my village remains vulnerable will be my fault for choosing to take this journey with Tai. If the creatures do strike again before it's over and someone dies, will that blood be on my hands?

I glimpse the mirror across the room—the one that held a reflection of me in Lady Jiangzhu's wedding ensemble. My stomach twists. I can't go back to being her yet—I *can't*. If her existence is to consume the rest of my life, then I should at least be allowed one final chance to claim glory as Liang Anlei.

Though I try telling myself that helping Tai save his people is the right thing to do, I can't pretend I'm going purely out of generosity. Already, my blood is humming with excitement. I picture myself cutting down Mowang in the Courts of Hell and triumphantly leading the people of Baiguang to freedom, and a grin creeps onto my lips. This may be Tai's quest, but that doesn't mean I have to stand by and let him be the hero. Like Warrioress, I could be the one to conquer evil and stand victorious.

I'm not giving up my chance at that, even if it means putting Dailan at risk. It's only for a little while—merely a week, if Tai's estimate is correct.

I leave the finished letter on the desk with my pendant then approach my trunk and grab my father's sword. I don't know if its magic will work in the Courts of Hell, but it's better than nothing. And there's a chance that Tai and I will encounter Ligui during the journey. I also take my clockwork pistol. Though only a few bullets enchanted with the same magic as my sword remain in its chamber, it could prove useful.

After changing into a new tunic and braiding my hair, I secure my sword to my back with a leather strap and stick the pistol into a holster on its side. I feel ready to take on every demon Hell has to offer.

I slip back out into the night.

By the time I reach the East Forest, the sun's first rays have faded the sky into a grayish blue. Getting out of Tongqiucheng took longer than I'd expected since Kang's men were still combing the city for the masked thief.

Now that I'm here, I realize I have no idea how to reach the lake. Uneasy, I stalk through the trees searching for anything that might guide my way—a sign, perhaps, or a well-worn path. I keep my sword out before me. Though daylight has begun broaching the darkness—and though I'm not far beyond the area guarded by Kang's bronze dragons—I can't be sure the Ligui won't strike. They've been unpredictable before.

Also, the person I've come to meet could easily choose to attack me.

Since it's hard to see through the forest's dense shadows, I risk shifting my sword into one hand to grab Anshui's spectacles. They're the only thing I brought other than my weapons. When I place them on my nose, the magic in the glass makes the woods look as if the dawn's pale light has already fallen through the leaves. Every way I look, all I see are trees, trees, trees. Since Kang's men were searching the forest immediately outside the city as well, I didn't dare stop until the last buildings at the edge of the city were well out of sight.

Now, I realize how foolish an idea that was. I should have stolen a map. In fact, there are probably lots of things I should have done to prepare for this journey instead of just grabbing my weapons and leaving a note. *I can figure this out . . . The lake can't be too far.*

My feet crunch against the forest floor, and the air is heavy with the scent of summer leaves.

"I see you've decided to help me."

Hearing Tai's voice, I whirl to find him leaning back against a tree with his long legs crossed at the ankles. Though he appears unarmed, he's probably concealing a weapon somewhere on his person. After the dirty trick he played on me last time, I wouldn't be surprised to learn he was using his carefree demeanor to mask his intentions.

But at least he showed up. I approach, still gripping my weapon. "What I've decided is that I'll do what it takes to get the River Pearl back, even if it means putting up with you."

He clutches his chest. "And here I was thinking you were pursuing me for the handsome face you made me reveal to you."

I roll my eyes, wishing I were witty enough to come up with a biting retort.

"What's that device you're wearing?" He cocks his head.

"Spectacles that help me see in the dark." I can't help adding, "My little sister made them."

"She must be a genius."

"She certainly is."

Tai's gaze turns to my sword. "Put that away. It's too light out for Ligui now. Unless it's me you're planning to kill?"

I'm tempted to threaten him into handing over the River Pearl; there's no reason *I* shouldn't be its keeper instead of him. But these woods are dense, and he obviously knows them better than I do. If he runs from me and vanishes into them, I'll never find him.

I shove my sword into the strap on my back. "Happy now?"

Tai pushes off the tree and gives me a wary look. "Follow me."

CHAPTER ELEVEN

THE HIDDEN SHIP

Morning reaches across Huimaohu, igniting sparks upon the lake's rippling surface. The crisp air smells of damp earth and lively greenery.

Sleepiness grapples my mind with sticky fingers, and I suppress a yawn. I can't believe how long this day has lasted, how many twists and turns it's taken. It was supposed to be my wedding day, the day that sealed my fate forever—instead I'm setting out on a quest worthy of Warrioress.

I find it funny that I once thought that I'd rather go to the Courts of Hell than marry Kang, and now I'm doing exactly that.

Tai pushes aside the tall grasses and wades into the water. I pause on the lake's shore, searching for the stolen vessel he claims to have hidden here. I thought he'd covered it in foliage, but from the way he's heading into the lake, that doesn't seem to be the case. Unless he just feels like going for a swim.

"What are you doing?" I ask.

"You'll see in a moment." Tai continues until the water reaches his knees.

I rake my gaze over his clothing, searching for the outline of a concealed weapon or the River Pearl, which he must be carrying. But he wears his tunic and trousers loose over his svelte figure, and I'm unable to make out anything for certain.

Tai lifts both hands and draws them across the air in a twirling pattern that almost looks like a dance. Sparks appear around him like a hundred brilliant fireflies, and the air shimmers. Moments later, a small ship glows into existence. A single mast rises from its bronze body, and the scalloped edge of the lone pale yellow sail gleams under the waking sun. Wide propellers poke out of the water.

I step into the lake, marveling at the shining vehicle. "You stole this from the viceroy?"

"I did." Tai looks up at the ship with a self-satisfied smile.

"How?"

"I obtained an invisibility potion from a spellmaster. All I had to do was sneak into the shipyard, toss the potion onto the ship, and fly off. The viceroy never even missed it . . . It's nothing compared to the rest of his fleet, and the shipyard supervisor was too scared to let him know it vanished."

"You used an invisibility potion?" I frown. Such magic couldn't have been easy to come by. Though simple magic-powered devices are commonplace, the rarity of ingredients needed for more potent spells means they're wielded only by the powerful; Dailan's spellmasters certainly wouldn't have been able to craft a potion that could hide an entire ship. It seems unlikely that Tai simply "obtained" one. "You stole that too, didn't you?"

Tai throws on an exaggerated look of indignation. "How dare you? I'll have you know the whole plan was the spellmaster's idea to begin with."

"Is this the same spellmaster you claim can make you a sword that can defeat Mowang?"

"Yes, that's right."

"Why is such a powerful person helping you?"

"My cause is noble." He winks.

I cross my arms. "Your cause may be, but you aren't—*thief.*"

His quick laugh sparkles through the air. "I never claimed to be anything but what I am."

Water soaks my trousers as I approach the ship. "How long ago did you steal this?"

"It's been almost three years, though I was searching for a way to free my people even before then. Considering all the trouble I went through, I find it funny that the answer turned up in my hometown."

"I thought you said your hometown was Baiguang."

"I said my *people* lived in Baiguang." He grabs a rope hanging over the ship's side. "It's where my mother's from. I was born in Tongqiucheng. When I was little, Mother used to take me to visit her family in Baiguang."

"Is she among those Mowang captured?"

"No. She died when I was six."

Though he tosses out the words casually, I'm sure there must be some grief behind them. I know all too well how deeply the loss of a parent can cut. I should say something. But no matter how many times I've had to offer condolences, I've never quite figured out how to stop being awkward at it. Somehow, my words come out wrong, and I always feel like my face isn't as sad as it should be. Just because I don't know how to express sorrow like everyone else, though, doesn't mean I don't feel it. "I'm . . . sorry to hear that."

"It was a long time ago." Tai turns his gaze toward the rope. "I don't know about you, but my feet are getting cold." He jumps out of the water and grabs the rope. As he climbs, his eyes keep darting toward me as if he's worried I'll attack.

I get the feeling he chose that moment to board the ship in order to keep me from asking any more questions.

After he pulls himself onto the deck, I climb the rope after him, my palms burning from the friction. Then I realize I'm rising faster than I ought to be. Puzzled, I look up to see Tai pulling the rope.

"What are you doing?"

"Giving you a hand."

"I don't need your help!" I glare at him. This is why I hate working with men—they always assume I'm the weak one. As a member of the Dailan Guard, I always avoided being partnered with men when possible because even though I beat several of them during our training duels, they could never acknowledge that I was as good as they were. If it's going to be the same way with Tai, then this will be a long journey indeed. "Don't you dare treat me like I'm weak!"

Tai opens his mouth as if to reply, then arches his brows. "Fine."

He releases the rope, and the force of the drop causes me to lose my grip. Startled, I yelp and land in the lake with a splash. Tai's laughter rings in my ears.

Hundan! Irritated, I pick myself up and wipe the water from my face. I scurry up the rope and onto the deck, where I find Tai leaning against the wheel.

He grins. "Have a nice swim?"

His mocking lights my fury, and before I know it, I've yanked off one soaked shoe and lobbed it at him.

"Hey!" He dodges, and the shoe bounces off the wheel. "You're violent when you're mad!"

"So don't make me mad."

"But it's so much fun."

I pull off the other shoe and raise it threateningly.

"All right! I'm sorry!" He holds up his hands. "Truce?"

"I accept your surrender."

"I am ever grateful, Lady." He clasps his hands in an exaggerated gesture of thanks.

I huff. "Don't we have a demon king to fight?"

"Of course." Tai scoops up the shoe I threw at him and hands it to me. "Now, if you can keep that to yourself for a few minutes, I'll launch the ship."

I resist the urge to hurl both shoes at his smug face. "Can you tell me where we're going yet?"

He rubs the back of his head.

"I'll tell you once we're airborne."

It takes every ounce of discipline I have to slip my shoes back onto my feet.

The ship's wheel is a lot more complex than I expected. Red and brown buttons bedeck its bronze surface, and four gauges stand before it, rising on metal poles from the wooden deck. Tai approaches a set of controls with protruding levers and blinking lights that curves around one side of the wheel. He takes a moment to bind his hair into a knot—like those I've seen in paintings of warriors from centuries ago. I watch closely as he presses the controls to start up the ship's engine, causing its propellers to spin in the water and lift the vessel. I don't like that I'm alone with him on a ship I can't operate.

Tai narrows his eyes against the brightening sun, which highlights the striking planes of his face. Wind blasts a few stray wisps across his forehead.

A flash of light catches my attention. Whirling, I glimpse something bronze coming into view over the treetops. Only a distant sliver is visible, but I see enough to know it must be one of the mechanical dragons that guard Tongqiucheng.

I gasp. "The patrols are coming! Hurry!"

Tai curses and reaches for a crank. Before he can grasp it, the oncoming dragon opens its metal jaws and spews a fiery blast in our direction. The blast hits the deck, sending us both hurtling through the air. A scorching wind engulfs me. I seize the wheel to catch myself, and it jerks to the right under my weight. The ship turns abruptly in response and I nearly fall over.

We're still ascending and I'm nearly eye level with the mechanical dragon. Though some distance lies between us, it's quickly closing the gap. Its jaws open a second time, revealing the blaze of the next blast glowing in the depths of its metal throat, a fire stoked by the machinery within. Heart pounding, I yank the wheel in hopes of maneuvering out of its path. The ship lurches, tilting to the left. It's only because

I'm gripping the wheel that I'm able to remain upright.

"Turn the blue crank!" Tai, who was thrown across the deck, struggles to find his balance on the pitching ship.

I spot the crank on the control panel. "What does it do?"

"Just turn it!"

"Why—" A second blast hits and knocks me forward. I desperately cling to the wheel as the spokes dig into my chest, surprised the ship's still flying. Considering the kind of firepower I've seen from Kang's bronze dragons, I'm guessing those on board this one aren't trying to destroy us—only stop us. The viceroy does want the thief alive after all.

Tai races to the controls and grabs the blue crank with both hands. "Why didn't you listen to me?"

I scowl. "Why didn't you tell me what it was for?"

Tai gives the crank a shove, but it only makes a quarter rotation. It must be heavier than it looks. The sounds of clunking gears and hissing steam rise from below, and a silvery sheen glitters around us. "It activates the invisibility spell, okay? The magic also muffles any noises the ship makes, so no one will hear us either."

"Why didn't you activate it when we took off, then?"

"It needs the engines to be hot, and it takes a few moments for them to warm up."

"If you knew that, then you shouldn't have deactivated the spell in the first place!"

"And missed the look on your face when it appeared before you?" He grins but keeps pushing at the crank.

I gape. "You idiot! You risked our lives so you could show off?"

He shrugs. "I didn't see anyone around at the time. Now, can you pull that orange lever to reverse this ship, or do I have to grow a third arm to save our hides?" He jerks his head at the lever.

I almost want to refuse just to spite him—especially since it's his fault we're in this situation. But our best chance at escape is to do something unexpected—if our pursuer can't see us, they'll assume we're still moving forward. "Fine!"

"Wait for my signal—the spell isn't fully active yet." His voice is strained from effort. He shoves the crank again and completes the circle. "Now!"

I yank the lever. The whir of the propellers becomes thunderously loud, and the ship lurches backward. The abrupt movement knocks me off my feet and I careen across the deck. My shoulder slams into the wooden boards, sending a shockwave of pain rippling down my body.

The ship jerks to a halt, and the propellers quiet to a hum. I jump up. The mechanical dragon, which was gaining on our stern moments ago, is now several feet in front of the bow and heading away. Its bronze reflection glides across the lake's surface while our ship hovers above the trees.

Tai grips the edges of the control panel like his life depends on it. A strained laugh tumbles from his lips. "That was close!"

I watch, relieved, as the departing dragon continues moving away from us. "Can all of Kang's ships turn invisible?"

Tai shakes his head. "The viceroy would never want to *hide* his fleet—he's all about awe and intimidation. I added the cloaking spell . . . The spellmaster showed me how to incorporate magic into the ship."

At least we won't have to worry about invisible patrols stalking us—assuming Tai's right. "Who exactly is this spellmaster you keep mentioning?"

"That's a secret."

"How many secrets are you going to keep from me? I thought we were supposed to be partners."

"Forgive me for not trusting a girl I just met . . . And who keeps trying to kill me."

I put my hands on my hips. "I've never tried to kill you!"

He lifts his eyebrows. "Sure you haven't."

"Well, I also just helped you get away from Kang's patrol."

"A deed that benefits you as much is it does me."

I have to consciously press my lips together to keep from baring my teeth in an animalistic snarl. "At least tell me where we're going. We're airborne now."

"I suppose we are." Tai peers into my face as if trying to read me. "The temple is just outside Baiheshan."

That's farther than I expected. Baiheshan is a province away—it would take weeks to reach by horse. But given the speed of Kang's ships, we shouldn't need more than a day or so.

In the distance, the dragon spews a fireball which explodes midair without hitting anything. They must be trying to flush us out.

I watch it nervously. "We should get out of here before they decide to look behind them."

"Agreed." Tai brushes a few stray wisps off his sweaty forehead and pushes a lever, and the propellers rev up.

The ship rises higher into the sky, but pitches so abruptly I nearly lose my balance. Machinery rattles and clangs, and the floor vibrates.

I may not be an expert in mechanics like my sister, but even I know that's a bad sign. "What's that? It sounds like the engine's damaged."

"I don't think so." Tai glances at the gauges before turning the wheel south. "Your erratic steering made it hard for them to lock onto a target."

"Are you certain? Maybe one of those blasts hit something important."

"The ship has made worse noises than this before. I've put it through a lot, but it's sturdier than it seems. Don't worry—I have everything under control."

The rattling ceases. I give him a skeptical look. "Shouldn't you check to see if anything's wrong?"

"It's fine, trust me," Tai says in an exasperated voice. "Engines rattle. That doesn't mean there's a problem. It smoothed itself out quickly enough, didn't it?"

I suppose Grandfather's mechanical cart worked well enough despite all the clunking sounds it made. Maybe it's the same with this ship. Still, I wish Anshui were here. She'd know what to do.

I walk up to the railing and keep a keen eye on the mechanical dragon as it disappears into the distance. My heart still quivers. Even after I can no longer see it, I keep staring in that direction in case it returns.

"You can relax." Tai calls to me from behind. "If they were going to catch up to us, they would have by now."

I turn to find him leaning back against the control panel. "Do you think they saw our faces?"

"I doubt it. They were still pretty far away when I activated the invisibility spell. We would have looked like ants to them. And the sail would have blocked their view."

"They must still be searching for us."

"True, but the sky is big, and we're both invisible and inaudible. To anyone not on board, this ship might as well not exist. I think we're all right for now."

I'm still on edge, but drowsiness twists its fingers into my head again. Though the cool air chills me through my clothes, which are still wet, I feel as if I could fall asleep standing up. I yawn widely, wondering how many hours it's been since I got any rest.

Tai looks at me. "There's a cabin below deck. With a bed. Also food and water, if you need them. Not that I'm trying to take care of you or anything . . . wouldn't want you to think I'm treating you like you're weak."

I narrow my eyes. "Good."

He sighs. "One of us is going to need to sleep at some point. And since the trip to Baiheshan will take more than a day, we should do it in shifts."

"Sure. You can go first."

"My day was a lot less busy than yours before I stole the pearl. I knew I'd be up all night, so I spent it sleeping. Which means I'm more alert and less likely to crash the ship into a mountain."

"We're miles from any mountains." I feel a smirk lifting my lips as he shoots me an irritated glare. But there's nothing to be gained from me standing here exhausted, arguing over nothing. Besides, if I sleep now, I can take the night shift later, and I'd be better at keeping an eye out for Ligui.

"Anlei—"

"All right! I'm going!"

As I cross the deck, I notice a wide hole with scorched edges gaping near the stern, exposing the ship's gears and machinery. I hope the cloaking spell is as effective as Tai claims. Another confrontation could destroy the ship's ability to fly.

A narrow doorway leads to a staircase descending into the lower part of the ship. There's not much down here—just a tiny cabin and a few trunks stuffed into the space beneath the steps. I shut the door behind me and slide my sword between the handle and the wall, forming a makeshift lock. I'm not stupid enough to sleep unguarded on a stranger's ship.

The bed is little more than a slab of wood with a bamboo mat and a worn blanket, but when I lie down on it, it feels like the most luxurious surface in the world. I keep my pistol close.

As I close my eyes, a soft noise whispers over me. It must be from the ship—the engine or maybe the whir of the propellers. But there's something eerie about the sound . . . it has a hollow, otherworldly quality entirely different from the ship's mechanical clunking and hissing. It's almost as if the voices of a hundred ghosts are all talking at the same time, but they're too vague for me to understand. Soon I give up trying, and sleep wraps its hands around my mind, swallowing me whole.

CHAPTER TWELVE

THIEVES

W hen I open my eyes, a strange copper ceiling greets me. I sit up with a start, seizing the pistol by my side before I remember where I am, why I'm here.

A flying ship, stolen from the viceroy's fleet. A young thief on a fantastical quest. And a decision so wild, I can hardly believe I made it.

Yet not a trace of regret clouds my mind, which is as clear as daylight now that I'm no longer exhausted. I had plenty of opportunities to turn back, so if I've lost my sense of reason, then the absurdity has become my new reality.

I stand and stretch, my muscles aching from last night's running and climbing and fighting. My clothes are still damp, and I make a mental note to push Tai into a lake if I get the chance. *The idiot. I'll probably kill him myself before Mowang gets the chance to try.*

Strangely enough, the prospect of fighting the demon king doesn't frighten me. Maybe it's because I've battled so many Ligui that death no longer scares me. Or maybe it's because the notion still feels too bizarre to be real.

A soft humming noise wafts through the air, too hollow to be from the ship's machinery. I vaguely recall having heard something similar before I fell asleep . . . something that reminded me of ghosts' whispers. Though I can't make out any words, the sound fills me with sadness, as if something invisible is crying out in pain.

The humming fades away. Shivers run down my spine. *Was* it a ghost? Some other supernatural being? Or merely a trick of the wind?

I pick up my sword, sling it across my back, and head out of the cabin, tucking my pistol into its holster. A slight tremor rumbles beneath my feet; I try to recall if the ship was always this shaky or if it's gotten worse since I fell asleep.

When I reach the deck, I shield my eyes from the bright mid-afternoon sun and glance around for Tai. But I don't find him at the wheel. Instead, he sits against the metal control panel, eyes closed and head bowed. Clearly, I wasn't the only one tired out by last night's adventure. A yellow light glows from the center of the wheel, which stands still as the ship sails through the sky.

Careless fool! What if Kang's patrols had happened upon us? The cloaking spell wouldn't have kept a stray blast from hitting the ship and revealing our position.

I move to wake Tai, but notice his right hand clenched across his stomach. Is he clasping the River Pearl? Or maybe he tucked it into a hidden pocket?

I could easily take back what he stole. Unarmed and unconscious, he appears completely vulnerable. That's his own fault for falling asleep unguarded with a stranger on board his ship.

But Tai's still the only one who knows how to operate the ship. Though I might be able to threaten him into obeying my commands, I doubt I'd succeed for long. He's proven to be slippery. Chances are he'd either steal the pearl again—or I'd have to restrain him and figure out how this flying contraption works myself. Even if I wanted to continue the quest, I doubt Tai's spellmaster would help me. I'd have to turn back.

Perhaps that would be the clever thing to do: take the pearl and secure my people's protection whatever the cost. But I'm not ready to do that.

Crouching, I shake Tai's shoulder. "Tai!"

He opens his eyes and blinks against the sunlight. His mouth spreads into a lopsided grin. "If you're trying to steal the pearl back, you're doing a terrible job."

My conscience pricks me. "I considered it."

His smile falls. For a moment, he regards me with a confused expression. "I couldn't have blamed you if you'd tried."

"Yet you fell asleep anyway." I raise my brows. "Does that mean you trust me?"

"Or I'm lazy. Father always warned me that idleness would be my downfall. Though few could match his level of diligence."

Though I know he won't give me a straight answer, I can't help asking, "Who is your father?"

He gives me a slantwise look. "Is this an interrogation?"

"It's only a question!"

"Then I suggest you stop asking."

I huff. What is it about his past that's so secret anyway? Or is he so distrustful of me that he won't even answer a simple question?

He stands and turns to the controls. "We're on track to reach Baihe-shan tomorrow morning. The temple is in the mountains, but the city is in the valley below. I'll have to hide the ship in its outskirts, since I can't exactly land on a cliff."

I know he only changed the subject to avoid telling me anything more. But I'm not giving up so easily. "Is your father from Baiguang too? Or Tongqiucheng?"

Tai crosses his arms. "Did you not hear my suggestion?"

"How can you expect us to work together when you won't answer the most basic of questions?"

"Simple. We journey to the temple, we get the sword from the spellmaster, and then we dive into the Courts of Hell and defeat Mowang. None of those tasks requires me to tell you about my family."

I clench my fists. I suppose all that matters for our quest is who we are here and now—not where either of us comes from or who our families are. "Fine." I peer over his shoulder. "Can you show me how the controls work?"

"Since it's a straight path from here to our destination, the ship can fly itself until we reach it. And I plan to do the landing." He tilts his head. "Why do you want to learn, anyway?"

"I don't like being stuck on a flying ship I can't control."

"Your ignorance is my guarantee. As long as I'm the only one who knows how to fly the ship, you have to stick with our agreement."

"Don't be so sure. I could always hold you hostage and *make* you do my bidding."

The corner of his mouth lifts. "You had your chance to do that, but apparently you have too much decency to attack someone who's asleep."

"Then that *decency* should be enough for you!" I draw a deep breath. *Discipline* . . . "There's a good chance we'll run into more trouble. If anything happens to you, I need to know how this ship works."

He narrows his eyes in consideration. "Fair enough, I suppose. I'll—" He turns abruptly back to the controls. Cursing under his breath, he seizes the blue crank, which is bent at a different angle than it was previously.

"What's wrong?" I ask.

"The invisibility spell deactivated by itself. Something must be broken."

My jaw drops. "I told you—" I break off. A silhouetted shape approaches on the horizon and it's growing bigger by the second. "I think there's another ship!" I swallow hard. *And they can see us . . .*

"No problem." Tai shoves the crank back into its previous position. "Now they can't see us anymore." His gaze lands on one of the gauges, and his eyes widen. "I don't understand . . . "

"What?"

Before he can answer, the approaching vessel fires. It's now close enough for me to see that it's a small single-mast ship like ours—except armed with a long cannon. The explosion rocks the deck. Surrounded by heat and the smell of molten metal, I tumble uncontrollably. My grasping hands fail to catch anything until I slam into the railing.

The ground tilts, and wind howls past my ears. Panic rises up my throat. We barely escaped before—how in the world are we supposed to get away now? I don't know who I hate more—Tai for neglecting the ship's damage or myself for believing him when he claimed everything was all right.

Ignoring my aching ribs, I try to stand but can't seem to regain my footing. I narrow my eyes against the gust. Tai clings to the control panel with one hand and grasps at the wheel with the other, but his attempts to steer only cause us to jerk erratically. The other ship is now on top of us—actually *on top of us*. Its menacing form, silhouetted against the bright afternoon sky, hovers just above our mast. But it seems to be rising, up and away from us . . . until I realize it's not the one that's moving.

We're falling.

A thunderstorm of curses blows through my head. "*Now* do you see a problem?"

Tai laughs. The arrogant fool actually *laughs*. "It would be just my luck that the invisibility spell fails as one of Kang's ships is approaching."

I scowl. If I die because of his carelessness, I'll spend the rest of eternity haunting him.

I make another attempt to stand on the crooked floor, but a great lurch sends me stumbling back into the railing. My head bangs against the wood, and my eyes fill with stars. Fear slithers beneath my anger. I can't have escaped Tongqiucheng only to be blasted out of the sky so soon after. There must be something I can do to salvage this situation. Rustling noises crash into my ears, followed by snaps and cracks. Then I see the green—leaves poking through the railing and branches reaching across the deck.

The ship stills. Without the whirring of the engine and the roaring of the wind, the air suddenly feels empty. I climb slowly to my feet. Rubbing my sore forehead, I look around.

The ship crashed into some trees. Judging by the downward angle of the deck, the vessel dove into the branches; though it's close enough to horizontal that I'm able to move across it, it feels like I'm walking on a steep hill. Clouds of white steam billow from the ship, nearly obscuring a few wisps of black smoke. I wrinkle my nose at the sharp stench of burned metal.

I expect to find Tai by the controls, but he's nowhere in sight. "Tai?" I look around wildly. Could he have fallen overboard? Sudden horror seizes me. No—surely I would have noticed if that were true. Maybe he went below deck. I race to the stairs. *"Tai!"*

"You called?" Tai appears at the bottom, holding a bronze staff with a leather strap dangling from it.

Relief cascades down my chest. "Are you all right?"

"Yes, I'm fine." He cocks his head, the traces of an amused smile on his lips. "You seem awfully worried . . . Does that mean you would miss me if I died?"

The relief turns to irritation. "Of course I was worried—about the River Pearl. If something happened to you, I might never get it back." I step back onto the deck and look up. The other vessel descends smoothly toward us.

Anxiety grapples my gut. The viceroy must have ordered half his fleet to search for Tai. *Or is it me they're after?*

He probably commanded his men to search for his wayward bride as well as the thief. If they catch me, they'll drag me back to Tongqiucheng in shame. It will be even worse if they realize I helped Tai escape . . . I don't want to think about what the viceroy would do to me for that. And they'll send Tai to his death while his people remain trapped in Mowang's infernal realm.

What do we do now? I glance around. We've landed in the canopy of a forest at the edge of a vast river. Wind from the approaching ship's whirring propellers sends ripples skittering across the water's surface, and gold light flashes off the shapes of soldiers on deck—they must be cyborgs. Treetops stretch across the horizon in the other direction. Even if we could evade our would-be captors, we're in the middle of nowhere. We might walk for weeks without reaching civilization.

I turn to Tai. "Is there any chance the ship can fly again?"

"Doubtful." His mouth remains at a cocky angle. "That blast tore a hole clean through the side. We should get out of here before they board." He starts forward.

"Wait!" The other ship looks so similar to ours, it could have been poured from the same mold. That means it can't hold too many people. "How many soldiers would a ship like this one carry?"

"Maybe three or four, plus a pilot. This was meant to be a scout ship." Glancing at the vessel—and the soldiers on board—he reaches into his tunic, retrieves his gray rag from a hidden pocket, and ties it over his nose and mouth.

I should hide my face too. If the cyborgs recognize me, they'll know I'm helping the Masked Giver. Viceroy Kang would see that as a betrayal, treason even. What would he do to Dailan in his wrath?

I duck into the stairway. I'm about to rip at my hem when Tai nudges me.

He holds out a second rag. "Here. I'd hate for Kang's men to think I was kidnapping their future Lady Jiangzhu."

I'm surprised he thought far enough ahead to bring a second mask. When I tie it on, a faint musky scent reminiscent of sandalwood and peppercorns wafts from the cloth. It's unexpectedly pleasant.

At least now the cyborgs will only see that the Masked Giver has an accomplice. Their future Lady Jiangzhu could be in another province for all they know.

I look over at the treetops again. As far-fetched as the plan forming in my mind is, it seems preferable to getting lost in the woods. "Could you fly their ship?"

Tai stares at me.

It's probably only for a second or two, but with the other ship closing in on us, every moment is precious. "Well, could you?"

An incredulous laugh bubbles past his lips. "You want to steal a ship from under Kang's cyborgs?"

"You stole this ship to begin with, didn't you? It can't be that hard!"

"I'll have you know—"

"*Tai!* We don't have time for this! Can you fly their ship or not?"

"Yes." He narrows his eyes. "What's your plan?"

The patrol vessel is near enough now for me to clearly see the glowing mechanical eyes of the soldiers waiting on its deck. "There's a hole in the side of this ship, right?"

Tai nods and gestures down the stairs. "See the light from our new window?"

A patch of yellow light sits at the bottom of the steps.

"Do you have a rope below deck? And a grappling hook?"

His face brightens. "Of course I do. I see—you want to wait for the soldiers to board our ship, and while they're here, climb onto theirs."

"Exactly." I rush down. "They'll probably leave at least one guard and the pilot behind. I'll take care of them. You take over the controls. Understand?"

"Very well. You'd make an excellent pirate, Lady."

I can't tell if that's meant to be a compliment.

A jagged hole gapes in the wall beside the small room, partly blocked by a fallen beam and pieces of twisted machinery. Tai swings into the area beneath the stairs and snatches the lid off one of the wooden trunks. A rope ending in a grappling hook lies coiled inside. He tosses it to me.

As I check the knots on the hook to make sure they're secure, a loud clunking noise sounds from above. It's soon followed by pounding footsteps; the soldiers are boarding. Time is short.

I rush to the hole in the wall, climbing over the fallen beam and scattered debris, and peer out. A narrow copper plank bridges the distance between the hovering patrol ship and this one, though it's toward the bow, and we're practically at the stern. Ridges band the plank's surface—it must telescope in and out. Two soldiers are in the middle of crossing. From where I'm standing, I can make out the wheel of the other ship, the pilot standing behind it, and a lone guard pacing across the deck.

Tai approaches, slinging his staff onto his shoulder. I lift the hook, preparing to throw it, but freeze. What if someone spots me as I'm climbing? I'll be completely helpless.

My hand drifts to my clockwork pistol. It doesn't have many enchanted bullets left, and I'd hate to waste them here when I might need them to fight Ligui. But the flares aren't limited . . .

Grabbing the weapon, I flick my thumb over the switch to make sure it's set to fire flares. "Take this." I shove it into Tai's hand. "It'll shoot flares. They probably won't hurt anyone, but they're bright enough to cause a distraction."

He holds up the pistol. "I always did like fireworks."

I give the rope a few good swings and then let it fly. The hook seizes the patrol ship's railing. Cold sweat pours down my face as I swing across. It's quiet so far. That means no one must have noticed—

A bright red flare breaks the calm, and shouts pepper the air. Whatever Tai's doing, I can't afford to lose focus and look back. The patrol ship's bronze hull sits inches from my nose, and wind from the spinning propellers whip my braids across my face.

When I pull myself onto the deck, I half expect the guard to be waiting, and I'm almost disappointed when no one confronts me. Then I see why—red flares explode from the damaged ship, keeping the cyborg soldiers from entering the doorway to the below deck area. Tai must be firing up the stairs, which is great for keeping the soldiers from spotting me, but how am I supposed to let him know that it's his turn to cross?

I glance back at the hole. To my surprise, Tai stands before the opening, waving his hands. I swing the rope back to him. I'll ask what he did to the pistol later.

Meanwhile, the lone guard stands at the end of the plank between ships, staring at the action. I yank my sword from its strap. He won't notice Tai if he's too busy fighting me.

I sprint up to the guard and take a swing. He's quick to block, but the element of surprise works to my advantage. Those cyborg enhancements give him strength, but that doesn't do him much good when I'm too quick for him to catch. I dodge, and his blade whooshes past me. Before he can regain his footing, I send a sturdy kick into his gut.

The guard stumbles onto the plank. By now the soldiers on the other ship have spotted me; one of them moves to cross, but the plank retracts before he can step onto it. The guard on my side strikes at me again, and as I duck the plank finishes retracting with him still standing on it. He grabs the railing with his metal hand. I jam my hilt into his fingers, and his grip loosens. He tumbles into the lake below.

A second splash sounds a moment later. I whirl to find Tai running to the controls from the opposite side, his staff in his hand.

"Where's the pilot?" I ask.

"Cooling off in the lake." Tai drops the staff and shoves a lever. The vessel zips forward so quickly, I have to grip the railing to keep from stumbling.

I glance back. Our old ship lies tangled in the treetops by the lake and grows smaller by the second. My breath is short, and my mask suddenly feels suffocating; I yank it off as I look around for more of Kang's ships. Only the vast heavens greet me. We escaped—no thanks to Tai. I march up to him with a scowl. "You fool! Why didn't you listen when I said our ship was damaged?"

"Are you still upset about that?" He tugs his mask down. "Everything worked out."

"Barely! We could have been captured or stranded!"

"But instead we obtained a new ship with a smoother engine, thanks to your excellent plan." He grins.

I can't believe the nerve of him. Too bad I couldn't have dumped him in the lake with the guard and the pilot. "You're unbelievable."

"Why thank you."

Rolling my eyes, I slide my sword back into its strap. My empty holster gapes at me. "Where's my pistol?"

"Still distracting those cyborgs, I imagine." Tai's eyes glint.

"I tied one end of a string to the trigger and wound the rest around the propeller of a hovering lantern so the weapon would fire on its own."

If I weren't so irritated with him I might have been impressed by the trick. But it cost me one of my few defenses, and while I wasn't particularly attached to that pistol, it was still mine. "So we have one less weapon."

"Nothing's good enough for you, is it?" Though his lips remain curved upward, there's something taut about his expression.

I don't care if he's irritated with me. After all the trouble we faced because of him, he has no right to judge me. I stride across the deck, searching the horizon. Part of me expects to see more ships descend any moment, but even after I've completed a full circle of the small vessel, I see nothing.

Tai leaves the controls and heads to the doorway leading below deck.

"What are you doing?" I demand.

"Seeing what kind of food those soldiers had. I'm starving."

"How can you think about your stomach at a time like this?"

"A time like what?" He arches his brow. "We escaped. And everybody has to eat."

My stomach rumbles in agreement. Still, it doesn't feel right to worry about such a small thing. "I'd better stay up here and keep an eye out for Kang's fleet."

Tai waves his hand. "The whole point of a scout ship is to fly off alone. You worry too much."

"And your carelessness nearly got us caught!" I glower. "I'm never trusting you as a lookout again, even if it means I have to stay awake the rest of the journey."

"Your empty threats grow more and more amusing." He laughs and continues below deck.

I wish I could retort that it *wasn't* an empty threat, but realistically, I know it is. Seething, I scan the sky. The white clouds are so placid that it's easy to believe we're safe, but we have miles to go before we reach our destination, and I'm certain more trouble awaits.

My blood still pounds from the rush of action, and I wipe the sweat from my forehead. The scalloped yellow-brown sail billows proudly from the mast, which gleams as if newly polished.

I can't believe it—I actually stole a ship from the viceroy's soldiers. An involuntary laugh erupts from my lips, and I clap my hands over them. I can't let Tai see my rush of delight; he'll take that as proof that I was wrong to worry.

Is it awful of me that I'm almost glad we were spotted? With the immediate danger gone, I'm free to revel in my triumph. Even Mother's tales of daring brigands couldn't compare to what I just did.

Mother would be ashamed to know I turned to crime so easily. So would Father. My parents always emphasized the importance of rules and laws. I draw a solemn breath. Stealing a ship and leaving those soldiers stranded was *not* heroic. It may have been necessary, but I shouldn't take so much joy in my actions. However, I can't bring myself to feel shame either.

I pace across the deck, the lessons my parents taught me ringing in my head. Laws exist to protect people, and without them, there would be chaos. I promise myself I'll do my best to avoid breaking more.

But chances are, stealing this ship won't be the last crime I must commit on my way to the Courts of Hell.

CHAPTER THIRTEEN

A RIVER LIKE HOME

G littering stars peek through hazy clouds. Only the ship's hum and the wind's song keep me company, since Tai's below sleeping. As I gaze at the bright moon, I think about the beings that dwell in its light; though the Yueshen haven't been a part of my life for years, their absence still haunts me.

The ship's control panel blinks like fireflies, and the yellow glow of the wheel reminds me of a hearth. They're the only illumination on board, since it would have been risky to light the lanterns. I wanted to snuff out even these specks of light, but neither Tai nor I had the mechanical expertise to do so without risking damage.

Tai spent the rest of the afternoon showing me how the controls work. I still don't know *everything*—it would take more than a few hours to learn how to control the ship completely. But I know enough. According to the gauges, we've slowed since the wind died down.

The propellers keep us going, though, and we'll still arrive at Baiheshan before noon.

I approach the bow and watch the dark land below glide by. Despite my calm surroundings, I keep my senses alert. Even under the cover of night I feel exposed.

Tai emerges from below deck with a wide yawn. "Anything interesting down there?"

I lean back against the railing. "You didn't rest for very long."

Suddenly an icy sensation blooms through my chest. For a moment, I can't figure out why, and then I hear it . . . the eerie whispers, the ghostly humming. Though I'm on board a different ship, the haunting sounds seem to have followed me. They fade after a few seconds, but the chill lingers.

"Did you hear that?"

Tai nods. "I used to hear them on board the other ship too. I have no idea what it is . . . the first time I heard it, I thought it was the Yueshen."

I frown. "The Yueshen have been gone for years."

"I know, but I still hoped." He shrugs. "Maybe some aspect of the viceroy's magic gave his ships life. Once, I swear the voices called out my name. But I probably imagined it."

I glance up the ship's bronze mast, wondering what kind of supernatural being would cling to a ship. Maybe they *are* ghosts . . . Maybe Viceroy Kang once used this ship in a battle and those are the spirits of the enemies he or his men killed.

Tai leans against the railing beside me. A strange melancholy seems to have descended over him. The bright spark has vanished from his eyes, and there's no trace of his usual teasing smile.

"What's wrong?" I ask.

"Nothing." He gazes up at the moon. "I just miss the Yueshen."

"I do too." It's said that the Yueshen were the descendants of an ancient village whose inhabitants purified their souls so well that they left their earthly bodies and ascended to the moon. I hope that's where they are now. "My sister says she met one once—a girl who braided her hair and twisted her ribbons into knotted animals."

"She's lucky." Tai smiles. "Have you ever seen one? I mean, a visible one?"

"No, but I once saw one of Grandfather's little copper butterflies vanish into thin air and heard a girl giggling. It always seemed strange to me that beings who were supposed to be purer than humans would steal."

"The original Yueshen may have been pure, but even lunar spirits change across generations. Trust me, they're no purer than the rest of us." He says that like he knows it for certain.

"Have you ever encountered them?"

"Mother used to tell me stories about them."

"My mother told me stories too." Wind blows a wisp of black hair across my face, and I tuck it behind my ear. "I always liked the ones about the Yueshen warriors who'd help humans fight monsters."

Tai nods. "I also liked those, though my favorite tale was about a Yueshen girl who fell in love with an earthly prince."

"I didn't know you were a romantic," I tease.

"You'll find I'm full of surprises."

"That's not hard when you refuse to answer half my questions."

"That still leaves you with half."

I shake my head. "So what's the story?"

"That's one I can answer." Tai gazes up at the luminous moon. "There was a Yueshen girl . . . not royalty, but she might as well have been, since she was the daughter of the Yueshen king's most trusted advisor. As a child, she was a wild little thing who often played tricks on humans." A fond smile lifts his lips. "One of her favorite victims was a young prince. He was a genius at magic—a favorite pupil of the realm's greatest spellmasters. He cast a spell to trap her, but it only lasted long enough for him to glimpse her face. She retaliated by stealing his most prized possessions. Soon, it became a game for them . . . She'd try to take his things or make a mess of his room or otherwise bother him, and he'd try to catch her. Eventually, they became friends, and, as they grew older, they fell in love. But whenever he tried to touch her, all he'd feel was mist."

"What happened to them?"

"She petitioned the king for the magic to turn her human. Though he refused at first, she wouldn't give up until he granted her wish. It took more power than the Yueshen had ever used in a single spell before to give her the ability to exist in both realms, but once the spell was cast, she could shift between human and Yueshen forms at will."

"It sounds like this story has a happy ending."

"It does. She and her prince were united on Earth." A sorrowful look glimmers in Tai's eyes. "I wish she—and all her kind—were still around."

"So do I." I sigh, thinking about all the untouched ribbons my sister left out for her Yueshen friend. "What do you think happened to them?"

He gives a noncommittal shrug. "I don't like to speculate about it."

"I always thought they retreated into their lunar kingdom when the Ligui started attacking."

"That's possible."

"Maybe Mowang *sent* the Ligui after them," I muse aloud. "Maybe when we confront him in the Courts of Hell, we'll learn the truth."

"Maybe."

I gaze out into the dark horizon, trying to picture what Hell will be like. It still doesn't feel real to me, like a place I'm actually going to. But once I get there, I intend to make Mowang answer for all he's done—not just for trapping Tai's people. The Ligui are creatures of Hell, which means Mowang is ultimately the force behind them. Who knows . . . maybe with their king gone, the Ligui will retreat? Then Dailan won't need outside protection, and I won't have to marry Viceroy Kang.

It doesn't hurt to hope.

The tops of green trees roll across the land and trail into the distant blue-gray mountains on the horizon. Baiheshan, the White Crane Mountain, looms tall above the rest. According to the navigational instruments on the ship's control panel, we're about twenty miles away. The city at the base of the mountain—also called Baiheshan—looks like colorful scattered pebbles from here. I squint at the mountain, trying to make out Baiheshan Miao, the temple where Tai's spellmaster lives, but all I can see are gray stones jutting between swaths of green leaves.

Below, sunlight bounces along the surface of Baihejiang, the White Crane River. I lean my elbows against the railing. The merry ripples fill me with a sense of calm, and I crave the touch of flowing water. In Dailan, I was never more than a few houses away from the nearest stream.

According to Tai, several large caves yawn along the wide river. The plan is to steer the ship into one of them and hope that's enough to conceal it, then walk the rest of the way so no one will suspect we're anything more than ordinary travelers. There's just one path up the mountain, and you can only get to it by going through the city.

Tai glances at me from behind the ship's wheel. "What kind of food do you want me to steal for you when we reach the city? I'm guessing you're as sick of *mantou* as I am. What about pork buns? Ooh, or a duck!"

I cross my arms. While subsisting on the plain white buns Tai found in the ship's stores has been frustrating, I'd rather eat a hundred of them than let Tai steal to feed me. "First of all, I don't need *you* to provide for me. And secondly, there won't be any stealing. Not while I'm around."

He leans one elbow against the ship's wheel and crosses his legs at the ankles. "You didn't seem to mind when you stole this entire ship."

Heat rushes to my cheeks. "That was different! We were escaping danger. And the viceroy has plenty of ships—it's not as if he'd miss this one little scout vessel."

"Tell yourself whatever you want. The truth is, you're shaping up to be an excellent criminal." He winks.

I turn away, certain my face is redder than the rising sun. My parents didn't raise me to steal from others. But they *did* raise me to *help* others, and I'm sure they'd agree that someone's life is worth more than a ship. Thinking about it that way, taking this one wasn't such a crime.

"If you don't want to steal, then I hope you have some coins in that tunic of yours. Or were you planning to beg?" Tai strokes his chin. "You look too clean to be a beggar. You'd have to rub some mud on your face to make it convincing."

I resist the urge to smack him. "For your information, I'm going to *earn* enough money to feed us."

"Who'd hire a pretty girl like you off the streets? And as *what*?" He lifts his brows.

If he's implying what I think he's implying, then he deserves that smack a hundred times over. But though he tries my patience, I find it in myself to be mature about this. One of us has to be.

"My sister and I are acrobats. Our parents used to take us to neighboring villages to perform." It might not be the best idea to purposely draw attention with my act when Kang's men are still looking for us, but that's a risk I'll have to take. Baiheshan is outside Viceroy Kang's province, so it's possible his men won't even be there. As long as I keep a sharp eye out, I should be fine. "Most of the time, we'd make the streets our stage. I plan to do just that."

"How much can you make doing tricks in the street?"

"Enough to buy us a meal or two. Without inviting trouble or depriving someone else."

He clutches his chest. "You wound me with your words! You know I only steal from those who wouldn't miss what I took. And I never get caught."

"I caught you, didn't I?" I smirk.

"Only because you had help. But I'm curious about these tricks of yours, so we'll try it your way first. If you don't make enough, I'll steal whatever else we need. Deal?"

"No, because I'll earn more than what we need."

"Aren't you arrogant."

"Look who's talking."

He grins. "At least I'm not arrogant enough to think that we can walk into Baiheshan without people wondering who we are. A young man and a young woman traveling together would cause a scandal . . . unless we were married." He extends his hand. "Will you be my fake wife?"

I lift my eyebrow. "Or unless we were related. How about I be your fake sister instead?"

"And here I was thinking you'd like pretending to be a married woman. You're so eager to wed, after all."

Though he apparently meant the quip as a joke, his words cause a strange sting in my chest. I'd managed to forget for a little while that I'm doomed to marry a man I despise. The thought of spending the rest of my life serving Viceroy Kang still makes me sick. It's not something I can joke about.

And it's something Tai would never understand—not that I care to explain. I scowl and walk away. Anger burns in my heart, and I'm not sure if it's aimed at the viceroy or at Tai for bringing him up.

"Wait!" Tai runs ahead of me, blocking my path. "I didn't mean to offend you."

"What did you mean, then?"

"I . . . " He shrugs with a helpless expression. "I don't know. I'm sorry."

I blow out a breath, reminding myself that he has no way of knowing how much horror I feel each time I think about marrying Kang. "Don't talk about my engagement ever again."

"I won't." A strange look crosses his expression—almost like pain.

Needing to change the subject, I say, "Now that we're practically at Baiheshan, can you tell me about this spellmaster we're meeting? Who is he?"

"*She* is from the Southern Continent, a long, long way from here." Tai's voice is light. "And her name is Ibsituu Bekele . . . except in her culture, given names come first. So when you meet her, call her Ibsituu."

The prospect of meeting someone from the distant Southern Continent is enough to banish all thought of Viceroy Kang. Both Mother and Father used to tell me and Anshui stories about the people from that far-off land. It's said they have brown skin and speak a language that sounds like stones rolling down a creek. Like people from the West—those odd foreigners with their yellow hair and harsh tongues—they sometimes travel to the Empire of the Pearl Moon for trade. But of course none make it to a village as remote as Dailan.

"Ibsituu." I try out the unfamiliar syllables. "I thought you said your spellmaster was a man."

"I never said that." Tai's eyes twinkle. "You assumed."

I knit my brows, mentally retracing our conversations, but have trouble remembering the exact words. I wonder what else he might have hidden this way . . . by feeding me incomplete information and letting my assumptions fill in the rest. And what other misconceptions I might have about him as a result.

A ringing sound chimes from the direction of the ship's wheel. Knowing that it means we're approaching our designated coordinates, I stride toward the controls. Tai follows and glances at one of the gauges.

"Time to start our descent." He pulls a lever, and I step out of the way as he turns to the wheel.

I watch him manipulate the levers with curious fascination. He showed me how everything works, but it's different seeing the machinery in motion. The press of a button, a turn of the wheel, the flick of a switch—a dozen little things that go into bringing the small ship closer and closer to the river until it skates gently upon the water.

The deck rocks back and forth, and I grip the railing to keep my balance until the ship steadies. The mouth of an enormous cave gapes against the side of the rocky mountain. Thin green vines with narrow leaves grow rebelliously against its grayish brown surface, draping down over the opening. Tai turns the wheel, and the ship glides inside. Every splash that hits my skin as the propellers churn the water feels like a gift.

The vines graze the sail as we enter the cave. All of Dailan could fit inside. Sharp formations that look like teeth jut from the arcing ceiling, and I feel like we've sailed into the mouth of a gargantuan beast. Water stretches into the darkness ahead, but considering I can see the stones and mud beneath it, it can't be very deep.

The ship halts. "This is as far as we can go," Tai says. "Not as good as an invisibility potion would have been, but it'll do. Give me a minute to secure the ship, and then we can head to the city."

I glance toward the mouth of the cave. The area we landed in seemed isolated, but a flying ship is a pretty visible thing. "I'm going to scout ahead to make sure no one spotted us."

"Suit yourself." Tai waves dismissively, not bothering to look up from the control panel.

I double check to make sure the strap of my sword is secure. It will make me more conspicuous than I'd like to be, but I'm not going anywhere without it. Besides, I need to use it as a prop for my Warrioress performance. A knot digs into my shoulder—I tied the scrap of cloth Tai gave me to use as a mask to the strap. It's best to keep it handy in case I need to hide my face again.

Finding the rope stashed by the bow, I toss its end overboard. It lands with a splash. As I climb down, I half expect Tai to try some prank like the one he pulled at Huimaohu, and I'm almost disappointed when I reach the bottom without incident.

The cool water, which reaches my knees, feels like a god's touch against my skin. I savor it as I wade toward the rocky riverbank. The sun is strong enough outside the cave that I should be dry long before we reach the city.

The river glistens beneath its rays. I picture the River Dragon, with his red-green scales and curling tail, swimming beneath the surface. How lucky he is to spend his days free like that!

I walk along the bank toward the ship's stern, which sits so close to the cave's opening that sunlight brushes the railing. I draw my sword in case I spot trouble. The ship's whir ceases. Without it, the air feels blissfully still. Only the songs of distant birds and the soft whisper of a breeze break the silence. Tranquil water stretches with brownish-green hues into the horizon, and the shadows of distant mountains stand proudly above it.

A great splash disturbs the quiet. I gasp at the sudden cold of mud and water hitting me. My troubled heart races from the shock, and I look around wildly.

I hear Tai's laughter before my eyes find him, standing a few feet away with his bronze staff clutched in one hand. A rope dangles from the ship's stern.

"You should have seen the look on your face!" He cocks his head. "You *do* kind of look like a beggar now that you're covered in mud. Are you sure you don't want to give that a try?"

He must have climbed down the ship's back and landed right next to me on purpose . . . another prank. I snarl, infuriated. *"Hundan!"*

Tai's eyes widen. "It was an accident?"

"You lie!" I throw down my sword and lunge at him.

Tai dodges me and sprints onto the shore, dropping his staff. I dash after him.

"Accident! *Accident!*" he exclaims between laughs.

"You rotten, pig-headed idiot!" My irritation froths over, and I chase him out of the cave and up the grassy riverbank outside.

He zigs abruptly to try to throw me off, then zags to avoid me again. I recognize his trick the third time and cut him off. I launch myself into him, grab him around the middle, and tackle him to the ground.

We land roughly, with me on top of him. My head bangs into his back. He flips over and tries to push me off, but I grasp his shoulders and pin him down.

Instead of fighting back, he holds up his hands with a sheepish grin. "Mercy?"

I suddenly realize how ridiculous this situation is. For a second, I stare incredulously into his eyes, then I burst out laughing. What was I planning to do once I caught him?

He laughs with me, and we both revel in the silliness. I double over, which brings my face close enough to his to feel his breath on my cheeks.

"*Shagua!*" I smack his shoulder. "I told you not to make me mad!"

"And I told *you* it's too much fun!" His eyes dance with merriment.

"I hate you."

"No, you don't."

I roll my eyes. "No, I don't."

"Does that mean you like me, then?"

"No." I pause. "Maybe. A little."

"I'll take it." His gaze catches mine. "I have a confession."

"Oh?" I feel like I should look away, at something—anything—else, but his eyes are too magnetic.

"The day you came to Tongqiucheng . . . it was no accident that you spotted me from your carriage. I was looking for you."

"What do you mean?"

A small smile flickers across his lips. "Rumors were flying that though the viceroy's new bride was just a village girl, she was so brave she fought the Ligui. That she was like a modern-day Warrioress. I couldn't believe it. I'd heard that some of the remote villages were using women guards, but it never seemed believable until I heard them talking about a real, living girl who was heading into my city. It hit me how incredible this girl must be to fight monsters known to kill the best of warriors."

I bite the inside of my cheek. I should be preening at the flattery, but instead, part of me wants to disappear. Other than my little sister, no one's ever . . . *admired* me before. My heart hammers, and I tell myself it's from the sprinting.

"I had to see you myself, so I went to watch the viceroy's convoy arrive. Of course, then I couldn't resist an unguarded coin purse, but when you looked at me . . . " He chuckles. "You know what happened next."

A small laugh escapes me. "Thief."

"Guilty."

I lean down toward him, drawn by some invisible force that yearns to get closer. The what and why don't enter my mind—all I know is now. His warm breath rustles the wisps of hair framing my face as he lifts himself up on one elbow, bringing himself even nearer to me—so near I can feel the heat of his lips. Never once does he break his gaze, and I suddenly feel like I'm tumbling, tumbling, tumbling into his dark eyes, not knowing or caring why.

An abrupt clunking noise breaks my trance. I look up, startled. Whatever spell held me vanishes—I'm suddenly back in the real world.

I scramble to get off of Tai, realizing how inappropriate my actions were. I'm not a little girl; I can't tussle with boys like a child. Mother would scold me harshly if she'd seen me like that.

What I need to do now is retrieve my sword, which I abandoned by the river, and find out what that noise was. What if it's Kang's men catching up to us?

I rush to grab my weapon from the water's edge. The clunking noise sounds again, this time accompanied by hissing. It sounds like a machine, but I don't see anything. "What was that?"

I expect Tai to be as alarmed as I am, or to at least make some offhand comment about it. When only silence greets me, I look back to find him still reclining on the grass, propped up on one elbow. A strange look fills his face. Though his eyes watch me, his mind seems a million miles away.

"Tai?"

He blinks. "I guess we both look like beggars now." He stands and brushes dirt from his clothes.

The clunking shakes the air yet again, this time louder, closer. I take a few steps up the riverbank and notice the narrow dirt road carving the land. Cresting a nearby hill is a mechanical wagon. It looks more like the one Grandfather built than one of Kang's mighty vehicles. Watermelons fill the back, and a tanned, gray-haired man in a cone-shaped bamboo hat sits behind the controls. He certainly isn't one of Kang's cyborgs, and he doesn't look armed either. With his humble clothing, it's more likely he's a local farmer going to sell his wares in Baiheshan.

If I can flag down the wagon, then we can reach the city much faster. But what if he spots the ship in the cave? I glance back at the vessel. Shadows hide all but one bit of railing, and the vines dangling over the opening further obscure it. The sooner we get to Baiheshan, the sooner we can take to the sky again, and the less likely someone will be to stumble upon it by accident.

I sling my sword onto my back and sprint up the hill. *"Xien sheng!"* I call for the driver.

The wagon halts, and the man turns to me. "Whose daughter are you? What are you doing all the way out here without supervision?"

"She's my sister." Tai, striding up to the road with his staff in one hand, answers before I can. "Our father sent us to run errands in the city. Can you spare some room for a pair of poor village siblings?" His words carry so much sarcasm, even I can hear it.

But they're apparently good enough for the man in the wagon, because he grunts and says, "Sure, if you can find room in the back. Don't knock off any of my watermelons."

"*Xie xie.*" Tai climbs onto the wagon and gingerly crawls over the watermelons to find a spot among them.

I choose to balance myself on the wagon's narrow back edge rather than get any closer to him.

The man yanks a lever on the wagon, and it sputters to life. Steam pours from the back, fogging the landscape before me. I stare ahead anyway, determined to look anywhere but at Tai.

CHAPTER FOURTEEN

THE STREETS, THE STAGE

Baiheshan looks like the child of Dailan and Tongqiucheng. Like Dailan, rivers cut through the heart of the city and bridges decorated with intricate sculptures of tigers and lotuses span the water, some made of stone and others of wood. One looks so much like a bridge in Dailan—with its simple arch and rounded rails—that my heart aches for home. Yet the city's scale and size remind me of Tongqiucheng. Elaborate storefronts line wide streets, and market stalls crowd dense alleys. Mechanical wagons chug along, but unlike in Tongqiucheng, no automatons or clockwork creatures roam about. Such technology must be rarer here.

The people of Baiheshan carry a different air than the elites of Tongqiucheng, and the men here all wear their hair in different styles. Most sport a queue—the Imperial style—but many also wear a topknot like Tai's—the ancient warrior's style. And still others, dressed in a monk's simple white robes, have no hair at all.

No wonder Tai was unconcerned about his "foreigner hair" making him stand out. Apparently there are many foreigners in Baiheshan, which is close enough to the roads leading from the West to have seen many travelers. We're also far enough from Tongqiucheng that whatever fear drove him to hide his face before is no longer a factor, since we've walked past several city guards without incident. So far, I haven't seen any sign of Viceroy Kang's presence and conclude that his search hasn't reached this city. I only hope I'm right.

I look around for an open part of the street I can perform in. A few Westerners pass us, dressed in odd-looking trousers and even odder tunics that are open in the front and have another, thinner tunic inside. Though not all of them have yellow hair—some have brown hair and others black like citizens of the Empire—their unusual facial features make them stand out. Sharp, pointy noses and jutting chins. Round eyes with thick lids. Hair even shorter than Tai's that hugs their scalps. And, depending on what parts of the West they come from, their languages sound like anything from a goat's bleat to a flute's melody.

"How long does it take to pick a street corner?" Tai, walking beside me, sounds nonchalant. Since we boarded the wagon he's been acting as if nothing happened.

I choose to do the same. "There's a strategy to it. You need an area that's crowded so you'll attract plenty of onlookers, but not so crowded that they won't see you through the masses."

An empty area sprawls before the back wall of a building. It's perfect—right in front of a bustling street, yet not blocking any storefronts. And I don't see any other street performers around.

"This will do." I speed into the spot then unstrap my sword. Eying its sharp edge, I wrap the leather strap around the blade; the last thing I want is for the sword to fling out of my hand by accident and impale an onlooker.

Tai watches with a bemused expression. "Do you really think this will work?"

"Yes," I reply, even though my heart whispers, *No*. I haven't performed in the streets since I was twelve, and back then, I had Father and Anshui with me. In Dailan, the audience consisted of only my friends and neighbors. I also don't have the set pieces I need for my usual Warrioress routine, so I'll have to improvise. All that traveling and fighting has left my simple outfit somewhat bedraggled and far from impressive. Then again, the last time I performed with my full regalia, I wound up attracting unwanted attention that led to an even more unwanted marriage proposal. Perhaps it's better this way.

Once my blade is bound, I raise it high and echo the words Father once used to draw crowds. "Everybody, listen here! Have you ever heard the story of Warrioress? Of course you have—who hasn't? But have you ever seen it performed by a living, breathing girl who can embody all the skills of the great lady fighter of the Yueshen?" As people start turning to me, I plaster a wide grin onto my face, imagining how Father used to do it and trying to emulate his confidence. "Watch me bring the great Warrioress to life before your very eyes!"

Though my muscles quiver with nerves, I hold my head high. I can't let anyone see me waver, especially with Tai watching. A handful of onlookers form a semicircle around me, and he stands among them, still holding that bemused expression, but there's also a look of curiosity and wonder in his eyes. I can't tell if he's admiring me or silently mocking me. Probably the latter.

The audience is much thinner than the ones Anshui and I used to attract. I choose to attribute that to the fact that I'm the one calling for attention, rather than my imposing father. Still, there are at least a dozen people here, and if each of them—or even most of them—chooses to give a coin, then that's enough for lunch at least.

"Have you ever heard the story of Warrioress?" I repeat, sweeping my sword to the side. Though my heart flutters, I speak with confidence.

I catch Tai's smile in the crowd, and somehow, that energizes me. He said he'd steal our next meal if I didn't earn enough. I'm not about to let him win.

Since I don't have my usual bamboo pole to leap onto, I'll have to do something else to start the act. I lay my sword on the ground. "She was the daughter of a Yueshen prince and his beautiful bride—a pair so pure, Heaven granted them the powers of the stars."

To illustrate the unearthly beings from the sky, I spring up and flip through the air, then let the energy carry me into a second flip. Soft, scattered applause speckles the air.

"But the evil Mowang grew jealous and, with his dark magic, cursed them so that any children they bore would fall to Earth and be trapped in a human form."

To illustrate the fall, I rush to the wall and use the momentum to carry me upward. For a moment, I'm weightless as I run up the wall like a spider. I flip over my head, land on both feet, and spin to face the crowd. Another spattering of applause follows.

I fold into the ground, forming a little ball. "The place where the infant Yueshen princess landed was once a battlefield, and the ghosts of the great warriors who'd died there took pity and raised her." Slowly, I rise, picking up my bound sword. "With their training, she learned to fight as well as any man—and better than most!"

Flip, tumble, turn . . . I toss my sword from one hand to the other and let my body explode into fireworks of movement. But though the small crowd applauds heartily at my tricks, they've grown no larger. Disappointment rumbles in my gut.

"But the girl knew she couldn't stay among the spirits forever. So she left the protection of the ghost warriors to seek out the humans." I walk in a large circle, using the opportunity to catch my breath. For effect, I swing my sword by my side. "Mowang, realizing how powerful she'd grown, sent a demon soldier to kill her the moment she struck out alone."

I raise my sword, preparing to switch roles and act out the demon soldier's part.

"And he attacked!" Tai leaps out of the crowd, swinging his bronze staff.

I whirl toward him, startled. My sword instinctively whips up before me. He catches its bound blade with his staff, and suddenly, we're face-to-face.

What does he think he's doing?! I glare at him.

His lips quirk, and he sweeps my weapon to the side. Spotting his staff slashing toward me, I move to parry. Claps of approval ring in my ears.

I want to yell at him to get out of my way, but with the audience watching, all I can do is make the most of the situation. When he strikes again, I dodge, then do an elaborate flip before striking back.

In the corner of my eye, I glimpse more people approaching to see what the commotion's about. *It's working . . .*

Still, if Tai wanted to participate, he should have asked instead of interrupting my performance. I strike at him again—none too gently—and he ducks. The moment I glimpse him moving to attack me, I leap into a back handspring. The sword in my hand nearly causes me to teeter, but I land on both feet. Channeling my annoyance, I launch a dramatic, whirling series of attacks. It's all theatrical, but I wouldn't mind if a few of those blows actually whacked his limbs. Tai blocks me, but this time, I manage to drive him against the wall.

Instead of allowing himself to be defeated as the demon soldier was, he ducks under my arms and rushes toward the crowd.

"Ladies and gentlemen!" he exclaims. "The story you've heard is incomplete!"

What's he talking about? I watch him with narrowed eyes.

"The one known as the demon soldier was not always a minion of Mowang." As Tai continues, his expression takes on an exaggerated air of tragedy. His tilted brows, pouting mouth, and elongated vowels are rather comical, and I stifle a laugh. "He pledged his allegiance to the demon king in exchange for the power to protect his village from invaders. But though that oath bound him to Hell, he was not evil at heart."

That's not part of the story! I open my mouth to protest his twisting of the myth but stop when I notice that the crowd has grown to twice its original size—and is watching with rapt interest. Apparently they don't care that Tai's making things up. Part of me is glad to have their attention, but a bigger part remains irritated.

"Great Warrioress!" Tai spins to me and drops to his knees, that melodramatic look of sorrow still distorting his face. "Will you help me escape my curse?"

I huff. "I thought Mowang sent you to kill me."

"I have no wish to obey his order. I only wish to be free . . . Please, my great, powerful, beautiful Warrioress, will you help an unfortunate, cursed soul?"

I scowl, wondering what I'm supposed to do now. *When in doubt, turn to your audience*, Mother told me once. *They'll let you know what they want.*

Glancing at the crowd, I ask, "Should I aid an agent of the demon king?"

Several people shout their approval. Perhaps they've heard this story so many times they're curious for an alternate ending. Or perhaps it's Tai . . . an aura of effortless charm clings to every action he takes. He makes everything he does seem natural, easy.

I look down at him, and his eyes glint with mischief.

"Will you help me, Warrioress?" He exaggerates his pout even further, and it's all I can do to keep from bursting out in laughter despite my annoyance.

I decide there's no harm in indulging the audience with a new version of the myth. "Very well." I reach out my hand. "Get up. You look ridiculous."

Soft chuckles ripple through the crowd. Tai clasps my hand, and I pull him up. He meets my gaze with that smirk of his. It feels so familiar by now, I don't know if I want to laugh or smack him. His warm grip lingers around mine, and I find myself strangely reluctant to release him.

I swing my bound sword. "How do we lift this curse?"

"Mowang used his dark magic to seize my beating heart from my chest." Tai clutches his chest and staggers backward. "He keeps it in an enchanted box guarded by monstrous serpents. If we can defeat them and retrieve it, I'll be free!"

"Oh?" I lift one eyebrow. His tale is nonsensical; Mowang's been known to do a lot of wicked things, but ripping out hearts isn't one of them. "I thought you said it was your soul that Mowang held."

"One's soul is bound to one's heart—surely you knew that?" He swings his staff. "They journeyed to the Courts of Hell and confronted the demons within!"

Tai's staff becomes a whirlwind as he expertly spins it between his hands, then over his head, then around his shoulders in a dizzying flurry. The crowd applauds, but he's not done yet. He tosses it high into the air and, while it's aloft, kicks his legs over his head in an aerial cartwheel. After landing, he catches the staff and points it at the audience with a firm, dramatic flourish.

The crowd claps loudly, clearly impressed. He flashes me a grin, as if expecting me to be as well. I have to admit, he's skilled with a staff. But I'm not about to let him steal the audience's approval when it's me they came to see.

I shake my head. "We'll never defeat them at this pace. Let me speed our progress."

I snatch the staff from him then whirl both it and my sword by my sides, turning them into a pair of propellers. The staff is significantly longer than a second sword would be, but I hold myself steady so no one will see that it's shaking my balance. I spin in place, passing both weapons around my body and over my head. Finally, I toss them both up and perform the same kind of aerial cartwheel that Tai just did—except I do it twice. I catch the sword and staff and—just for good measure—throw them up again and jump up in a double flip. The moment my feet touch the ground, I snatch both from the air and end with a powerful pose, the sword above my head and the staff out before me.

Roars of approval erupt from the crowd. I glimpse Tai staring at me with an expression of awe, and this time, it's my turn to smirk. "Though the soldier fought bravely, any skills he possessed Warrioress could perform twice as well—if not more." I toss him the staff and put my hand on my hip, daring him to do better.

He bows his head. "Of course, the soldier knew he was no match for the legendary Warrioress."

A sense of satisfaction courses through me, and it feels somewhat strange, almost unreal. He just admitted defeat—something no man has ever done with me before. Part of me wonders if Tai's willingness to concede is part of the performance, but the look of admiration and respect shining in his eyes seems genuine. Something warm glows in my chest, and my smirk melts into a different kind of smile.

"Even the best could use some help." I toss my sword from one hand to the other as an idea hits me. "It would be more efficient to defeat the monsters together, don't you think?"

Tai, apparently taking my cue, begins spinning his staff again. "Indeed, it would."

I slash my sword and perform a series of kicks while Tai, at the same time, whirls his staff over his head. For a few moments, we each show off our talents. He turns his staff into a maelstrom of moves while I fly through the air with my flips and handsprings.

Cheers and applause fill my ears, and I grin. Tai catches my eye, then tosses me his staff. I snatch it and whip both weapons around me. Wondering what he'd do with it, I pass my sword to him.

He doesn't miss a beat. The instant the sword lands in his grasp, he begins slashing the air in rapid, dizzying movements. I keep twirling the staff, but steal a few glances in his direction. Though he's not as quick as I am, Tai can certainly handle a blade. His arms are fluid as he slices at an invisible enemy, and I wonder where he trained. There's no way he learned these skills on a whim—someone must have spent years teaching him. Was he a soldier once?

Tai catches my eye again and throws my sword back to me. I grab its hilt then toss both weapons so I can perform one last flip. I catch them midair before stabbing the ground as I land.

"They defeated the monsters!" I force energy into my voice despite my heaving breaths. As I rise, my legs feel wobbly.

Applause thunders through the crowd of onlookers, which is now so dense I can't see the street through them.

"The soldier took back his beating heart." Tai clutches his chest and doubles over with melodramatic flair. He glances at me, and a wicked grin lights his face. "The moment he returned to his human state, he realized he was desperately in love with Warrioress."

Hun shen me dan?! I bite my teeth to keep from yelling the curse aloud. Hot fury engulfs me. Does he *always* have to make fun of me?

"That's a pity, because, as we all know, Warrioress would go on to brave many more adventures *alone*." I shoot Tai a glare. "And after defeating many more enemies, she would marry a great king."

Tai drops his expression back into that farcical pout. Still clutching his chest, he sinks to the ground. "The unfortunate soldier spent the rest of his days pining after the magnificent woman who freed him, until finally, he could take the sorrow no longer and died of a broken heart."

I want to smack him so badly I have to clench my fists to stop myself.

Groans rumble through the crowd. Alarm seizes me . . . We can't leave them with a disappointing ending. No one would give us any coins, and all that work would have been for nothing.

Before I can come up with a way to salvage the situation, Tai springs up. "I take it you don't like the way this story's supposed to end?"

A flurry of head shakes peppered with more groans passes through the crowd.

"Would you like a new story, then?" Tai's lips curve. "A different take on the legend?"

Nods. Cheers. Exclamations of approval. What's *wrong* with this crowd? Warrioress's way is set—her story's been written a thousand times. Everyone *knows* what becomes of her—a marriage to a mighty ruler, a lifetime spent behind the walls of his palace after she gave up her adventuring ways to be a good queen, wife, and mother. People aren't supposed to make up new endings to old legends. It's practically blasphemy.

But the crowd doesn't seem to care. Tai's alternate myth has them enraptured. An unexpected sense of envy snakes through my gut at the way he enamors people without even trying, whereas even on my best days, I'm about as likable as a thorn bush. When I perform, it's my skills people come to see, not *me*. It's probably why the crowd was so small before Tai stepped in, why after our sister acts, Anshui was always the one who received the most applause, even though I performed the harder tricks. Too bad the viceroy saw only my performer self and not the thorn bush.

"A new story it is!" Tai whirls to face me. "Beautiful Warrioress, this humble soldier offers you his devotion for all eternity." He clasps his hands in a pleading gesture and sinks to his knees. "Will you accept my hand in marriage?"

I clench my jaw, imagining how my character would respond. "The great Warrioress would not love a man just because he wanted her to." I give him a disdainful look. "He'd have to earn her favor."

"And so he shall!" Tai stands and winks at me, and I resist the instinct to roll my eyes.

"How?" I demand. "By slaying monsters and bringing her treasures? Remember, Warrioress defeated many, *many* monsters on her own and had no need for knickknacks!"

"Of course. How could one forget?" His expression warms, and he takes my hand. His eyes meet mine, and that strange pull draws me in once again—though toward what, I don't know.

A wave of heat rolls over me, and my pulse hammers so loudly I wonder if the entire audience can hear it. I must have performed harder than I thought . . . must have worn out my body more than I imagined.

"The soldier was well aware that he was no match for Warrioress's skills." Though he's speaking to the audience, Tai's gaze remains on me.

"He knew he could never be worthy of such a legend, and that he'd always be in her shadow. But his love was so true, he did not care."

He places one hand on my cheek, and my breath catches. For a moment, I forget where I am, what I'm doing.

"All this humble soldier had to offer was his unconditional respect and devotion, and he hoped it would be enough." His voice softens, and he sounds so sincere I wonder if he was an actor as well as a soldier in the past he won't tell me about. Or perhaps it's part of being a thief—this ability to cast illusions without magic.

Because that's all this is—illusions. He's playing a character, just like I am, and I hate that I have to remind myself of that. I must be sinking too far into my role, because my heartbeat quickens at his words. But I'm not Warrioress and never will be. And he's certainly not this ridiculous piece of fiction he improvised.

"Marry him!" A woman's voice bursts from the direction of the crowd.

"Yes, marry him!" another audience member cries.

A laugh explodes from my lips. It's ludicrous how invested the audience is in this impromptu perversion of a legend, but why do I care so much? After all, it's just a story. And if having Warrioress marry the soldier—who somehow became a romantic hero instead of the first demon she defeated—will prompt them to give us more coins, then I shouldn't care.

"Very well." Throwing on a carefree expression, I look at the crowd. "After he spent years and years proving his love, and after she came to realize that having someone so devoted was rather nice, Warrioress agreed to marry the soldier."

"And they went on to have many, many more adventures together," Tai adds. "Traveling the world and taking down evil wherever they went."

Worried that he'll stretch this performance out even longer, I say, "The end!"

I back away from Tai, yanking my hand from his, and lean forward in a quick bow. The sounds of clapping hands and approving shouts tumble toward me, and I grin. The thrill of applause sweeps through me and knocks away my worries for a moment.

Tai steps forward and bows as well. Though he smiles for the audience, he seems . . . faded. The usual spark has vanished from his eyes, and there's something forced about his grin.

I feel like there's a great, wide . . . *something* . . . standing right before me that I'm just not seeing. I'm not sure I want to see it.

Something about it scares me.

CHAPTER FIFTEEN

HIDE YOUR FACE

A spicy burst of rich, pungent flavor explodes on my tongue, and though my eyes sting, I savor the sensation. I've never eaten anything that tasted so powerful before. Apparently, the boiling oil of this beef dish wasn't hot enough, and the cook had to make it even hotter with pointed red peppers. Those who run this restaurant come from the Lunan Province in the southwest, which is famous for its spices. I can't decide if that makes this food delicious or just painful, but either way, I'm enjoying the challenge of eating it.

We still haven't spotted any sign of Kang's search party, which I can only guess means they haven't made it as far as Baiheshan yet—maybe they're methodically combing through Sijiang Province first before moving beyond its borders. But there's no way to know for sure, and we shouldn't linger. I quicken my pace.

Across the worn wooden table, Tai leans back in his chair with a quizzical expression. "You're sure this is the first time you've tasted Southwestern food?"

I'm busy stuffing rice into my mouth to relieve the heat, so I simply nod in response.

"You must've been *really* hungry then." He glances at my now-empty bowl, which is red from chili sauce. "It takes most people a few tries before they can stomach spicy beef."

I swallow my bite. "I'm not most people."

"That's true." He looks away.

Since we concluded our street performance, he's been unusually muted. As we went through the audience collecting coins—more than enough to pay for lunch and the next several meals—I threw several self-satisfied comments in his direction to gloat. After all, I'd proven myself right, and he wouldn't be stealing anything. Instead of mocking me as usual, he simply smiled.

He remained similarly faded as we hunted the streets of Baiheshan for a suitable place to eat. I was the one who picked the rickety little restaurant run by a Lunan family—I've always wanted to try their famously spicy dishes. It surprised me when he didn't comment on my bold choice.

"What's wrong with you?" I blurt. "You've seemed off since the performance."

"I'm tired." He lifts his shoulders. "Takes a lot of energy to fight imaginary monsters."

I narrow my eyes, unconvinced.

"*Zen me le?* I'm not allowed to get tired?" A teasing spark lights his gaze, and though I know whatever's coming will probably infuriate me, I'm glad to see its return. "I see. You find it as much fun as I do when I make you mad. Don't worry, I have plenty more ways to do so."

"I'm sure you do." I keep my voice flat and unimpressed.

He leans his elbows on the table. "You seemed to like the new direction I took Warrioress's story."

"Because the audience did! Why did you do that anyway?"

"For fun." The corner of his mouth flickers, but falls before the smile completes. "It always bothered me how the legend of Warrioress ended. I love how it begins—a lone youth taking on the world against all odds. You'll laugh at this, but I always wanted to be her."

I arch my brows, surprised. "Not many men would admit that."

"I'm sure many more think it than would say so." He grins. "Anyway, every version of the tale I ever heard ended with her marrying a king. After that, the story was just . . . over. As if she vanished once she got married. I always wished I could change it."

I'd never looked at Warrioress's story that way before. It was always told as though becoming a great queen was her ultimate triumph. But Tai's right . . . there are no stories about what she did after she married. It's as if her life ended at the bridal carriage.

That's the future I face as well. Gloom settles over me as I recall the image of Lady Jiangzhu—the painted face that scarcely looked like mine. She's not a person . . . she's a fine-looking object to be commanded, hardly different from one of Kang's automatons.

"Anlei . . . " Tai nudges my arm.

I look up, and he flicks his gaze to the left without turning his head. His expression is firm—it must be something serious. I glance in the direction he indicated then quickly turn back around.

One of Kang's cyborg soldiers is hovering outside the restaurant.

The glowing yellow eye and gleaming bronze arm, whirring with gears, are unmistakable. My whole body tenses.

How did they find us? They couldn't have followed our ship . . . I would have noticed. If the viceroy's men had made their vessels invisible, they'd have descended on us a lot sooner. We'd never have made it to Baiheshan. The viceroy must have sent his men to *every* city in search of clues after learning about Tai's stolen ship. I wonder if the men we left stranded had some mechanical means to send a message telling the viceroy of our last known whereabouts. Could someone have spotted the ship we hid in the cave? If they did, and the viceroy's men reclaim it, how will we ever make it to the Courts of Hell?

We have to leave. Since the cyborg stands by the main door, I look around for another way out. My gaze passes over the restaurant's plain walls and across the beat-up tables and chatting diners. It lands on the small doorway leading to the kitchen. The restaurant's owner—a full-figured woman with a high bun and round cheeks—emerges from it, her long blue tunic swaying around her knees as she brings someone their tea. She probably wouldn't mind a few extra coins in exchange for letting Tai and me slip out the back.

I turn my eyes back to Tai and incline my chin toward the door. Tai glances at it then nods.

Tongqiucheng must be empty of soldiers because all of them seem to be here. I can't turn a corner without seeing a cyborg. Locals and foreigners alike ogle at the half-man, half-machine beings. Two bronze ships, each with three masts supporting wide tawny brown sails, hover on giant propellers above the city. Long ropes dangle down their sides.

I'm grateful for the sheer number of people on the main road. With every step I take, someone bumps into me or I'm forced to dodge a rattling cart. It's a miracle anyone's able to move through this clogged-up place. But Tai and I chose to take the city's busiest road because the multitudes provide cover.

As we weave through market stalls and throngs of people, Tai wraps a rag over his face, leaving only his eyes exposed. I untie the cloth looped around the strap carrying my sword and bind it around my own face. A few passersby throw us odd looks. Unfortunately, the masks seem to be making us more conspicuous.

"How far until we're out of the city?" I murmur.

"Not far, but leaving might be a problem." He jerks his head to the right. "See that gate?"

I crane my neck to see over the crowd. A wide street lined with storefronts stretches toward an elaborately carved stone gate. Curving designs reminiscent of a cloud's wisps hug the tall, arched doorway flanked by tiered fountains down which streams of water skip. Beyond it, a narrow road winds up the mountain, whose emerald peak pierces a sheet of white clouds. I glimpse the distant rooftop of the temple nestled into its side.

That must be the road we need to take. But two cyborgs stand by the gate, peering at everyone who walks through it. Not that there are many who do. The area is fairly empty compared to the density of the rest of the city.

"That's the only way to the temple," Tai murmurs. "We could try to get out another way and circle the city, but I have a feeling the other roads will be watched as well."

I nod, silently cursing our misfortune. Perhaps the safer thing to do would be to remain in Baiheshan for the time being. But how long would we have to hide? I wouldn't put it past Kang to order his men to search every hub of civilization from here to the Southern Continent and stay there until the thief is caught. Waiting him out could take time—time I don't have. The longer it takes Tai and me to free his people, the higher the chances that another Ligui attack will descend on Dailan before I can return the River Pearl and secure the viceroy's protection.

Besides, I don't have that kind of patience. *There's always a way* . . .

My gaze lands on the narrow river snaking through the city, the one crossed by the simple bridge that reminded me of Dailan. As far as I can tell, no cyborgs patrol its banks. A handful of simple wooden boats glide along its serene surface, carrying bulging woven baskets, and a stench rises from the water, powerful enough to wrinkle my nose even through my mask. The sewage and garbage of a whole city must be rotting in there. Apparently for that reason, several of the boaters wear masks as well.

No wonder no one's stopped Tai and me. Though it might be unusual for someone to keep their mask on after leaving the river, it's probably not unheard of.

Several unused boats sit beside one of the bridges, and an idea strikes me.

"Follow me," I murmur.

Tai knits his brows but doesn't speak as I lead him in the direction of the riverbank. Glimpsing a cyborg soldier, I turn my face away and squeeze past a horse-drawn wagon toward a small market stall selling cone-shaped bamboo hats; I pause briefly to trade a coin for one. The merchant seems surprised when I fail to haggle. He cocks his eyebrow at our masks but doesn't comment.

If Kang's cyborgs question him, he could point them in our direction, so I zigzag into the crowd so he won't know where we're heading.

"What's your plan?" Tai whispers.

"The river." I secure the hat to my head. "We'll take a boat. Since they're not looking for a woman, I'll steer while you hide in the back."

"Oh, so you're stealing again?"

"Renting." I narrow my eyes. "We'll leave our remaining coins behind for the owner. And I'll dock it someplace obvious once we make it past the city limits."

Tai arches his brows. "The boat's owner won't see it that way."

"Do you have a better idea?"

"I wasn't saying yours was bad. Just pointing out that you may be as much a thief as I am."

I choose not to answer. As I approach the riverbank, a twinge of guilt pierces me, but a person's life is worth more than any object.

A narrow boat sits under a wide bridge, anchored to the riverbank by ropes tied in elaborate knots that might have presented a challenge had I not grown up in a river village. Several large, empty baskets fill the back. *That works.* My heart pounds as I draw closer, and I silently pray that the owner won't come back for it anytime soon. The bridge's shadow soon covers me.

"Give me your staff." I hold out my hand.

Tai complies. He keeps watch while I undo the knots. When I finish, he crawls into the back and ducks down. Knowing my sword will make me stand out, I place it down beside him before arranging the baskets to cover him. I leave the small bag of coins we earned from our street performance under a rock, then push off, hoping the boat's owner will find it. There's no way to guarantee that someone else won't steal the money, but it's better than not trying at all.

Hopping into the vessel, I push the staff along the bottom of the shallow river, sliding the boat along the water. My breath quickens as I spot a cyborg on the bridge above. I duck my head, hoping my hat will cover my face. Even with the mask on, I fear they'll recognize my eyes.

They don't know we're here, I remind myself. *As far as they know, I'm just another resident of Baiheshan.*

Unsure of where the river leads, I risk a glance up. The mountain towers in the distance, and though I'll have to lead the boat upstream, I can still get us closer to the temple if I follow the water in that direction.

I push along the bottom of the river. Tai lies completely still, but his presence seems to fill the space around me. I pray Kang's men won't sense it too.

A cyborg paces along the riverbank ahead, questioning one of the boaters who glides past. My heart seems ready to leap out of my chest as I draw closer, and I push the boat further toward the opposite bank, hoping he won't notice me.

His yellow eye meets mine. "You!" He waves his arm in a beckoning gesture. "I—"

"You have no authority here!" A man in the long, embroidered robe of a civil officer marches up to the cyborg, his black queue swaying from beneath his round hat. "Viceroy Chu demands to see you and all your kind at once!"

As the cyborg proceeds to argue with the official, I blow out a breath.

Keeping my head bowed, I continue pushing the boat forward, wondering how long my luck will last.

Anshui's spectacles do a decent job of letting me see through the dense trees at night, but enough shadows remain to make me tense. Though Tai and I have been trekking through this forest for hours since leaving the boat behind, we seem no closer to the temple. Since we have to fumble our way through the wilderness—it would have been far too bold to take the road—I can only hope that we're still heading in the right direction.

I glance at Tai, who's a few paces behind me. "Any idea how long it will be?"

"No. I've never had to take this route before."

My whole body aches from everything I've put it through today, and my stomach rumbles, reminding me that it's far past dinnertime. But we can't afford to slow down—not when it's night and we're exposed. "Baiheshan Miao is protected by barrier spells, right?"

"Yes," Tai answers. "Though I've never heard of any Ligui here. As far as I'm aware, they only attack Sijiang Province."

"I wonder why that is. Part of me wishes they *would* attack someplace else so maybe the Emperor would believe our messengers."

"I'm pretty sure the only reason he doesn't believe them now is because the viceroy doesn't want him to." Tai's tone darkens. "It would look bad for him if the rest of the Empire knew that his province was under attack and he had to seek help."

"So he let my village suffer for the sake of his reputation?" I knit my brows, outraged.

"That's my theory."

If Tai is right, Kang might as well be responsible for what the Ligui did to Dailan. By refusing to send help or allow anyone else to come to our aid, he let those monsters kill our people. Yet we still have to grovel to him for help. And I still have to marry him to ensure he will. It all seems so wrong, and I yearn for some kind of justice. But what can I do? Small villages like Dailan are at the mercy of the powerful. The Emperor barely even cares that we exist.

"How do you know so much about the viceroy?" I ask.

"I don't know any more than most."

"But your face means something to his soldiers. You would never have made it out of Baiheshan unseen without me, which means I as good as saved your life today. Considering I helped you escape Tongqiucheng and the scout ship, that's *three* life debts you owe me. The least you can do is tell me the truth about who you are."

Tai purses his lips. I'm not sure if he's looking away because it's too dark for him to see where I am without the benefit of Anshui's spectacles, or if he's deliberately avoiding my gaze. "My identity is a secret I've guarded all my life, and I swore an oath to keep it that way. It's not something I can confess." I start to protest, and he holds up his hand. "You can press me all you want, but I won't break my vow."

If an oath binds him, then asking him to break it for the sake of my curiosity would be wrong. At least this means he'll likely keep his oath to me about returning the River Pearl when he's done with it.

"Why didn't you tell me about the vow before?"

"I'm too used to keeping secrets." He shrugs. "It's just who I am."

Before I can respond, a smoky wisp, dark even against the shadows, catches my attention. I shove Anshui's spectacles into my pocket and seize my sword.

"Ligui," I whisper to Tai. They must be expanding their reach if they're showing up in Baiheshan. I'm disturbed, but I don't dwell on it. I'm too used to the unexpected—when you live in a village where Ligui might invade every night for a week then go months without appearing, you adapt to randomness. "Stay close. I'll take care of them."

My heart clenches at the blackness around me. It's so dense I widen my eyes just to make sure they're open. I've never fought on terrain like this before—a forest so thick even the moonbeams fail to break through. I wish I could have kept Anshui's spectacles on, but I don't trust them not to fall off. Though the only Ligui attacks I've witnessed have been waves of monsters descending on places with many people, Mr. Liu—one of the few Dailan messengers to make it back—once described how two appeared before him when he was traveling alone on a deserted road.

A Ligui's cry rings out to my left, and I whirl, slashing my sword. Several powerful arms, each holding a dagger, flail from what looks like a dozen torsos standing on a multitude of legs. Scores of glowing white eyes glare at me from its many heads. It looks as if someone bound the shadows of several large, knife-wielding men together, and they're doing their best to escape.

The rush of action pounds through my veins. Dark blades stab down toward me, and I quickly parry. Magic crackles from my sword with each blow. Seeing an opening, I thrust forward and slice upward, cutting one of its many torsos up the middle. Its multitude of heads shriek at once, and the sound shakes me to the bone. But the torso—and the flailing arms attached to it—vanishes.

In the corner of my eye, I spot another Ligui forming, but with this multi-headed thing still coming at me, there's nothing I can do but pray that Tai's able to find shelter somewhere—though where, I don't know. There aren't any barrier spells out here. And he's as good as unarmed without an enchanted weapon.

I try to quicken my movements. Heat winds around my skin. After slicing off another of the Ligui's arms, I take off one of its heads. Screeches and shrieks grate in my ears so loudly I can barely hear the crackle of my sword against the thing's knives.

A blade crashes down toward me. I dodge, but the movement throws me off balance. Pain lances through my left arm as a different blade slices my skin. Before I can recover, yet another blade comes at me. Though I manage to block it, the force sends me flying backward into a tree.

My neck snaps back, and my head bangs against the trunk. Total blackness surrounds my vision.

A moment later I'm on the ground, but I don't remember hitting it. My sword lies by my elbow—when did I release my grip?

Ignoring my injuries, I grab my weapon and spring up, ready to finish the fight. But the Ligui is gone. Did I do enough damage that it dissolved while I was briefly blacked out? Puzzled, I take a few steps forward. Distant crackling catches my attention. Gold sparks bounce between two trees. *What in the world?*

Another screech explodes behind me. I whirl in time to see a burst of sparks spew forth. A dark mass undulates several paces ahead. Parts of it dissipate, leaving behind a familiar figure.

The Shadow Warrior. This is the third time he's appeared in a few days—is he following me? Why?

The Shadow Warrior's glowing white gaze meets mine for an instant before he vanishes into the shadows, robbing me of yet another chance at revenge. Familiar rage crashes against my heart, but a sense of confusion accompanies it. The other Ligui seem to have disappeared as well. But where did they go?

Something taps my shoulder, and I spin, raising my sword. It catches Tai's staff.

"Hey! It's me!" He pushes down my blade. "I think they're gone . . ."

I listen for the shrieks of the Ligui, but hear none. "What was all that about?"

"I don't know. I destroyed two—I think that's all there were."

"No, there were at least—wait, you destroyed two Ligui? With what?"

He glances at his staff and spins it once. "This contains just enough magic to treat Ligui as if they're solid."

My jaw drops. "You had an enchanted weapon this whole time? You should have told me!"

He angles his mouth. "I'm sorry, I wasn't trying to hide it. It just never occurred to me to mention it."

"You stole that from someone, didn't you?"

"Would you believe me if I said it was a gift?"

"No." I snort. "Anyway, we should hurry." I slide my sword into its strap and move to pass him, but he catches my shoulder.

"You're injured."

I glance at my cut. It may sting and bleed, but it hardly counts as a wound. "No, I'm not." I shake him off, pull out the spectacles again, and continue through the woods. When I realize he isn't following, I turn. "Are you coming?"

Tai approaches with something white and glowing in his hand: the River Pearl. Catching my gaze, he moves it behind his back. "Don't try to steal it."

"If I'd wanted to do that, I would have already. What are you doing with it?"

"A dragon's magic is supposed to have healing powers." He holds the pearl up. "I think I can do something about that cut on your arm."

"Half of Dailan has tried to use the pearl for healing. It never did anything."

"They didn't read the ancient scroll I saw at the viceroy's palace." He peers at the gleaming relic. "I don't know if this will work, but it's worth a try if you'll let me."

Deciding there's no harm in it, I hold out my left arm and pull the sleeve back to reveal the bleeding gash running from my wrist to my elbow. "*Hao ba.* Go ahead."

Tai draws closer and takes my hand, wrapping warm, strong fingers around mine. I find his touch unexpectedly comforting. He brings the pearl toward my cut until it hovers so close I can sense its energy flowing into my skin.

He closes his eyes, and I peer into his face curiously, wondering what he's doing.

A stinging sensation prickles down my arm. Startled, I try to pull back, but he tightens his grip around my hand. A warm, invisible force pulses across my skin. I gasp as white light from the pearl streams down into my wound like water flowing over a rock.

After a few seconds, the light fades, leaving behind unblemished skin. I stare in shock. "How . . . How did you do that?"

"It worked?" Tai opens his eyes and releases my hand. "That's . . . fantastic." Though he speaks with his usual light tone, an odd, somewhat disturbed look crosses his expression. "I told you this was more than a useless relic." He gives the pearl a toss and slips it into his tunic.

"You didn't answer my question!" I can't stop staring at my arm. There's no way that should have worked; I've witnessed Dailan's spellmasters try and fail to unlock the River Pearl's powers again and again. How did this strange boy succeed at what they couldn't? "What did you *do*?"

He knits his brows. "To be honest . . . I don't know. There were words on the scroll . . . I can't explain it, but when I thought of them just now, I felt the pearl heat in my hand. I guess that was the magic waking."

"What did the scroll say?"

"It wasn't the words themselves that mattered, but the emotion they invoked." He shakes his head. "Like I said, I can't explain it."

I narrow my eyes, but confusion colors his expression. Apparently there are powers at work here that even he doesn't understand.

"I need to see that scroll."

"Well, if you need a thief to steal it for you, I know one who'd be happy to take the job." Tai flashes me a grin.

"I'll keep that in mind."

So the River Pearl has magic after all . . . a kind powerful enough to latch onto someone who did nothing more than read some words. No wonder Viceroy Kang wants it so badly.

For the first time, I start to believe that the pearl really *can* be used to defeat the demon king. Now that I've seen the magic, the fact finally hits me—*we're going to fight the demon king.* A strange mix of excitement and fear runs through me as the weight of what we're going to do finally lands. But though my heart trembles, this changes nothing.

I've come too far to turn back now.

CHAPTER SIXTEEN

THE SPELLMASTER

B y the time we reach Baiheshan Miao, dawn is spreading its first glisks across the sky. Exhaustion weighs on me from a whole night of walking through the forest. We would have made it here sooner if we'd known where we were going—the road from the city to the temple takes only three hours to walk—but with nothing to guide us, it's amazing that we found our destination at all. The sight of the temple's wide, tiered roofs energizes me, and I pick up my pace.

A stone wall surrounds the temple. As I approach a round door, Tai rushes past me to the entrance. He must be as eager for this part of our journey to end as I am.

The door swings open before we reach it. A tall woman of a deep brown complexion with cool undertones stands beneath its wooden frame. She looks like no one I've ever seen before, and I warn myself not to stare. Her long white tunic, worn over a white skirt that reaches her feet, drapes down from one shoulder and is belted by a woven sash of dark blue lined with thin, brightly colored stripes. A string of large wooden beads drapes down her neck. Her prominent cheekbones slope toward a firm jaw, and brown eyes gaze at us from beneath black brows. Though her head is shaved like most monks', she wears a band of black-and-white beads across her forehead.

Tai greets her with a grin. "Ibsituu. It's good to see you again."

"I'm glad you made it back." Her low voice seems to glow like jade, and her accent makes her sound like she's smoothing down each word she speaks, rounding their sharp corners. Though her skin is as firm as my own except for subtle lines by her mouth, her patient eyes suggest that she is significantly older than I am—perhaps older than my mother. She gestures for Tai to enter with one long, narrow arm, and her expression warms. "Come inside. You must be exhausted." Her gaze lands on me. "And who are you?"

I approach. "Liang Anlei."

"She's the only reason I made it here at all." Tai smiles at me.

"I see." Ibsituu's eyes gleam. "And yet the hardest part of your journey has yet to begin. I take it you found the final piece, then?"

Tai produces the River Pearl in a movement so quick I don't see where he pulled it from.

After accepting it with both hands, Ibsituu closes her eyes. "Yes . . . I feel the River Dragon's power. How did you obtain it?"

"He stole it from me." I cross my arms. "I'm here to make sure he defeats Mowang and gives it back when he's done."

She barks out a laugh. "You possess uncommon generosity and courage, Liang Anlei."

My heart glows at the praise. *"Xie xie."*

"Bie ke qi." She walks into the courtyard. "I assume you two are the reason Viceroy Kang's cyborg soldiers wanted to search the temple last night. Viceroy Chu's men stopped them, and as far as I know, the two viceroys are currently negotiating via messenger for Kang's right to conduct a search here. You should be safe for now, though I don't recommend you stay long."

"Good to know," Tai says. "Did they happen to mention a stolen ship hiding in a cave?"

Ibsituu arches her brows. "What happened to the invisibility spell I gave you?"

I let out a derisive noise. "That ship crashed because Tai wasn't paying attention. We had to steal a different one."

He shoots me an irritated look. "It was just bad luck. I—"

"I don't care." Ibsituu gives Tai a chastising glare. "I hope you haven't come to ask for another one. Invisibility potions take time to create."

Tai's mouth drops into a sheepish expression.

"As for your initial question," she continues, "do you think all this bureaucracy would be necessary if they'd found your ship? It would have been evidence enough that there was a dangerous thief in this province, and Kang's men would be free to hunt him as they pleased."

I exhale. At least we won't have to attempt to reach the Courts of Hell on foot—assuming no one discovers the ship before we return. "We don't have a lot of time."

Ibsituu nods. "Come with me."

I walk beside her. Rows of long, one-story wooden buildings with sloping roofs that flick up at the corners stretch before me. Narrow wooden beams streak the wide windows, latticing each at firm right angles. A wide stone staircase marches toward a towering pagoda with brilliant red and gold walls. Serene statues of gods and goddesses sit along the paths, their legs folded and their hands posed gently before them with curving fingers. Traces of golden sunlight brush the brightening sky, and a crisp breeze ruffles my hair.

A group of white-robed monks sit on the floor inside one of the houses, whose wide doors sit open. Their eyes all appear closed—they must be meditating. The sounds of soft, distant chanting trickle past my ears. Three women in blue robes—two that appear to be from the Empire and one with Western features—emerge from one of the pagodas and speak quietly among themselves. From the few words I catch, they seem to be discussing ancient spiritual teachings.

A sense of calm surrounds the entire place, and I let out a contented sigh.

"It's beautiful, isn't it?" Ibsituu smiles at me. Following my gaze, she nods at the women in blue. "Their school of thought prizes tranquility. That's why they dress in the color of the calm sky. Those of us who wear white and shave our heads follow teachings that value truth and simplicity. Though I like to keep a few pieces of my ancestral homeland with me." She touches her beads. "While we are the largest group here, this temple is home to many philosophies, and everyone who comes is welcome to their own beliefs. The only rule is that we respect each other. I wasn't looking for this temple when I first came to the Empire of the Pearl Moon, but once I arrived, I knew it would be a while before I left."

"Where did you come from?" I ask.

"The answer to that is complicated. I was born in a place called Mwezi, a nation also named after the moon, though that's not where my family originated. I left home to seek adventure and knowledge and to find new ways to improve my abilities. I spent a lifetime traveling across the Southern Continent and into what you call the West before I discovered Baiheshan Miao. I like to think it was destiny that brought me here."

"Mwezi." I savor the new syllables and wonder what it must be like to live there. For a brief moment, I fantasize about traveling to the Southern Continent someday, but I stop myself when I remember that Lady Jiangzhu won't be allowed to leave her husband's palace, let alone the Empire.

"I don't know if I'll stay here forever." Ibsituu slides open the door to one of the buildings and steps over its high threshold. "No one's destiny is set, no matter how certain it may seem." She gives me a meaningful look as she says that, and I wonder if she somehow used her magic to see what I was thinking.

I follow her into a wide room that reminds me of the houses back in Dailan, with its plain walls and large windows. She approaches the simple wooden table and settles down in the chair before it. Other than a wooden shelf holding a number of rolled-up scrolls, they're the only furniture in sight. A long bundle wrapped in white cloth sits before her.

Tai leans his staff against the wall. "Is that what I think it is?"

Ibsituu nods. "I've all but completed it since I last saw you. Go ahead, unwrap it."

Tai unwinds the cloth to reveal a gleaming weapon of bronze and silver. Intricate patterns interwoven with winding symbols snake up the blade, glittering with magic. Even from here I can sense the supernatural power pulsing within the metal. The wide cross-guard curves upward, and a bronze serpent spirals around the grip toward a gaping ring that looks just the right size for the River Pearl.

That must be the enchanted sword that can defeat Mowang. My fingers itch to wield it. Though this is Tai's quest, part of me hopes I'll be the one to sink that blade into the wicked demon king.

"It could destroy most supernatural evils as it is." Ibsituu holds out her hand, and Tai passes the sword to her. "But not Mowang—yet."

She places the River Pearl in the ring at the end of the sword and cups both hands over it. Bowing her head, she closes her eyes and knits her brows with concentration. Sparks burst from her hands, but not the golden kind I'm accustomed to seeing; this magic is a brilliant blue, as if someone shattered the summer sky. They leap higher and higher before pouring into the weapon. A low hum fills the air as the sparks wind around the blade, and I can sense the power of the magic. A shiver frosts my skin.

The sparks fade. Ibsituu sinks forward with a long exhale, resting her forehead on her hands, which still cup the pearl. I glance at Tai uncertainly. He furrows his brow—he's as confused as I am.

A moment later, she sits up, her eyes weary. "It is done." She gestures at the sword. "A great evil is seizing this nation, and if it isn't stopped, your people won't be the only ones to suffer. Take the weapon. Drive it through Mowang's heart—that will destroy his body."

Tai grips the hilt, staring in awe at the blade. "I don't know how I could ever repay you."

"I don't create such things for profit." Ibsituu flicks her wrist dismissively. "Not anymore." Seeing my questioning look, she continues, "Using magic to create has always been my passion. The more complex and intricate the spell or item, the better. Even if I don't intend to use them myself, I enjoy making them."

I nod. Anshui once told me something similar.

"When I was younger, I would create nearly anything for the joy of the challenge," Ibsituu goes on. "People would come to me with requests and offers of lavish rewards, and I would accept if I found the project interesting, even though not everyone who sought me was the type I wanted to work for. Now I am more discerning, and I keep the true extent of my abilities quiet. To those outside the temple, I am but a simple monk with some knowledge of magic, and the others here respect my privacy enough not to question what I do with my time. I only reveal my power and offer my aid to those who deserve it—to heroes or those about to become heroes." She turns to Tai. "I believe in your cause . . . and in you."

Tai beams, and jealousy pricks my chest. He gets to be the hero of his story, seeking out great spellmasters like Ibsituu, robbing viceroys to get materials for his quest, and ultimately becoming the savior of his people. When they tell this tale, I'll be nothing more than a brief mention—that girl who assisted him for a while before vanishing into matrimony. And what of my story? Who will hear about the girl warrior from a small village who defended her people with her sword before being forced to do so with her hand?

A light bump on my arm draws my attention back to Tai, and he holds out the sword to me. "Here. I know you want to hold it."

I can't deny that. His fingers brush mine as he passes it to me. Some of the sword's magic must still be sparking, because an odd sensation tingles through my hand.

I raise the enchanted blade. It's heavier than my father's sword, but better balanced. The hum of its energy flows up my arms, and I feel as if I'm holding a solid bolt of lightning. My entire body clamors to whip it about to see what it can do, but there's not enough space, and it would be disrespectful to wield a weapon here, even to test it.

Now that the River Pearl is a piece of this weapon, I can sense its power reaching toward me from the sword's pommel.

"Magnificent, isn't it?" Ibsituu stares up at the blade. "Perhaps it sounds arrogant to say so of my own creation, but it is my finest."

"You're sure this can defeat Mowang?" I ask.

"Yes. I created it from a unique combination of magic I gathered from around the world during my journeys. I dare say I'm the only person who could have crafted it. Alas, I am not a trained fighter and would not fare well if I tried to wield it myself." Her expression sobers. "I must remind you that Mowang cannot be *killed*, only rendered incapable of interacting with the living until he regenerates."

I run my finger along the blade's intricate grooves. "Will destroying him stop the Ligui?"

"I cannot say. I believe an opening between Hell and Earth is allowing them to escape their realm and enter ours. Defeating Mowang might not be enough to close it."

I frown. "What created that opening in the first place?"

"Again, I cannot say. Perhaps Mowang can tell you when you meet him. If you ask nicely, he may answer."

"I guess—" I stop when I notice the joking glint in her eyes. She shares a conspiratorial look with Tai, who chuckles. "Very funny."

She stands. "You must be tired. Come, I'll show you to the guest rooms."

Both my aching body and drowsy head agree, but the longer our ship remains in that cave, the more likely it is that someone will spot it. "Thank you, but we should head back to the ship."

Ibsituu frowns. "How do you expect to operate it if you're too tired to see straight? I can't imagine you slept last night."

As if on cue, Tai yawns widely. "She has a point, Anlei. Don't worry. No one will find it."

I'm not so sure about that, but I also understand how bad an idea it is to try escaping while impaired by weariness. Especially if we run into Kang's men. "Very well."

Ibsituu heads out the door, and I follow.

"Can I have that back now?" Tai reaches for the sword, and I reluctantly let him take it.

An excited chill shoots up my spine as I think that soon I'll be facing the greatest evil of all. I can almost see the Maw of Hell yawning before me—that infernal gate at the base of Heihuoshan, the Black Volcano. Considering how quickly the stolen ship brought us to Baiheshan, we'll likely reach it in less than two days.

As I fall asleep remembering the tales Father once told me of the Courts of Hell, I find myself strangely eager to see them for myself.

I step out of the temple's small guesthouse. Not much lay inside its plain wooden walls—only a few rooms with simple beds covered in bamboo mats and earthen water basins in the corners. The sun still shines brightly, silhouetting the pagoda across the courtyard. I stretch, wondering how long I was asleep. After a day-long adventure that spilled past the night and into this morning, I passed out on that bamboo mat moments after closing the door behind me. Since the door to Tai's room remains closed, he must still be sleeping. I push it open to wake him so we can return to the ship as soon as possible.

Sleep softens the lines of his mouth, and the gentle light seeping in through the shuttered window traces the curve of his cheek. That he failed to hear me enter means he must still be exhausted. After all we've been through, I don't blame him. I close the door behind me. We'll both be better off if he gets the rest he needs.

I wander across the courtyard, drinking in the serenity of Baiheshan Miao. Everything seems to pass slowly here, from the way the monks glide across the grounds to the gentle chants and prayers whispering on the breeze. It's almost as if this place exists underwater, with currents adding grace and patience to each movement.

A voice catches my attention. Recognizing Ibsituu's fluid accent, I follow the sound to the pagoda. She kneels inside, her head bowed as she whispers something to the enormous golden statue of a goddess in a towering headdress and flowing robes. The sweet smoke of incense curls toward the ceiling. Red-brown columns surround her, carved with gilded characters. Concentrating hard, I focus on one, hoping to glimpse their meaning. The strokes flip and twist in my mind despite my efforts to will them into stillness. I make out just enough to realize it's a proverb about tranquility before giving up.

Ibsituu stands and bows, then approaches me with a smile. "Awake already? I wasn't expecting you to be up until dinnertime. Did you dream of anything?"

I think back to the jumble of images that flashed through my mind just before I woke. Considering how vivid my nightmares can be, I was grateful for the harmless randomness. "Nothing that made sense."

Ibsituu steps out of the pagoda and walks toward one of the buildings—the same one where she enchanted the sword. "Very little seems to make sense these days. The Ligui arrive and the Yueshen vanish . . . I'm certain these events are connected, but I do not know how. I was asking the Goddess of Wisdom to grant me the focus to discover the answer."

"I always thought the Yueshen fled back to the moon."

Ibsituu shakes her head. "Before the Ligui came, they were already disappearing. One by one, little by little . . . consumed by a dark force."

I shudder. "That's horrible."

"Indeed." She steps into the building. "But you did not seek me to hear about unsolved mysteries. What were you looking for?"

"I . . . don't know." I shrug, unsure what drew me to her in the first place.

"Come, you must have had a question."

"I guess, if you don't mind me asking . . . What's it like to travel so far? I've always wanted to see the world."

Ibsituu approaches the wooden shelf and gazes across the many scrolls. "I'm not sure how to answer that. Traveling is my way of life. Venturing into unfamiliar lands is as normal to me as staying home is to many. Like my parents and their parents before them, I've never felt bound to any land."

"Is this common among your people?"

"Not particularly. From what my parents told me, my ancestors were unique in their restlessness."

"My ancestors were restless too." I recall the stories Mother told me about her days in the traveling troupe. "My father's roots are in Dailan, but my mother . . . I've never met anyone from her side of the family. They're still out there, traveling the world, but I have no idea where they are."

"It sounds as if you and I have something in common." Ibsituu looks away with a sorrowful expression. "I never meant to lose touch with my family, but I was very single-minded when I was younger. I would obsess over something I was studying or creating and forget to respond to their correspondences. Or I would impulsively decide to travel somewhere and neglect to tell anyone where I was going. It took me years to realize what I was missing, and though I eventually managed to reestablish correspondence with my parents and siblings, I have nieces and nephews who grew up without knowing me and have already left their parents for their own adventures."

Mother once told me something similar—how she probably has cousins she'll never meet. If by some miracle I am to escape my marriage and fulfill my dream of seeing the world, I'll probably have to leave her and my sister behind. *Actually, I already have.* "I guess separation is the price of adventure."

"Yes." Sighing, Ibsituu turns back to the scrolls, pulls one out, and, apparently finding it to be the wrong one, shoves it back in. "But I don't regret the path I chose. I've found it to be very fulfilling. Each time I came to a new place, I would absorb as much as I could until I felt there was nothing more I could learn, and then I would move on to the next. Across nations in the Southern Continent, northward into what you call the West, then eastward to the Empire of the Pearl Moon . . . I might linger for years in one place, but I always know it is temporary. Even this"—she gestures toward the door, indicating the Miao—"and what I've done for you and Tai in creating that sword are just stops on a journey that will take a lifetime . . . and possibly more."

"That sounds wonderful."

"It certainly is, though it can also be trying. Still, I aim to explore as many places as I can, both earthly and supernatural."

"Why not accompany us to the Courts of Hell, then?"

"I must admit, I was tempted. However, the journey will be danger-ous, and as I mentioned before, I am not adept at combat, nor do I wish to be. Though I have spells I could use as weapons, I am not a fighter—I am an intellectual." She grabs another scroll. This must be the right one since she pulls it out. "Also, I started working on a new spell while waiting for Tai to return with the River Pearl, and I do not wish to abandon my work for someone else's adventure. This is Tai's quest, after all."

I grimace at the reminder. "I wish I had a quest of my own."

"Oh, but you do. And soon you will find it."

I want to believe her, but I feel so trapped by the future Kang forced upon me that it's hard to imagine a different one.

Ibsituu spreads the scroll across her desk.

"What is that?" I ask.

"I need to put the finishing touches on the map that will lead you to the Maw of Hell." She reaches into the folds of her skirt and produces a small sphere that looks as if it's woven from copper twigs. Jagged cracks in its surface reveal intricate clockwork within. "I meant to finish it earlier, but it's one of many things I am working on and it didn't seem urgent until you two showed up here."

I peer at the object. "How is that a map?"

"It's drawn to the power of the great infernal gate. Trust its guidance. When you reach your ship, it will lead you there."

"But . . . how?"

"Heihuoshan resides in another dimension, and reaching the portal is more than a matter of traveling in the right direction. The map will lead you in seemingly random directions, but your ship's jerking dance will be part of a ritual that will take you to the right spot. When you finish, it will guide you on a similar trip back. Perhaps you will return with some of the answers I've been unable to uncover." She places the sphere on the scroll, covering it with her hands, then closes her eyes.

I stare as the characters peel off the scroll and float up before her, blue magic glittering from the edges of their black strokes. She lifts her hands, and they dive into the sphere like a hundred dragonflies. A blue halo briefly appears around the sphere. When it vanishes, several tiny, barely visible characters march across the sphere's surface.

Ibsituu opens her eyes. Her posture appears more sagged than before—she must be tired. She gestures at it. "There, it is complete."

I pick it up, feeling the magic humming within. I'm one step closer to facing Mowang, and this enchanted device will take me to him. I may be borrowing this quest from Tai, but that doesn't make me yearn for victory any less.

CHAPTER SEVENTEEN

HEIHUOSHAN

"Anlei! Hide!" Father points at the giant water pot standing outside our door.

Glimpsing a black shadow swooping down from the star-speckled sky, I scramble to obey. Fortunately the clay pot is nearly empty, and I barely cause a splash as I leap inside. Terrified, I curl myself into the tiniest ball I can.

Clanging and crackling noises ring out above. My anxious breaths echo against the pot's clay walls. Through the opening at the top, I catch flashes of Father's blade and the sparks flying from it. I remind myself that he's the best fighter in Dailan and can defeat any adversary, even a Ligui shaped like a warrior.

Father staggers backward against the pot, grasping it for support. The Shadow Warrior slashes his throat, and I see every drop of blood that spills. It drips onto me, hot and sticky.

I press my hands to my mouth to contain my screams. Tears stream down my face. Father collapses sideways, vanishing from sight.

The Shadow Warrior stares down at where Father fell. His glowing eyes convey disdain. After a moment, he flies up, and I see the white crescent on his neck. It looks almost like a mocking grin.

Trembling, I try to climb out of the pot. I knock it over instead and come spilling out along with what little water was inside. The clay shatters against the cobblestones where Father lies lifeless in the street. I can't hold it in any longer . . . I'm crying, I'm screaming . . .

"Anlei!" Tai's voice rings in my ears.

Blinking, I find him peering down at me with concerned eyes. The small lantern of the below-deck room gives off a gentle glow that highlights the worried creases in his forehead. I must have cried out in my sleep. Cold sweat pours down my face, and my hands quiver. No matter how many times my nightmares force me to relive the night Father died, I can never get used to it.

I sit up on the narrow bed and try to appear calm for Tai. "I'm fine." I recall the events of the past day—making our way back to the city and being relieved to overhear that Kang's men had been ordered back to their ships until the dispute between viceroys could be resolved. Returning to our ship, which mercifully remained where we left it, and waiting for the cover of night to take off. That's what matters: the present. "How long until we reach Heihuoshan?"

"Another half a day at least." His expression doesn't change. "And don't lie to me—you're anything but fine right now. You're shaking."

I tense, hoping to steady myself. "It was only a nightmare."

"What did you see?"

"It doesn't matter."

"It does to me." Sighing, Tai crouches, bringing himself down to my level. "I know we haven't known each other long, but we've been through a lot together and . . . I care about you. If something's troubling you, I want to help."

My heart startles at the sincerity in his tone. Gone is the usual joking Tai, the one who won't take anything seriously. For the first time, I feel as if he's being completely honest with me. Still, I'm so used to keeping my fears a closely guarded secret that I don't know how to be honest back. "You . . . can't."

"Why not?"

"It's personal."

"And you still don't trust me?" A hurt look flashes across his eyes. "Anlei, I know I have my secrets, but I've never been dishonest with you. I wish you wouldn't treat me as you would a stranger."

His words remind me of what Mother once told me, about how I've never really trusted anyone as a true friend. I can't explain why I am this way . . . Perhaps in my efforts to be strong like Father and hide any signs of weakness, I've erected a wall between myself and everyone else. Perhaps that's why people in Dailan called me selfish.

"It isn't you," I murmur. "I've always been this way. I'm not used to . . . sharing. I'm not very good at being around others."

"To your credit, you've managed to put up with me." Tai's mouth quirks. "I'm known to be rather difficult."

A small laugh escapes me. "At least you admit it."

"Oh, I'll admit to being a lot of things. My father had a whole list of criticisms he'd throw at me when he was displeased. To be fair, he was mostly right. He's a stern man, but not an unjust one. Some of his favorites were foolish, impulsive, troublesome . . . I can't deny any of those."

"I've been called those things too. Also selfish, undisciplined, and blunt."

"Only an idiot would think you're selfish after all you've gone through for your village. And I like that you're blunt. One never has to wonder what you're really thinking, and that's a rare trait. In fact, I think it's brave that you always speak your mind." He smiles.

I glance away, unsettled by a flutter in my heart. "Other than my family, no one's ever liked me for who I am."

"I could say the same, minus the family part."

I turn back to find him staring past me, a sad tinge clouding his face. "Is your family . . . gone?"

"No, they're around—or they were until Mowang took them. They just don't like me very much. Most of the time, my father was the only one who would put up with me." Though his tone is light, I wonder if he's using it to mask his sorrow.

Hoping to learn a little more about him, I ask, "What's he like?"

Tai strokes his chin, and I can tell he's deciding how much to reveal to me. "He has a heart of steel—firm, disciplined, and brave. He and I disagree on a great many things, but I try to respect his reasoning. He's good to those he cares about, even if he doesn't visibly show affection. To him, actions matter more than words or gestures."

"He sounds like my father." My heart aches as I picture Father's face. He didn't smile much, but that didn't mean he wasn't happy. "I hope your father—and the rest of your people—are all right."

"I hope so too." Tai leans a little closer. "Was your father a warrior like you?"

"Yes. He taught me some of his combat skills to improve my Warrioress act. He meant to teach my sister too, but she was only eight when he died—too young to hand a blade to." I blink back a sudden onslaught of tears. "I was only twelve, so he didn't have a chance to teach me how to truly *fight*. There's so much I wish I could have learned from him."

"I'm sorry." He reaches as if to take my hand but hesitates and withdraws.

I'm surprised by the twinge of regret that pierces me when he does. Part of me longs to speak more of Father and let the tears I'm holding back fall. But I don't know if I'm ready to be that vulnerable in front of Tai. So I change the subject. "Did you learn to fight from your father?"

Tai shakes his head. "He didn't have time to tutor me himself. Though he sometimes gave me advice." His eyes grow distant, and a fond smile creeps onto his lips. "Once when I was very young—maybe six—I found my way into the room where he stored his weapons. I wanted to know what it was like to be a great warrior like Father, so I took a staff from its rack. I couldn't control it and ended up knocking down many of the bladed weapons stored there. Father, of course, was furious. But not because I'd made a mess—he told me he feared I might have harmed myself. The next day, he brought me a staff of my own—one more suited to my size—and told me that if I was going to wield one, I had to learn to treat it not as a weapon, but as a limb. An extension of my body rather than a thing I hold. Even though it was a long time ago, I remember those words each time I pick up a staff." A wistful look crosses his expression. "I, too, wonder what I could have learned from my father if he were around. Especially since he *could* have been but chose not to be."

"I'm . . . sorry to hear that." I purse my lips and wish I knew what else to say.

Tai shrugs. "He always had more important things to worry about than me. I grew accustomed to it. So here we are, a pair of renegades who have managed to earn the disapproval of just about everyone."

"At least we approve of each other."

He widens his eyes in an exaggerated expression of surprise. "Did you just say you approve of me?"

I grin despite myself. "Don't let it get to your head."

"Too late, it already has."

It suddenly hits me that since he's down here with me, no one's keeping an eye out for Kang's search party. I rise abruptly. "Don't you have a ship to watch? I should have known better than to give you a second chance at that."

Tai stands with a laugh. "As if you could have made good on your threat to stay awake the rest of the journey."

I scowl. "Kang's men are still looking for us. If you don't go back to your post at once, I'm taking back my approval."

"All right, I'll leave you alone now." He moves toward the door, but his eyes linger on mine. "Whatever nightmares you're battling, I hope you conquer them."

It's not until after he's left the small room that I realize I didn't use my sword to secure the door before I fell asleep.

The copper sphere Ibsituu gave us—the "map" to the Maw of Hell—hovers a few feet before me at the bow of the ship. Blue and gold sparks leap from its metal surface as I watch it keenly, not wanting to miss a single turn. I still find it hard to fathom that such a simple-looking object could carry so much power. The Maw of Hell is said to lie at the end of the world; Tai and I would hardly be the first humans to reach it, but it's not exactly a common destination.

The map remained still—a mere trinket in appearance—as we made our way back to the ship. But the moment Tai ignited the engines, it sprang to life and settled before the wheel, floating in the air like a butterfly.

I risk a glance away from the sphere to check for any other ships. So far, the area we're flying through seems fairly deserted. Still, a nervous knot remains in my gut. If we're spotted, there's no place to hide.

Emerald earth streaked with rivers sweeps toward the blue horizon. I wonder what land we're passing over—whether this is still part of the Empire of the Pearl Moon or if we've crossed into another nation. Since the sphere steered us in erratic zigs and zags, I've lost track of how far east or south or west or north we've flown.

The sphere darts to the right and quakes in place. I twist the wheel in the direction it indicates, and machinery clangs and whirs as the propellers adjust to the new direction. Above me, the scalloped sail twists on its high mast. The wind picks up, speeding the ship, and I savor the rush.

"Are we there yet?"

Glancing back, I spot Tai emerging from below deck and rubbing his eyes. "If you need more rest, feel free to continue sleeping."

"Careful, I might take you up on that."

"*You* be careful, or I'll take Ibsituu's sword and slay Mowang alone before you wake." I throw him a teasing smile.

"You would." He shakes his head as he approaches.

A flash of purple light streaks the sky just as the sharp stench of sulfur crashes down upon me. An abrupt rumble shakes the deck, throwing me off balance. My hands slip from the wheel, and I stumble backward.

Strong arms catch me as the ground stabilizes. Despite the unnatural purple lightning, I feel safe. I look up in time to see Tai flash a grin at me, and strange heat rushes through my skin.

I quickly regain my footing. "What just happened?"

"You fell. I caught you. No need to thank me."

"This is no time for jokes!"

"It's the perfect time for jokes. Who knows if we'll survive this? It'd be a shame if we spent our final hours being glum."

"If we weren't already heading to Hell, I'd toss you in myself."

The sky has turned from blue to black, though the purple flashes are bright enough to continue lighting the ship as if it were day. We must be getting close. At least Kang's search party won't be able to follow us into this otherworldly realm.

I approach the bow. Heihuoshan juts before us, distant but nearing. Orange lava bubbles up its peak and streams down its steep sides, forming a wide lake at its base. It looks every bit as terrifying as in the illustrations Mother used to show me, but I refuse to be intimidated by the sight. The surrounding land is entirely devoid of life. Yellow and brown stone stretches into the horizon in every direction, carved by canyons and pierced by towering rock formations. No trace remains of the greenery that surrounded us moments ago.

As we draw closer to Heihuoshan, I glimpse a wide, yellow arc stretching across its base—the gateway. Something dark moves before it. Considering its size compared to the mountain's, it must be enormous.

The Maw of Hell . . . and the demon that guards it. A tingly mix of fear and excitement shoots up my spine. I'm about to walk into a legend.

"This is it." Beside me, Tai glares at the Maw of Hell. The fierce determination in his expression gives his face a striking intensity. "Are you ready?"

"Of course." I wrap my hands around the leather strap carrying my sword. "Are you?"

Rocky ground crunches beneath my feet as I land beside the ship. With no body of water to anchor it on, we had no choice but to leave it hovering a few feet above the ground.

Beside me, Tai gives Ibsituu's sword an experimental swing before tying it to his belt, using a piece of rope looped around the hilt. The River Pearl glows against his tunic, and the surrounding darkness makes its brilliance more acute.

Rocky black land stretches before us, a lifeless plain broken only by jutting pillars of stone. Neither the sun nor the stars illuminate this desolate place—only streaks of purple lightning. Heihuoshan stands a field's length away, the glowing gateway to Hell arcing across its front. Even from here, I can see the Guardian pacing before it.

I march forward. From the stories I've heard, the Guardian is not an evil being. He may be a demon, but he only exists to do his duty: keeping the demons of Hell within and keeping all others out. Yet he must have failed in some capacity since the Ligui managed to escape. Maybe I can learn how while I'm here.

There have been plenty of tales of humans—and Yueshen, including Warrioress—who have journeyed to the depths. Each depicted the Guardian as a bureaucrat, a reasonable and intelligent being who can be negotiated with. Though my instinct is to cut down anything in my way, I remind myself of those tales as we draw closer. Since the Guardian is said to be as powerful as Mowang in many ways, it would be better not to expend my energy—or risk failing—before I reach the target.

"Just so we're clear," Tai says, "do *not* run up to the Guardian and start hacking him to pieces. We don't want him to sic his demon dogs upon us before we've made it inside."

"I wasn't planning to!" I shoot him a slantwise look. "Do you think he'll grant us an audience with Mowang?"

"We'd hardly be the first." Tai shrugs. "I'll say I'm here to negotiate for my peoples' release. That should be reason enough for him to let us through."

"I hope so."

The Guardian towers over us as we approach. I crane my neck.

Dressed in a warrior's armor, he's almost human in shape. But his grotesque red face, with its protruding fangs, giant eyes, and sharply slanting brows, reveals his demonic nature. Black talons protrude from the long fingers gripping a glowing orange staff. Spotting us, he bends down on one knee to get a closer look.

"What brings you to the Maw of Hell?" His low voice shakes the ground.

I expect Tai to answer, but he doesn't. The Guardian peers right at me with his penetrating black gaze. I suck in a breath and glance to the side, wondering where that quick mouth of Tai's is when we need it.

"Do not look away when I am speaking to you!" The Guardian leans closer. "Answer me."

I straighten. Though terror courses through my veins, I won't let any of it show on my face. "My name is Liang Anlei. I am here to negotiate with Mowang for the release of the people of Baiguang and to learn why demons are being allowed to escape to Earth."

"Is that so?" The Guardian furrows his brow. "I have not heard of these matters."

That's strange. The Guardian is supposed to be aware of all major happenings in the Courts of Hell so he'll know who to let in and out. I also find it odd that Tai doesn't respond. I reach over to nudge him, but my hand meets empty air.

I jitter, fumbling for words. Why am *I* the one doing the negotiating? "I assure you, it's true—"

"Wretch!" The Guardian's roaring voice shakes the ground so hard I stumble. His eyes flash red, becoming twin fireballs above his snarling mouth.

I seize my sword, wondering what I could have said to enrage him so, but then I realize he's not looking at me anymore—his giant hand now grips a squirming Tai around the waist.

"Did you think you could sneak past the great Guardian?" The giant demon squeezes his fist around Tai.

What happened?

The Guardian flings Tai to the ground. He lands hard, a pained cry escaping his lips.

"Tai!" I rush over with half a mind to kill him myself. "What—"

"Gun kai!" The Guardian waves one enormous arm in our direction. "Get out and never return!"

Tai stands, though he seems a little unsteady on his feet. "Guardian—"

"How *dare* you address me?" The Guardian leans down, his face inches from Tai's. "You are a dishonorable rat! *Gun kai!*"

He rises to his full height and slams the end of his staff into the ground. The impact shakes the earth so hard I fall backward. Tai lands beside me.

I scowl. "What were you *thinking?*"

Loud barks fill the air. I twist to see several demon dogs crawling down the sides of Heihuoshan, their fangs and eyes glowing yellow. Pointed ears top their broad heads, and their muscular red bodies ripple as they move.

Ta ma de! Cursing, I spring up. We'll have to hack our way in after all. I'm better at hacking anyway.

One of the demon dogs launches itself at me. Eager for action, I arc my sword, slicing it in half, and quickly jump out of the way. A pained howl explodes in my ears as it dissipates into red smoke.

A flash of white catches my eyes. Tai wields Ibsituu's sword, fending off two of the demon dogs. But he doesn't notice the third that leaps at him from behind. Its huge paws land on Tai's shoulders, pinning him to the ground.

"Tai!" Panic floods my chest. I race over. Tai struggles to free himself, the monster on his back must be too strong.

It's going to kill him. It's going to *kill* him.

The demon widens its fanged mouth. I lunge at it, throwing every ounce of strength I have into the jump. A feral cry bursts from my throat as I sink my enchanted sword into the monster.

As the wisps of smoke dissolve, I grab Tai's arm and pull him up. A powerful welling makes my eyes sting, and I don't know if it's from rage or relief.

Demon dogs pour down the sides of the fiery mountain, flowing alongside the lava. Their growls rumble like thunder across the dark landscape as they approach at a menacing walk. The Guardian stands before the gate with his arms crossed, looking down at us with disdain. It's a warning . . . he's giving us one last chance to leave before ordering them to tear us apart.

As much as I hate to surrender, there are simply too many. Even I can see that.

Tai doesn't seem to—he starts forward, as if to charge at them.

I seize his arm. "Don't!" He tries to yank himself free, but my grip is too tight. I glower at him. "I swear by the Gods of Heaven and Earth, if you don't come with me, I'll knock you out and drag you back to the ship!"

He scowls but glances back at the advancing demons. A look of defeat descends into his eyes.

I march toward the ship, pulling him along. He jerks his arm hard and manages to free himself this time. I'm tempted to grab him again to make sure he doesn't try anything stupid, but since he heads in the same direction as me, I refrain.

I feel like my role has inverted somehow . . . *I* should be the one exploding with action despite the obvious foolishness. In the Dailan Guard, I was always the one who had to be held back by my more practical teammates. Yet if I'd let my usual instincts take over this time, we'd both be dead.

Behind me, the demon dogs continue barking. I quicken to a run. By the time I reach the ship, I don't hear them anymore. The Guardian must have called them back. I guess the stories about him being a reasonable being were true then; he could easily have shredded us instead of letting us go.

Not that it matters much since we failed to enter the Courts of Hell.

I pull myself onto the deck and glance down at Tai, who is climbing up behind me. I snatch the rope and yank him up as hard as I can until he stumbles onto the deck beside me. "*You* were the one who told *me* we should negotiate. Why did you try to bypass the Guardian?"

"I saw an opening." Tai strides to the bow, his expression stormy. "He was focusing on you . . . I had a chance to slip by."

"So you were going to leave me behind?"

"No, that's not—"

"Then *what*?"

"From where I stood, I could see the torments beyond the gateway.

My people are inside . . . I could *feel* it. I couldn't stand the thought of them suffering a moment longer, so I made my move." He rakes his hand through his hair, which has come loose from its topknot. "I'm sorry. I realize now that it was a mistake."

"A mistake that could have killed us both!" I clench my fists. If I hadn't slain that demon dog in time, if he'd died . . . I fling the thought from my head. It hurts too much to even consider. "We had a plan. How dare you abandon me?"

"I wasn't—That's not what I was doing!"

"Oh? What did you think would happen if you succeeded? I would have had to deal with the Guardian's wrath alone! I thought I could trust you as a partner, but it looks like that was *my* mistake."

"I didn't think of that. I didn't mean to . . . " He sinks against the railing and looks away. "Again, I'm sorry. I don't know what came over me."

"That's not good enough!"

"How many times must I apologize?" The look he gives me is half angry and half pleading. "I wasn't thinking, okay? Those are my people—my family—trapped in the Courts of Hell, suffering right in front of me. How could I turn away?"

I start to retort but stop myself. Barely a week has passed since I abandoned Pinghua to pursue the Shadow Warrior. She survived—no thanks to me—but that doesn't change what I did. I let the hunger for justice overwhelm my sense of reason. I'm in no position to judge Tai for doing the same.

He bows his head. Usually so assured and arrogant, he suddenly seems vulnerable. "It was only an instant—I barely took a step before the Guardian caught me. But in that instant, I failed both my people and you. I . . . I'm sorry. I wish I could take it back."

Though I haven't quite forgiven him yet, I hate seeing him so defeated. I wish I knew what to do, what to tell him.

Tai may have cost us the most straightforward way into the Courts, but we can't give up. The peple of Baiguang are counting on us. "We haven't failed yet. We can find another way in."

Tai gives me a sad smile. *"Xie xie."*

"What are you thanking me for?"

"For saving my life. Again. And for . . . being here." His eyes meet mine, and I wonder what it is about them that always seems to pull me in. There's something strangely beautiful about the way he looks at me—not just the striking planes of his face, but the warmth in his expression, the meaning in his gaze.

My pulse hums at an uncomfortable pace. I turn away. The Maw of Hell still gapes before us, and the Guardian still stands in our way. I pull Anshui's spectacles out of my pocket and fiddle with them absentmindedly. A yellow flash glints in one of the lenses. I pause. *What was that?*

Perplexed, I peer at it and realize that a tiny piece of Heihuoshan, a mere speck at this distance, glows through the lenses. Intrigued, I place them on my face.

The speck becomes more of a circle, rippling against the rocky mountain. I take off the spectacles again, and it vanishes.

"What's going on?" Tai approaches.

"Take a look." I hand him the spectacles. He places them on his face. I stifle a laugh at how ridiculous they look, with their stacks of round lenses and clicking gears. Do I look that peculiar when I wear them?

Tai catches my eye and grins. "Do I look smarter?" He lifts his chin with an exaggerated expression of seriousness.

"Even a bird mask would make you look smarter," I tease, glad the tension between us seems to have dissolved. For now.

"Birds *are* intelligent creatures." He casts his gaze at Heihuoshan and furrows his brow. After a moment, he approaches the ship's control panel and grabs the telescope tucked against the side. When he returns, he holds it up against the spectacles. "Something's moving . . . "

"Can I see?" He hands me both the spectacles and the telescope. I put the lenses back on, press the telescope against the lens, and take a closer look. Familiar black wisps rise out of the glowing yellow circle. "Those look like Ligui . . . Is that the portal they use to escape into our realm?"

"Perhaps." Tai strokes his chin. "And perhaps they're not all the portal will allow through."

I nod. The same thought occurred to me . . . Apparently there is more than one way into the Courts of Hell. What's more, the Guardian didn't seem to know how the Ligui were escaping to Earth. If this is the same portal they're using, then it must be somehow beyond his view.

I walk up to the rope leading down the side of the ship. "All right, let's give this another try."

CHAPTER EIGHTEEN

THE COURTS OF HELL

A vast cavern yawns below me. The screams of tortured souls ring in my ears. Scaling the side of Heihuoshan was no easy feat—the incline was so steep, I was sure my lungs would explode from the effort—yet it was nothing compared to what we're about to face.

What looked like a yellow circle from a distance turned out to be wide hole in the mountain's surface, and that supernatural glow was the light of Hell spilling out. Without the spectacles, it looked like a crater. If we hadn't known it was there, we could easily have fallen in and tumbled uncontrollably through the fathomless depths.

Infinity stretches beyond the portal. A long stone walkway extends forward with no end in sight. Just layers upon layers of spaces and scenes, as if someone cut up a painting depicting the Courts of Hell then stitched it back together at random. Other walkways lie perpendicular or upside down relative to the one before me, and demons stroll along each in every direction. There's no sense of up or down. Many hover in the space in between, their grotesque faces contorted in wicked glee as they torture the sinners. Demon judges, with their elaborately embroidered robes and hideous fanged faces, preside over each of the torments, sending sinners to the appropriate demons for their punishments.

In some corners, demons use ice to freeze the sinners, then shatter them, then revive them only to do it all over again. In others, they flay the screaming humans bit by bit, as if they were peeling oranges. Some sinners are pierced with hooks, dangled by their skin until it rips. Some are disemboweled, shredded, torn apart by the demons' claws. Others are burned with fire, or forced into boiling liquids, or ground by machines, or thrown onto beds of knives . . . I swear to myself that I'll be a better person if I survive this. Nothing is worth being damned to this place.

Though Mowang's demon subjects inflict horrendous torments upon sinners, he isn't the one who decides who gets punished or how. Only the Heavenly Gatekeepers decide who's to suffer in the Courts of Hell. When a person dies, their spirits go before celestial judges, and those deemed sinful are marked for damnation. Once they reach the Courts, they're judged again to determine what manner of punishment would suit the crime.

But Tai and I are not marked. Even though Mowang rules this place, neither he nor his demons can torture anyone without permission. That doesn't mean he'll follow the rules, though.

Drawing a breath, I step through the portal with Tai.

"Mowang certainly has a sense of style." Despite the smile on his lips, his eyes betray his fear.

"Don't worry, I'll protect you." I swing my sword, and the act of bravado emboldens me. It's easier to have courage when someone's counting on you. "Any idea where we're supposed to go?"

Tai shakes his head. The glow of the River Pearl in his sword attracts the eyes of some of the surrounding demons, but they appear too occupied doling out their assigned torments to do more than look. "I couldn't exactly find a map for an infinite realm that's always shifting. Even Ibsituu doesn't have that kind of knowledge."

Finding Mowang in this abyss seems impossible. But we must. Even if Mowang abided by the laws of Heaven and forbade his minions from exacting punishments meant for sinners upon the innocent people of Baiguang, being forced to witness all this horror—forever, with no respite, while being deprived of the life you were meant to live—is a fate no one deserves.

The acrid stench of smoke and sulfur fills the air. An odd swirl of scorching heat and biting cold stings my skin. My hair sticks to my sweaty neck as I make my way across the walkway, wondering what I'm even looking for.

A blue-skinned demon digs its claws into Tai's shoulders. He barely has a chance to cry out before it pulls him off the walkway.

"*Tai!*" I rush to follow but halt at the edge. All I see are the sickening torments of sinners being impaled, boiled, and worse.

"You can't take him! He hasn't been damned *you can't take him!*" Something feels ready to explode from my throat, and I don't know if it's a scream or a sob. Gritting my teeth, I search the depths.

A flash of light—what looks like the glow of the River Pearl embedded in the sword—catches my eye. Tai could still be holding it.

I leap off the walkway before fear can stop me, launching myself toward that glow.

I'm falling—falling—falling—

Images of Hell whip past. Of judges sentencing sinners, of sinners weeping and begging for mercy that will never come. Of demons cackling as they inflict pain, delighting in the suffering around them.

The same blue demon that took Tai materializes before me. Though I'm still tumbling through infinity, I slash my sword at him. "Where's Tai?"

"Sinners are dealt as they deserve." The demon answers in a sing-song voice, spreading its mouth in a hideous, fanged grin. "What's your sin, my lovely?"

"You can't take him!" I slice my blade through its torso.

The demon explodes into smoke, but its cackle rings in my ears even after it vanishes.

I twist through the air, searching desperately for any sign of Tai. In every direction, all I see are the gruesome torments of Hell. Birds picking organs from still-writhing bodies, acid drop by drop eating away at skin, stones crushing sinners beneath slowly growing piles. The sights sicken me, but I search each face and am relieved when I recognize none.

With nowhere to land in this unending pit, I keep falling. I'll never find Tai this way. I cast my gaze around for a way to stop. Spotting a vertical slab of stone, I grasp it with my free hand.

The whole world shifts. What was vertical becomes horizontal, and I find myself hanging off a walkway similar to the one I jumped off. I pull myself onto it.

"Anlei!" Tai's voice rings in my ears.

I whirl. "Tai?"

An agonized scream rips past my ears—was that him?

My legs carry me across the stone walkway at top speed, though I don't know where I'm going. All I know is that Tai's voice came from this direction—nothing else matters. I can't let him be tortured here. He . . . he doesn't deserve to suffer. He may be an infuriating, pig-headed, slap-worthy idiot, but he's far from wicked. No demon can have him—not while I'm around.

A column of flames rises before me. I jump back. It vanishes, and in its place stands Tai, bound by chains and screaming as the blue demon drives a dagger into his stomach.

"No!" I try to lunge forward but find I can't move. I thrash and flail as hard as I can—but I remain frozen despite my efforts.

The demon drives his blade into Tai again and slowly carves a zigzag down his torso. Blood pours from his body, and his cries shred my heart. A scream rips from my throat. Tears fill my eyes. I pour every ounce of effort I have into trying to free myself from whatever spell has me trapped. But it's no use—I might as well have turned to stone.

This is your fault . . . A deep, haunting voice floats through my head. The column of flames reappears, engulfing Tai with its infernal fingers. His face contorts, and each scream pierces my heart like a thousand knives. *This is your fault* . . .

"Stop!" The useless word tears from my mouth. I watch, helpless, as the flames consume him, until only ash remains. Yet I still hear his screams in the distance. He's worse than dead—Hell has claimed his soul.

The spell releases me. I collapse forward. Sobs wrack my body. I've failed. I've failed more spectacularly than I thought possible. Tai is gone—they've destroyed him. And they'll destroy him again, and again, and again, forever, because this is Hell. They may call themselves Courts, but there's no justice here.

There will be a reckoning. I squeeze my eyes and send a prayer to the Gods of Heaven, begging them to intervene. *Their laws have been violated . . . Mowang has allowed his demons to take one who isn't damned. They have to help . . .*

No one can help you. That deep voice invades my mind again, and the face of the blue demon appears. *You deserve all you suffer.*

It's in my head . . . How is it in my head? *You can't touch me! I'm not a sinner!*

Are you sure?

Get out! The blue demon fades, leaving only the darkness of my mind.

I inhale sharply. I'm not finished yet. Mowang must answer for what he's done. When I find him, I'll demand that he release Tai as well as his people.

I open my eyes then jump up with a start.

I'm no longer in the Courts of Hell. I'm home—in Dailan.

The familiar water of Dailanjiang shimmers before me. Shocked, I drag my gaze across the sloping rooftops.

A bone-shattering screech rips through the air. Ligui surround me, so dense, their darkness obliterates the view of my village. I spring into action but find myself once again grappled by a spell.

No . . . no . . . no . . .

Screams fill my ears. One by one, Ligui rip apart everyone I know—my mother, my sister, my fellow guards . . . *everyone.* And I can't stop them. I do nothing as they behead Mother, as they smash

Anshui's skull. I do nothing as Headman Su and Pinghua and everyone I ever knew fall into their evil clutches.

Cries scratch my throat, and tears stream down my cheeks.

This is your fault . . . You left them to this . . .

The blue demon appears in my head again. It's right. I let this happen. I left my village behind, and I chose to let them remain unguarded so I could chase glory with Tai. And I failed him too. I led him into the Courts of Hell thinking I could protect him, and I was wrong.

This is your fault . . .

Heat licks my skin. I cry out as the scorching agony spreads through my entire body.

This is your guilt. The blue demon cackles. *See how it burns?*

The spell releases me again. I find myself in a heap on the ground, writhing in agony as the fire engulfs me.

This is your fault . . . This is your guilt . . . You deserve this . . .

I did this. I left my family, my entire village—

I left to save them. That one thought shines clear though my pain, loud and bright. *I sacrificed my dreams so the viceroy would protect them.*

You abandoned them to go on an adventure with a thief . . .

I may want adventure, but I'm also helping Tai save his people. I clench my fists. The demon—it's doing this to me. This is its way of torturing me—burning my body the way guilt burns my heart. But that guilt has no place in me. I may not have made the perfect choices, but I regret nothing.

You deserve this . . . You deserve this . . .

No! I force myself to stand despite the excruciating heat. I'm still gripping my sword—I can take down the creature that's torturing me.

"Where are you, coward?"

I still see the riverbank, still witness the Ligui tearing my village apart. None of this is real . . . I'm in the Courts of Hell, and the blue demon took it upon itself to sentence me. But it had no right.

"Face me!" I swing my sword. "Where are you?"

Wicked laughter rings through my ears. The demon's vague form materializes before me, as if the air is water and it's a reflection from afar.

I start toward it but double over as a new wave of heat strangles my body. I scream. The pain is so all-encompassing that it's all I can do to keep from sinking into the ground.

I glimpse the blue demon before me. The sight of its cackling face ignites my anger. I manage to straighten, raising my sword.

But before I can strike, a bright silver blade sprouts from its chest. The demon screeches and explodes into smoke. The image of Dailan explodes as well.

I'm back on the stone walkway. The heat vanishes. I blink in shock at the sight of Tai standing before me, wielding Ibsituu's sword.

"Anlei!" He rushes toward me.

So much relief and joy pours through me at seeing him alive that I find myself falling into him. I wrap my arms around him, savoring the feel of his body against me—the solidness, the warmth. He's real. Nothing else I saw before was, but *he* is *real*. I bury my face into his shoulder, too glad to care about anything else. I haven't lost him after all. His head rests against mine, and his breath rustles my hair. Inhaling deeply, I breathe in his scent. I hold him tight, and somehow, that makes me feel whole.

What happened? How is he here?

Realization dawns upon me. That wasn't him the blue demon

destroyed—that was a mirage. Just as Dailan was. The blue demon created both hallucinations to torture me. I don't know when the real world faded and the demon's world took over—did it start the moment I saw it take Tai? Was everything that happened after an illusion? Whatever the case, the blue demon was responsible. But Tai robbed me of my revenge just as I was about to seize it.

"Why did you do that?" I pull back. "I had it!"

Tai stares at me. "You were screaming—I saved you!"

"*I* was going to save me. I didn't need you to interfere!"

"I know you didn't." His eyes blaze like twin black flames that burn deep into my heart. "But don't ask me to stand there and do nothing when something's torturing you. You may be strong enough to bear that kind of pain, but . . . I'm not."

I hold his gaze but feel my scowl softening. My mind flashes back to those awful moments when I thought the demon was torturing Tai. Even if they were mirages, the pain they caused me was all too real. "I understand." I sigh. "What happened to you?"

"I don't know. One moment, I was beside you, and the next, I was clawing my way out of an ice pit."

"Stay closer next time." Though I'm still shaken, I do my best to throw on an expression of confidence. "I'll keep the demons away."

"I don't doubt it." He smiles, and a warm feeling glows in my chest.

What do we do? If we continue as before, we'll wind up in the same spot—getting caught by demons who don't follow the laws of Heaven. We could wander forever and reach nothing.

But this is Mowang's realm. He can appear wherever he wants. Maybe it would be easier to make him come to us.

"Mowang!" I holler. "You have violated the laws of Heaven! I am Liang Anlei, and I am here as the hand of justice! Come, face me! Or are you afraid of a mere human?"

Tai looks impressed. "Not a bad idea." He turns to the chasm and exclaims, "Mowang! You—"

A great rumble cuts him off. Purple and red sparks dance before us then burst into a brilliant explosion of magic and color.

Mowang rises from the infinite pit, a figure so enormous my stomach clenches. His monstrous yellow eyes stare down at us from his crimson face. White fangs jut from his blue lips. Lines of green streak his face in grotesque patterns. None of the paintings I've seen of him captured the extent of his evil. Two clawed red hands protrude from the long sleeves of his black robe.

My muscles quiver. I tighten my grip around my father's sword to keep my fear from showing. I'm facing Mowang—*Mowang*. The demon king himself. The master of the Courts of Hell.

Mowang leans down, his fiery eyes meeting mine. "A peasant girl who imagines herself a warrior." He whips his gaze to Tai. "And a half-breed." The corner of his mouth curls.

I glance at Tai, wondering what that means. Tai's attention remains fixed on Mowang, anger glittering in his eyes.

"You have my attention." Mowang draws himself to his full height. "Now, what do you want?"

CHAPTER NINETEEN

THE DEMON KING

The ground turns from gray to deep orange. The air shimmers, and the world shifts. I'm now standing in a giant room elaborately decorated with gleaming sculptures that look as if they are carved of black jade. They depict demons with grotesque faces, sharp claws, and menacing eyes. Some stand along the yellow walls, but many more protrude from large columns. What those columns are holding up, I don't know, because their tops vanish into a haze of black smoke.

Something white and glowing moves behind the smoke. Narrowing my eyes, I realize that those pale, vague figures are people. Men and women and children crowd against the fog, peering down at us. They must be ghosts, and this must be the demon king's throne room. It looks just the way Mother described it in her stories, except even more intimidating than I imagined. Most of the place is empty, and the sheer amount of space is unnerving.

Mowang didn't appear before us—he transported us to him. He stands before his throne—a massive red chair that looks like thousands of screaming faces piled on top of each other.

I shudder but keep my chin high. I can't believe I'm making demands of the demon king. "Stop the Ligui from escaping to Earth, and release the people of Baiguang!"

The demon king lets out a low, menacing chuckle. His yellow eyes shift to Tai. "Baiguang? Is that what you told her?"

Confusion pecks at my mind, but I ignore the questions. Mowang is said to be tricky; he could be playing mind games.

"You have no right to hold them!" Tai's voice shakes. "Release them *now!*"

He points his sword upward. I realize that he's indicating the people behind the veil, and horror floods me as I give them a second look. Those aren't ghosts at all—they're the living people of Baiguang, trapped by supernatural forces.

Mowang arches one thick, black eyebrow. "Heaven has not interfered thus far, and I do not take orders from half-breeds." He glances at me. "Or peasants."

I scowl. "You can't hold the living. Your rule is only over the damned!"

"These people may be among the living, but who's to say they aren't damned?" Mowang's lip twists into a hideous grin. Though his voice isn't loud, its resonance shakes the floor. "And who's to say I'm working against the will of the gods? Perhaps by holding these beings here, I'm serving their will. Perhaps I'm protecting the rest of the living from a much worse fate."

"Liar!" Tai's eyes blaze with so much wrath they could melt an entire winter's snowfall.

My own anger burns hot enough to incinerate whatever ground would remain. How dare Mowang be so glib? "Enough of your tricks!"

Mowang leans down until his enormous face is just a few feet in front of us. A wave of heat blasts me. "While I enjoy my tricks, I never act without reason. You think that destroying my body will save your little world, but you are mistaken. Now, begone."

He waves one giant hand, as if to brush us away.

"No!" Tai strikes at him with Ibsituu's sword.

The River Pearl's glow explodes with white sparks. Mowang recoils. His face contorts, and his eyes flash as the sparks gather into the form of the River Dragon—his curving body and snapping jaws. The image dissipates, but its shape is burned into my memory forever.

I stare at Ibsituu's sword, awed. Tai's eyes widen with surprise.

The silver blade crackles as white light glows from the intricate symbols engraved in the metal. The power pouring from the pearl resonates in my very soul and fills my core with brightness and energy. I swear I can hear the River Dragon's voice saying, *Back away, Mowang.* His voice reminds me of the vibrations that continue shaking the air after someone beats a drum.

Mowang must hear him too because his monstrous scowl deepens further. "This is my realm. You have no power here!"

A small smile plays on my lips despite my fear. Dragons are among the mightiest of all supernatural beings. They're practically gods—certainly greater than any demon, even the one who calls himself king. Perhaps Tai and I stand a chance after all.

My nerves hum, harmonizing to the River Pearl's uncanny voice.

I know Mowang won't call the other demons to his aid. He wouldn't be the king for much longer if he needed help defeating two humans, even if they wield a dragon's magic.

It's just him and us—with the River Dragon on our side.

As Mowang raises his mighty arm to strike again, I charge at him. I may not be wielding the River Dragon's power, but I know he's here with me. I can *feel* his presence.

A blade materializes in Mowang's hand—one so black it consumes all light. A great gust of air knocks me backward and pins me to the ground, its howl filling my ears. I squeeze my eyes against its sting.

Fury burns in my blood. I stab the ground with my father's sword and push with every drop of strength I have. Faint popping and hissing noises surround me, and the weapon heats in my hand. Its magic must be at work. Using the sword as leverage, I push and push.

Finally, I manage to rise. The wind vanishes. I open my eyes to find the air shimmering with golden sparks. Mowang and Tai battle on the other side of the throne room. The demon king towers over Tai, and with his enormous size, it would seem he could flick Tai away. But the River Pearl's magic helps balance the scales. Its white glow surrounds Tai, creating a halo shaped like his silhouette that's as tall as Mowang with a blade just as great that crackles and clangs against the demon king's.

I speed toward the dueling pair, and my soul clamors for action. I *will* have justice today. Tai may wield the River Pearl, but this is my chance at glory too.

Tai drives Mowang back toward one of the massive carved pillars. Seeing an opportunity, I leap onto the pillar and climb the carvings.

Both Tai and Mowang are too busy to notice. Halfway up, I'm high enough that Mowang's back stands just out of reach. I have no qualms about striking a supernatural enemy from behind. Demons have no honor, and so they don't deserve fair combat.

I push off the pillar, holding my sword out in front of me and aiming for his shoulder blades. The tip of my blade hits its target but bounces off, and the force sends me hurtling through the air. My back impacts the pillar, knocking the wind out of me. Before I fall, a giant hand pins me against the column. At least my arms remain free to move. But when I stab Mowang's wrist, the blade bounces back so hard the hilt flies from my grip, and my weapon clatters to the floor.

Panic rises up my chest. Why did I think I could do this? Only legends can defeat Mowang, and I . . . I'm just a village girl who partnered with a thief.

I spot Tai lying on the floor, held down by Mowang's enormous black shoe, which gleams like the scales of a deadly serpent. Ibsituu's sword lies just beyond the reach of Tai's grasping fingers. A white halo, vaguely shaped like the River Dragon, swirls around the blade.

Mowang peers down at it, arching his brows with disdain. "Are these your champions, River Dragon? Pathetic."

His giant palm pushes into my stomach, making it hard to breathe. With the carvings pressing painfully into my back, my failure weighs on me. I've proven worthless in this fight. Tai's gaze flicks up to the black veil, behind which his people hammer and scream, begging for freedom.

A new wave of fury blossoms through me. Mowang's duty is to punish the damned—*not* to harm the living. If the gods won't stop him, then I will. I grip two protruding statues and writhe under Mowang's tightening grasp. Pain lances my whole body as I grind my bones against the pillar's carvings. The demon king watches, his white fangs gleaming. He's enjoying the spectacle of me squirming.

I heave myself upward. A cry escapes my lips as I succeed in sliding beneath his grasp. It's hardly a movement—barely an inch up and to the side, but it's enough for my body to find a groove in the carving behind me. I take advantage of it and twist.

"Anlei!"

Tai flings Ibsituu's sword up to me. Mowang reaches for it, but I grasp its hilt first. Its energy pulses up my arm, setting fire to my veins. My lips split into an eager grin. *I* wield the River Dragon's magic now. At last, it's *my* turn to be the hero.

I slash at the giant hand holding me. The blade sizzles against Mowang's skin, and a rancid smell explodes in my nose. He releases me with a cry. I tumble downward. With my free hand, I seize one protruding carving. Tai still lies pinned beneath the demon king's enormous boot. He screams in pain as Mowang drives his foot harder into his chest.

"Let him go!" I swing the enchanted sword at Mowang.

Brilliant light explodes around its blade, extending its reach by more than twice my height. The sword's light blasts Mowang's chest, sending him flying back. He hollers as he crashes against the ground. I struck a blow to the *demon king*. Never have I held such power before, and I savor every drop with wicked glee.

Tai scrambles to his feet. Mowang rises in a movement so abrupt he seems to simply blink into his standing form. He moves toward Tai.

"Don't touch him!" I push off the column. The moment I hit the ground, the world around me shrinks. Or rather—I've grown. A white haze surrounds me as I find myself standing eye-to-eye with the demon king. I'm not a mere peasant any more. I'm the bearer of a dragon's magic and the hero tomorrow's storytellers will sing of. "This is your last chance, Mowang! Release Tai's people, and call the Ligui back to Hell!"

Mowang's lip curls. "Even if you strike me down, my subjects will continue their work, and I will regenerate quickly enough. A hundred years is nothing to an immortal."

He swings at me with full force. My enchanted blade clashes and clangs against his dark weapon. Since it's clear he won't give me any answers about the Ligui. I see no reason to hold back. I relish each attack. He will pay for every life his demons took from my village.

Yet none of my blows manage to land. He keeps blocking my blade, and each time I feint, he knows what actual move I'll make and strikes to compensate. I'm quick enough to keep him from hitting me, but I can't seem to do any damage. Worse, he's an immortal incapable of tiring, while my limbs begin to grow weary. Sweat runs down the side of my face, and my heart pounds like an insistent fist beating down a door.

Frustrated, I lunge at the demon king, hoping the sheer energy will drive past his defenses. Mowang uses the opening to strike me in the gut. Or rather, what feels like my gut. A great force knocks me back, and the white haze vanishes. I'm my diminutive human size again. I stumble to the ground, suddenly feeling like a fool.

I glimpse Tai at the top of one of the columns, holding my father's sword. He swipes the blade at the black veil imprisoning his people, but it has no effect. The River Pearl's magic can defeat Mowang's—maybe if I can slice open the veil, Tai's people can escape while I hold off the demon king.

I sprint to the pillar and climb as quickly as I can. Mowang stabs his blade toward me. As I move to block, the white halo reappears, as if the River Dragon can sense my intentions. With my sword locked against Mowang's, I continue climbing, shifting my body and letting my blade slide against his. The white halo extends, making it easier for me to keep moving without changing its position.

When I'm halfway to the top, Mowang pulls back. I fall forward but manage to keep my grip on the column. He takes a swing. I parry and stab forward, aiming for his heart. The white light impacts his stomach and throws him backward. He lands with a howl. I curse. A little higher and I would have destroyed him.

"Anlei!" Tai clings to the column with one hand, holding my father's sword in the other. He drops it and reaches down to me.

I should throw him Ibsituu's sword. He's already at the top, and I still have halfway to climb. But I don't want to let go of the River Pearl's magic. I was *so close* to ending Mowang. Am I doomed to be the supporting character in Tai's story?

Mowang blinks back into a standing position. He raises his weapon.

I draw my sword-wielding arm up to swing—and throw the blade to Tai.

I release my grip on the pillar a second before Mowang's weapon impacts the side I was just clinging to. Grasping desperately, I catch one of the protruding sculptures a few feet down. The glowing white blade slices through the smoky curtain above, and sparks explode from the gash. A translucent man emerges, hovering in the air. Silvery light reminiscent of the halo around a full moon surrounds him. I stare in awe. He wears his black hair as Tai does—tied in a knot at the top of his head. A woman emerges behind him, her long black hair pinned in an elaborate style with tresses flowing down from beneath intricate buns. She, too, is translucent, and her long dress trails behind her as she soars to freedom. More and more of their kind fly down one by one.

Mowang's great roar shakes the cavern. The ghostly beings flood his face with light, attacking with some kind of magic. As Mowang tries to swat them away with his blade, Tai leaps from the column.

The glowing white sword sinks into Mowang's chest. Sparks of red and yellow erupt from the spot, and the demon king's scream shatters the air. My bones shake under its cacophonous volume.

It cuts out as his body dissolves into smoke—just like the Ligui I've fought so often.

That's it—we won. Tai might have struck the final blow, but I'm the one who gave him the opportunity. I'm a hero, too.

We've defeated the demon king.

We've become legend.

CHAPTER TWENTY

PIECE OF BOTH, PART OF NEITHER

I stare at the spot where Mowang stood, unable to believe what's happened. The demon king is gone, defeated. Perhaps not forever, but still—we did that.

Shaking myself out of my stupor, I climb down the pillar and scoop up my father's sword from where it landed on the ground. Tucking it back into its strap, I look around for Tai. He threw himself off . . . What happened to him?

I open my mouth to call his name, then freeze.

He remains where he was when he drove the blade into Mowang— hovering in midair. His body has turned translucent, like those of the beings that emerged from the smoky black veil. The same silvery glow clings to him as he watches them.

The veil, meanwhile, has vanished. The translucent beings pour down, and their shouts of joy and relief ring bright. Some blink out, vanishing abruptly. Others revel in their newfound freedom, darting around like fireflies. The cavern walls, once yellow like firelight, now glimmer silvery blue like the moon.

Yueshen. My jaw drops. *So this is why they vanished.*

The sight of the mysterious lunar spirits takes my breath away. It's as if someone captured moonlight and molded it into the shapes of hundreds—no, thousands—of people, each ethereal and beautiful. Once, I would have counted myself lucky to glimpse even one reflected in a mirror at night. To be surrounded by so many—it's wondrous. Tears spring to my eyes. I wish Mother and Anshui were here to witness this.

Tai flies as freely as they do and glows the same lustrous hue. He . . . he's Yueshen too. He catches my eye, and his grin recedes. He swoops down toward me. "Anlei—"

"You *liar!*" I point one accusing finger at him. "You told me—"

"I told you my people were from Baiguang—white light. I never said we were human."

"You never said you *weren't* human!"

"That's the oath I mentioned—I swore I'd never tell a human the truth of my origins or of my Yueshen abilities."

He glances over his shoulder at the throne. Yueshen dive into the frozen screams carved into the black stone and vanish. He gestures at the spot. "We should get out of here. There's a portal at the throne's base."

I continue staring at him. I still can't quite believe what I'm seeing.

He gestures impatiently. "Anlei!"

Snapping out of my daze, I look over at where he's pointing. All I see are infernal carvings until I pull Anshui's spectacles from my pocket. Through their lenses, a yellow circle appears in the air by the throne's base. Beyond it stretches the lifeless landscape surrounding Heihuoshan.

My instincts carry my feet toward the portal at a run, but my eyes remain fixed on Tai, who flies beside me in his ethereal form.

"I can't believe you hid this from me." As I step through the portal, I think back to our past conversations wondering if I missed something. Rivers of lava flow to either side of me, and heat wraps its thick cords around my skin. In the distance, I glimpse the ship. Not seeing any demons, I slow to a walk. "Mowong called you a half-breed . . ."

Tai floats beside me as I head toward the ship. He nods with a wistful smile.

"That story I told you about the Yueshen girl and the human prince . . . it was true—except my father wasn't actually a prince. My mother saw him as one, though. She could shift into human form and, after their marriage, he was granted the ability to shift into Yueshen form. I was born to live between worlds. We were happy . . . but then an accident took her. The Yueshen never wanted anyone to know it was possible for a human to gain their powers, and her death—which happened while she was in human form—sealed their decision. That's why they made me swear never to tell a human who I really was or what I could do. But I had no choice but to shift forms after attacking Mowang, and now you've seen me for yourself." He spreads his hands. "My oath is moot."

Anger and curiosity wrestle for dominance in my mind. I don't know if I want to yell at him for keeping his true nature a secret from me when I've risked my life—and my village's safety—for him, or if I just want to know more about him. "Did you *want* me to know?"

"Not at first." Tai drifts a few inches closer to me. "But the more time we spent together, the more wrong it felt to keep my secret. If I hadn't sworn on the souls of my ancestors that I'd do everything in my power to keep a human—any human—from knowing the truth, I would have revealed this form to you earlier."

I give a disgruntled nod. "Do you prefer being Yueshen?"

He shrugs. "Flying is fun, but I've spent more of my life as a human. Since I'm not fully one of them, the Yueshen won't let me live in their kingdom. And sensations are . . . muted. I could put my hand on a flame and sense only a slight twinge."

"What does it feel like to touch another person?" Curiosity gets the better of me.

"I don't know. I've never been around another human long enough in this form to try it." He holds out his hand to me. "Let's see."

Hesitating, I lift the spectacle off my eyes, then touch my fingertips to his. But all I feel is mist . . . something warm and present, yet ethereal. It's the kind of comforting heat that settles on one's skin on a humid summer day. "You might as well be air."

"You . . . are certainly there." Tai tilts his head. "Yet not fully so . . . It's like touching water. You can cup it in your hands, but it easily slips out. I suppose this is why Yueshen can't lift anything larger than a sword." The glow fades around him, and the colors of his face saturate. He's human again—and his hand is warm against mine. His lips quirk. "That's better."

Heat rushes into my cheeks. I pull away and ball my hand behind my back.

Beings of light whirl across the dark, lightning-streaked sky. This is the stuff of legends—descending into Hell, destroying Mowang's physical form, freeing the Yueshen from their unjust captivity. It's a story Tai's people will tell their children and grandchildren. And I'm a part of that. Because of what we've accomplished here, a piece of me will always be immortal.

But only a piece.

While Tai's quest has ended in triumph, mine lingers on. Mowang may be vanquished—for now—but Hell and all its infernal inhabitants remain. The Ligui will continue ravaging Dailan, and I'm still the only hope for my village to receive the protection it needs.

I glance at Ibsituu's sword. Though the River Pearl's luster remains bright, the supernatural light that surrounded it during the battle has gone. I feel as if a light has vanished from me as well. My fate remains the same as it was before. The bridal carriage is still waiting for me in Tongqiucheng.

Tai holds the River Pearl sword out to me. "Take it."

"About time." I accept the weapon. A weight sits on my heart as I realize I may have wielded a weapon for the last time. Unless I run into Ligui on my way back to the viceroy's palace, I'll probably never fight again.

Tai glances from the sword in my hand to the one on my back. "You look as if you could take down an army alone. Are you sure you have to go back to marry the viceroy?"

"Dailan is still counting on me." A glimmer of hope shines in my heart. "But once Viceroy Kang hears of what happened here, he might allow me to fight in his army instead of sitting in his palace."

Tai lets out a dry laugh. "You may have become a legend, but that still makes you a story. And stories are often doubted."

"You're saying he won't believe me?" I grimace. "You tell him, then."

"He wouldn't believe me either. He wants me dead, remember?"

My heart sinks. To Kang, Tai's still just a thief. I glance up at the Yueshen, who are quickly blinking out, no doubt transporting themselves back to their realm of moonlight. They don't seem to care that I helped save them all from a terrible fate. Still, perhaps one of them could help convince the viceroy of the truth. "Everyone here saw me—surely if enough of them tells Kang about what I did, he'll believe me."

"Good luck convincing them to help. They aren't exactly fond of humans. But you shouldn't have to convince the viceroy of anything. After all you did, you shouldn't have to return to him."

"This changes nothing." I pause in my tracks and stab the River Pearl sword into the ground. "Mowang said the Ligui would keep attacking. I still need Kang to protect Dailan—I can't defend them alone."

"Don't marry him." Tai grips my shoulders. Without his usual teasing glint, the intensity of his eyes is startling. "I know you can't love him. If it's for honor, embrace the dishonor. If it's for power, well, you already have a different kind of power. Just, please, don't marry him. He'll destroy you."

I stare at Tai, my gut twisting. The pounding in my heart intensifies, and my breaths grow short. He's right—I spent little over a day in the viceroy's palace, and I became a shadow of myself.

But this was never about me. It was always about my home, my family. Tai knows that . . . I've told him enough times. Anger crackles in my soul—something deeper than the mere irritation Tai sparked in me before. Does he honestly think I *want* to marry the viceroy?

Or does he believe I'd abandon my people?

Either way, the wrath coiling up my veins is so strong, it's all I can do to keep from hitting him hard. I tighten my hands around the sword, fearing they'll ball into fists and fly without my permission.

"I told you before not to talk about my engagement." I barely manage the words through my clenched teeth. "My way is set."

He releases my shoulders and backs away. "Enjoy it, then."

"Go to Hell."

"We're already there."

When I realize the irony of my insult, a new flash of rage ignites within me—though I don't know if it's directed at Tai, the viceroy, or myself. I stare at the weapon in my hands. The River Pearl had the power to vanquish Mowang, but not the power to change my fate.

It occurs to me that it's still stuck in a hilt. I consider bringing Kang the whole sword but realize that would mean having to admit to aiding the thief.

I look back at Tai. "Can you take the pearl out of the hilt?"

"I'm afraid not." Tai's returned to his usual carefree demeanor, as if nothing we just said happened.

"I thought the Yueshen were masters at magic."

"They are, but I'm not." He lifts his shoulders. "I am a half-breed, after all."

I try to discern what his tone might be conveying. "What does that mean? You looked like one of them to me."

"I can take their shape, but I don't possess all their powers. I—"

"Tai!" A Yueshen woman floats down toward us, her black brows arched over sharp black eyes. She looks older than Tai, but not by much. Her strong cheeks and broad mouth carry an air of authority. "What are you doing with that human? You swore an oath!"

Tai throws her an irritated look. "Anlei obviously knows the truth. You could show her a bit more courtesy." He gestures at the woman. "This is my cousin Suyin."

Suyin glances down at me with a look of disdain. If there's any familial resemblance between her and Tai, I don't see it. Not only does her round face contrast Tai's prominent cheekbones, but she lacks any of Tai's good-natured charm.

She glowers at him. "You were about to tell her about your Yueshen abilities, which you know is forbidden. *Especially* after what happened to your mother. How dare you?"

Tai glares at her. "It's not—"

"You will tell the human girl no more. By breaking your oath, you would shame not only yourself, but your ancestors as well. It's bad enough that you let her see you transform. Your mother would weep to see her son so dishonorable."

Tai turns his gaze to the ground.

I scowl at Suyin. "Why do you hate me? I just met you!"

"It's not you she hates." Tai shakes his head. "It's humans. According to them, my father lured my mother to Earth then failed to protect her there. And Mowang claims he imprisoned them because of humans, though he didn't mention why." He throws his cousin a furious look. "But she should be thanking you for saving our people."

"If it weren't for her kind, we wouldn't need saving." Suyin's tone is light, but from the way she looks at me, I might as well have been personally responsible for her imprisonment in Hell.

"What are you talking about?" I march up to her. "*Mowang* trapped you!"

Suyin gives me a frigid look, then waves her hand at Tai in a beckoning motion.

"Come. There are Yueshen matters I must discuss with you."

Tai hesitates. "I still have business here."

"No, you don't." Suyin gestures at the ship. "Your human friend has a way to get home."

Ignoring her, I turn to Tai. "Why *did* Mowang trap your people in the first place? You never explained that."

"I don't know," Tai says. "I wasn't there when it happened . . . I only found out because Suyin managed to escape long enough to tell me that Mowang was rounding up all of our kind. He used his magic to cast a net and draw the Yueshen into his domain. But it didn't work on me because the spell was meant for spirits, and I'm half human." He glances at his cousin. "Do you have any theories?"

"That is what we must discuss." Suyin lifts her brows. "*After* we return to our realm."

"*Your* realm." His expression darkens.

Suyin lets out a biting laugh. "This again? You're too old to whine about living on Earth."

"If Earth is my place, then I have no reason to leave."

Suyin's jaw hardens. "Our people just escaped Hell and are running around in confusion. They need us—why would you linger here? For *her?*" She looks down at me. "I suppose you want to see her safely home."

I clench my fists. I want to knock her teeth out. "I don't need anyone's help."

Tai gives me an apologetic look. "Anlei—"

"Go! She's right." I jerk my head at Suyin. "Your quest is over, and now I must complete mine."

"I wasn't going to abandon you."

"This was always where we were supposed to part ways." A sudden pain stabs my heart as I realize I'll probably never see him again. I always knew I'd have to return to Tongqiucheng, hand over the River Pearl, and marry Viceroy Kang, but . . . but I never thought . . .

Why should I care? Tai is merely someone I agreed to help. Now that the journey's finished, there's no reason for us to linger in each others' lives.

Tai clears his throat. "Are you sure you know how to fly the ship on your own?"

I give him an irritated look.

"I need a verbal affirmation so that if you end up crashing it, I have a witness who can testify that it wasn't my fault." He gestures at Suyin. Though he appears to be resuming his usual maddening jokes, there's a weight to his voice.

Part of me wonders if it's because he doesn't want to leave me—but that's ridiculous. Maybe we didn't kill each other on this journey, but we were never meant to be more than temporary allies, and I don't understand why his leaving is affecting me so much. I give him a haughty look. "Without you to distract me, I'll fly it better than you ever could have."

"Enough!" Suyin holds out her hand. "Tai, are you coming or not?"

Tai hesitates, his gaze fixing on me. He parts his lips, as if there's something he desperately wants to say. Then he shakes his head with a mirthless laugh. "I wish you a happy marriage." He shifts into Yueshen form and takes Suyin's hand. They vanish in a flash of white light.

"Hundan!" I yell at the empty air where he stood. "Good riddance to you!"

My words ring across the empty land. Though thunder rumbles above, the space around me feels eerily silent. The very air seems hollow, as if someone sucked the life out of it.

I stick the River Pearl sword into the strap beside my father's blade and march toward the ship. After a moment, I quicken to a run. This realm is stifling me; I need to get out *now*.

By the time I reach the ship, I can barely breathe. My legs are sore from running, and I almost don't have the strength to pull myself up the rope. I rush to the ship's wheel. Gritting my teeth, I turn to the control panel and flip its copper switches.

Even after I take off and follow the map back into the terrestrial realm, the hollowness remains. Neither the hum of the engine nor the colors below fill the lonely void around me.

CHAPTER TWENTY-ONE

TO COME

Wind whistles past my ears as I steer the bronze ship through the clouds, heading back toward the river outside Baiheshan. Though I've learned how to control it, it still feels like it belongs more to Tai than to me.

He doesn't need it anymore, now that the Yueshen are free. He doesn't care that it's the reason he was able to save them at all, that it carried him loyally to the completion of his quest. He just—left it behind. Like he left me behind. Without even a real farewell. Yes, I told him to leave, but . . . how could he be gone so easily?

A powerful swelling rises behind my heart. What's wrong with me? I have no time for such idle sentimentality. The sky around me is fading fast, which means the Ligui could appear, and there's still the danger of Kang's fleet.

I set the controls to instruct the ship to keep traveling forward on its own. I suppose I could have done that hours ago, but I preferred the control of steering it manually. If nothing else, it kept my focus occupied during the long, empty hours.

The pale moon hangs in the darkening sky, becoming clearer and clearer as the sun's last rays fade away. I search the white halo ringing its almost full shape, trying to discern the beings that live within. Their apparent disdain for humans taints the image I had of them before. I hope more of them are like Tai than Suyin.

I wonder whether the sky's dark enough for the light to count as moonlight. What if the Yueshen appear in a reflection? What if Tai does?

I have no business dwelling on him when I still have a duty to fulfill, but even though that quest is over, I can't stop my mind from dragging me backward.

I feel the walls of fate sealing me in once again, as they did when I was staring at my reflection before what would have been my wedding. Except nothing will interrupt me this time. I can't *let* anything interrupt me. Kang would not tolerate any more hindrances; it will be challenging enough to convince him to forgive me for running off, even if it was to return something he considers his.

A breeze whispers across the deck. Ghostly voices waft through it. A chill envelops me, and I tense. The voices seem to come at me from everywhere and nowhere at once, filling my ears and ringing in my head. Yet I hear no words, and soon they fade to silence, leaving me to wonder.

The tiered roofs of Baiheshan Miao glow under the midday sun. The journey took longer than I'd hoped—a full three days. After spotting distant shapes on the horizon, I took a roundabout route in case they were part of Kang's search party. I didn't dare sleep until after I'd hidden the ship back in the cave by Baihejiang, which I did in the dead of night to avoid being seen by Kang's patrols in the area. I hadn't wanted to waste time resting after, but my exhausted body won the battle.

This time, no wagons were heading into the city, and I had to walk the entire distance. By the time I arrived, it was dark. I'm not familiar with the road, and without Tai to guide me, I feared I'd get lost if I trekked through the woods. Furthermore, Kang apparently received permission for his cyborgs to comb the city, and evading them slowed me down. At least none are currently searching the temple.

Ibsituu greets me at the temple's gateway. "It's good to see you again. Your timing is good too—Kang's men departed earlier today and shouldn't return for a while." Her gaze slides past me, and I know she must be wondering where Tai is.

"Tai left with his people." I wipe the sweat from my forehead, hot after hours of walking under the summer sun.

"I know. I felt it when the Yueshen returned to their kingdom in the moon."

"Did you know who Tai was?"

"I did." Ibsituu gestures for me to follow as she walks into the temple's courtyard. "Not because he told me, but because when I met him, I sensed immediately that he wasn't fully human. A simple unmasking spell revealed his true nature, but I promised I wouldn't tell anyone who didn't already know." She steps over the threshold into her room. "You shouldn't blame Tai for keeping his identity a secret from you. The Yueshen have never trusted humans; they are the descendants of purified souls and see those left on Earth as inferior . . . petty, greedy, cruel." She snorts. "They seem to have forgotten that pride was the first sin their ancestors had to relinquish to ascend."

I mirror her wry expression.

"Of course, not all think that way," Ibsiuu continues. "Tai certainly doesn't. But though he lives between worlds, he is still bound by the Yueshen's laws. I'm sure you haven't seen the last of him." Her lips form a teasing grin. "I assure you, his thoughts are dwelling on you as well."

Heat creeps up my cheeks. "I don't think so."

She arches her brows at me.

"I didn't come here to talk about him." Huffing, I pull the sword containing the River Pearl from the leather strap binding it to my back. Its blade scrapes against that of my father's weapon. "Could you undo whatever spell you used to bind the pearl to the sword? I need Viceroy Kang to think I chased the thief across the country and returned immediately."

Ibsituu accepts the sword with both hands and releases a regretful sigh. "Are you sure this is necessary? I'd rather not take it apart."

I give her an apologetic look. "I'm sorry. But I don't know how I'd explain the sword to Kang without revealing that I helped the thief escape."

"You could claim that by the time you caught up to the thief, he'd already embedded it in the sword . . . " Ibsituu shakes her head. "But that would be too much power to grant Viceroy Kang, and it may expose my true talent to him—something I do not wish for. I suppose the pearl was stolen from your people to begin with, so it's only right that it should be returned in its original condition." She settles down in her chair and places the sword on the table before her. "Did Mowang say anything to you when you confronted him?"

I shrug. "Nothing true."

"Oh? What lies did he tell?"

"He said that by holding the Yueshen, he was protecting the rest of the world." I let out a derisive noise. "Tai didn't take well to that."

"Interesting . . . " Her gaze becomes contemplative. "Mowang may be wicked, but he never does anything without reason."

"That's what he said too. Do you know what his reasons are?"

"Perhaps he was speaking of the great shadow looming over the Empire of the Pearl Moon. I thought Mowang's defeat would lift it, but instead, it seems to have grown heavier."

"A shadow . . . " I lean toward her. "Does it have to do with the Ligui and why they keep attacking?"

"I don't know, but it seems the Ligui were not under Mowang's command. In fact, he may have felt threatened by their growing presence. Unfortunately, I've yet to learn where they're coming from."

"Aren't they coming from Hell?"

"Apparently not. Some may cross in and out of Hell, but that's not where they originate from." Ibsituu scowls. "Mowang's defeat was supposed to restore the balance of the world, but there's a darker, crueler force at work. Whatever the demon king's intentions, he was slowing the spread of the Ligui, and without him, they rage free."

"But how—"

"I don't have all the answers." She gives me a stern look. "I've told you all I know."

"Sorry," I mumble.

"It's been frustrating." She shakes her head. "I've used my most powerful spells, but the truth evades me. Meanwhile, the innocent continue to suffer. I heard news of another Ligui attack just this morning."

Guilt unfurls in my heart. Destroying Mowang may have freed the Yueshen, but it condemned others to the Ligui. "Where was the attack this time?"

"A small village far from here. I only learned of it because a mechanical pigeon arrived in the city with a note begging for aid. I believe it was called Dailan."

My face goes cold. I'd hoped the Ligui would stay away from my village long enough for me to marry Kang and secure his protection. Instead, by helping destroy Mowang, I may have somehow released the very monsters I hoped to protect them from.

Dailan has survived many such attacks before. I breathe deeply, forcing myself to remain calm. "Was there anything else?"

Ibsituu meets my gaze with a sympathetic expression. "That was your village, wasn't it?"

"Yes. Will Baiheshan be sending anyone to help?"

"The note wasn't asking for defenders . . . It was asking for shelter for refugees. It appears there's not much left to defend."

No . . . I feel as if I've just fallen on a field of spikes. If I hadn't accompanied Tai on his quest, if I'd taken the River Pearl from him when I had the chance . . . I might be married by now. Those mechanical dragons would have been patrolling the sky, and Dailan would still stand. *What about Anshui? Mother? Are they even alive?*

I bolt up so fast my chair rattles. "I have to go."

"Of course." Ibsituu waves her hand over the River Pearl. "But you will need this . . . I will not take long."

She gives the sword one last long look, as if committing it to memory, before closing her eyes. Blue magic swirls at her fingertips, which she brings down to the hilt. My heart hammers with agitation as I watch.

Discipline, Anlei. Father's voice rings in my head, and I picture the stern look he would have given me. *The River Pearl is moments from your reach. Dailan's people still need the viceroy's protection. They're seeking refuge in Baiheshan, but cities don't like opening their doors to a flood of strangers.*

I focus on the mental image of my father. *Protection for Dailan is the bride price Kang was willing to pay if I married him. He still has to keep that promise. He has to let them into his city.*

I repeat those thoughts, using them to anchor me to the floor while Ibsituu completes her rituals. Though I still intend to return to Tongqiucheng, I decide to stop by Dailan first. I have to at least know if my family survived.

After what feels like an eternity, Ibsituu says, "It's done."

She hands me the pearl. The sword lies on her table, and though its carvings remain as beautiful and intricate as before, its blade has lost its luster, and the round hole in its hilt looks like a gaping wound.

I accept the River Pearl, and the hum of its energy pulses through my skin.

I tear out of the temple and down the mountain, praying to whichever gods might be listening that my family survived the consequences of my mistakes.

CHAPTER TWENTY-TWO

A RETURN

R ed rays from the sinking sun glaze Dailanjiang, making it appear like a river of blood. As I lower the ship toward the glistening ripples, I tell myself over and over that my worst fears can't have come to pass. The ghostly whispers of the ship sift through me like frozen rain. I feel as if a hundred haunted souls surround me, asking something of me—but not saying what. Whatever magic the viceroy used to enchant this ship, it must have disturbed the dead.

Dailan appears on the horizon as I glide down toward the water. A strange rush fills me—the warmth of home coupled with the chill of fear. The fading light silhouettes everything. From this distance, it looks as it always did—a cluster of low buildings carved by glimmering streams and surrounded by green swaths. A smile tugs at my lips. Though the length of my journey can be counted in days, I feel as if I've been gone for too long. I've seen so much, experienced so much.

It's as if I lived an entire lifetime since I said farewell to home.

As I draw closer, the details become clearer. I furrow my brow, unwilling to believe what I'm seeing. The buildings don't look dark because they're shadowed . . . they're the charred remains of burned wood. What looked like walls from a distance turn out to be the skeletons of buildings with collapsed roofs filling the space between blackened beams. A fire has ravaged my village.

How did this happen? The Dailan Guard was still strong when I left it. And though Ligui have been known to start fires by knocking over torches, ours is a village surrounded by water. My heart clenches with sorrow and anger, and my eyes sting. This is my nightmare from the Courts of Hell come to life—me helpless and unable to save the home I love. My gaze claws over the ruins of my village for any sign of hope.

I find it in the figures that move through the littered streets, salvaging whatever they can from the wreckage.

A handful of people cluster along the riverbank, drawn by the sight of the flying ship, but I don't see my family among them. As soon as the ship touches the river, I grab a rope and jump overboard. Cold water splashes up my entire body as I wade to shore, cursing the current for slowing me.

"Anshui! Mother!" I step onto the shore. Shocked exclamations from the villagers buzz past me—they thought I was the viceroy or his men returning. I ignore them.

The wooden gateway over the main road is gone, reduced to cinders. A sob rises up my chest. It's only a thing, but it was a piece of my home. *"Meimei! Ma!"*

"Jiejie!" Anshui emerges from the wreckage of a house and rushes to

me. "It *is* you! How are you here? Were you flying that ship?"

I catch her and hold her in a close embrace. "Yes. I heard about what happened to Dailan, and I had to return."

"You received one of my mechanical pigeons?" She releases me. "I sent one to every city I could think of."

"*You* made it?" Pride swells in my chest. "That's amazing."

"I was the only one left who knew how. The spellmasters . . . They joined the Guard in defending the city, using magic as weapons. But . . . the Ligui . . . they were too strong." Her eyes glisten. "Did the viceroy send you to lead his men to protect us?

I smile at her innocence. "I wish that were true, but I flew alone."

Her face falls. "We can't stay here. The fire destroyed so much . . . We'll starve."

"What happened? Where is Mother?"

"The Ligui attacked two days ago. There were more than we've ever seen before . . . They overwhelmed the Guard and crashed through the barrier spells. The only reason any of us survived is because they attacked near dawn, and the sun rose in time to drive them away. They seemed determined to destroy everything, seizing every source of fire and spreading the flames everywhere. I've never seen them so vicious before. We lost so many . . . They came to our house . . . " She stares at the ground. "I used a pistol to hold them off, but I'm not a warrior like you. Mother's hurt . . . I don't know if she'll make it."

The words sit at the edge of my mind, refusing to sink in.

"I tried to protect her." Tears stream down Anshui's face. "But when I wasn't looking . . . I'm sorry."

My eyes sting. I arrived too late. I don't know what to say, so I just pull Anshui back into my embrace.

She sobs against my shoulder, hot tears soaking my tunic. "Why hasn't the viceroy sent his bronze dragons to protect us yet? I thought after we gave him the River Pearl we were supposed to be safe . . . "

"No one told you what happened in Tongqiucheng?"

She shakes her head. "Is he on his way? If you received my pigeon, that means he received the message too, right?"

"I didn't receive the one you sent to Tongqiucheng . . . I heard about the one in Baiheshan."

"What were you doing in Baiheshan?"

"It's a long story . . . "

Though I long to wake Mother, if only to say hello, I know she needs rest. Her skin is paler than white ash, and the bandages wrapped around her limbs, chest, and head send guilt lancing through my heart. I kiss her forehead. Her soft breath tickles my face.

Anshui puts a gentle hand on my shoulder. "Come. We can check back later and see if she's awake. I'm sure she'll be happy to see you."

I rise from my kneeling position and let my sister guide me around the other injured villagers who lie on thin mats spread across Headman Su's house—the one structure that survived intact. My vision blurs, and I squeeze my eyes.

The dead number in the dozens, which, for a small village like ours, might as well be thousands. I don't know how we'll bury them all when

Dailan is already stretched so thin between salvaging and caring for the injured. Grief weighs on my heart so heavily I fear it will drag me into the ground, leaving me a weeping heap.

I pass Pinghua on my way to the threshold, and a sharp mix of sorrow and relief courses through me. The last time we fought together, I abandoned her to pursue my own revenge; she's always been such a fierce fighter, but she was injured in that fight. Is that why she's here now, lying unconscious with bloody bandages wrapped around her leg and face? Yet at least she's alive . . . There are so many I once knew that I haven't seen since returning to Dailan. I dread to think of where they might be.

"I'm so sorry," I whisper.

Anshui gives me an annoyed look, but her eyes are sad. "How many times are you going to say that before you accept that this isn't your fault?"

"But it is." I wander down the street, not really heading in any direction. Gold lines of barrier spells glimmer around the edges of Headman Su's house, and I wonder if they'll be enough to protect the injured inside. The sky fades above us, the blue hands of twilight blotting out the pink of sunset. Soon, darkness will rise, and the Ligui could return again. But who will defend what's left of Dailan? Only a handful of guards remain, including me.

The River Pearl, sitting at the bottom of the cloth bag slung over my shoulder, bounces against my hip. Earlier, Anshui sent her last mechanical pigeon to Tongqiucheng to tell Kang that it's here. If we're lucky, he'll receive the message and return with his flying armada, though that might take a few days. I want to shove the relic into his hands so he'll grant my people his protection.

"Kang's fleet would be here now if I hadn't gone with Tai," I murmur. "Our village wouldn't have been burned . . . so many would still be alive . . . "

"You couldn't have known."

"I knew it was a risk. I shouldn't have let him go the night he stole the pearl."

"If you hadn't, the Yueshen would still be trapped by Mowang." Anshui glances up.

I follow her gaze. The moon shines bright. I can't help picturing Tai up there right now, soaring across that far-off realm. "I suppose. And Tai would never have given up on the River Pearl. He would have found a way to steal it again—or been caught trying. Kang would have executed him." A shudder runs down my spine, and it brings me some comfort to know that at the very least, Tai and his people are safe. "Still . . . I don't know if freedom for the Yueshen was worth the price."

Anshui gives me a stern look. "You did the right thing. And when Mother wakes, she'll tell you the same."

My sister's willingness to forgive me so easily warms my heart.

"There's no sense in dwelling on what already happened." Anshui places a hand on my arm. "I hope I get to meet Tai someday."

Irritation pops up my chest, though not at her. "That's not going to happen. Our quest is finished, and he's gone."

"I don't believe that. Neither do you."

"What's that supposed to mean?"

"Just that you talk about him an awful lot, and I have a feeling he's doing the same up in the Yueshen's realm."

Ibsituu said something similar, and it irks me that both she and now my sister seem to think there's some lingering connection between me and Tai. "Why do you say that?"

"It's obvious, *shagua*." A playful spark lights my sister's eyes. "You're completely obsessed with him."

My jaw drops. "I am *not!*"

"Then why do you keep talking about him?"

"You wanted to know about my journey, didn't you? He's the reason any of it happened."

She throws up her hand. "If you were any denser, you'd fall right through the earth! That conversation ended an hour ago, but you keep bringing him up."

"That's only because I can't get him out of my thoughts!"

Anshui smirks. "*Jiejie*, what do you think love is?"

I blink at her, not knowing whether to laugh or smack her. She's being completely ridiculous—I'm not in love with Tai! How could I be when half the things he does make me want to throttle him?

My sister giggles. Though it's at my expense, it's good to see her happy again. "Is he handsome? He sounds handsome."

"You're being foolish," I grumble.

A red flare explodes in the sky, and a man's distant shout rings out. All humor vanishes from Anshui's face. I stare in disbelief at the bloody stain against the clouds. How will we protect the survivors of the last Ligui attack with so few of us able to fight?

I grab my sword from its strap. "Anshui, get inside."

She seizes the pistol tucked into her belt. "I can fight too."

"You can't—"

"Yes, I can. I already did."

I stare at her in disbelief. She's never been a fighter—in fact, this is the first time I've seen her hold a weapon she wasn't tinkering with. Yet three days ago, she defended our house because I wasn't there. *But she's only thirteen.* "Go! You aren't trained!"

"Do you think the Ligui care?"

A black wisp draws my gaze. I whirl in time to face a shadowy being that materializes before me—a multi-limbed monster with gaping mouths screaming from three heads. Flailing arms ending in grasped swords swipe at me.

Enraged, I lunge at it. "*Gai si!* Haven't you done enough?"

A shot rings out. The thing screeches as yellow light spews from the spot where the bullet hit one of its heads. Anshui's aim is true; I shouldn't have doubted her. But I still hate that she's out here, forced to fight because she's one of the few people left who can.

I attack with renewed fury. I have to destroy this Ligui before it reaches my sister. My sword crackles against the creature's shadowy blades, and gold sparks fly. After ducking to avoid a blow, I swing upward and slice through one of its torsos.

A second shot from Anshui destroys one of the two remaining heads. As the creature stumbles, I thrust my sword into the shadowy mass. The last smoky wisps of the Ligui dissolve. I glance at Anshui. Terror fills her face, but she keeps her pistol raised as if ready for more.

Shots from other guards pierce the air. The clang and crackle of enchanted swords whirl on the wind. A black cloud covers the moon—I gape as I realize it's actually a swarm of Ligui. Already I can tell that there are too many to fight, too many to drive back.

Rage pulses through my veins at the cruelty of fate. The River Pearl sits in the bag on my shoulder. It's all we needed to ensure Dailan's protection, yet I'm too late to deliver it.

A Ligui materializes in the shape of a lion a few feet away. Four dragonfly-shaped shadows flock around it. There's no one else in sight.

I charge. As long as there's still breath in me, I won't let anything harm my sister. I slice and swing in every direction, attempting to battle all five enemies at once. Anshui's shots pop through the dark, and sparks spew from the dragonflies' wings. Acrid smoke whirls around me. An abrupt swipe of the lion's paw sends me tumbling to the ground, and I taste metal.

Before I get a chance to recover, the shadowy lion explodes, and the dragonflies scatter. The clunk of metal and the whirring of propellers blow down toward me. A bronze dragon snakes through the air above. Kang must have received Anshui's first message—not enough time has passed for him to have received the one telling him about the River Pearl. Maybe he came because he fears he'll never get it if there's no Dailan left to protect.

I exhale. Explosions of enchanted fire rock the ground and pierce the sky with their yellow light.

"Jiejie!" Anshui, now standing behind the enchanted barrier of the headman's house, gestures for me to join her.

I start toward her but glimpse a human-shaped Ligui disappear around a corner ahead. The sight of the white crescent glowing on his neck sends anger surging through my veins. Does the Shadow Warrior keep reappearing just to torment me?

I race after him. Kang's dragons won't be the ones to take him down—it will be me. That raw, gnawing need to destroy him seizes my entire being. Nothing will stop my revenge this time.

As I draw closer, he spins to face me. I strike with a fierce cry. He catches my blade with his own shadowy weapon. His white eyes meet mine as magic snaps and crackles from our locked swords.

I shove forward, forcing him back. Rage hums through my core.

"Anlei! Stop! It's me!" Though darkness obscures any movements of his mouth, his voice is bright and clear—and familiar.

I've never heard a Ligui speak before. I didn't think it was possible.

This must be a trick. Without hesitating, I swing again.

"Anlei!" He blocks my blade.

The shadows fade from his face, and pale moonlight spills onto his familiar features.

Shock radiates through me. I stare, frozen in place. This *must* be a trick—this *must* be.

Because it's Tai who stares back.

CHAPTER TWENTY-THREE

SEIZED BY FATE

It's a trick—I won't fall for it. The enemy I've sought to destroy and the boy I risked everything to help—they *can't* be one and the same.

My sword remains pressed against his weapon. When he shifted into human form, the black blade transformed into a bronze staff—the same one he carried during our journey.

This thing might look like Tai, but it can't be him. That it would use his image against me reignites my wrath. I attack with full force.

"Anlei!" He dodges.

"*Coward!* Show your true face!" My sword clashes against his staff as I drive him back.

"This *is* my true face—it's been me this whole time!"

"*Liar!*" The tip of my blade nicks his cheek.

I freeze at the sight of red blood trickling down his face. Ligui don't bleed. Supernatural beings don't bleed—only humans do.

"It's me, really." Tai gives me a pleading look. "I'm sorry—I wanted to tell you before that I can shift into shadow form, but Suyin stopped me. I should have ignored her."

I stare in shock. "You—You're a Ligui?"

"No. I only look like one in my shadow form. This happens because I can't become fully invisible like the other Yueshen."

"Can they become shadow as well?"

He shakes his head. "I only do because my powers are partial."

Part of me is still convinced this must be a trick. I keep my sword ready before me, but he doesn't attack, doesn't transform into another kind of monster, doesn't do anything except watch me. His expression is one of earnest apology, tugging at my heart, begging me to believe him.

Tai is the Shadow Warrior . . .

The entire time I knew him, he was lying—even more so than I already knew. It was one thing when he was concealing his identity as half Yueshen, but now that I know he's the Shadow Warrior as well . . .

Why is it that every time we meet, you're trying to kill me? Those were among the first words he spoke to me . . . I thought he was referring to the time I pursued him as the Masked Giver. But now I recall how the Shadow Warrior's eyes smiled at me when I confronted him aboard Kang's flagship.

Now that I see the truth, it seems so obvious that those were the same eyes that teased me throughout our journey to the Courts of Hell. No wonder the Shadow Warrior appeared so often—he was Tai all along. Tai, the boy for whom I risked my life and the lives of everyone I knew. For whom Dailan suffered so his people could be free. The boy I laughed with, performed with, fought with. The boy I foolishly let myself trust.

He was a lie—all of him. The Tai I thought I knew never existed.

Because he's also the monster that killed my father.

Perhaps he thinks the truth about his identity will save him from me, but he's just sealed his fate. I will destroy him—send him back to the Courts of Hell where he belongs, except this time as a sinner to suffer all the tortures we witnessed.

I swing at him hard. Shock lights his eyes as he blocks. I almost want to laugh. Did he really think I'd let him go? Did he take me for a soft-hearted fool who'd release a murderer because she once considered him a friend?

Somewhere in the world, there's a person who would seek a reason to forgive him. Who would cling to the illusion of him created onboard a ship in the sky and in the streets of a strange city. Who would trust in the boy whose sense of fun could lighten her own heart as she both delighted in and raged at the jokes he made. Who would toss away any sense of betrayal and instead try to understand, to sympathize.

That person is not me. If that makes me a monster as well, so be it. I strike and strike. *"Why?"*

"I came to Dailan for the River Pearl but had to flee when Kang's fleet arrived." He speaks between quick breaths, and his staff clashes against my blade. "I tried to steal it again on the flagship, but then—I encountered you, and something about you fascinated me. It was the way you fought—with a passion and grace worthy of Warrioress. That's why I had to see you when you came to Tongqiucheng."

Is he mocking me again? The monster! Now I know why he killed my father. He must have been after the River Pearl then as well. It was what he needed to defeat Mowang, and he didn't care who he had to cut down to get it. He must have tried again and again over the years, spying on our village until the Ligui attacked, and then using the creatures to mask his efforts. He was only lucky enough to avoid me until that night when Kang arrived with his dragons.

His luck has run out. He won't escape me this time.

Red tints everything; all I see is rage. I attack relentlessly, striking and stabbing and swinging with the ferocity of a thousand armies. His efforts to stop me aren't enough to keep me from driving him into a wall.

His staff keeps my blade from cutting off his head. I press my sword against it as hard as I can. If I press hard enough, I'll force his staff into his throat, and he can die smothered by his own weapon.

"Anlei!" His desperate gaze meets mine. "What do I need to do to earn your forgiveness?"

"You can't," I growl.

"Why do you hate me so much?"

"Do you really not know?" A strange, humorless laugh explodes from my lips. "You killed my father!"

I turn my sword against his staff, hoping to catch his neck. He shoves back, sending me stumbling away. His shocked eyes are as round as the moon. I spring forward again, but instead of defending, he shifts into his shadow form and soars into the sky.

Spotting a nearby column, I climb it as fast as I can.

An explosion shakes the world around me, causing me to lose my grip. I land on my back. Buzzing sounds in my ears, and my head throbs from where it hit the ground. I glimpse a second explosion taking out a Ligui a few feet away and squeeze my eyes against the brilliant light.

When I open them again, Tai is gone, no doubt retreated to the Yueshen's realm. I'll never look at the moon the same way again. The weight of defeat sits heavily on my chest, and I remain on the ground, wishing the dirt would swallow me whole.

I let him escape again, and this time it's worse . . . because I can't tell myself that I did everything in my power to stop him. Despite all my rage, despite all his lies, that was still Tai before me. Though I attacked as hard as I could, my blade kept finding his staff—not his body. Something held me back.

That soft-hearted fool—part of her is a piece of me, and it was just enough to let him escape. Because though I want to see him only as the Shadow Warrior, he's . . . he's *Tai*.

Tears stream down the sides of my face as I remain prone, staring at the bronze dragons winding through the sky. They're tears of anger at myself and at the boy who betrayed me. Tears of grief for the Tai I thought I knew—the one I wish existed in place of the lying, murdering wretch who tricked me into thinking he was a hero. Tears of shock and tears of pain . . . I want to rip my heart from my chest and crush it to bits.

Where was the glimpse of darkness that should have warned me to his true nature? And why was it absent again, just now, even after the truth became clear? Maybe if I weren't so bad at reading people, I would have seen it.

I don't want to believe any of this. But there's only one shadow being that bears a white crescent on his neck, and he said himself that the other Yueshen can't shift into this form. He also confessed that he was the only one of his people who escaped Mowang's capture—and it was because he was half human.

No other being in the world could have been the one I saw cut my father's throat.

I can't believe I let myself be so fooled.

Quick footsteps pound the dirt, and the Ligui's screeches pierce the air. But I remain on the ground, defeated in a way I'd never thought possible, anchored in the dirt by my shattered heart and flowing tears.

I can't let anyone see me like this. Any moment, one of the other remaining guards—or worse, my sister—might stumble upon me.

I inhale deeply, breathing in the smells of sulfur and smoke and river water, and push off the ground.

"Lady Jiangzhu!" One of Kang's cyborg soldiers approaches at a run. It takes a moment for me to recall that *I* am Lady Jiangzhu—or will be once I'm married. He seizes me by the arm. "I'm so glad I found you. Come with me. I'll take you to the viceroy."

I let him drag me forward, too weary to shake him off.

Kang's sharp eyes flick up and down my body, his lip twisting with disgust. He sits on a wooden throne, an ornately carved thing with abstract curving patterns and dragon heads peeking out from elegant swirls. Rich embroidery of colorful dragons covers his long blue robe, but though his official garb and stern expression radiate authority, he no longer scares me. I've evaded his soldiers and stolen his ship, fought my way through Hell, and conquered the demon king. He may still hold power over me, but I will not tremble before him.

Headman Su stands behind him. Though he holds himself erect, his lip twitches nervously behind his gray beard.

Kang's eyes narrow. "When Su begged me to intervene after receiving Dailan's message, I was inclined to refuse. What kind of alliance can be forged when the promised bride leaves without permission?"

"Did you not read the note I left for you?" I arch one brow. "I went to pursue the thief that stole the River Pearl."

"Where is he, then? That's the ship he stole from my scouts on Dailanjiang, is it not?"

There's no point in denying that. But I don't have to tell the whole truth either. "Yes. I found it in a river cave—he'd hidden it there while he went to steal food." My prepared words roll easily off my tongue. They're all technically true, and I hope that means the cyborg soldier standing behind me won't be able to use his powers to detect any falsehood.

"The thief got away, but not before I reclaimed the pearl. I took the ship so I could return sooner with it." I reach into the cloth bag on my shoulder and produce the glowing white relic.

A startled look flashes across Kang's face. Su's bushy brows shoot up into his crinkled forehead. I lift my chin in triumph.

Kang drags his gaze over me again, but this time a hungry glint sparks in his eyes. "I shouldn't have underestimated you, my beautiful Warrioress."

Though it sounds like a compliment, his words make me uncomfortable. "I take it you still want to marry me, then? With this as part of the deal?" I hold the River Pearl up a little higher.

Kang's tongue flicks over his lips in a movement so subtle I almost don't see it. He reminds me of a snake tasting the air. "I honor my agreements. Why did you not come to me at once?"

"On my way back, I heard of what had happened to my home." I keep my words curt. "I had to come here—I needed to know if my family had survived."

"Understandable." Kang's tone is cold.

"Dailan still needs your protection. But as you can see, there's nothing left here. We can rebuild, but with the fields destroyed, my people will starve unless given refuge."

"Then I will grant it." Kang stands and approaches. "There is enough space aboard my ships to house all your refugees. In time, I will help your village rebuild." He reaches into his sleeve and pulls something out of what must be a hidden pocket. When he uncurls his fingers, I find my jade pendant sitting inside. "You left this behind as a promise that you'd return. By taking it back, you close the circle."

He slides the cord over my head. His breath fouls the air around me, and his fingers on my neck might as well be spiders. Bile rises up my throat. He's turned a precious memento from my father into a symbol of my bondage.

He grabs my chin. "Of course, the quality of my wife indicates the quality of our alliance."

Nausea coils through my stomach. He wants to know that I'll be obedient, dutiful. A decorative flower pot or a plaything or a servant depending on his whims. But Dailan already suffered once because of my mistakes, and I can't let that happen again.

I grit my teeth. "As I said before . . . If my people have your protection, then you'll have your bride."

Kang's lip curls. "Good."

CHAPTER TWENTY-FOUR

WHISPERS OF TRUTH

The night passes swiftly outside my window—too swiftly. Warm summer wind breezes into my room as the viceroy's flagship cuts through the clouds. I glimpse one of the other ships, a wide vessel with enormous propellers and three tall sails scalloping toward its deck, and I wonder if my mother and sister are aboard it. All who remain of Dailan fly with me tonight, to be sheltered in Tongqiucheng until arrangements can be made to rebuild the village.

I suppose I should be grateful, but can't bring myself to be. Perhaps it's because Kang's "generosity" was bought and paid for by an ancient relic and an unwilling bride.

The small ship Tai and I once stole together passes across my view. Hovering lanterns, which we never used for fear of being seen at night, illuminate the cyborg soldier behind the wheel. I turn away as anger slices me like a hot knife. How could Tai have led me to believe he was my friend when all along, he was my father's murderer? Did he not even recall the crime? Has he killed so many that one villager's life was nothing? Who *is* he?

Memories tug at my heart—of us journeying together as allies, as friends, as . . .

I tell myself that they're lies—all of them—that every nuance of Tai's character was nothing more than an act designed to deceive me into helping him, but though I repeat these thoughts over and over, they don't feel real. I still want to believe in the boy I thought I knew.

I'm an even greater idiot than I thought. Tears of rage prick my eyes.

I wish I could block out the moon forever. Sinking into the wooden chair by the wall, I bury my face in my hands.

Anlei . . .

I start at the sound of my name, spoken in a ghostly whisper. That voice—it was my father's. It rings in my bones, just as it did the last time I was aboard the viceroy's flagship. Just like the other whispering voices aboard both stolen ships. Yet while those sounds held no words, my name is clear.

Anlei . . .

"Father?" I look around, wondering if it really is his ghost this time. Or maybe it's my guilt speaking, asking how I could have failed him so thoroughly. Not only did I let his murderer get away again and again, I actually helped him. Befriended him. Trusted him.

If I ever see him again, I'll finish this once and for all. I clench my fists. But something about the thought feels wrong. It was one thing when I sought revenge against a faceless Ligui. Now that I know it was

Tai the entire time . . .

Why should that change anything? Just because he showed himself to be part human doesn't mean he's not the same monster that killed Father.

The next time I encounter him, I'll remember that.

My mind floats in a fog of weariness and sadness. I don't think I slept at all during the day we journeyed back to Tongqiucheng aboard the viceroy's flagship. At least this time he didn't parade me through the city, opting instead for a quiet return in the drowsy hours before dawn. I hoped to see my family when we arrived, but one of Kang's automatons quickly led me into a carriage to take me into the palace. From what I've heard, the villagers are being settled in temporary quarters on the other side of the city.

Now that night has fallen again, I'm finally alone. No more servants trying to dress me up like a proper lady. Preparations are being made for a second attempt at the wedding ceremony, which is to take place tomorrow. I try not to think about it, or about what will come after.

I cross my room, wishing I could appreciate its beautiful décor. Wooden carvings of orchids adorn the tall bed frame, and latticed bronze lamps hover near the ceiling, their tiny propellers whirring softly and giving off subtle sparks.

A sudden movement in the window catches my eye. I jump; there's a pale, translucent figure hovering outside.

It's Tai in his Yueshen form, his staff clutched in his hand.

I automatically reach behind me before recalling that my sword's no longer strapped to my back—it lies at the bottom of my trunk. I bolt toward it and seize its lid.

"Anlei!" Tai flies into the room. His body becomes solid as he shifts into his human form. "I'm not here to hurt you!"

"Why did you come armed, then?" I grab my sword and whirl to face him. "I know that's no staff you wield!" I strike.

He holds up his weapon in time to block mine. "I only brought it so you wouldn't kill me before I had a chance to speak. Looks like I was right about needing it." Tai's mouth lifts into a humorless smile. "Can you let me live long enough for me to explain?"

"Explain what? How you've been lying to me since we met? How you killed my father in cold blood?"

Tai looks me straight in the eye. "I did *not* kill your father."

"*Liar!* I saw you!"

"You saw a man-shaped figure with a white crescent on his neck, right? It may have looked identical to my shadow form, but it was someone else."

I shove my sword against his staff, forcing him to step back. "You're the *only* half-Yueshen—you said it yourself!"

"I'm not the only one with partial Yueshen powers."

I start to speak but hesitate as I wonder if there might be some truth in his words.

"I'm not the murderer you seek—my father is." Tai's voice is taut. "It's the only possible explanation for what you saw five years ago. I swear, I didn't know. When he married my mother, the Yueshen granted him the ability to shift as I can so that they could both travel between realms. And like me, he can't turn invisible. He can only become shadow. I didn't want to believe it, but I do believe *you*, and if you saw a shadowed man with a white crescent on his neck . . . there's only one person that could have been."

I narrow my eyes. My heart clamors to believe him, but I remind myself that he's lied before and could be lying again.

"You don't believe me." Tai's jaw tenses. "After everything we went through together, how could you believe I'm a murderer? If nothing else, think of the facts—five years ago, I was only fourteen and barely knew how to wield a sword. Your father was an experienced soldier—I could never have bested him in battle."

"You've lied and lied and lied." I glare. "How can you expect me to trust you now?"

For a moment, he just stares into my eyes. I don't know if it's anger or pain or frustration or all three that color his expression, but I won't let him seize my sympathy when he doesn't deserve it.

"What I told you is true. And I'm willing to stake my life on it." He steps back and releases his staff. It clatters on the floor.

I tense my arms in time to keep momentum from driving my blade into his neck. *Why did I stop?* If I'd just let the force push me forward, I would have ended him already. But enough doubt scratches at my mind that I don't regret hesitating.

"I know I lied to you before, and for that, I'm sorry." Tai holds up his hands. "I understand now that I shouldn't have . . . that despite my oath, I should have found a way to let you know the truth of who I am. But I'm not lying about this. I swear to you by the Gods of Heaven and Earth, I did not kill your father. It was my father who did." He takes a step forward, bringing himself inches from my blade. "If you really don't believe me, then kill me now and end this."

Blood pounds in my ears. I swore I wouldn't believe his lies anymore, but . . . what if he's actually telling the truth this time? My heart screams for me to believe him, to lower my sword and stop threatening my friend. *Friend? What kind of friend tells so many lies?* I remain frozen with my blade to his throat.

"I've spent my whole life lying because of what I am." Tai's voice is strained. "No one could know that I was half Yueshen—that was the oath my parents swore when I was born. It's an oath that bound me before I knew what oaths were. When my mother died, my father went mad with grief—ordered all memory of her destroyed because it was too painful to think about the past. But he couldn't destroy me, and so he hid me instead—treated me as he would a bastard. I'm so used to *being* a secret that speaking the full truth feels . . . foreign. But I should have known better." His gaze bores into mine. "I swear to you, Anlei, from now on, I'll only speak the truth to you. And that is an oath I shall value above all others. If my cousin or anyone else claims this dishonors my ancestors, then they do not understand what true honor is. After everything you've done for me, you deserve my honesty."

The remorse in his tone seems so genuine, and every word he speaks rings with truth. I feel it in my gut, in my heart.

He *didn't* kill my father. He couldn't have. The certainty sits like a mountain in my mind, solid and immovable. Relief cascades down my chest, warm and comforting. I've never been so glad to be wrong.

"I could have killed you." I let my sword sink onto the floor. Glimpsing the small scratch on his cheek from where I previously drew blood, I look down. "You could have avoided me forever—why did it matter what I thought?"

"If you need to ask that, then it's better you don't know."

I glance back up and cock my head. But a more important question arises. "You said your father killed mine—who is he? Where can I find him?"

Tai's lips contort into a cynical smile. "You're about to marry him."

CHAPTER TWENTY-FIVE

THE END OF LIES

M y fist tightens around my sword. "If this is another of your jokes . . . "

"I wish it were." Tai spreads his hands. "I swore I wouldn't lie to you anymore, and I meant it. My full name is Kang Taiyue . . . named after the sun and the moon. My mother, of course, was the moon, and my father . . . she always called him the sun in her life." A sad smile flickers across his lips. "This is why I hid my face. If my father knew that his own flesh and blood had robbed him, he'd see it as the ultimate betrayal. Far worse than the actions of a commonplace thief. I didn't want to cause him that kind of pain."

Shock pulses through my body. Viceroy Kang . . . the true Shadow Warrior. I'm betrothed to the man who murdered my father. "Why did he do it?"

"He was after the River Pearl. He must have used a Ligui attack as cover, and your father must have gotten in his way. I'm so sorry . . . I knew he'd killed on the battlefield, but I had no idea he was capable of coldblooded murder."

Fury burns hot in my chest, but something stronger keeps it from bursting onto my tongue—something that reminds me that Tai's been innocent this whole time, and I nearly killed him for nothing. "No, I'm sorry. I should have listened before trying to kill you."

"I think a part of you sensed the truth even so." His mouth quirks. "If you'd really wanted me dead, I'd be dead."

I smile in spite of everything. "Why did Kang wait five years before trying to get the pearl again?"

"I think he realized back then that the River Pearl couldn't leave Dailan, but not why. I can only guess, but . . . it seems that five years ago, he was hunting down every significant magical object he'd heard of. After he failed to get the River Pearl, he must have dismissed it in favor of something he thought more powerful. But recently, he came across the ancient writings I told you about, the ones revealing just how strong the River Pearl's magic is. That's why he came back—and was so bent on succeeding this time."

"What about you? Why did you arrive the same night that he did? And why in your shadow form?"

"I wear that form for the same reason I wear a mask: to keep anyone from knowing who I am. Because of my oath, I had to hide my Yue-shen abilities from humans. But sometimes I need to fly, and it's easier to go unnoticed in my shadow form. If I were spotted, no one but my father would recognize me, and even he might not see the crescent on my neck and might mistake me for a shadow or a Ligui. So after I read the scroll and realized that my father was after the same relic I needed to free the Yueshen, I stowed away aboard one of his ships to reach Dailan. I thought that once I got close enough, I could race ahead and reach the pearl before he did. Of course, that was before I knew a spell prevented anyone from taking it out of the village."

"Why didn't you transport yourself instantly?"

"Like invisibility, that is a Yueshen ability I lack."

"But you can fly."

"Yes."

"Why did you need the ship, then?"

Tai shrugs. "I'm not as fast as a ship. Also, flying is tiring. Why do you travel by horse or cart when you can walk?"

I knit my brows and try to weave all the pieces of truth he's handing me into a tale that makes sense. "Masked Giver, Shadow Warrior, half Yueshen, viceroy's son . . . How many people are you?"

"Just one. I've gone by many names, but . . . I'm only Tai. I'm not an actor—I wouldn't know how to behave like someone else." His gaze meets mine, drawing me into their dark depths. "You know me, Anlei. There's only one me to know."

I nod, understanding. Even when they called me Lady Jiangzhu and dressed me in silk, even when I wore costumes and called myself Warrioress on stage, I was still Anlei.

I can't believe I'm about to marry my father's murderer. The thought of vengeance has simmered beneath my skin for five years, and it will last until I avenge my father and fulfill my oath. Now that I know who my target is, the need burns so fiercely it threatens to incinerate everything else I am. Especially since, in giving Kang the River Pearl,

I handed him the object my father died to keep away from him. The realization makes me nauseous. Did Kang know when he chose me that he was picking the daughter of one he murdered? No—of course not. When he chose me, he didn't even know my name.

I wonder how the viceroy would react if I told him the truth. I intend to tell him—right before I kill him.

I stride toward the door.

Tai rushes to cut me off. "Where are you going?"

"To avenge my father." I step to the side.

"Don't!" He blocks me again.

I hold up my sword. "Get out of my way."

A wry grin twists his lip. "So you're back to wanting to kill me."

Irritated, I lower the blade and shove him out of my way. "It's not you I want dead."

"I know—and I can't let you do this." He seizes my shoulder.

"What—"

"He's still my father. If you try to kill him, I will stop you." His dark eyes crackle, and I realize he means his words every bit as powerfully as I meant mine.

"He's a murderer—you said so yourself!" I throw his hand off. "He must face justice!"

"I know there's no forgiving what he did to you and your family, but . . . I can't let you—or anyone—kill the man who gave me life."

"Why do you defend him when he doesn't care about you?" My words taste like acid. "He tried to erase you from existence—did he even visit you after your mother died?"

A devastated look fills Tai's expression, and regret bites my soul.

I wish I could roll my words back behind my teeth like a spool of thread spilled on the floor.

"I barely saw him." His voice softens. "But he's . . . he's my *father*. My blood. The only family I have on Earth. He has more important things to do than coddle me. Ruling the province, fighting in the Emperor's border war, growing his armed forces—he's a *viceroy*. Even if he wasn't there for me, he saw that I was taken care of. I've always respected him. And I find his absence easier to take than my Yueshen relatives' disdain."

I recall the way Suyin treated him, as if she were a high-and-mighty princess and he a lowly commoner. Yet she was the only one who spoke to him at all.

How lonely Tai's life must have been, caught between worlds. Never Yueshen enough for his relatives on the moon. Yet too much so for his father to bear looking at him after his mother's death.

That he'd be so determined to protect his murderous father both surprises me and doesn't. Surprises because Tai seems determined to remain loyal to a murderer. And doesn't because . . . that seems so very much like something he would do. He may lie to cover his identity, but he's true to those he considers his own. He dove into Hell and crossed swords with Mowang himself out of loyalty to his people. I faced the same danger and gave him the victory—out of loyalty to him. I guess we're more similar than I thought.

The question is, which is stronger—my loyalty to my father or my loyalty to Tai?

The dead are to be honored, but the living are to be cherished. Father's words, spoken years ago, echo through my mind. *Many choices come down to love or hate. Choose love, every time.*

Thinking of it that way, I don't have a very complicated choice before me. Is my hatred toward the viceroy more powerful than my love for a friend?

The word *love*, even as an unspoken thought, causes my heart to leap higher on its next beat. I tell it to hush.

Even if Tai stood aside, I could hardly kill the Viceroy of Sijiang Province so abruptly. He's guarded night and day. The automatons wandering the hallways and courtyards would sound the alarm if they spotted an armed intruder in his section of the palace. In fact, I'm lucky none of them were near enough to hear my argument with Tai. Chances are, I'd fail in my quest for vengeance—and end up dead or condemned for my troubles.

And then there are my people. That the viceroy holds their fates in his disgusting hands makes me want to burn this whole place to the ground. They're what bind me to him. I wouldn't put it past him to accuse my people of conspiracy and execute them mercilessly. Even if I succeeded, his heirs would seek vengeance.

I drop to the ground, my legs melting beneath me, and my sword slips from my grasp. Too many thoughts and revelations have crowded my head in too short a time. Too many emotions have shaken my core. I dig my fingers into my hair, as if that will help me get a better grip on my thoughts.

"What do I do?" Tears prick my eyes. "Every fiber of my being wants the viceroy dead, but because he's your father, I can't kill him. Even if I could, my whole village would suffer the consequences. And I still have to marry him tomorrow . . . they're all counting on me to seal our alliance. After that, my life will be over."

Tai sinks down beside me. "We can find some other way to protect your village . . . You don't have to give your life to him. You don't have to . . . " He swallows hard.

"After the marriage, I won't see you again, will I?" It seems like such a stupid thing to worry about when my choice is between marrying my father's killer or risking my peoples' lives. But as I picture my miserable future under the viceroy's roof, I know that Tai's absence will make it feel even emptier.

"I'm not allowed in the main areas of the palace." Tai's voice is low. "That wouldn't keep me away, but my finding you wouldn't free you either. Please, don't marry him."

"And let my people suffer?" I press my palms into my eyes. "I wish Mowang had killed me in the Courts of Hell. Then at least I would have received an honorable, glorious death."

I feel his arm wrap around my shoulder, and his touch carries all the warmth of summer. It's the one thing that seems capable of easing the excruciating ache in my soul. I lean into him. His other arm encircles me, pulling me into a close embrace. I feel his breath rustling my hair, hear his heartbeat against my body. For several moments, we just sit there, and blissful nothingness descends. My mind empties of thoughts as I let Tai's presence take me whole, filling the hollow spaces within me and pushing back the darkness.

But nothing's eternal except Heaven, and eventually, reality returns.

Come morning, someone will arrive at my room to prepare me for my wedding. I'll still have to don that red dress and veil, still have to step into that bridal carriage to be made the property of an evil man.

And all because he wanted the River Pearl. He killed my father to get it, and now, he'll be killing me as well.

"What does he want with it anyway?" I wonder aloud.

"Shen me?" Tai's voice is soft, and he keeps his arms around me.

I reluctantly pull away, and immediately the world feels colder. "The River Pearl. Why was Kang so determined to have it? And with such urgency?"

"I don't know. That was something his writings didn't reveal to me."

"But you didn't see all of his writings."

"No. Only a very small part, I suspect."

I stand. "Where does the viceroy keep these writings?"

"Whatever he wants with the River Pearl—he can't have it. Not when it's the reason he killed my father. If I can't have my vengeance, then I at least deserve answers."

"You do. I'll take you." He crosses the room and picks up his staff. "Bring your sword. You'll need it."

"How come?"

"Automatons guard his secret archive, and it lies outside the palace. I tried passing through the walls before, but there's magic in them that blocks me. We'll have to break in. It's a great risk—are you sure you want to do this?"

I purse my lips. It will be too late to cover our tracks once we destroy the automatons. Kang will know for certain that someone infiltrated his lair. I might avoid getting caught, but then again, I might not.

But if I don't do this, I'll go mad. I'll strangle Kang the moment he lifts the bridal veil from my face. Channeling my fury into seeking answers is the only hope I have. I thought I'd do anything to protect my village's safety, but I never imagined I'd be forced to marry my father's murderer.

If I can find out why Kang wants the River Pearl so badly, at least I'll know what my father died for. Maybe it will help diffuse my wrath.

And maybe I can find a way to undermine the viceroy's plans without him finding out. If I can avoid getting caught, it's possible I'll be able to return and see the marriage through.

But if not—so be it.

I give Tai a firm look. "Let's go."

CHAPTER TWENTY-SIX

THE TOMBS

S tone lions stand at attention along the wide road, their carved manes streaming down weather-worn backs. Though it's hard to make out the details in the darkness, I can tell they must be very old. Rain has smoothed down sharp claws, and wind has chipped away at powerful jaws. Yet their age makes them all the more majestic as they watch over what travelers may journey to the Sijiang Tombs. Built by emperors of the previous dynasty hundreds of years ago, they flow with the grace of the old style. It's simpler and more rigid than the elaborate, curving designs I'm used to, with powerful lines molding bold shapes.

My sword bounces against my back as the mechanical wagon I'm riding in hits a bump. Gears clank and steam hisses, but since we're miles from the nearest town, it's doubtful anyone will hear us. It's forbidden to build homes within a wide radius of the Tombs; they're as isolated as a place can be. That's probably why Kang chose them to house his secrets.

According to Tai, his father uses an underground passageway beneath his office to access a hidden chamber within the tombs where he keeps his writings and his most powerful magical objects. Considering how many hours we have been traveling, that passageway must be long indeed.

"How did Kang build such a tunnel?" I wonder aloud.

"He didn't. It was dug generations ago as an escape route in case of an attack or an uprising." Tai glances at me from the seat beside me as he shifts a lever to keep the vehicle on track. Fortunately, our first flying ship wasn't the only vehicle he'd stolen from his father over the years. It would take at least a day—probably more—to reach the Tombs on foot. Anshui's spectacles, which I lent him, sit on his nose—two large, round lenses decked out with smaller lenses and gears that look rather absurd. Especially since they're slipping.

An amused smile splits my lips.

Tai flashes me a grin. "Your sister's marvelous device is quite fashionable, don't you think? Every noble from here to the capital will be wearing them by this time next year—even during the day."

"Don't be ridiculous." I shake my head. "Did you always know about the tunnel to the tombs?"

"I'd heard rumors about its existence, but Father always insisted that it caved in decades ago and no longer existed. I believed him—until the day I spied him opening a hidden door in the floor of his office. He shifted into his shadow form and flew down into the darkness. I wanted to follow or to go in after he'd left, but his automatons were always standing guard."

I nod. Those automatons are still watching Kang's office, which is why we're heading to the tombs the traditional way—the way traveled by pilgrims wishing to pay tribute to the rulers of the past.

"How much farther do we have?" I ask.

Tai knits his brows. "I can see the gate ahead . . . you probably will too in a moment."

I open my eyes as wide as I can, focusing on the dark path before us, but though the moon is bright, it's not enough to illuminate the horizon. All I see is a small piece of road leading into black swaths. "How long did it take you to figure out where the tunnel led?"

Tai rubs the back of his neck. "Almost a year. I was hoping to find something in my father's secret archive that might help me free the Yueshen. I couldn't enter it from his office, so I had to find it from the other end—the tombs. I snuck out whenever I could, sometimes flying and sometimes driving this thing"—he raps his knuckles against the wagon—"to explore until I discovered a hidden tomb that wasn't mapped in any of the palace's records. When I saw the automatons guarding the entrance, I knew I'd found the right place. I was going to find a way to sneak past them, but the very next day, I learned about the River Pearl. Let's hope they're the only things guarding the tomb."

"I doubt we'll be that lucky."

When we reach the gate to the Sijiang Tombs, we leave the vehicle just beyond the vague shadow of its tiered roof. As I follow Tai across the wide, open grounds, I yearn for sunlight so that I might get a clearer look at these eternal homes of ancient rulers. Though darkness obscures the magnificent structures, I feel their grandeur all around me. I pause in awe of stone gateways carved at sharp angles and embellished with twisting, tapering designs. Of great buildings—large enough to be houses but serving as entryways and monuments—that must shine bright with red and green and gold in the day. Of statues of stern gods dressed in flowing robes and tall hats. Each item was placed deliberately to evoke a sense of balance. I'm sure entire libraries could be filled with the methodology used in the design.

Several paces ahead, Tai glances back at me. The yellow light from a single hovering lantern, suspended by propellers, traces the confused look on his face. "What's wrong?"

"Nothing." I rush to catch up. "I've just never seen anything so grand in my whole life."

He smiles. "Magnificent, isn't it? I'll show you around during the day sometime. There's so much to see."

"I won't have that kind of freedom after we're done here. If we're caught, I'm finished. Even if we're not, Kang won't allow me to go anywhere."

His expression darkens. He turns away and gives the lantern a slight nudge to push it along. I follow him in sullen silence, wondering how I'm going to face the consequences of my choice tonight.

We approach an uneven path lined with rough, stacked stones. They form a tall pair of walls that seem to push back the earth. A towering, arched door, which appears embedded in a hill of stone, stands at the end. Beyond that lies the final resting place of a noble family from yesteryear. And beyond that, down a passageway no one would think to travel, lies Kang's secret chamber.

Uneasy, I pull my sword from its strap. The door's red paint is chipped, and small bronze domes bulge from its surface. A pair of enormous metal rings hang from its center. The doors look too heavy to move, but I reach for one of the rings anyway.

"No need for that." Tai approaches the stones lining the path, leans his staff against them, and feels along the edges. Digging his fingers into the cracks around one of the stones, he pulls until it comes loose. He jumps out of the way as it lands on the ground with a *thud*.

I peer over Tai's shoulder as he reaches into the crevice. A set of switches sits inside, and he flips them one by one. Gears clank and whir as the doors spread toward me like a pair of outreached arms. Only black lies beyond their grasp. Their movements are slow and clunky, and the thumps of machinery sound louder than thunder.

As soon as the space between them is wide enough for me to fit through, I grab the hovering lantern and speed inside. Wind buzzes through the lantern's propellers. Tai follows.

A cool draft wafts toward me as I enter a cavernous space lined with smooth, gray stones. High walls rise toward an arched ceiling. It looks plain next to the ornate carvings outside, but the somberness of its simplicity matches its purpose. Five large, rectangular structures encased in red lacquer sit against one of the walls.

"Do you know who lies here?" Though I'm speaking no louder than usual, my voice sounds like a shout against the stillness, and my words bounce off the walls.

"A minor noble and his family," Tai answers. "He was one of the rare individuals not directly related to a past emperor to receive a place in the Sijiang Tombs."

"He must have performed a great feat to have been granted such an honor."

"I'm sure he did. Still, this is a lesser tomb compared to those of the higher nobles and the emperors. It's probably the least visited—I'm guessing that's why my ancestors chose it for their secret tunnel." Tai strides to the opposite end of the cavern. A slender wooden door—indistinct and easy to miss—sits against the stone walls. He taps one of its narrow hinges. "Take a look."

It takes me a moment to realize he's indicating a tiny space between the door and the wall. I pull the lantern as close as I can and peer through.

Three bronze automatons stand clustered in the narrow passageway beyond. Each holds a sword. They appear skeletal, with narrow limbs no wider than bones. Exposed gears are visible within their torsos, which look like brass cages with flat, horizontal bars. Unlike the painted automatons that served Kang, these have blank plates for faces. I drag my eyes down the metal frames, wondering how I'm going to destroy opponents that don't appear to have any vulnerable spots.

"This is as far as I made it," Tai says. "When I saw the automatons, I knew I'd need more than my staff to get past them."

"Well, now you have me." I give my sword a confident swing. "How does this door open?"

"I . . . haven't figured that out yet."

"Alas." I raise my blade over my head and bring it crashing down on the door. A burst of wood chips and red sparks flies up. The door must be guarded by magic as well. The force from the impact ripples up my arms. It feels good to destroy something—especially when it's standing between me and the answers I need. Jagged shadows play along the edges of the deep groove I created. I yank the sword out and prepare to swing again.

Tai shoots me a surprised look. "Sure, why not?" He raises his staff. The weapon shimmers as if underwater and transforms into a sword with a broad, silver blade etched with twists and swirls. They look like they could be writing in ancient characters.

Though I knew his staff hid a second purpose, my eyes nevertheless widen at the transformation. "Did Ibsituu make this weapon too?"

"Actually, it was Suyin who enchanted it. That was years ago, before she and the rest of the Yueshen were imprisoned by Mowang. It was a gift for my thirteenth birthday."

I tilt my head. "Really? I thought she didn't like you."

"She doesn't. But she's still my family, and I'm still hers. She told me she made it for herself but erred in one of the spells, and so I could have it since it was flawed anyway." He shakes his head. "I knew better than to believe her."

I'm not sure I understand Tai's reasoning, but his relationship with his cousin is his business.

We take turns hacking at the door, sending splinters and sparks flying. Beneath the thuds, the cracking of the wood, and the sizzle of magic, the sounds of mechanical whirring hum to life. The noise sends excitement pulsing through my veins.

My next hit widens the hole enough for me to glimpse the glowing amber lights of the automatons beyond. They must be activating.

I grab Tai's shoulder before he takes the next swing. "That should be enough."

He cocks his head with a puzzled look as I back away from the door, then lifts his brows. "Be my guest."

I cross one leg behind the other and leap sideways into the door, using the extra force to launch myself off the ground and driving my heel into the fragmented wood.

I barely have time to regain my footing before a bronze sword descends upon me, glinting from the glowing yellow eyes of the automaton that wields it.

CHAPTER TWENTY-SEVEN

PASSAGEWAY TO TRUTH

T he air glitters with the orange and yellow sparks of magic impacting magic. Energy and heat thrum through the air. The automaton presses down on my weapon, and I push back as hard as I can but can't seem to make it budge. Beside me, weapons clang and crackle as Tai engages a second.

The machine's mechanical eyes glow gold, but otherwise, it has no face. Just a smooth, copper mask. An unnatural, yellowish-green light shines below, but I don't dare look down to find its source. I twist to free my sword from under its blade. My heel hits something solid behind me—the wall. Without my sword to brace against, the automaton stumbles. I glimpse exposed gears whirring on the back of its head. Encouraged, I raise my sword high and strike down.

Though my edge impacts, all that does is fill the air with snapping noises and white flares. My mechanical adversary whirls so abruptly that it wrenches my sword, still caught in the gears, from my grip. A second machine swings at me. Gasping, I drop and feel the whoosh of the blade over my head.

"How are you doing over there?" Tai's voice rings out over the noise of clashing metal, whirring gears, and crackling magic. "I think I prefer fighting Ligui. How about you?"

"I'll take a Ligui over these metal monstrosities any day!" Glimpsing my sword protruding from the first automaton, I scramble to seize the hilt. I'm forced back when the second lunges at me.

"They seem to like you more than me. I ought to be offended."

"Do you *ever* stop joking?" I dive at my sword and reach it this time. The moment I yank it free, the second automatons strikes again. A cry of rage and frustration explodes from my throat. I stab its torso, driving the point of my blade between bronze bars. It stops against grinding metal gears.

"Look out!" Tai leaps to my side and blocks another automaton's sword. The bronze blade is close enough for me to feel the heat of its magic. Their crossed blades spark inches from my forehead.

My weapon—still braced against the gears—shifts upward. Something gave. "Hold them off—I have an idea!"

"Only if you ask nicely."

"*Tai!*"

"That didn't sound like a question." Tai's shoulder bumps against mine as he fends off oncoming blades.

I ignore his lopsided grin. Using my whole body to push, I drive my blade up into the automaton's gears. Horrible screeching noises grate against my ears. Tai's strange laugh ripples through the passage-way—what in the world does he find funny now? The automaton's metal body spasms, causing its weapon to jerk erratically. I find satisfaction in each crack of a breaking gear and dig my weapon deeper. The automaton's sword falls. Popping and sizzling noises erupt, and what looks like tiny threads of white lightning radiate from its torso and flow down my blade. An uncomfortable sensation—like a million bees buzzing under my skin—rushes up my arms, and a clink like shattering glass jangles for a brief moment. My sword abruptly slices all the way upward, piercing a gap in the automaton's metal shoulder from below. The machine collapses toward me, its yellow eyes fading to blackness.

Grinning, I yank my sword and kick the broken thing backward to free my blade. Wisps of black smoke seep from the fallen machine's torso.

"So that's how you destroy them." Beside me, Tai speaks between gasped breaths.

I move to defend him from an oncoming strike. "Your turn!"

Tai stabs the automaton closest to him. My world becomes a blur of blades as I hold off the attacking machines. Blood pounds in my ears and it hits me how idiotically I acted when I focused all my energy on destroying the first automaton. This would be a lot easier if I didn't have to worry about keeping those blades away from my vulnerable partner.

But I've started noticing a pattern in their movements. These machines possess no skill; they can only rely on the power of their strength to hit, hit, hit. That makes them predictable.

The damaged automaton's weapon falls, clanging as it hits the ground. A small bud of relief blooms in my chest. The passageway rings with snapping noises intertwined with the jangle of metal hitting metal. Finally, the automaton collapses.

As I parry the last machine's blade, Tai buries his sword between the bars of its torso. The heat rising from my skin seems powerful enough to fuel an engine, and I don't know if it's from the exertion or the anger. When the last bronze sword falls, I raise my blade over my head and bring it crashing down into the machine. The blow doesn't do more than dent the exposed gears, but it feels good to release some energy.

After the automaton's eyes dim, Tai throws me an incredulous look. "And I thought I was the reckless one." Though his words emerge smoothly, he speaks them between panted breaths. "I can't believe you left me to fend off three blades!"

"I knew you could handle them." I wipe the sweat from under my bangs.

Tai shakes his head. "You're welcome for saving your life."

"You're welcome for saving yours."

The warm light of the lantern, still hovering at the passageway's entrance, illuminates the crooked tilt of his grin. I feel my own face mirroring the expression as triumph swells in my chest.

The sense of victory dissolves as I glimpse black shadows swirling around the broken machine. I recall how smoke seeped from the first one I destroyed. Now it hits me—that wasn't just any smoke.

Inhaling sharply, I lunge at the materializing Ligui. A piece of it takes the shape of a boar's head, which lets out a great shriek as my blade stabs the blackness. But the rest of the thing keeps gurgling upward and forms a monster with ten heads conjoined at the torso.

Each resembles the silhouette of a different animal.

Tai's blade silences the boar head mid-screech. I step to the side to dodge a swiping claw—one of many. My back bumps up against something warm and solid: Tai's back. Though this Ligui is one entity, it's so large, with so many flailing appendages and snapping jaws, that it seems to surround us. Fury sharpens my vision, but the red edges are missing. I'm not fighting alone, not battling out of sheer rage. This time, I have a partner to rely on, and his back pressed against mine gives me a sense of security.

The walls shake from the creature's screeches, but after I drive my blade into the creature's side, it melts into the air. The echo of its cries hasn't yet faded before I glimpse another Ligui. A stream of black pours from the second automaton.

By the time I reach it, it's taken the shape of a large man. My sword finds its shoulder—prompting a great cry—but it doesn't strike back. Instead, it flies out the passageway's entrance.

A crackling noise spews from behind me. I spin. Tai decapitates a Ligui shaped like a giant lizard. More emerge from the broken automaton, erupting like an explosion of black smoke. Many are human-shaped. While that isn't unusual, I'm surprised to see them race toward the doorway, and their screams sound more like voices than the usual unnatural screeches.

One flies in a zigzagging pattern and morphs into a four-legged creature. Its human-shaped head remains, and I raise my sword, but it doesn't attack. It stumbles a few steps and morphs again—four legs joining into a single body as it becomes an enormous serpent. My eyes widen. It's as if the Ligui doesn't know what form to take.

Spotting more blackness rising from the third machine, I whirl. Tai destroys one Ligui before it can materialize. I slash the next—shaped like a human-sized fox—before its sharp claws can hit me. I spot something float toward Tai and move to hit it, but he catches my arm.

My confusion turns to shock as I realize what I'm facing. It's not the featureless blackness of a Ligui . . . It's a translucent woman. Her face is twisted into a grotesque mask—one eye enormous and bulging out of its socket, the other dragged down to her cheek by dripping bags beneath it. Her upper lip twists over gnashing teeth. Yet her nose and jaw appear . . . normal. Black patches obscure swaths of her body. Her arms are twisted at odd angles, like the gnarled branches of a dead tree, and her legs flail beneath the hem of a long, gray skirt. But the lines of silvery light crisscrossing her neck and hands carry a familiar gleam . . . The gleam of the Yueshen.

She darts away, then stops abruptly and spins, her long, black hair swinging over her shoulder. "I . . . found them . . . " Her voice is a rasping whisper. "All of us . . . in darkness . . . "

She screams and darts out the passageway.

"Wait!" Tai zips past me, glowing in his Yueshen form.

I sprint after them, but I'm not fast enough to keep up. I slow to a walk and stare out into the night beyond the tomb's wide door. Both the woman and Tai are already so far away I can't see them.

Questions hammer at my mind. Those Ligui *emerged* from the automatons—were they there the whole time? But how? Come to think of it, the automatons behaved like Ligui. They attacked without thought and without mercy with no regard for their own survival. Like the supernatural beasts, those mechanical terrors were things of pure aggression. Could the Ligui have possessed the automatons?

But that last one . . . she looked like a cursed version of a Yueshen woman, almost as if someone had tried to bind her body to that of a Ligui. I wish I could have questioned her.

I wonder how long I'll have to wait for Tai to return. Sweat pours from my forehead, and the breeze flowing in through the tomb's entrance brings welcome relief. A minute later, I spot a shadow flying down toward the tomb. I instinctively raise my sword, but lower it again when I realize it's Tai, returning in his shadow form. The white crescent glows on his neck. I swallow hard, as if I could swallow the automatic hatred the sight of it sparks.

This isn't the being that killed my father. The shadows fade as his feet touch the ground, and I relax at the sight of Tai's face.

"I couldn't find her," he mutters. "The moment she left the tomb, she vanished in a flash of silver light . . . like a Yueshen."

"Was she one of them—one of you?"

He furrows his brow. "She was no Ligui. Except . . . something's happened to her, and she's no longer fully Yueshen."

"How? And what was she doing in Kang's automaton?"

"I've never heard of any magic that could trap a Yueshen. Except . . ." Tai trails off. Even in the dim light, I can see his expression darkening.

I gasp. "Except the story you told me about your parents. Your father . . . he trapped your mother when they were young."

"It was only a game." Tai squares his shoulders. "We should continue." He speeds back to the passageway.

I rush to keep up. "Your father has been dealing in darker magic than anyone could have imagined. We both saw those Ligui emerge from the automatons. I think they *were* the automatons—somehow, they possessed and powered the machines."

"That's impossible." Tai seizes the lantern.

I step over the broken machines. "This is *his* secret chamber we're going to, and those were *his* automatons guarding it."

"Really? I'd forgotten."

"That's not funny!"

Tai laughs—a humorless, cynical laugh that puzzles me. "It must have been unintentional. Perhaps he was experimenting with strange new magic and didn't realize what the consequences would be."

"That's ridiculous, and you know it."

"Of course it's ridiculous! *Everything* about this is ridiculous! My father using Ligui to power machines? I've spied on him my whole life, but I've never seen anything that would explain him using forces of evil."

"That's probably because he was most guarded with it—or because you were only seeing what you wanted to see." I grab his shoulder and force him to face me. "*Bendan!* It's obvious what happened!"

Tai laughs again, and this time, he laughs so hard, he leans back against the wall. Some kind of madness must have gripped him, because I see nothing humorous in any of this.

"What's *wrong* with you?" As I step toward him, I notice a blood-stain darkening the upper part of his right sleeve. "You're injured!"

"Oh, right." He glances at his arm.

"Why didn't you tell me?" I stick my sword in its strap and rip at the hem of my tunic.

"I was a little distracted."

As I finish tearing a strip of cloth, I recall how he'd laughed while fending off the three automatons—and back when I first met him and hit him in the gut. "Do you always laugh when you're hurt?"

"It's either laugh at the absurdity or scream at the pain. I'd rather laugh." Though his mouth remains bright, there's a strained look in his eyes.

"*You're* absurd," I grumble. He doesn't protest as I examine his cut. He leans his head back and stares at the blank rock above us, still but for a slight flinch as I feel the edges of his wound. It's deeper than I'd hoped. I bite my lip and bind the wound as tightly as I can. "You need a doctor."

"We're not exactly in a position to fetch one."

"You should head back to Tongqiucheng. I'll continue alone."

He gives me a look that says that's the most ridiculous thing I could have uttered. "I'm not going to bleed to death. And I haven't come this far to turn back without answers."

That's exactly what I would have said in his position. I nod. "Then we'd better hurry before you lose enough blood to faint. I don't want to carry you out of here."

"Being carried actually sounds rather nice. I should have asked that automaton to aim for a deeper vein." After what he said about laughing and screaming, the grin he gives me suddenly seems tainted. It's no longer the carefree, irreverent expression I took it for. I wonder how many other laughs and smiles he threw on to conceal some kind of hurt.

We continue down the dark passageway. Only shadows accompany us, and the lantern isn't bright enough to illuminate the end. My mind keeps traveling back to the cursed Yueshen woman. Kang must have trapped her—but how? And was he the one who cursed her, or had she already been cursed, and whatever dark magic was meant to draw Ligui drew her in as well? And then there were her strange words . . .

"Who did the Yueshen woman mean when she said 'I found them'?" I wonder aloud.

Tai purses his lips. "When she flew away, she said, 'The vanished were with me.' I thought maybe . . . "

"What?"

Tai sucks in a sharp breath. "Before Mowang trapped them, the Yueshen had been disappearing without explanation. They would leave home one day and then . . . never return. It started many years ago—before my mother died—but no one has ever been able to find out what happened to them. And it wasn't just a few—it was dozens, which grew to hundreds."

I purse my lips. "Ibsituu told me about that. I thought Mowang was taking them."

"So did I. I thought I'd find them with the others in the Courts of Hell. But even after we defeated Mowang, they were still missing."

"You think the cursed woman was among the vanished, and that she'd been to wherever they were taken."

He nods.

"She emerged from the automaton . . . " I step in front of Tai. "What if Kang is the reason for the disappearances? What if he trapped them and cursed them—perhaps trying to use them as he does the Ligui?"

Tai's face spreads into an odd, humorless grin. "You don't know what you're talking about. My father would never do that—he married a Yueshen woman, remember? They're family to him. We don't even know for certain if the Ligui were part of the magic he used in the automatons."

"How *stupid* can you be?" Some kinder part of me warns that insulting him will only do harm, but my frustration shouts over it. "We saw the same thing!"

"Do you realize what you're accusing my father of?" Flickering shadows from the floating lantern contort his strange, pained smile. "Imagine if it were *your* father we were speaking of. What would you do?"

"My father would never—"

"Exactly."

I'd forgotten—again—that Kang is more than a ruthless viceroy to Tai. Dark magic, using Ligui, trapping and cursing innocent Yueshen . . . this is the kind of wickedness only Mowang should be capable of. The idea of Kang possessing such evil comes easily to me, but . . . that's Tai's *father*.

There's more than one idiot in this tomb tonight.

"I'm sorry." Not because I think I'm wrong, but because of how callously I acted.

The smile fades from Tai's face, and I see fully the agony in his eyes. The disbelief, the willful denial that someone he loves could be capable of such evil. That's when I realize that everything I said . . . he knows it as well as I do. He just doesn't want it to be true. I hope for his sake that I'm wrong.

Whatever the case, the truth lies beyond the shadows obscuring the passageway's end.

DARKER THAN HELL

I expected to walk into some kind of study, perhaps a cramped library stuffed into a cave. Instead, I face a cavern that seems as wide as the Courts of Hell. Infinite darkness stretches beyond the lantern's meager light, which flashes off gleaming surfaces and offers a tantalizing glimpse of what might stand before us. Something shimmers like water ahead, and I wonder if we've stumbled upon an underground river.

"I think I preferred the Courts of Hell," I murmur. "At least there we knew what we were dealing with."

"Are you saying my father is worse than the demon king?" Tai approaches, a carefree look settled firmly on his face.

I choose not to answer and take a few slow steps forward. The darkness doesn't budge. I can see the entire sphere of light cast by our one small lantern, and it doesn't illuminate anything. I shudder at the enormity of the space. Yet the hollow echo of my footsteps indicates that there must be walls—an end somewhere.

I'm about to pull Anshui's spectacles from my pocket when the cavern blooms to life. Splashing noises pepper the cool, dank air as glowing bronze lanterns rise from a vast lake stretching before me. With their round shapes, they remind me of a million fireflies. Tiny propellers hum softly as they scatter throughout the darkness, bit by bit pushing it back with their golden light.

I stare with awe and disbelief at what they reveal: a great armada of bronze dragons and flying ships. Golden brown sails scallop down proud masts, and grand propellers protrude from the sides of broad hulls. The larger ships are decorated with the heads of dragons or tigers or phoenixes, while the smaller ones look almost identical to the little single-mast boat Tai and I rode upon. The waving bodies of the dragons curve out of the water and dip back down, forming glittering arches. With their raised metal heads and yawning mechanical jaws, they look as if they're screaming at the sky.

I'm so overwhelmed by the sheer number, I almost don't notice that some of the machines appear unfinished. One ship near the shore is little more than a bronze skeleton housing complex engines. A dragon not far from it sits with the wide doors open, exposing the metal tubes winding through its body like veins. Enormous as this fleet is, Kang apparently isn't finished.

Considering the landscape outside, this must be the hollowed-out inside of a mountain—and machines fill nearly the entire space. They make Kang's current fleet appear tiny . . . In fact, I'm sure the Emperor's own navy is not so great. Though the ships and dragons currently sit deactivated on the water's still surface, the sight of such power to destroy makes my heart quiver.

The Emperor would never allow such a force to exist. Enough news trickled to Dailan for me to know that the Emperor dislikes it when regional governors grow too powerful and forbids anyone from wielding magic greater than his own. With this armada, Kang could conquer entire nations. The Emperor would be furious if he knew.

I turn to Tai. "Did you know about this?"

"Of course not." His eyes are round. "That explains why he needed the River Pearl. Can you imagine how much magic it would take to power this fleet?"

Whispering voices chatter past my ears, speaking sharp syllables but lacking words. It's as if someone ripped a language apart and scattered its beads. Yet there's a desperation to the sound. A frosty sensation tiptoes down my spine as I'm reminded of the similar whispers I heard on board Tai's ship.

Release me . . .

I whirl toward Tai, who shoots me a puzzled look.

"Did you say something?" he asks.

I shake my head. "What was that?"

Light . . . I beg you . . . Give me light . . .

From the confusion on Tai's face, I know he heard it too.

Darkness . . . So much darkness . . .

The whispers shimmer with an uncanny quality that chills me to the core. Tensing, I look around, but I see only lifeless machinery, still water, and silent stone.

I recall the otherworldly voice—the one that sounded like my father—that called to me on board Kang's flagship. That was the closest sound I'd heard to these voices . . . But what does that mean? Are the dead trying to reach us?

Where am I? Where am I? Where am I?

Free . . . Set me free . . .

I've lost the light . . . Can you help me find it? I've lost the light . . .

"Any ideas?" A slight quiver in my voice betrays my nervousness.

"My father is preparing a fleet that can conquer the world." Tai shrugs, but his grip tightens around his sword. "He must have been very noisy while constructing it, since apparently he's awakened the dead."

I peer at the unfinished dragon. The exposed machinery inside—a mishmash of gears and tubes and cylinders and wheels—fascinates me. "He couldn't have built all this alone."

"And yet, I have a feeling he did. If he'd hired laborers, he would have had hundreds—no, thousands—of people who knew what he was up to. Swearing them to secrecy would only do so much to keep so many contained. Not to mention the budgeting nightmare that would come from paying them . . . can you imagine trying to hide such a cost from his treasurer?"

I huff. "So you think he hollowed out a mountain and hammered together a fleet of flying ships by himself? Even if he did, who's going to fly them?"

"Well, he *is* brilliant at magic. Perhaps he created a spell to make them build and fly themselves."

I start to retort but pause when I realize he's probably right. Magic is greater and more complex than anyone can imagine—Anshui told me that once.

Since I'm not going to get any answers by staring, I march along the edge of the lake in case there's more than a fleet here.

Tai jogs to catch up. Tawny light from the hovering lanterns covers every craggy wall, leaving hardly any shadows. Since they only activated when Tai and I entered, Kang must have enchanted them to illuminate upon detecting a person's presence. If he were to come down to the cavern, he'd know right away that someone's here. We need to move quickly.

A small one-story building comes into view. It's more akin to the humble houses of Dailan than the magnificent tiered structures of Tongqiucheng. Abstract patterns of red and green and blue zigzag along the trim, and carved dragons frame the open doorway.

Tai dashes to it. I shove my sword into its strap and follow. By the time I arrive, he's already inside and examining a copper device. It looks like a spherical cage protruding from the end of a metal cylinder. Intricate symbols, similar to what Ibsituu carved into the sword that defeated Mowang, snake across its golden body. And it's the right size for the River Pearl.

"What is that?" I ask.

"No idea. It was just lying here." Tai gestures at the wide, lacquered desk before him.

A high-backed chair, decorated with graceful swirls, sits behind it. The one-room building is filled with shelves. The dark wood slashes downward at harsh right angles. Brown dowels protrude from the ends of yellow and tan scrolls. Curious, I seize one and unfurl it on the desk. The bound strips of bamboo clatter against the table, adding their voices to the strange symphony of whirring lanterns and continuing whispers—some that carry odd words, and some that only convey desperation and fear.

Let me go . . .

Tell me why . . . Why . . .

Please . . . It's so dark . . .

I do my best to focus on the black characters inked across the scroll. But they swim and swirl before me—like they always do—and my heart thunders. Concentrating hard, I trace each stroke, forcing my mind to perceive characters instead of jumbled symbols. But my progress is slow.

Beside me, Tai stares at a scroll he pulled from one of the shelves. This one is made of paper, and it crackles as he spreads it.

I lean closer to the one I'm examining, as if that might help me read better. Eventually, I'm able to piece together the meaning of the first column of characters—it's a poem, an ode to the power of steam. While that seems useless, there are still several columns to go.

Meanwhile, Tai rolls up his scroll and grabs another one.

"What did that one say?" I ask.

"Just a description of a steam engine. How about yours?"

"I'm working on it." I go back to my deciphering, wishing Anshui were here. She'd absorb all these characters in a heartbeat and tell me not just what they said, but every possible interpretation of the text.

Tai rolls up the next scroll. He glances at me, and his brow furrows. "Didn't realize you were an admirer of poetry."

I scowl. "There might be more than poetry here."

"Is now really the time to become a literary critic?"

Heat rushes to my cheeks as I realize that he's already read the entire scroll at a glance—and that it really is only a long poem. Which I would have realized before wasting so much time if only my brain weren't so averse to the written word.

I roll up the scroll, shove it back into the spot I took it from, and grab a second.

Meanwhile, Tai has unfurled another. This one has diagrams, which I can understand much easier. The brushed black lines look like the inner workings of an automaton.

"What does that say?" I ask.

Tai shakes his head. "I was hoping it would tell me what the Ligui have to do with the automatons, but it's an early prototype. It still has placeholders for the types of magic to be used."

I spread the scroll I grabbed. Though I hate to ask, I know he'll read it much faster than I could—and at least tell me if it's useful before I waste my time perusing it. "What about this?"

"A treatise on Imperial politics . . . It says so right in the title. Can't you . . . ?" He trails off and pulls his lips in.

He's wondering if I'm illiterate. It's not an outrageous assumption, considering that half my village can't read. Father, who spent so many painstaking hours teaching me despite his peers saying it was pointless to teach a girl, would weep if he knew. I powered through those lessons, powered through my tears of shame and frustration, but though I absorbed the knowledge, it never came naturally to me.

Now that I know that Tai's the viceroy's son, I realize he comes with a whole host of assumptions that he wouldn't have if he were born as poor as I am.

"I *can* read. It's just difficult. Characters don't speak to me the way they're supposed to. That's all." I roll up the scroll and shove it back into its slot. "I'm not a simpleminded peasant."

Tai places a hand on my shoulder. "I would never think that of you. I'm sorry if I insulted you—that was not my intention."

I exhale, deciding to accept his apology.

We spend the next several minutes looking through scrolls, hoping to find something that might explain what we've seen. Meanwhile, the whispering voices continue scratching at my consciousness.

Why . . . Why won't you liberate me . . .

Dark . . . I must destroy the dark . . .

Can nobody hear me . . .

A strange laugh escapes Tai. "Oh, Father. You're so predictable."

I peer down at the bamboo scroll before him. It stretches across the entirety of the table, yet its end remains rolled in his hand. "What is that?"

"A plan. My father is apparently aiming to use this fleet to over-throw the Emperor and install himself as ruler. Not surprising, really. The Emperor wouldn't stand a chance . . . His forces are embroiled in the Border War, and he has nothing that can compete with a flying armada. Still . . . "

Despite his light tone, the dismay is plain in his eyes, and I can hear what he would have said: *Still, I hoped it wasn't true.*

Just having this secret armada constitutes treason—which is pun-ishable by death. The right thing to do is obvious: warn the Emperor of Kang's betrayal. And from the look in Tai's eyes, he knows it too.

"Your father isn't who you think he is." My words sound hollow, even to me.

Tai gathers up the scroll with such fury, I fear he'll rip it to shreds. But he only returns it to its rolled state. It looks so innocuous—a fragile column of paper and ink—that I can hardly imagine it contains the downfall of a nation. "Father used to say he could run this country better than the Emperor. I thought it was idle talk."

He slams the scroll onto the table and buries his face in his other hand. His shoulders shake, and for a moment, I think he's crying. But then I hear muffled laughter behind the palm pressed to his mouth.

I don't know what to do. The answers are clear to me—Kang intends to overthrow the Emperor. I may not have any particular loyalty to the Emperor—especially since he ignored Dailan in its most desperate hour—but I've seen enough of Kang to fear his ascendance.

He must be stopped. It's not even a choice to me—it simply *is*. Any hesitation I might have for Tai's sake evaporates. I could sacrifice my own revenge for him, but this . . . this is bigger than either of us.

And he knows it. That laugh—that harsh, cynical, tortured laugh—tells me so.

"*Tai!*"

He inhales sharply. "There's more. This new fleet is different from the one he currently commands—it can fly itself without need for human operators. And it can be controlled as one unit, though this doesn't say how."

I press my hand against my forehead, unable to imagine how much magic it must have taken to build such a thing. "How long did this take him?"

"According to the dates on the scroll, he's been planning this since before my mother died . . . " He shoves the scroll at me. "Here. I might burn it by accident."

He strides to the doorway. My heart aches for him. I wish there were something I could do, but comforting people has never been my strong suit. I'd probably make things worse.

Clutching the scroll, I contemplate what to do next. The Emperor must be warned—but how? The capital would take weeks to reach. Meanwhile, Kang's sure to notice that his plans have gone missing. With his flying ships, he could easily beat me there; for all I know, he could twist things to cast *me* as the traitor. And my people would suffer from Kang's retribution.

One question nags at me: *What is Kang waiting for?* His armada may not be complete, but surely he has enough to act. My mind wanders back to the River Pearl . . . how hungry he was for it, how much magic it holds. But it couldn't be what he needs to activate the armada—after all, he flies the same ships now, though in smaller numbers.

"Anlei! Over here!"

I run toward Tai's voice, following the curving shore of the underground lake. The bow of a massive barge protrudes past the water, blocking what lies beyond. When I round it, I stop in my tracks.

Tai stares at rows of mechanical beings identical to the ones that attacked us in the passageway. They stand in perfect lines, their faceless heads watching the lake with dead mechanical eyes. Their numbers must be at least ten times—no, twenty times—the entire population of Dailan.

Just the sight of so many makes me dizzy. "This . . . This is the army he's going to conquer the Empire with."

"Why would he need it?" Tai approaches the machines, his eyes wide. "He has so many loyal soldiers . . . and people with cyborg enhancements are stronger than purely mechanical automatons."

"Soldiers could question or even resist," I muse aloud. "Machines would do whatever he says, no matter what."

"And they couldn't leak his secret."

"But *we* must. Tai, we have to warn the Emperor at once." I place my hand on his arm. "This isn't about you or me anymore."

Tai stares at the ground. For several moments, he doesn't speak, and a muscle works in his clenched jaw. I watch him, my hands tight around the scroll. If he doesn't agree, I'm prepared to complete this mission on my own, even if he tries to get in my way. But my heart tells me it won't come to that.

Meanwhile, the voices continue swirling around us.

Just one ray of light . . . I beg you . . .

Tell me who I am . . .

Free me from darkness . . .

Finally, Tai gives a single, sharp nod.

I release a breath. I hadn't realized how tense I was until that moment. I turn to leave, but stop in my tracks when I hear the latest whisper.

Tai . . . Cousin . . . Is that you? And the human girl . . . Anlei . . .

CHAPTER TWENTY-NINE

VOICES

*D*arkness . . . So much darkness . . . Cousin . . .

Her voice is whispering, distant, like an echo without a call attached to it. Yet she feels near.

"Suyin?" Tai glances around wildly.

Who speaks to me from the darkness?

"Suyin! Where are you?" Tai searches his surroundings with quick, birdlike jerks of his head. "Suyin!"

Tai . . . Anlei . . . Is it really you?

Why is her voice among those of the strange ghosts that seem to haunt this cavern? Who *are* they? Ghosts have been known to wander tombs before, but Suyin can't be among them . . . Could she? "Is she . . . ?"

"She's alive. I just spoke with her yesterday."

"Are you sure?"

Tai's expression hardens, and he turns away without answering.

I hate to think that Suyin might have died suddenly and somehow joined the underworld chorus surrounding us. Yet if she's alive, how could—

"Remember the cursed woman in the passageway? What if there are more like her trapped inside these machines, and *that's* whose voices we're hearing? What if Suyin is among them?"

"That's impossible. She's family—my father's own niece. Do you really think he'd curse *her*?" Tai lets out an incredulous laugh.

"Of course he would!" My mind reels with a mix of excitement and horror. Excitement because the pieces are clicking into place—and horror because of what it would mean. There are so many voices around me—uncountable, impossible how many. If each belongs to a cursed Yueshen, then that means Kang has trapped numerous people—so many, he *must* have been responsible for the Yueshen who went missing before Mowang captured them.

Tai shakes his head at me and wanders down the rows of automatons. I want to knock him out of his denial, and the surest way to do that is to find Suyin. Though I should be racing to the capital with the plans we found instead of worrying about this, I can't abandon Tai—not now.

Cousin . . . If you're there . . . Bring me light . . .

Suyin's whispering voice seems to be everywhere and nowhere at once, wrapping my ears from every direction. She, like the Yueshen woman we encountered in the passageway, must have been cursed and bound to one of Kang's machines. I shiver. No one deserves that fate.

I draw closer to the automaton army and grab my sword in case they spring to life. But they remain motionless as I wander past them. Lanterns bob in the air, causing yellow sparks to dance upon their bronze limbs. Behind the rows of mechanical warriors, I spot several partially formed automatons lying side-by-side on the ground. Some are only torsos with their bars splayed and gears exposed. Others have only one or two limbs attached, or are only a head and an arm connected by a shoulder. The automatons closest to them are not part of the formation, but face away from it—toward their incomplete artificial comrades. And their fingers, instead of clutching swords, end in gleaming tools.

Are they building others of their kind? Did Kang enchant his machines to multiply? That would explain how he has so many. And if he could enchant an automaton to create another automaton, then it's certainly possible that he could enchant them to create more complex things— like mechanical dragons and flying ships. *That must be how he's building his fleet. It's clever . . . If only automatons work for him, then there's no risk of someone turning against him and warning the Emperor.* If Kang weren't using his brilliance for such vile purposes, I might be impressed.

You . . . Human girl . . . You . . .

"Suyin?" I whirl, but find nothing behind me. Yet that time, I was certain the sound *was* coming from behind . . . There was something more pointed about it.

Here . . . I'm here . . .

Definitely right beside me—the automaton to my left. I drive my sword through the machine's torso before my mind has a chance to catch up.

"Anlei!" Tai rushes toward me.

I look up in alarm, expecting to see the automaton's eyes light up. But it remains dark, deactivated. I exhale sharply and angle my blade upward. Since I'm only holding it with one hand—the scroll remains in my other—the action takes more effort. My muscles quiver from the strain. The cracking sounds of breaking machinery pop around me, but no sparks burst from the machine.

By the time my blade pierces through the automaton's shoulder blade, Tai is beside me. He swings his sword in time to decapitate an emerging Ligui before it can settle into its animalistic shape. I kick the automaton to free my weapon. My blood rushes, anticipating action.

But none comes. Instead, a human-shaped shadow speeds upward, releasing an agonized wail. More shadows pour forth, and though I strike at them, they ignore my blows as they flee. Like the Ligui in the passageway did.

What looks like steam pours from the fallen machine, taking the form of a translucent man as pale as moonlight and shimmering like water. Unlike the cursed Yueshen we saw previously, he looks entirely human, with a tall nose and a graying queue.

He doesn't acknowledge us, instead dissolving into nothingness with a long, haunting sigh.

"He . . . wasn't one of your kind, was he?" I ask.

"Yes and no." A warped smile curls Tai's lips. "He wasn't Yueshen, but then again, neither am I—fully, at least. He *was* human, and so am I—partly. Though unlike him, I'm quite alive."

"He was a *ghost*?"

Before Tai can reply, another being emerges from the automaton. At first, I think it's another Ligui—and it certainly looks like one, with its shadowy, falcon-shaped body—but then it shifts, stretching into a human woman. Except her face is twisted and deformed, with her nose higher than both eyes and her mouth spread across her chin. Her lips move, but no words emerge—only garbled syllables. Her whole body darkens and shrinks. I gasp. She takes the shape of a falcon once more, her limbs compressing and contorting. But parts of her body remain translucent instead of turning to shadow. The falcon's wings are elongated hands, and both of the bird's eyes appear human even as a sharp beak protrudes from what would have been a nose.

The creature opens its beak and lets out a high-pitched shriek that's somewhere between a Ligui's screech and a woman's scream. It—or she?—zips past us.

I gape as the being weaves between the floating lanterns.

"Cousin?"

I whip back toward the automaton in time to see Suyin emerge from its bronze body. She looks the same as she did the last time I saw her, but her frantic expression robs her bold face of its authoritative air. Though she's translucent and glowing, she appears dimmer, as if someone tossed a black veil over her.

"Suyin!" Tai shifts into his Yueshen form and floats toward her.

She opens her mouth as if to speak, but widens it into a yawn and thrusts her hands out toward Tai's neck as she lets out a piercing scream.

Tai grabs her wrists. *"Suyin!"*

She kicks at him, still screaming—no, screeching. I raise my blade, but before I can act, Suyin freezes abruptly. "Tai? Are you Tai?"

"Last time I checked." Tai releases her wrists.

I regard Suyin, wondering what happened to her. She *appears* fine, but she just emerged from a supernatural trap that also held Ligui and . . . and what, exactly? Ghosts of dead humans and cursed Yueshen who could shift into animals?

"You." She points at me with a shaking finger. "You're human . . . You're *human!*" She springs toward me, her eyes filling with a feral rage.

I hold up my sword, but Tai tugs her back before she reaches me.

"Suyin!" He gives her hand a jerk, and she spins to face him. "What's wrong?"

"Earth . . . I was drawn to the earth . . . " Suyin relaxes, and she glances at me. "Anlei?"

I nod, unsure of what to make of any of this.

Suyin digs both hands into her flowing black hair. "The earth was a great magnet, and I a tiny scrap of metal . . . I, a tiny . . . " She looks at her translucent hands. "Am I a ghost?"

"You're Yueshen." Tai's voice is calm, but his brows are low with confusion.

"Of course . . . many of us were." Suyin's eyes widen. "Tai! Cousin! You found me!" She faces me again. "You're the human girl who helped free us from Mowang! What's your name?"

"You just said it." Whatever happened to Suyin when she was trapped, it's causing her to forget who she is—and what everything is.

She arches her brows. The expression is disdainful, but at least she appears in control of herself again. "Have some respect when speaking to a Yueshen noblewoman, Anlei." A panicked look fills her eyes. "I must speak quickly, before the madness returns."

"What—"

"Listen!" She cuts me off. "I was drawn to the earth by a strange force that overpowered my will. I couldn't think, and I didn't know what was happening. Everything went black, and when I woke, it remained so. I was in total darkness, unable to move and barely able to speak. Most of the time, I couldn't hear anything either, though I sensed the silent screams of the others trapped with me. Once in a while, I'd hear snatches of the world. I started forgetting who I was. All I knew was that I was trapped, and that I had to attack, but I couldn't move alone. I was no longer me, but an extension of a monster. Then I heard you . . . both of you . . . I tried calling to you, but I didn't know if you heard me. After that, light flooded everything." Her words become quick, breathless. "Some of those around me were Yueshen as well—we couldn't speak with each other, but I felt the connection. But they were broken, twisted into something nearly unrecognizable. And they kept twisting and twisting until there was nothing left of who they were."

"So they were cursed?" Tai asks.

"We were all cursed the moment we were drawn into the darkness." A strange glint fills her eyes, and she darts upward.

"Where are you going?" Tai chases her as she flies toward the cavern ceiling, where the other beings that emerged from the automaton are now clustered.

Suyin stops abruptly. She dives toward me, her mouth stretching into a scream, but she freezes before she lets it out, a look of horror filling her expression. "Something . . . It keeps tugging at me, telling me to join the others, and that we must attack."

"The curse." I think back to all the beings that emerged from the automatons, and I realize something. It's so bizarre that I want to dismiss it at once. Yet after what I saw, I can't deny it.

I glance at Tai, who now stands on the ground beside Suyin, wondering if it occurred to him too.

Tai meets my gaze. "The Ligui are Yueshen, aren't they? That's what you want to tell me, right?" He bursts out laughing.

I stare at him in bewilderment.

He doubles over and sinks to the ground, dropping his sword. "You're right . . . Of course, you're right . . . I kept hoping I'd find something to prove you wrong, but it's all right here . . . " He buries his face into his knees, his shoulders shaking. "And to think, all that time I was wondering what happened to my people, the answer was right in front of me . . . " His words dissolve into mirthless laughter.

Kang created the Ligui. He built traps to draw spirits into his machines, using them to power his inventions. Some were spirits of the dead, and some were living spirits—the Yueshen. *That's* the great secret behind his genius—and it must be the darkest form of magic. Any rage I've felt toward him before seems like mere flickers of light next to the enormous conflagration burning my veins.

Inside the traps, the spirits lose themselves, their minds poisoned and destroyed by the dark magic. Suyin had only been trapped for a matter of hours, but she was already starting to forget who she is. As time passes, the tortured spirits must evolve into Ligui . . . and those that escape the machines attack the living.

That means Kang is responsible for every Ligui attack I've ever defended against. For every death suffered. My mind flashes back to those moments on the viceroy's flagship when I thought I heard my father's voice. Horror pours into every crevice of my being as I realize that it probably *was* him, trapped in the walls of the ship, lost in the dark magic. And the ship Tai and I took across the sky—that was powered by the same evil.

My stomach coils with disgust, and guilt pierces my chest. All those whispers we heard—those were ghosts and Yueshen . . . the very people we were going to rescue.

My blood calls out for Kang's. Not even the sun itself burns as hot as my wrath. I want to destroy him through and through, want to throw him into the Courts of Hell and watch demons inflict as much pain upon him as he ever caused the world.

Tai's mad, humorless laughter rings through the cavern. He knows as well as I do what his father wrought, and not even the strongest loyalty could hold up his denial.

Sorrow fills my chest, pushing past my rage. I hate Kang with every fiber of my being, and yet . . . I find no satisfaction in knowing what he's done. No sense of triumph at uncovering his deeds, no righteous victory at revealing his true nature. I want . . . I want it to not be true. I want him to be the man Tai hoped he was—a stern but just leader, a war hero, a caring father.

But no amount of wishing will bring that illusion to life, and we can't let disbelief keep us from action.

"Tai!" I shove my sword into its strap and lean down toward him, but when I try to touch his shoulder, my hand passes right through. He's in his Yueshen form.

His face remains buried in his knees, and his shoulders shake with muffled but uncontrollable laughter.

"*Tai!*"

I glance at Suyin. She seems herself once more, but her eyes keep darting upward to the other spirits circling near the cavern ceiling. "Suyin!"

She snaps her gaze toward me. "Yes?"

"Are you . . . you again?"

She lifts one sharp black brow. "If I weren't, you would know."

At least her cold arrogance means she's in command of her mind. The effects of the curse must be fading. "I need you to do something, and it's important." I hold up the scroll containing Kang's invasion plan. "Kang is planning to conquer the capital and install himself as ruler. These are his plans—proof of his treachery. I need you to deliver them to the Emperor." As a Yueshen, Suyin can transport herself to Zhongjing instantly.

Suyin crosses her arms. "The Yueshen do not trouble themselves with human politics." I start to retort, but she holds up a hand. "But Kang is our enemy too. I'll see it done."

I give her the scroll.

She glances at Tai and hesitates. "You'll get him out of here?"

"Of course."

She flies away, becoming a silvery streak as she zips toward the cavern's entryway.

I draw a sharp breath and kneel beside Tai, who's still laughing madly. "Stop it! Why do you keep laughing?"

Tai glances up at me, his mad grin more tragic than any tears could have been. "Because it's what I do. When you grow up unwanted, you start wondering if you'd be better off without the world. If you take your situation too seriously, every deep river, every sharp blade starts looking like an invitation to freedom. And so I laugh instead . . .

I laugh at the absurdity that is my life."

The words pierce my heart. I wish I knew how to take his pain away.

"I should have just let you kill him. He's a dead man anyway. You might as well have gotten your revenge." The color in Tai's face fills in as he returns to his human form. "My father needs to die."

"He's *evil*." I don't know what else to say. I want desperately to say something kind, to alleviate a pain I can't begin to understand, but my capacity for words is limited in the best of situations, and now it fails completely.

"I know." He tips his head back, and though the twisted grin remains on his face, his eyes glisten. "I think part of me always knew. He's never been what you might call 'good.' Intelligent and strong, but never kind or compassionate. Still, I wanted to believe everything he did was ultimately for the best. It's as if there were two of him—the viceroy the world saw and the father I believed he was. I'd tell myself that the latter was his true self and that any cruelty he showed was because of politics or some other force, that it wasn't really *him* . . . My mother loved him, after all. Enough to leave her people for him . . . perhaps he was different before she died. I was too young to really know, but . . . I remember joy. I remember love."

"Why are you telling me this?"

"I don't know." Tears spill down his cheeks, and he presses his palms into his eyes. "Because you're here, and I'm not considerate enough to ask whether you even care."

"Of course I do! Just because I don't know what to say doesn't mean I don't care."

"I'm not used to people caring about me." He drops his hands and inhales sharply. "I was raised by a rotating series of people who worked for my father. He was the one constant in my life, and I clung to that. I needed to believe he cared in his own way. My Yueshen relatives made it clear they didn't. As a child, I asked them if I could live with them. Father could barely look at me after Mother's death, and I thought they could take me to a new home. But they told me I wasn't one of them—that I'd never be one of them. So . . . that makes me no one."

"Everyone's someone." I hate how useless my words sound. "We . . . shouldn't stay here."

Sighing, Tai pushes off the ground and slowly picks up his weapon. "I want to believe that despite everything, there's still good in him. Though I guess it doesn't make a difference now."

Something catches his attention, and he sprints past the rows of automatons and toward the cavern wall. I spring up and race after him, wondering if a new kind of madness has possessed him.

He approaches a small cave hollowed into the wall. Within it lies a small shrine of red lacquer built to look like a miniature temple. Gilded stripes decorate its triple-tiered roof, the corners of which flick upward and end in little gold dragons. Beneath it sits a delicate porcelain noblewoman wearing a blue tunic decorated with blooms over a floor-length white skirt. A large headdress embellished with flowers forms a crescent over her head, and tassels dangle by both of her ears. Behind her, large gilded characters stream down the walls.

Beneath the shadow of the cave stretches a pristine box of the purest glass I've ever seen. Inside lies a woman—the same beautiful woman whose porcelain figure sits inside the shrine, dressed in the same garb. Her pearl-white skin is flawless. She's not a girl, but she's not old either. Black brows arch over closed lids with long lashes, and there's something familiar about her face—the angular chin, the broad mouth. Her hands are folded over her stomach. She looks as if she could be sleeping.

Though we *are* in a tomb, I've never seen anyone buried in glass before.

Tai's sword falls from his grip and clangs against the rock. He drops to his knees, pressing one hand against the glass.

"Mother . . ."

Kang must have used magic to preserve her body. Tai inherited most of her features—her sharp cheekbones carve across his face. But he said she died when he was only six. I find it disturbing that Kang kept his dead wife down here with him as he worked on his plan for conquest. He must have been more than in love with her—he must have been obsessed.

"I–I don't understand." Tai stares in shock at the lifeless woman. "My father told me she died in a boating accident . . . they never found her body . . . "

I crouch beside him. "He must have lied."

Tai shakes his head. His lips quirk into a humorless grin, and pained laughter explodes from his lips. His mouth widens as if he's trying to form words, but none emerge.

I hesitate, then place my hand on his shoulder. "Tai . . . "

He collapses against my shoulder, and the laugher dissolves into sobs. I wrap my arms around him and hold him close. What could I possibly say to make this better? What do you tell someone who's watched his world shatter layer by layer, each revelation crueler than the last? I've never felt so powerless in my life. His tears soak my clothing as I hold him tight, hoping my heartbeat will speak for me when my tongue can't. *Gods of Heaven and Earth, please take his pain away . . .*

"You have no right to be here." A low, ominous voice rumbles from behind.

Tai and I both look up, startled. Kang emerges from the stone beside the shrine, passing through it as though it were water.

CHAPTER THIRTY

THE ARMADA

K ang glares at me, his expression as black as his obsidian robes. Hatred bursts through my chest and overwhelms my senses. I jump up, seize my sword, and charge at him, eager to rid the earth of a treasonous murderer.

An automaton appears before him, emerging from that same sheet of rock, and blocks my blade. I twist to free my weapon, but a second—and then a third—and then a fourth—seep out of the cavern wall. The next thing I know, I'm battling a flurry of bronze swords while Kang strides away as if I ceased to exist.

Wrath and frustration threaten to rip apart my insides. I parry and dodge and strike back as hard as I can, but my blows do nothing. The only way I can stop them is to dig my blade up their torsos, but I can't do that alone.

"Tai!"

He remains kneeling by his mother's coffin, but the tears have stopped. Now, he's as still as a statue. I want to go over there and shake him back to reality, but with four automatons after my blood, I can't.

"Stop." Kang's voice, distant yet booming, echoes throughout the cavern.

The automatons freeze and stand at attention.

Still enraged, I plunge my blade into the torso of the nearest one, finding satisfaction in the popping and sparking of shattered machinery. When the Ligui emerge from the broken machine, I relish slicing them to pieces. But no sense of triumph accompanies this victory—I've wasted my energy on a still machine.

Gears clatter and machinery whirs as the mechanical army awakens. Their eyes ignite with yellow light. A sinking, sickening sensation fills my stomach.

"Don't be so foolish as to think you can fight your way out of this." Kang approaches with a disdainful expression. He clutches a copper device before him—the one we spotted in the building. Except now the River Pearl glows in the center of the metal cage. A cloud of white sparks glitters around the machine, as if someone pulled down the stars and clustered them all around this one thing.

Even from this distance, I sense its power humming in my bones. It's a low, subtle vibration, somehow alive.

The sounds of splashing call my attention to the lake. The bronze ships stir to life, propellers spinning and engines whirring. Steam rises in a great white cloud from the fleet, surrounding the floating lanterns. Metal clunks as the bronze dragons shift in place, awaking from their slumber. The ghostly voices grow louder. A shiver wracks my body.

"It's a shame." Kang pauses, still several yards from me. "I was rather looking forward to our wedding."

I scowl. "Your plan has failed. We've already warned the Emperor."

"Yes, I know." His calmness sends a shiver down my spine. "All that means is that I'll have to mobilize tonight—somewhat ahead of schedule, but no matter. The Emperor may know I'm on my way, but he won't have the means to stop me."

"How did you know?"

Kang gestures at the spot on the wall where he emerged. "This portal connects the cavern to my palace, making it essentially an adjacent room. When I retired to my chamber, I heard you through the wall telling the Yueshen girl to take my plans to the Emperor."

"She's your *niece!* How could you trap her like that?"

"I have no control over who the traps capture, so she shouldn't take it personally. Not that it matters. I learned years ago how little family means to some people." He glances at Tai, who remains crouched by his mother's tomb. "Like you. I know that you were the Masked Giver. What kind of son steals from his father?" He turns away with disgust and strides toward the lake, shimmering for a moment before settling into a translucent, glowing form—a Yueshen form. "I declared that those responsible for the River Pearl theft would be arrested for treason. My decree holds. You will both be publicly executed, and the Dailan villagers will be cast out of my city."

I find it almost laughable that he's accusing *us* of treason. I'm not the least bit surprised that he would so quickly turn me from bride to prisoner, but the casualness with which he spoke of executing Tai is chilling. How can this cruel, heartless man be Tai's father?

The three automatons that accompanied Kang stir back to life. Their swords clatter to the ground, and they reach at me with grasping metal hands.

I raise my sword, but pause. Fighting these things would be useless; I can't destroy them alone, and even if I could, more would replace them. As much as I hate running instead of fighting, sometimes that's the only choice.

I sprint to Tai and seize his arm, dragging him up. "*Kuai pao!* Come on!"

Tai looks at me with wide, confused eyes still wet with tears. I run, thinking he'll follow, but stop when I realize he's not behind me.

Instead, he soars across the lake in his Yueshen form, heading toward Kang.

What does he think he's doing?

The automatons rush at me. I dash forward, though I don't know where I'm going. The machines' clunking footsteps pound the rock. The space between the cavern's wall and the lake's edge narrows until only a few feet remain.

Sensing a movement behind me, I spin to find an automaton reaching for my arm. I dodge and kick its torso hard. It stumbles into the lake and vanishes beneath the surface.

I keep running but look back to see if it emerges. Its bronze fingers grasp the rock at the water's edge. Though it pulls its head up, it seems to be struggling to get out. *It can't swim!* With two other automatons close behind and another five joining the chase, my best chance for escape is to take a dive.

Before I can jump, a metal hand grasps my upper arm. Though

I yank with all my strength, I can't get free. I swing my sword in a desperate attempt to escape. Metal clangs uselessly against metal.

"Father!" Tai's voice rings through the cavern.

I look up to see him landing on the deck of one of the great ships. Kang, back in human form and still holding the device containing the River Pearl, ignores him. He strides toward the bow, flanked by two automatons that must have already been on board.

"Father!" Tai grabs Kang's shoulder, but his hand goes straight through.

I knit my brows, every bit as confused as Tai appears to be. The Yueshen are incorporeal to humans, but not the other way around. Tai should have been able to at least touch his father, as he was able to touch my hand outside the Courts of Hell.

Tai's body solidifies. In his human form, he runs up to Kang and grabs him again. This time, his grip lands. Kang spins to face him.

"Did my mother know?" Tai's voice is raw. "Did she find out about your dark magic? Did you kill her for it?"

To my surprise, Kang's face melts into an expression of sorrow. "I loved her with every fiber of my being." His voice is so unexpectedly gentle I almost wonder if he's someone else. All the cruel power and wicked strength he usually carries drains from his body, and he sags under the weight of grief.

The rest of the cavern seems to sag with him. Propellers stop spinning, machinery ceases to hum. The automatons grow still. Even the metal grip on my arm loosens.

On the deck of the ship, Tai glares at his father. "Answer me!"

Kang heaves a great sigh, and I'm surprised by how . . . human . . .

he appears. He's no longer the demon-like monster I percieved. "I spoke the truth when I told you her death was an accident. Yes, she found this place, as you did. And like you, she objected to my methods. I tried to make her understand . . . My dream was for us to rule together as Emperor and Empress. But she wouldn't listen . . . She tried to fight me, and I defended myself . . . I never meant for her to die."

Tai's expression crumples in shock and grief. His sorrow is so palpable even from here, I feel it stabbing my own heart. The truth was obvious from the moment we found his mother's body, but Kang's confirmation makes the reality even harsher. A stinging sensation crawls into my eyes, and I wish I were an almighty god who could rewrite reality to fix the past.

"Every time I look at you, it's her I see," Kang continues. "That's why I could never bear to be near you—because each time I saw you, I relived her death."

Behind my surprise, rage simmers in my core. Kang killed his wife—accident or not. I didn't think it was possible for me to hold any more hatred toward him, but the well seems endless.

Kang places a hand on Tai's face. "You're a piece of her, my son. I should have known you would betray me as she did."

I barely glimpse the flash of metal emerging from Kang's robe before he drives a dagger into Tai's stomach.

A scream rips from my throat.

Tai staggers backward, and a bloodstain blossoms across his tunic. Kang turns away, his expression cold. The two automatons seize Tai's arms and drag him to the railing. He seems too stunned to resist as they throw him overboard.

Energy explodes through my veins, fueling a burst of strength powerful enough for me to yank my arm free. The automaton reaches for me, but I dodge and leap into the lake. Cold water engulfs me.

The ships' propellers hum back to life. All I know is that I have to reach Tai and *now*. I swim toward the ship, only realizing several strokes in that I'm still holding my sword with one hand. I tread water and rush to stuff it into the strap on my back. Water splashes into my mouth, bitter and cold.

The weapon weighs me down, but I force myself forward. Tai floats several yards ahead of me. He appears limp, and I pray to the Gods of Heaven and Earth that I'm not too late.

Around me, the ships and mechanical dragons propel closer to shore and lower their gangplanks. Automatons file onboard in neat rows. A few remain behind and pace along the water's edge, waiting for me to return to shore.

Ahead, Tai sinks beneath the surface.

No, no, no . . .

My heart drums to the rhythm of *kuai dian! kuai dian!*, urging me to move faster. I dive underwater and force my eyes open. Light spills through the water in coppery shafts—enough for me to see his silhouetted form a few feet ahead. Dark blood swirls around him. I grab his motionless wrist, tug him toward me, and hook both arms under his shoulders, pressing his body to mine. Kicking hard, I pull him with me as I swim upward.

My head breaks the lake's surface. I gasp for air. Tai hangs limp in my arms, but I refuse to believe he's dead. Water blasts from the propellers of one of the ships, spraying my face. I cough and look around frantically. Where should I go?

Ships rise from the lake. They fly toward the cavern's dark ceiling and knock into the floating lanterns. Mechanical dragons snake into the air, belching steam. A crack appears in the cavern's ceiling, and a ray of sun pierces the shadows. More cut across the dark in jagged lines. Tiny pebbles, hardly bigger than grains of sand, rain down. The cracks turn to holes, which widen and widen to let in the dawn.

The shattered rock slides harmlessly off the machines but stings my skin. I bow my head and squeeze my eyes. Several get into my mouth as I breathe hard, trying to sustain my strength. I can feel it fading all around me from the effort of staying above the surface with the weight of my sword on my back and Tai in my arms. But I won't let go of either. One is all I have left of my father and the other . . .

Even if Tai's already dead, I can't leave him here to sink into dark waters.

He's not dead . . . He can't be . . .

The rain of pebbles stops. I open my eyes to see that nearly the entire hollow mountain has vanished. The sky stretches above me, pale blue and streaked with clouds. Dawn's first light glints off the tall masts and highlights the curved sails of Kang's fleet. Mechanical dragons swim gracefully through the sky.

The sight is at once magnificent and horrifying—a beautiful monster waking to destroy the world.

CHAPTER THIRTY—ONE

WILLING SPIRITS

Water sloshes across my face. I'm sinking, and it's taking more strength than I have to keep myself and Tai above the surface. I look around again, wondering if I can swim to a far shore before the automatons waiting along the near one can catch up.

Though most of the armada has taken off, a few vehicles remain. These must be the ones that were too unfinished to function, with their skeletal hulls and their lack of sails. The nearest one is a bronze dragon with a circular door gaping open in its side. It looks complete, but must be missing some engine or another to have been left behind. Whatever the case, it's far from the shore.

I swim as hard as I can with Tai in my arms. With each flailing kick, I'm sure I'll find myself towed under the lake by weariness. But I somehow make it without drowning.

I drag myself into the giant machine and pull Tai in after me.

Coughing and sputtering, I collapse beside him. My limbs feel as if they're made of stone, but I force myself to sit up. Tai remains motionless, lying face-up where I left him. My eyes burn, and I don't know if the wetness on my cheeks is from the lake or from tears.

"Please . . . "

I press my ear against his heart. A faint *thump* sends relief pouring through me. But it's short-lived as I notice all the blood staining his tunic. I may have saved him from drowning, but I can't stop the flow. He needs a doctor—no, a miracle.

He's as good as dead, and I can't do anything about it.

My sob reverberates against the dragon's curved walls. My heart hurts so much I want to rip it out and throw it into the lake. If I could somehow siphon off part of my life to preserve his, I would.

This isn't over yet. The fight isn't done—his heart still beats.

Above, early rays gild what remains of the cavern walls.

The walls . . . They're gone. Tai said there was magic in them that kept him from passing through them in Yueshen form, and I recall how Suyin, instead of vanishing, flew to the passageway. But if the walls are gone, perhaps the spell is too . . .

"*Suyin!*" I call for her because she's the only one I know who might be able to reach us. "Help! It's Tai—he's hurt! Help! Somebody! Please . . . *wo qiu ni . . .* "

A brilliant light shaped like a woman's silhouette appears, hovering above the water just beyond the dragon's doorway. For a moment, I think it's Suyin, but the light dims to reveal Ibsituu, floating with a silvery halo surrounding her white clothing and wooden beads.

I gape. "Are you Yueshen too?"

She smiles warmly. "No. But I recently perfected a spell that allows my spirit to leave my body temporarily. It's the one I was working on before you arrived at the temple— with all the strangeness in the spirit world, it seemed necessary. My physical self is still in Baiheshan."

I marvel at her abilities . . . I've only heard of people leaving their living bodies in legends before. Though I want to ask how she found us, I swat the question away as her gaze lands on Tai. She presses one hand against his forehead. Blue sparks dance from her fingertips.

Tai's eyelids flutter open. "Ibsituu?"

"I'm here." Her expression falls as she glances at his wound. "But your injury is beyond my ability to heal. Only the River Pearl's magic can save you—you must tell us what you saw when you read Kang's scroll about it."

Tai lets out a dry chuckle, which turns into a cough. "It won't work."

"Why not?" I ask. "You used it on me—how did you do it?"

He shakes his head.

Ibsituu's brow crinkles. "Come, Tai. This is no time to be coy."

"Sure, it is." He looks like he's trying to grin. "Now I get to take my secrets to my grave."

Ibsituu harrumphs. Her fingers flicker through the air, and Tai abruptly freezes in place. Magic glitters around his body, surrounding him in yellow and white flashes.

I glance up at Ibsituu. "What did you do?"

"I was tired of his jokes, so I froze him in time."

I stare at her.

She smiles. "It was clear he wasn't going to answer our questions, and none of us have time for his foolishness. My spell will keep his condition from worsening." She twists her wrist, and his eyelids fall shut. "There. Now they won't dry out while he waits."

"For what?"

"For you to save him. Like I said, only the River Pearl can heal this wound. When the spell breaks, it will be as if only an instant has passed. We can worry about asking how he made it work then. The spell won't last very long—not much longer than my astral projection—but at least it gives him a chance."

"How will I unfreeze him if you're gone?"

"The spell will wear off on its own—probably within the hour after I vanish."

I tap my fingers against my arms. "Kang has the River Pearl on board his flying ship. How am I supposed to get it alone?"

"You are not alone—you have me." She sits back on her heels. "I was drawn to this place by a great surge of dark magic, and when I arrived, I heard you calling. What happened?"

I explain what we discovered, speaking so quickly my words nearly collide into each other. I tell her about the automaton army and the plans to seize the Emperor's throne, and about how we concluded that Kang must be capturing spirits to power his machines, but that trap curses them to become something monstrous . . . Ligui.

Ibsituu angles her mouth into a sardonic smile. "It appears Tai was safe from those traps for the same reason he was safe from Mowang's: because he's half human. The trait the Yueshen disdain him for is also what's saved him from their fates."

I almost find that funny. "I don't really like the Yueshen, but I don't want them to suffer either. This has to stop."

She nods somberly. "It's all coming together now. Since we last spoke, I learned that the Ligui were summoned by someone on Earth, creating a tether between our world and the realms beyond. But I couldn't trace the tether's origins. All I knew for certain was that if it were severed, the Ligui would snap back to where they belong, and we would be free of them."

"That means Kang is the tether."

"Yes. The Ligui are bound to his life. To create the machines you spoke of, he would have had to force the spirits to behave as those machines would. The curse within the trap must force them to channel pure aggression and to move as one unit. That's why the Ligui attack at random and often in great numbers. It's also why some appear to be multiple creatures bound into one. They are not conscious beings."

That explains why their actions seemed so random. They had no purpose, no life—they were stripped of their souls, reduced to nothing but destructive instincts. "And they take the shapes of animals because they've forgotten who they are," I muse aloud. "Does this mean they're all damned?"

Ibsituu spreads her hands. "I don't know. I wouldn't think so—the Heavenly Gatekeepers would not be so cruel as to damn souls that were cursed by another. I believe their lives end when they become Ligui, but their souls are kept from moving on by the tether. It's possible that by slaying them, you were releasing them."

I think back to my days with the Dailan Guard. No matter how many we destroyed, whatever infernal source forms them seemed bottomless. "How are there so many? I know destroying the machines releases them, but Kang couldn't have had so many machines destroyed, could he?"

"His magic must not be strong enough to hold them forever, and the ones that escape become the creatures we've faced. They wander aimlessly as smaller groups until they're near enough to a swarm to be drawn in. You mentioned that a dozen spirits emerged from each automaton. That must mean his ships take hundreds, if not thousands. And he has to keep replenishing his machines with new spirits. I suspect that most are spirits of the dead rather than Yueshen." Ibsituu purses her lips. "Mowang captured the Yueshen because he knew someone was using them to develop a dark magic that could rival his own. Like me, he sensed the shadow over the land, and like me, he couldn't pinpoint where it was coming from. He was, in a way, protecting them, though in his mind, he was depriving an unknown rival of a fuel source."

"So by freeing them, we actually put them in worse danger." If Tai were conscious, he'd surely laugh. I almost want to. After all we went through to rescue the Yueshen from the Courts of Hell, it turned out that doing so risked sending them to a worse fate.

But none of this talk about the mechanics of Kang's evil has helped me figure out how to stop it.

"Can you fly me to the armada?" I ask.

"I'm afraid not." Ibsituu sighs. "I can cast spells, but otherwise, I cannot interact with the physical world, and casting a spell to give you flight would require different skills from the ones I currently posess— just as you may be talented with a sword but not a crossbow."

A silver light appears above the lake's center, materializing into Yueshen. Suyin stands at the front, and dozens of Yueshen men and women cluster around her, their long robes flowing. "Tai!" She whips her gaze around. "What happened to the fleet?"

"Suyin!" I wave.

She glances at me and vanishes. An instant later, she appears before me. Her eyes flick to Tai. "What happened to my cousin?"

"He tried to confront Kang. Ibsituu cast a spell to keep him from getting worse, but only the River Pearl can heal him."

"I should have known Tai would do something foolish," she scoffs.

My nostrils flare at her callousness. "Why you—"

"We're worried about him too." Ibsituu cuts me off and gives me a meaningful look.

I frown and try to figure out what I missed. Suyin certainly doesn't *look* concerned. Yet she did return for him, I suppose.

Suyin tosses her head. "Anyway, I delivered the message to the Emperor then gathered my people so we could destroy the machines and free any more of our kind trapped in them. Where did they go?"

I gesture toward the sky. "They left."

"Then we'll find them."

"Wait!" I exclaim before she can blink out. "Tai was in his Yueshen form when he confronted Kang, and Kang was human. Tai passed right through him."

Suyin arches her brows. "That can't be."

Ibsituu faces Suyin. "And who are you to declare what magic can and can't do? I know of a spell that can shield a human from the touch of any spirit—living or dead. Considering what Kang was working with, he certainly would have cast it on himself. Otherwise, the very Ligui he created would have killed him years ago."

Suyin frowns. "So none of us can kill him?"

"One of us can." Ibsituu shifts her gaze to me.

I lift my chin. "Get me to his ship, and I'll bring him down. Can you . . . transport me there?"

"No," Suyin scoffs. "That would take more strength than any of us possesses."

"Possess . . . " I turn to Ibsituu. "This machine was built to be powered by spirits—living or dead."

"Now there's an idea." Ibsituu pans her gaze around the mechanical dragon's metal interior. "Kang bound unwilling ones because it's easier to control than to persuade. But that doesn't mean willing beings couldn't move it."

Suyin lets out a high laugh. "You must be delusional! I just escaped from one of those traps—why would I return?"

"If you'd let me finish, you'd understand." Ibsituu crosses her arms. "You were cursed because Kang forced you. A willing spirit, one who consciously entered a machine, would not face the same torments. We would only need to listen when we heard the machine's commands. And I say 'we' because I, too, am currently in spirit form and will happily possess this machine to get Anlei to Kang. But I cannot do it alone. Neither can Anlei confront Kang unassisted."

"I'm more than a match for him!" I bite out.

Ibsituu cocks her brow. "I meant that he will be guarded."

Right . . . Kang would never leave himself alone and vulnerable. I'm not delusional enough to think I could cut down an army of automatons to reach him.

"We came prepared to fight." Suyin gestures at her people. "We will destroy whatever stands in our way."

"But remember, only Anlei can kill Kang." Ibsituu holds out her hand. "Will you join me in carrying her to our common enemy?"

Suyin purses her lips.

My heart pounds. "We don't have much time. If we don't leave now, we might not catch up." I find my eyes drawn toward Tai, still lying frozen at my feet, and silently add, *And the spell might wear off before I have a chance to get the River Pearl . . . which means he'll die.*

Suyin throws me a haughty look and vanishes.

"Suyin!"

Before I can say anything else, she reappears, accompanied by the other Yueshen, who form a shimmering wall of people behind her.

One of them—an older man with a graying topknot—turns to her. "This is the human girl, my lady? Are you sure she can destroy Kang?"

"Are you questioning me?" Though he's taller than her, Suyin manages to look down at him nonetheless. She whirls toward Ibsituu. "Tell us what we must do."

From the outside, the round window before me looks like the dragon's right eye. I gaze down at the controls beneath it. Though the mass of colored buttons, flashing lights, and bronze levers appears chaotic, a closer look tells me they're not so different from the ones I used on the ship I flew with Tai.

My heart quickens at the thought of him. He's still lying on the floor in the center of the dragon—there wasn't exactly a bed nearby, and I wasn't about to leave him behind.

I sense the living presence of the spirits around me. Ibsituu, Suyin, the Yueshen warriors—they're in the walls, the floors, the controls. They're the soul of this artificial beast.

I rev up the engines. If I understood Ibsituu correctly, that will also send a command to the spirits inside the dragon, and some combination of their movements and the machinery will cause the vehicle to activate.

I push a lever, commanding the dragon to rise, and twist the speed dial to maximum. I only hope I'll be able to catch up to Kang.

The dragon roars to life. Machinery whirs and magic crackles as it rises, carried on the backs of the spirits possessing it. Though I'm the only one standing behind these controls, I'm not alone. Once we get close enough to Kang's ship for me to board, Ibsituu, Suyin, and a half-dozen Yueshen she selected will emerge from the walls and join me in the fight. The rest will continue propelling the dragon and use it to keep the other ships in the fleet from assisting Kang.

The cavern and landscape outside streak into a blur of color—brown and green bronzed by the rising sun. Moments later, I'm in the sky.

The dragon stabilizes, hovering steadily in a sea of clouds. Ahead, I spot Kang's armada flying in the direction of the sun—eastward toward the capital. I'm surprised it's near enough to be within eyeshot.

I steer the dragon toward the flying fleet. Though it's been hours since I last rested or ate, I've never felt less tired. The dragon picks up speed, though I haven't touched the controls—the spirits must have seen the fleet as I did and sped up the pursuit. The machine now has a will of its own.

Outside the window, the dragon's enormous bronze jaws open. A fireball shoots out from between them, blasting toward the fleet. It hits one of the smaller ships at the armada's rear, and flames consume the vessel's sail. I watch it burn. That's one less to worry about. The dragon fires again, but misses widely. I spot a joystick and give it an experimental twist. The dragon's head—the part of the vehicle I'm standing in—jerks abruptly, and I nearly lose my balance. I tug the joystick more gently and align the dragon's jaws with the next closest ship.

Yellow fire streams from the machine. The Yueshen don't seem to need my command to know what to do.

Cannons protrude from the vessels ahead. One of Kang's dragons twists to face me. Realizing it means to attack, I seize the wheel and turn it hard. The blast impacts the side of my vehicle, sending me flying into the wall.

I grasp for something—anything—to hold onto while the mechanical beast pitches, either reeling from the other dragon's fireballs or trying to dodge them. The movements are frantic, directionless. The floor tilts, and I trip. My thoughts turn to Tai, who's probably being thrown across the vehicle too. He's frozen in time, but would that keep him from being injured when he lands against the metal floor and walls?

Anlei! You must take control! Ibsituu's voice whispers past my ears. *We can fire when you need us to, but we need direction!*

Gritting my teeth, I make my way back to the controls and seize the wheel. The other dragon approaches from the left. I grab the joystick and twist the dragon's head to face it.

"Fire!" I yell.

A stream of yellow explodes from my dragon's jaws and hits the enemy machine. What remains of its head—now a charred mechanical skull with exposed engines—turns toward me. I rush to steer my vehicle away from it, dodging its blast.

The metal beast flails. I turn the wheel, bringing my dragon alongside the other.

"Fire!"

A blast tears through the other dragon. This time, it's enough to rip apart what remains of the head—the control center. The rest of the machine remains airborne, but thrashes about erratically. A satisfied smile curls my lips. I've won my first victory against the armada.

A cannon from one of the remaining ships launches a blast at me. I turn the wheel but fail to evade the shot; the impact shakes the vessel, and I cling to the wheel's spokes to keep from falling. I try to aim the head of the dragon I'm piloting, but its movements are shakier than before. *The machine's damaged.*

Our one mechanical dragon can't defeat the armada when we're so outnumbered. I have to find Kang. *That's* what matters—not battling individual vehicles.

I focus on evading the attacks instead of firing back, hard as it is to pass up the opportunity to destroy. I think about Tai and how any moment, Ibsituu's spell could wear off and he could bleed to death. My heart pounds to the rhythm of *kuai dian! kuai dian!* as it urges me to hurry.

My one advantage seems to be speed. Perhaps having willing spirits helps the vehicle move faster. Or perhaps Kang is unconcerned with my catching up to him.

I weave the dragon between vehicles, dodging cannon fire and scanning the fleet for the ship I saw Kang board earlier. My guess is that it's at the front, leading the rest.

A glimmer of gold catches my eye, and I risk a glance down to see what it is. Several mechanical oddities zoom toward the fleet. Bronze phoenixes and metal butterflies—the kinds of flying novelties built to adorn festivals and amuse children, except much larger. They speed toward the fleet and crash into Kang's ships. Though they don't do much damage, they draw the cannons away from me.

My eyes widen. "What are those?"

The Yueshen have possessed them as well. Ibsituu's voice is barely audible through the rumble of the engines. *Suyin sent a messenger back to her people asking for help. This is how they answered.*

"That's amazing." At least the diversion will help me keep this dragon flying a little while longer.

Another blast shakes the floor. The ominous clunks of machinery surround me. A metal panel rips off the ceiling, and cold air blasts my face. I grip the controls so tightly my palms hurt.

Then, I spot it—the viceroy's flagship. The same dragon-headed vessel, with its majestic masts, enormous propellers, and tiered buildings that took me from Dailan. I would have noticed it if it were among the armada in the cavern . . . It must have been stored elsewhere, with the smaller fleet the Emperor knew about and condoned.

No wonder I was able to catch up. Kang didn't head to the capital immediately, but stopped to fetch his flagship. My lip twists in a wry grin. His pride will be his downfall.

Another panel flies off my vehicle. My mind turns with alarm to Tai and how he's lying vulnerable in another part of the dragon. If this machine goes down, he'll go down with it.

The dragon's head jerks abruptly without my command, and the jaws yawn open.

"No!"

It's too late—the fireball explodes against the flagship. I stare at the flames in horror. Destroying the flagship would mean killing Kang, but for all I know, it could destroy the River Pearl as well.

The flames dissipate. To my surprise, not a single scorch mark mars its gleaming hull. I twist my mouth, uncertain whether to be relieved. It appears that the viceroy built an indestructible ship.

No wonder he took the time to get it. He must have infused the flagship with additional powers to guard it against attacks. Perhaps he even anticipated that his own creations might be used against him. But that doesn't mean I can't board and confront him one-on-one.

The only way to get from my ship to his is to jump. My stomach plummets, but I haven't come this far to let fear stop me. Besides, people are counting on me. The spirits trapped by Kang's dark magic, the entire Empire . . . and Tai.

Thinking of him steels my determination. The enormity of all that's at stake weighs on my soul, threatening to overwhelm me, but focusing on one person gives me clarity. The thing that will save him is within reach.

Nothing will stand in my way. Nothing.

I bring the dragon closer to the flagship until I'm near enough that the deck appears to be only a few yards in front of the window. Cyborg soldiers pace across it. They must have joined Kang when he fetched his flagship. They'll be tougher foes than the clumsy automatons were.

I glance at the open space where the panel tore off. It's large enough for me to climb through. If I can crawl onto the dragon's snout, I can make the leap to Kang's ship.

Cannon fire blasts toward the dragon's side. I twist its body without changing the position of its head to avoid a direct hit.

"Keep the dragon in this position!" I shout over the noise. "I'm going to board the ship. Those of you who are joining me—now's the time."

Ibsituu seeps from a wall near the opening, her calm expression incongruous with the chaos around me. Yet fierceness radiates from her eyes. She lifts her hands. A bolt of blue lightning sparks between her palms. She appears more transparent than previously, and my eyes struggle to differentiate between her white clothing and the bright sky behind her.

Beside her, Suyin materializes with six Yueshen—three men and three women. Though none wear armor, I can tell at once that they're warriors. Clad in long, belted robes of bright green, they hold themselves with the practiced focus of soldiers.

Suyin gives me a quick nod and blinks out along with the Yueshen warriors.

Ibsituu places a translucent hand on my shoulder, though I can't feel it. "I'm reaching the limits of my astral projection, but I will remain as long as I can."

I swallow hard.

This means I have less than an hour to get the River Pearl and save Tai. I doubt I'll last that long on Kang's ship anyway.

"Good luck." Ibsituu soars to the flagship, where the Yueshen are already throwing silver spells at the cyborg soldiers.

I clench my jaw and duck through the hole in the wall. I turn to face the dragon's side, my back to the sky. Digging my fingers into the protruding edges of the panels—what looked like scales from a distance—I pull myself sideways toward the snout. My breaths grow quick and my muscles tight as I climb along the outside of the dragon. The ground below looks so desperately far away that the treetops blend into a carpet of green. Wind rushes past me, threatening to blow me off. I tighten my grip and narrow my eyes.

By the time I make it to the snout, my limbs are quivering. I ignore the feeling. Maybe if I pretend I'm okay, I will be.

The flagship's deck stretches beyond the dragon's snout. Though many of the cyborg soldiers are presently fending off blasts cast by the Yueshen and Ibsituu, several stand along the edge of the ship with their eyes fixed on me, weapons drawn and ready.

This is my death—I have no chance.

Still, I have to try. If I fail, Kang will conquer the Empire and impose his tyrannical rule upon everyone within its borders. A monster who killed his own wife and tried to kill his own son will never face justice. I'm the only one who can stop it, and I will not fail.

I crawl along the dragon's snout until I reach the tip. I glare at my goal—the deck, and the cyborg soldiers patrolling it. It's time to act.

The enemy is waiting.

I seize the sword from my back and spring off the dragon's snout with all the power my legs can muster. For a moment, I fly.

I raise my blade, hungry for action.

CHAPTER THIRTY-TWO

BATTLE IN THE SKY

I land on the deck. Before I even get the chance to straighten, the nearest cyborg brings his weapon down toward me. Gasping, I hold my sword out at a downward angle. When the blades meet, I immediately move, letting the other slide off. Fiery flashes burst from enchanted metal. I swing and catch the man in the side.

He cries out and doubles over. A fierce kind of gladness washes over me. Though this is the first time I've seriously wounded a fellow human in combat, all I feel is triumph. He may be a man, not an automaton or a Ligui, but he allied himself with the one who created those monsters.

Before the first man hits the ground, I find myself locked in combat with another two. Fury possesses my arms as the Yueshen possessed the mechanical dragon, and I let it flame brightly.

One of the cyborgs slices at my neck. I lean backward, arcing my spine. The blade passes over my face—and lands in the bicep of the other man. He's so close, his scream buzzes in my ears.

I twist out from under the blade and take advantage of the first man's distraction to stab him through the gut. Blood splashes onto me, hot and metallic.

A fourth soldier charges at me, and I prepare to face him, but a white blast catches him before he reaches me. The metal enhancements encasing his right arm explode with sparks and flames.

Whirling, I find Suyin muttering unintelligibly as she rhythmically spreads and contracts her fingers, between which brilliant white balls form. She punches both hands out, and one of the spells hits a cyborg in the leg, causing him to stumble forward. The other misses, but the deck catches fire where it lands.

Beyond it, I spy the magnificent tiered building in the center of the deck. Kang's chambers. He must be inside right now.

What feels like lightning zaps through my core, spurring me forward. But I only make it a few steps before an invisible force knocks into me. I barely manage to keep myself from falling.

A scream shreds the air. I whip my head to see Suyin doubled over in pain. Black scorch marks blot her robes. I stare, wondering what could have injured a Yueshen, and spot one of the cyborgs aiming a pistol at her.

I leap over, stretching my sword out between the barrel and Suyin. The cyborg fires again, and the projectile hits my blade. The grip grows hot. A scorching sensation pulses up my arms. I refuse to cry out even as the pain spreads into my shoulders and causes my muscles to quake.

The man shifts his aim and fires at me. A blue lightning strike hits his torso, and he falls backward. The shot passes close enough for me to feel its heat on my cheek.

"Anlei!" Ibsituu's voice booms above the din of fireballs and pistol shots, and I realize she must have been the one who saved me. "Remember your task!"

I nod and turn back to the building. The ornate trim glitters from the light of dozens of magic missiles zipping through the air, incongruently beautiful amid the violence. All around me, the Yueshen toss their fireballs and lightning strikes at the cyborg soldiers. Some fall, but many others use their swords to deflect, then fire back with their enchanted pistols. Kang must have prepared them to fight spirits.

Ibsituu dissolves like mist after firing one last bolt of lightning, and I know she's reached the end of her astral projection. Only Suyin and a few Yueshen warriors remain.

I sprint up the wooden steps—splintered and charred from stray blasts—leading to the building. The door bursts open before I reach the top.

Kang stands beneath its gilded frame, glaring down with cold, narrowed eyes. From this angle, their shape strikes a familiar chord, and the memory of the Shadow Warrior staring down at my father's fallen body flashes through my head. Though they were obscured by a supernatural white glow, I see those same eyes in Kang now.

A sword gleams in his grip, glittering with carved symbols and golden magic. He doesn't speak a word before swinging at me. I manage to block, but he has the high ground, and he leans into our locked weapons with the full force of his strength. My arms tremble. I try to twist out from under the attacking blade, but he shifts his position, keeping me locked beneath him.

My left foot slips back toward the edge of the step. Kang's lip twists into a snarl. His expression is one of disgust—as if he's stamping on a bug. I feel my body collapsing all around me. Maybe if I weren't exhausted from this endless day with its endless fights, I'd find the energy to free myself. But even my rage can't keep my knees from buckling.

Kang continues pressing his blade into mine, forcing my arms to bend. The edge of my sword is inches from my neck, with his blade crossing it so close to my face I can almost feel it.

Gods of Heaven and Earth, I'm going to die by the very sword I vowed to plunge into my father's murderer.

My foot slips again, and my heel dangles over empty air. Struck by a desperate idea, I jump backward, throwing myself over the edge of the steps.

Kang's blade slides down toward me, and its edge nicks my cheek. Wind stings my wound as I tumble to the deck below. A cyborg aims his pistol at me, but lowers it abruptly. I glance up to see Kang with his hand raised—a gesture that says stop. He wants to kill me himself. At least he won't cower behind his soldiers.

"Face me, Kang!" I raise my sword, fire sizzling through my bones.

Kang gives me a disdainful look. He slowly descends the stairs, his silk robes swirling in the wind. One of his long, loose sleeves flaps around his forearm, but the other sits heavily on his wrist. I recall the dagger that struck Tai and how it seemingly appeared from nowhere. That must be where he keeps it—I'll have to be mindful that he doesn't pull the same surprise on me.

My muscles quiver with a strange mix of exhaustion and excitement. The moment Kang's foot hits the deck, he lunges. I leap to the side and use my blade to smack his away. I start to attack, but a stray blast—whether from a cyborg or the Yueshen, I can't tell—flies toward me. I duck. The heat singes the top of my head.

The next thing I know, Kang is bearing down on me. I drop into a roll, narrowly avoiding his swing. By the time I scramble to my feet, his blade is upon me again, his hateful eyes glittering behind it. I hold up my sword in time to keep from being sliced in half, but his strength is too much for my exhausted arms. My blade flies out of my control, arcing over my shoulder.

I manage to keep my grip, but don't get a chance at a counterattack before I'm forced to defend again. He strikes over and over, his blade pounding into mine with the relentlessness of a typhoon. Each blow is deliberate, calculated. I swing wildly just to keep up my defenses.

Explosions ring in my ears. I'm vaguely aware of the remaining Yueshen still fighting the cyborgs. In the distance, the wail of strained machinery and the thwacking of propellers sound from the bronze creatures powered by the Yueshen as they try in vain to slow the fleet any way they can.

Kang drives me back and back and back until I can retreat no further. My heel finds the edge of a wall. He's forced me against one of the buildings.

Triumph flashes across his eyes. He lowers his blade.

I seize the opening and dive into an attack—only for his sword to meet mine in a movement so quick I barely feel the impact against my blade. With a rapid twist, he forces my weapon so far to the side, it rips out of my grasp.

Cold seizes every inch of me as I hear my blade clatter against the deck. Curses swirl through my head. How did I fail to see that coming?

Kang strides up to me. I try to back away—only to find myself pressed against the wall. His body is nearly against mine—too close for a front kick or a knee to the stomach. He shoves his blade against my throat, and it stings my skin.

But I refuse to accept defeat.

I refuse.

"What a waste." Kang stands so close, his disgusting breath rustles my hair. "You would have made a beautiful bride."

The words roil my stomach, and I spit in his face.

He scowls. "A quick death is too good for you. The only question is whether I have the patience to keep you alive any longer."

He presses his blade further into my skin, and I feel a hot stream of blood slide down my neck.

Then, I feel something else—his wide sleeve swinging against my collarbone. It's heavy—heavier than any sleeve should be.

The dagger.

I don't think—I just move. One hand dives into his sleeve and finds the hilt tucked into a pouch inside. The other punches out and shoves his blade back. Pain lances through my palm, but I don't care.

I dig the dagger into Kang's chest, shoving it in as far as I can.

Kang cries out in shock. Using the few inches left between us, I lift my knee and jab it forward into his gut, forcing him back.

The moment his blade is far enough from my throat, I duck under it. My gaze catches my sword lying a few feet away. I dive for it.

Kang, reeling but still standing, takes one more shot at me. I knock his blade out of the way and channel all the strength I have left into one mighty swing.

My blade slices through his neck. Blood spurts into my face.

It's delicious.

His head tumbles to the ground. The thud and the roll are like music, and the ensuing crash from the rest of his body falling forms a satisfying coda.

Kang is dead. The Shadow Warrior, slain. The murderer of my father, the captor and torturer of countless spirits, the traitor and would-be conqueror of the Empire—destroyed.

By me. Liang Anlei. The new Warrioress.

Brilliant yellow light explodes from Kang's head.

When it fades, he stands before me once more—translucent, but still menacing. A spirit. My heart trembles, but I hold my blade steady.

Before I can strike, a whirlpool of red and black smoke appears beside him. From it emerges Mowang, no longer giant and solid, but still terrifying in his grotesque power. His clawed hands seize Kang's shoulders.

"We had a deal, Viceroy." His low, rumbling voice thunders in my ears.

Mowang pulls Kang into the whirlpool. The viceroy lets out a long, howling scream. It cuts off—too quickly—as the smoke disappears.

CHAPTER THIRTY-THREE

HIDDEN CHARACTERS

I gape at the spot where the viceroy vanished. I almost wonder if I hallucinated it.

A sudden tremor shakes me back to reality. A red-tinted fog—one I hadn't realized was clouding my vision—dissipates, leaving my surroundings in startling clarity.

Ligui pour out of the deck, billowing like black smoke. But none attack. Instead, they race into the brightening sky and dissolve into the air. Other spirits soar among them—some that look like the cursed Yueshen I encountered in the cavern. And a few—very few—that just look like . . . people. Translucent and ethereal, yet recognizably human. These must be the ones that held onto their souls even through their imprisonment and torment.

And then I spot one that makes my heart ache and soar at the same time.

Father's face warms as his gaze lands on mine. "Anlei . . . "

He reaches a hand out to me.

"Father!" I race toward him, tears streaming down my face. Before I can reach him, he floats into the sky. *"Father!"* I grasp at the air beneath him, trying in vain to pull him down.

"I must go." He gives me a fond look as he falls into the light. "So must you. I'm proud of you, my daughter."

"Father, wait!"

His spirit vanishes into the sunbeams. I stare at the spot, overwhelmed by a flood of emotions I can hardly name.

The ground shakes again. The movement is so violent I barely manage to keep from falling.

"Anlei!" Suyin flies toward me with a look of alarm. "Get out of here, *now!*"

Her warning crashes down on me as I recall what was powering this ship. The spirits have been freed, released back to their realms now that Kang—the tether binding them to Earth—is gone. Without them, this vessel is about to plummet into the ground.

I need to jump back onto the mechanical dragon and sail off to safety. I dash across the deck, tucking my sword back into its strap. I nearly reach the railing before I recall who's waiting for me on that bronze beast.

Tai . . .

He'll die without the River Pearl, and it's still on board. This ship is a giant mass of metal and machinery, and it won't be the only one falling from the sky. How long would it take me to dig through the shattered mess and find the pearl once it's on the ground? Ibsituu said her spell to freeze Tai wouldn't last much longer than her astral projection, and that already ended. He could be bleeding to death this very moment.

I whirl back toward the building at the center of the deck. Not many cyborg soldiers remain, but the few that do appear too confused to attack. The ground rocks under my feet, and wind roars. We're falling—I can feel it. The propellers and machinery are slowing the ship's descent, but without the spirits, they aren't strong enough to keep it aloft. I can hear them sputtering, shaking, shattering.

I stumble across the deck, barely able to keep upright with the ground so unsteady. My body protests, telling me that my heart will explode, my lungs burst, and my limbs melt unless I sink into the ground and let weariness take over.

But I've pushed it this far. I can last a little while longer.

I have to crawl up the steps. When I reach the top, I'm rewarded by the sight of a celestial white glow within the confines of a copper cage.

The River Pearl. My heart leaps.

I'm going to make it. Tai's going to make it.

I grab the whole device—I can worry about getting the River Pearl out later. Racing back across the deck is much easier than making it to the building was. The flagship is now freefalling, and I'm running downhill.

Ahead, a bronze dragon races down in tandem, and I know it's the one powered by my Yueshen allies. Behind it, the mechanical phoenixes and butterflies and other oddities scatter across the red sky, hovering while Kang's armada falls hard and fast all around them.

I reach the railing. The dragon's snout is close. I climb onto the railing and push off—

My fingers graze metal but fail to find anything to cling to.

I'm falling.

Thunderous gusts whip over me. I squeeze my eyes, my face smarting under the lashes of my hair, which must have come unbound from its braids. But though I know I'm plummeting to my death, I'm no longer afraid. My heart hammers no more, and my breath no longer quivers.

I'm sorry, Tai . . . I failed you.

I release a long breath, though I feel like I'm releasing so much more. The weight of injustice from my father's death, the binding pressure of my forced marriage, the burden of my village's fate—it's all over now. I only wish I could have saved Tai.

Maybe someone else can . . .

I thrust my right arm upward, holding out the device containing the River Pearl. I keep my eyes closed against the harsh wind as I shout, "Suyin! I have the River Pearl! Please, take it to Tai!"

Something grips the other end of the device and I feel my whole weight drop onto my arm, which snaps straight. For an instant, I'm suspended in mid-air. But I barely have time to acknowledge the sensation before I'm back to falling.

"You called?"

The voice sends a jolt through my heart, and I force my eyes open.

Tai holds the other end of the device, falling alongside me. A crooked grin lifts his mouth. "That wasn't very nice of Ibsituu to freeze me without my permission."

Gladness floods me at the sight of him, but it quickly turns to panic as my gaze shifts to his bloodstained tunic. "What are you doing here?"

"I couldn't let you fall alone." Despite his nonchalant words, his voice is strained. "I woke in time to see you tumble, and I flew down to catch you. Well, sort of."

I flick my gaze over his body—it's solid. Which means he shifted into his Yueshen form to fly down to me and turned human again to catch me. "What's your plan then—fall to your death along with me?"

"Of course not. I can fly, remember?"

"But Yueshen can't carry—"

"I have a plan." Tai holds out his other hand, reaching toward me. "Do you trust me?"

I reach up to grasp it. "Yes."

His fingers close around mine, and I squeeze them tight, taking comfort in the warmth, the connection, the sureness. Blood from the cut on my palm slides down my wrist, but I don't feel any pain.

The howling gale forces my eyes shut again, but with Tai's hand clasped in mine, I feel safe. His fingers are an anchor, and whatever comes next, I find security in them.

Then, they vanish. Yet I still feel them—it's as if someone took away the flesh and bone and blood, but left behind the warmth.

My weight drops onto both arms, as if I'm dangling from the edge of a cliff. But the wind is gone.

I open my eyes to see Tai's translucent face smiling at me, glowing brighter than the rays of the sun around him.

The warmth disappears, and a yelp escapes my lips as I drop. But my feet find solid ground. I look around in surprise and realize that I'm standing on firm, wonderful earth. Green grass extends from under my feet toward a distant range of mountains.

Tai sinks down slowly, and I realize what he did. The Yueshen can't carry anything bigger than a sword in the physical world, but Tai managed to for just a moment—just long enough to stop my fall and save my life.

He returns to his human form and smiles broadly. Gratitude and joy flood me. I drop the device and throw my arms around him. I press my body to his and feel his arms encircle my waist. For a moment, I bask in the relief of survival and the bliss of his presence.

He collapses against me.

I'm suddenly aware of the wetness on my tunic—the blood spread from his wound. I lower him to the ground, my arms shaking under his weight. My strength is nearly depleted, but I scrape up what's left to grab the copper device and use my sword to pry open its cage. The River Pearl tumbles out, radiant as a full moon on a clear night. Its power pulses through my blood as I pick it up. "You're going to be okay."

Tai lies on the grass, staring up at the sky. His brows are tilted and his mouth tight, and I can tell he's trying to contain unspeakable amounts of pain. When he meets my gaze and lifts his lips, his smile is more tortured than any scream could have been. "My father's dead?"

I nod. My heart weeps for him, and when his eyes glisten, I know it's because, somewhere deep and hidden, he's crying for the father he thought he knew, mourning the man he could have been, grieving the redemption that never came.

"I'm sorry." My voice emerges as a croak. "I had to."

"I know." His eyes fall shut.

"Tai!" I seize his shoulder and shake it. His lids barely lift. I stifle a sob and hold up the River Pearl. "Tell me how to unlock its healing powers."

"It won't work." The words drift by on an exhale, so soft I nearly miss them.

"Tell me!"

"Just let me be." He looks back to the sky, and I wonder if he's searching for his father's ghost amid the sunbeams.

He won't find it there—Kang's in Mowang's clutches where he belongs. My blood burns at the idea that Tai might let himself die over grief for that vile man. I lean down toward him. "No! You can't let go of your life so easily. I fought too hard to save you!"

Tai's gaze turns to me, his eyes filled with pain.

Tears spill down my cheeks. "Please . . . why won't you tell me how to use the River Pearl?"

"Because it won't work. And it will be easier for you if you don't know."

"Don't know what? Whatever it is, at least let me try." A sob wracks my body. "Please . . . "

His lips quirk. "Very well. Since you're insisting and I'm dying, I guess I get to be a little selfish."

The tornado of questions in my mind could rip apart mountain ranges, but I bite my tongue.

"The ancient scroll . . . the one that revealed how to unlock the River Pearl's healing powers . . . " He speaks between labored gasps.

I lean down to hear better.

"When I healed you, I told you that all I did was picture what it said in my mind, and it worked. That was the truth . . . " His eyes fall shut.

"No!" I shake him hard. "You don't get to die. Not before telling me what that scroll said!"

He opens his eyes with a harsh laugh. Blood trickles down the side of his mouth. "Okay, okay. The scroll was written by a man who had been a close follower of the River Dragon all his life. When his wife lay dying, the River Dragon revealed the pearl's secret to him . . . and it was a poem. To unlock the pearl's healing powers, a person must picture the characters one by one as if speaking them in one's mind—and mean them. Unless the words are true, you can think them as many times as you want, and the pearl will do nothing."

"What did it say?"

When he recites the poem, each word carves into my soul.

Slips in strange, the dart
All, all, now takes part
What dark took from you
Take whole from my heart

It's a lover's poem. I don't know this one specifically, but I've heard a hundred like it. Sappy, yet . . . poignant. Because even if the words are weak, if the emotion behind them is true, they have the power to shake a person's world.

And this poem . . . Tai's saying that it's one he silently recited to me once. And meant it—the River Dragon's magic wouldn't have been fooled.

I stare at him, my chest heaving under my lungs' effort to contain my pulse. "But . . . but when you healed me . . . we'd only known each other a little while."

"And, if you'll recall, I said I didn't know if it would work. But it did . . . the River Dragon knew me before I knew myself. I kept silent because it was easier, but I guess there's no need for me to fear consequences anymore." He briefly closes his eyes, and when he opens them, their dark intensity pulls me into their depths. "I love you, Anlei."

My throat catches. I never even dreamed that anyone could love me—I never had time to indulge such a fantasy. I was always so focused on being as indestructible as possible, on becoming the best warrior I could be, and on seeking my revenge. Though I watched husbands and wives and young lovers show their affection for one another, I always felt like I was in another world. Love was for them, not me. Not because I denied myself, but because . . . it simply wasn't part of my existence.

I guess that's why I didn't see it when it was standing right in front of me, but now that Tai's confessed, a veil I didn't know was clouding my vision lifts from my eyes. I think back to all he did for me, all he said to me. All the unspoken words between us that left me wondering.

He loves me.

And I . . . I would sacrifice my life for him. More than that—my justice. If Kang hadn't been the tether binding countless souls, and if he hadn't tried to conquer the Empire . . . I would have let him live, just to spare Tai the pain.

And when I was in the Courts of Hell, the first hell visited upon me was his death. Because even the demons knew—without him, I would shatter.

Slips in strange, the dart

I form the characters in my head. Their strokes draw across the darkness of my mind, bright enough to rival moonlight. But they quiver, trying to swim away—I shut my eyes and focus on each curve, each angle, each line. They *will* stand still for me this time.

All, all, now is part

He said he loves me. How can something catch me so off guard but feel so true? What is love? Do I even know? I know of the stories and songs, but when it comes to me, to what's real . . .

What's real is that if he dies now, I'll break. I thought I'd felt every kind of pain when I lost my father, then thought the world had splintered what was left when I saw Dailan's destruction. Yet there was a piece of me I didn't know existed, deep and vulnerable and precious. It's the part of me that's connected to him, and if it breaks too—what will be left of me?

What dark took from you

I don't understand why. I don't understand why. But sometimes, it just . . . is.

Take now from my heart

Take it. Whatever it is—take it. The River Pearl's hum grows more and more intense with each moment. I feel its resonance in my bones. Invisible tendrils reach into my body and seize a piece of my soul. *Take it.*

I feel their silky threads wrapping around the innermost parts of me. My palms heat under the pearl's magic. A sharp tug yanks at my heart, trying to tear out a piece. I let it fly. For several moments, I'm overwhelmed by the sensation of light pouring from my heart, down my arms, and into the enchanted relic.

Then, it all ceases.

I open my eyes and peer down at Tai, who abruptly pushes himself up on one elbow. His brows are knit with a look between confusion and—and something else. Though his tunic is still stained, I can sense that the life has returned to him.

I lift the torn cloth. The injury is gone—healed. A smile spreads across my face. It worked. Hardly able to believe it, I run my hand across the spot where a wound should have gaped, but feel only the smooth, warm skin.

I meet his eyes, a thousand suns burning in my chest.

I fall into him. His arms wrap around me, and his lips meet mine.

EPILOGUE

Nothing can truly be fixed. Once broken, nothing will ever be as it was.

I'll never return to the innocence of the days before I watched the Shadow Warrior murder my father. Tai will never be the same person he was before learning how deep his father's betrayals ran. But we're resilient. And though you can't repair something entirely, you can mold it into something better.

That's how we choose to see Dailan as well. Though the new Viceroy of Sijiang Province—Tai's half-brother by one of Kang's other wives—was willing to let my people stay in Tongqiucheng, none of us belong there. I certainly don't. That place may look magnificent, but I was brought there as a prisoner, and so it will always be tainted for me. As for Tai—he might have spent most of his life in the city, but it was always a life of hiding, a life of deception. And legally speaking, he doesn't exist. That half-brother—still a child of twelve—rules under the influence of his mother, and she has no reason to welcome a potential challenger to her son's position.

But Tai never wanted to be viceroy. He's content with being nobody. And so am I.

I heave another load of supplies onto the back of a mechanical cart. It's one of many the new viceroy—or rather, his mother—donated to help my people rebuild. The sooner we're gone from Tongqiucheng, the better, as far as they're concerned. Our presence has placed a strain on the city, not only because we're outsiders, but because everyone knows that it was a Dailan girl who exposed Kang's treachery. Some even blame me for the unrest that's occurred since. Sijiang Province lost the Emperor's favor after what happened.

As far as the wider public knows, the Yueshen descended from the moon to stop Kang. Some have even embellished the tale by claiming the River Dragon made an appearance. Few—if any—mention me.

I don't care. Let those hungry for power jostle over fame . . . I just want to move on.

It will take a long time to rebuild Dailan, but the automatons the new viceroy's mother gave us should speed the reconstruction. I horrified everyone by stabbing one when she first presented them to us. No spirits emerged—these were purely mechanical. Though they aren't as strong or independent as Kang's were, I prefer them any day.

As for the River Pearl—the new viceroy's mother claimed it's cursed, and that it poisoned her late husband's mind. I don't know if she actually believes that or if it's an attempt to exonerate her household. In any case, most of Tongqiucheng believes her and wants nothing to do with it. And so Headman Su agreed to take it back to Dailan and return it to its pedestal in the River Dragon's shrine.

Something tugs at my braid. Startled, I whirl. But I know at once that it's Tai.

He pulls me into a kiss, and for a moment, I lose myself in his presence.

A snicker interrupts my bliss, and I turn to see Anshui making a face at me.

I smack Tai's arm with a grin. "*Hundan!* There are better ways of getting my attention!"

"But they're no fun." Tai smiles back. His gaze pans over to Headman Su, who narrows his eyes with a disapproving look. "I don't think your people like me very much."

"They aren't accustomed to outsiders." I shrug. "But my mother was once an outsider as well, and she made a home in Dailan. You can too."

"I have a better idea. Ibsituu sent a mechanical pigeon to say she's decided to return to Mwezi. She asked if I'd like to join her on the journey—and told me to ask if you'd like to come."

I purse my lips. "My people need me."

His fingers brush a wisp of hair from my cheek. "Do they?"

I glance past him at the horizon, stretching green and wide before high mountains. I long to know what lies beyond them, to see for myself the exotic lands I've only heard of in stories. Now that the Ligui are gone, Dailan won't need as much protecting. And I was never going to make a life as a fisherman's wife or anything. I never had to think about it before because my focus was on the village's survival, but now that it's safe . . .

I take Tai's hand. "Let's do it. And after we accompany Ibsituu to Mwezi, let's journey on."

His face brightens. "Sounds like a plan."

My blood races as I think about all the places we'll go, all the places we'll see. I feel . . . untethered. For so long, my life was dictated by forces beyond my control. Even when I sought justice for my father, I was controlled by a rage tied to another. But that's over.

From now on, only I define my destiny.

ACKNOWLEDGMENTS

Like every meaningful journey, taking a book from rough draft to published novel takes countless steps. Special thanks to everyone who's helped me turn *Stronger Than a Bronze Dragon* from a pipe dream into a real, live book.

Thank you to my amazing parents, Yonghua Wang and Jianqing Fan, for supporting my writerly adventures.

Thank you to my sister, Angel, for being my muse (whether you knew it or not).

Thank you to my fantastic agent, Dr. Uwe Stender, for believing in and championing this book.

Thank you to my wonderful editor, Lauren Knowles, for hammering this story into the best version of itself. And to Team Page Street for bringing this book into the world.

Thank you to Karissa Laurel, Brian Lynch, and Linnea Schiff for beta-reading early versions of this book and helping me improve it.

Thank you to everyone in the Jersey City Writers who came out to my critique session to help me hammer this story into shape: Beth Bentley, Joseph Del Priore, Allison Goldstein, Jonathan Huang, Rachel Poy, Kevin Singer, and Sara Stone.

Thank you to Ngiste Abebe, Àbíké Jacobs, and Sara Tadesse for your valuable insights as sensitivity readers.

Thank you to Purvi Patel for driving me to produce the words I needed. May you rest in freedom.

And thank you to everyone in the writing community who's been there for me over the years. There are far too many to name, which just goes to show that even when we're on our own journeys, we're all part of something greater.

ABOUT THE AUTHOR

Mary Fan is a hopeless dreamer whose mind insists on spinning tales of "what if." As a music major in college, she told those stories through compositions. Now, she tells them through books. Based in Jersey City, she can usually be found somewhere along the river.

Her novels include *Starswept*, an award-winning and critically acclaimed YA sci-fi novel, the *Jane Colt* sci-fi trilogy, and the *Flynn Nightsider* YA dark fantasy series. She's also the co-editor of the *Brave New Girls* YA anthologies, which are dedicated to encouraging girls to enter STEM careers and to raising money for the Society of Women Engineers scholarship fund. Her short works have been featured in many anthologies, including: *Love, Murder & Mayhem* (Crazy 8 Press), *Magic at Midnight* (Snowy Wings Publishing), and *Mine! A Celebration of Liberty and Freedom For All Benefitting Planned Parenthood* (ComicMix). Find her online at www.MaryFan.com.